A low rumble ~~~~~~~~~~~~~ it him off

With a grunt, Kane got back to his feet. He couldn't see anything moving in the waist-high grass, so he found a stumpy handhold in the bark of a tree and hauled himself ten feet up. That's when he noticed a pair of beasts tugging carts behind them. They were escorted by Watatsumi with rifles, and they looked as haggard as he felt.

"We've got a ride coming," Kane said. "At least, I hope they're friendly. They look all beat."

Kondo nodded, returning to the remnants of the tent. He found his radio and keyed it.

Kane rested his forehead against the bark, letting the Watatsumi's rapid Japanese wash over him. Things were pretty bad. Manta was incapacitated, and Remus badly wounded. He and his allies were banged up.

He hoped the medical facilities Ryugo-jo had were as good, or better, than those of Cerberus. They were going to need that kind of help. Because the Dragon Riders were not the true force assaulting the Watatsumi. The renegade Japanese dragon-men were only puppets.

There was something worse out there in this forsaken pocket of prehistory.

Other titles in this series:

James Axler
Outlanders®

SAVAGE
DAWN

A GOLD EAGLE BOOK FROM
WORLDWIDE®

TORONTO • NEW YORK • LONDON
AMSTERDAM • PARIS • SYDNEY • HAMBURG
STOCKHOLM • ATHENS • TOKYO • MILAN
MADRID • WARSAW • BUDAPEST • AUCKLAND

Recycling programs
for this product may
not exist in your area.

First edition February 2013

ISBN-13: 978-0-373-63877-2

SAVAGE DAWN

Copyright © 2013 by Worldwide Library

Special thanks to Douglas Wojtowicz for his contribution to this work.

Printed in U.S.A.

"When Pack meets with Pack in the Jungle, And neither will go from the trail, Lie down till the leaders have spoken, It may be fair words shall prevail."

—Rudyard Kipling

The Road to Outlands—
From Secret Government Files to the Future

Almost two hundred years after the global holocaust, Kane, a former Magistrate of Cobaltville, often thought the world had been lucky to survive at all after a nuclear device detonated in the Russian embassy in Washington, D.C. The aftermath—forever known as skydark—reshaped continents and turned civilization into ashes.

Nearly depopulated, America became the Deathlands— poisoned by radiation, home to chaos and mutated life forms. Feudal rule reappeared in the form of baronies, while remote outposts clung to a brutish existence.

What eventually helped shape this wasteland were the redoubts, the secret preholocaust military installations with stores of weapons, and the home of gateways, the locational matter-transfer facilities. Some of the redoubts hid clues that had once fed wild theories of government cover-ups and alien visitations.

Rearmed from redoubt stockpiles, the barons consolidated their power and reclaimed technology for the villes. Their power, supported by some invisible authority, extended beyond their fortified walls to what was now called the Outlands. It was here that the rootstock of humanity survived, living with hellzones and chemical storms, hounded by Magistrates.

In the villes, rigid laws were enforced—to atone for the sins of the past and prepare the way for a better future. That was the barons' public credo and their right-to-rule.

Kane, along with friend and fellow Magistrate Grant, had upheld that claim until a fateful Outlands expedition. A displaced piece of technology…a question to a keeper of the archives…a vague clue about alien masters—and their world shifted radically. Suddenly, Brigid Baptiste, the archivist, faced summary execution, and Grant a quick termination. For Kane there was forgiveness if he pledged his unquestioning allegiance to Baron Cobalt and his unknown masters and abandoned his friends.

But that allegiance would make him support a mysterious and alien power and deny loyalty and friends. Then what else was there?

Kane had been brought up solely to serve the ville. Brigid's only link with her family was her mother's red-gold hair, green eyes and supple form. Grant's clues to his lineage were his ebony skin and powerful physique. But Domi, she of the white hair, was an Outlander pressed into sexual servitude in Cobaltville. She at least knew her roots and was a reminder to the exiles that the outcasts belonged in the human family.

Parents, friends, community—the very rootedness of humanity was denied. With no continuity, there was no forward momentum to the future. And that was the crux—when Kane began to wonder if there was a future.

For Kane, it wouldn't do. So the only way was out—way, way out.

After their escape, they found shelter at the forgotten Cerberus redoubt headed by Lakesh, a scientist, Cobaltville's head archivist, and secret opponent of the barons.

With their past turned into a lie, their future threatened, only one thing was left to give meaning to the outcasts. The hunger for freedom, the will to resist the hostile influences. And perhaps, by opposing, end them.

Chapter 1

From his perch, Kondo had a clear view of the deforested lands around the growing fort-factory. As commander of security for the ventilation ports and aboveground manufacturing, the Watatsumi soldier was at once exposed atop a slender tower yet ready to direct his men and provide them with cover fire. He had to climb one hundred feet up a ladder to the observer's roost, where he had a full, 360-degree panorama of the isolated island plain for two miles to the horizon. The rifle settled beside him, the M95 Barrett, was built for such ranges.

The Watatsumi *bushi* were warriors trained in the way of the samurai, and honor was a way of life. Still, as in the day of the bow and arrow, through to the first use of muskets, the art of ranged combat was not neglected by their warrior code. Only the most foolish and petty of noncombatants would have called a *bushi* sniper a cowardly assassin. The truth was that a long-distance weapon did not make a man invulnerable to harm or timid in the face of danger. And danger there was—the subterranean Watatsumi were threatened by a cannibal offshoot that had remained aboveground and now attacked their former brethren.

The Dragon Riders had their own tools of distant death, and Kondo was a tempting target, even behind the low stone walls on the platform. The Dragon Riders knew that removing a Watatsumi sniper from his position as an eye in the sky gave them an advantage over the embedded defenders, both blinding them and removing an opponent who could strike them from a second flank.

Kondo knew his firepower could potentially prove effective on anything smaller than the nearly seven-ton acrocanthosaurus that the invaders had somehow summoned and trained, but only with the luckiest of brain shots. He wished that he could haul something even more authoritative than a .50-caliber sniper rifle up the ladder because despite the armor-piercing capabilities of the weapon, a mere half inch and two ounces of lead were only a pinprick to a massive, 6500-kilogram apex predator.

As it was, the Watatsumi were still at a disadvantage when it came to fighting the dinosaurs. Vehicles had been lost in conflict with the smaller, more agile creatures under the Riders' command, Utahraptors and deinonychus, the last of them being destroyed on first contact with no less than three of the thirty-five-foot-long monster acros when they first appeared five years earlier. While the Japan that the Watatsumi had lived under and escaped from had been considered the mecca of advanced technology back in the twentieth century, the weaponry they'd inherited from the Philippine redoubt and scrounged from home was not cutting edge.

Antitank rockets had been eschewed simply because, even with the split of philosophy among the Watatsumi and the Riders, neither side expected to need high-powered explosives for bunker busting. For 120 years, their defensive needs had been sufficiently met with assault rifles and swords and bows rediscovered by the reptile men. Before skydark the Watatsumi had been loathe to venture out among their Japanese kinfolk, but sneaking into U.S. military bases in Japan had been impossible. Even so, most of what would have helped was too heavy to be drawn out of the collapsing underground city or had been destroyed when the earth-shaker missiles caused rampant destruction in the Philippine redoubt they'd entered.

More than a century and a half had gone without the necessity to hold off six-hundred-pound predators capable of running at up to fifty miles per hour, let alone the acrocanthosauruses. Thus, as true warriors, the Watatsumi adapted tactics to maximize their available tools. So far, it had kept the battle even, but there was no advantage to either side. The Riders still managed to procure bows and arrows, which were utilized with deadly efficiency, capable of penetrating even the heavy-banded composite armor that the reptilian underground dwellers wore.

This armor—made of leather, polymer slats with chain and silk sandwiched between—had vastly reduced the horrific torso wounds inflicted even by the killing claws of the raptors. Kondo had seen too many friends with their limbs amputated by the razor-sharp natural weapons of the dinosaurs, and even that powerful armor couldn't withstand the crushing power of the acros' massive jaws. The Barrett rifle that he carried could generate six and a half tons of energy at the muzzle with one round. The bite force of an acrocanthosaurus was measured to be identical, according to damage done to jeeps and the shredded remains of Watatsumi who had struck. The only thing that would work against such jaws would be the tank armor that would also work against the heavy .50s.

And the Japanese dragon men barely had enough manufacturing room and capability to make simple automobiles. There had been one chance, a sliver of information dealing with remote mind control, which began their quest. They had first gone to Florida's wiregrass swamp and its Atlantic Undersea Testing and Evaluation outpost, and then to the Bahamas AUTEC prime base with its link to the Tongue of the Ocean base, where Kakusa had been hidden.

That was where Kondo had felt his name soiled, his conscience bloodied with the kidnapping and infection of innocent humans. No matter how guilty Orochi had been, no matter what Kondo had accomplished in ending Orochi's conspiracy and the assault of the foul beast that it had awakened, the *bushi's* soul was wounded.

Too many innocent people died as puppets of an angry, demon let loose from its bottle. Kakusa had been responsible for their killing, hurled with malicious abandon against Grant, Rosalia and the defending Watatsumi.

Those parasites needed to be stopped, and the monster directing them had no qualms about spending lives and spilling blood, even the blood of its own dying puppets. The pawns fought to the death, and even the destruction of their hosts didn't keep the parasites from separating to seek out new victims.

The infested people who had been freed of the octopoid creatures had been left either completely paralyzed or so suddenly despondent that they preferred suicide to continued existence. These were Orochi's and Kondo's own victims who had been impossible to save. In a way, Kondo wished that he could have died that fateful night, because he had betrayed his basic warrior's oath to protect the defenseless. True soldiers fought for a cause, and it was invariably the defense of their people. In the long run, that lifelong crusade did not involve the murder of the helpless.

Kakusa's involvement, Orochi's machinations, those might have alleviated the conscience of others, but they weighed heavily on Kondo. Especially with the death of his friend Fumio striking so close to his heart.

Despite the bright skies afforded by the veins of magma flowing through obsidian glass tubes, providing the equiv-

alent illumination of a sunny, clear day, Kondo's mood was
dark and clouded. His honor was smeared by those deaths,
and one other thing. In his efforts to gain his people assistance, he had shared the secret of Ryugo-jo with Grant,
a human he had come to see as a brother and comrade in
arms. It was only a moment of weakness, and he reached
out to his new friend, seeking a thread of hope.

Time had passed, and though he knew there were other,
more pressing matters, Kondo had to fight the pangs of
abandonment. He couldn't allow himself to feel betrayed.

"Grant has not forsaken us," he said aloud, knowing
that no one would be close enough to hear him, unless he
pressed the transmit button on his comm.

For emphasis, for further comfort, he punched himself
on the thigh. The brief jolt of pain, his anger at his own
wallowing in toxic doubt, cleared his mind.

If it hadn't been for that, he wouldn't have caught a
glimpse of a shadow flitting across one of the magma
ports.

That brief flicker of darkness drew Kondo's attention to
the thing suddenly diving out of the sky. He'd had barely
a moment to react, throwing himself to the floor of the
platform.

Instants later, a winged figure swept past, plucking
Kondo's twenty-five-pound rifle from its spot as if it were
a mouse in the talons of an owl.

A curse escaped Kondo's lips, even as he ripped his
handgun from the holster on his hip. He brought up the
weapon with lightning speed. With the main weapon gone,
and the sky sporting two more of the broad-winged assailants, he realized that the Riders had brought a new nightmare back from the past.

The exact species was unknown to Kondo, but they
were large enough and strong enough to fly even with

nearly thirty pounds of steel grasped in their talons. Given
the claws he saw on them, he could tell that they were capable of removing limbs from a person with one swift pass.

Kondo stiff-armed the pistol and opened fire, his pistol
barking loudly in the serene afternoon. Lead flew at the
two airborne creatures, but they were agile, breaking their
dive to avoid a hail of lead aimed at them. The reptilian
birds, whatever they were, had sufficient intellect to not
only avoid gunfire, but also disarm a sniper.

Kondo keyed his comm with his free hand, shouting
orders at the top of his lungs to give warning to the men
below. As he did so, his gaze fell to the horizon, and the
bulk of three giant apex predators loomed. His vision focused, fingers clawing a fresh magazine for his empty gun,
and he noticed the riderless deinonychus and the cannibals
mounted on their Utahraptor steeds.

The Dragon Riders had their own air force, and they
had been smart enough to send it ahead to take out the
sniper over watch that had given the Watatsumi a slight
edge in repelling them.

The odds were even now, but only if Kondo could continue fighting the airborne beasts.

"Acros and mixed raptors approaching from the north!"
Kondo alerted. "Protect…"

Movement, the rustle of feathers and scales, pulled him
away from the ventilation plant below. The airborne predator was mere moments away, and there was no way that
Kondo could aim and fire at the beast. His martial arts
training took over, and he knew the best way to avoid
being disemboweled was to get in too close for an enemy
to use his knife, or in this case, razor claws. He charged
to the rail and leaped at the creature.

Sky monster and soldier crashed together, Kondo's arms
wrapping around the thing's neck even as its bald head

thrashed at him. Needle-sharp teeth slashed at Kondo's face and neck, drawing blood, but it was nothing deep.

Now, there was no platform, merely empty air all around.

Twelve-foot spanning wings flapped violently, hoping to catch the sky enough to keep the pair aloft, but Kondo was much heavier than any rifle, and he smothered his opponent's vision and bent its neck.

Out of control, the pair wildly spiraled to the ground.

Kondo's vision blacked out to the sound of crunching bones.

Chapter 2

The Cerberus trio had been on a long journey, even without factoring in the instantaneous mat-trans jump from the Montana redoubt to a lonesome temple hidden within the forest. The surroundings were familiar, as the Cerberus warriors had been in the area before, but previously they had arrived in the belly of a transport helicopter. They had avoided the need to penetrate the thick undergrowth of the Kashmir jungles. In the two centuries since the twilight of humankind's dominance, the terrain that had once been filled with clear-cut forests or artillery- and grenade-blasted battlefields from international skirmishes had regrown, coming back with lush life, both flora and fauna rising in abundance. The animals of the subcontinent kept their distance from this trio of travelers, either too small to wish to confront or too intelligent to want anything to do with human contact.

At the front of the group was Kane, a man who had the sleek, supple muscles of a wolf combined with the cool, piercing glare that lit his gray-blue eyes. His brown hair was a sweat-plastered, tousled nest. It was trending toward being long, but he kept it cut off at midneck and trimmed to stay out of his eyes. He brushed the back of his hand along his bristle-covered jaw, perspiration splashing to the side as he flicked it away. His right arm was at rest, elbow held in close to his side, the folding machine pistol in its hydraulic forearm holster ready to snap into his hand at the first sign of trouble. He wanted to keep that arm free to deal with any sudden, unexpected but well-anticipated danger, so he did the majority of the forest hacking work with the machete clenched in his left fist.

He was glistening with sweat, despite the top of his shadow suit being tied around his waist. It wasn't because the garment was too warm; the suits had been designed to be environmentally adaptive, keeping their wearers warm even in arctic temperatures or cool in blazing heat.

Kane's senses were almost preternaturally sharp, and the body-hugging, weather-resistant shadow suit had never hindered him across a dozen adventures around the globe. Still, Kane didn't see the need to wear the suit for its cooling capabilities, nor its protection from light small-arms fire. The wilderness was as much a home to the former Cobaltville Magistrate, despite his being born and raised within the walls of the ville. Be it the forests of the Bitterroot Mountains, where his new home, Cerberus redoubt, was hidden, the deserts of the American southwest or northern Africa or the jungles of the subcontinent, Kane was equally comfortable. The air, as hot and sticky as it was, felt good against him, and the sheen of sweat on his bare skin made him feel human and real, not a piece of meat antiseptically wrapped within a plastic casing.

Behind him was a woman whose coppery-red hair was pulled severely back, plastered to her scalp and secured by elastic into a ponytail that kept her from feeling stifled and smothered by her blanket of locks. Her voluptuous torso was snugged into a blue, formfitting tank top, displaying her freckled shoulders and cleavage and laying bare the long, lean-muscled arms that had developed in the years since she had been merely an academic, recording and rewriting Earth's lost history in Cobaltville. Her job had been as an archivist, doing her work to both preserve and suppress knowledge, and it was a task made immensely easier by a photographic memory and an eager desire to learn. Her discoveries, however, had led her into her first meeting with Kane, who had his own curiosity about an artifact he'd discovered. The knowledge they'd unearthed had forced them from the megalithic tower and the rule of the hybrid baronys into the resistance movement led by Mohandas Lakesh Singh.

At the Cerberus redoubt, Brigid Baptiste became more than merely a deskbound student of the past. A true adventurer, she survived the battles with the barons and the inhuman aliens they had evolved into. She was already tall and lithe, but the years of her endeavors had transformed her into an athletic, skilled survivor and fighter against the forces of tyranny on Earth, and in worlds and dimensions beyond.

Brigid wasn't as drenched by perspiration as her companion, but then she wasn't engaging in the same incessant activity as Kane, who fought to carve a path through the Kashmir forest with all of his strength focused behind the three pounds of sharp-edged steel he wielded. To make up for the relative lack of labor, Brigid carried not only her gear, but also Kane's. It wasn't as demanding as slicing through vines, branches and saplings, but her lower back and legs were starting to complain.

"I always wanted to be a Sherpa," Brigid muttered to herself as they continued on.

A growl drew her attention in the wake of a leafy smack of a branch that had whipped over her head, missing it by an inch.

"Bakayaro!" Grant bellowed in response to being struck in the face yet again. "Kane, if I find out you're deliberately aiming at me, I swear…."

Brigid had to clamp her hand over her mouth to stifle

a paroxysm of laughter at the giant ex-Magistrate's complaint. She observed Grant's continuing education in the Japanese language, courtesy of the many lessons provided by his lover, Shizuka. She was the leader of the wayward samurai known as the Tigers of Heaven, based on New Edo, an island off what used to be the California coast.

The enormous black man was six foot four and more than 225 pounds. His size was compounded by the fact that most of that weight was assembled in his broad, powerful musculature, making it difficult for him to find clothes or armor that fit. This day Grant had rolled up the sleeves of his shadow suit to bare his forearms, allowing the air through to cool his skin.

"Okay, Baptiste," Kane said, pausing in his assault on the jungle. "What did he just say that made you snort like a pig?"

Brigid looked back to Grant, seeking approval. Grant nodded. "Go ahead and give it to him."

"In effect, it was a one-word response that loosely translates to English as 'what are you, an idiot?'" Brigid stated.

Kane raised an eyebrow, looking to Grant. "That's some cleaned-up language from you."

Brigid cleared her throat. "Trust me. It's not. The south end of a northbound horse is involved."

Grant smirked. "I'm really loving Japanese. Just one word for a minimum seven-word response is pure gold."

Kane grinned in response. "Got to love efficiency. No, I was not aiming for you."

Brigid leaned in closer to Kane. "No smart-ass comments? What, did you overheat in there, Kane?"

"Maybe some alien moved into his brain," Grant said. "Poor fucker, he must be awful lonely in there."

"Ha. Period. Fucking. Period. Ha," Kane responded.

He turned to get back to work when Brigid interrupted him yet again.

"Okay. That Zen attitude is uncharacteristic for you," she said. "Grant and Shizuka don't even show that, and she's teaching him Zen archery!"

Kane turned back, wedging the point of the machete into the ground. "I've got things on my mind."

He mopped his brow. "We're here to try to find where the Watatsumi might actually be, and we're coming to Hannah and the Nagah for more clues. The last time we were here—"

Brigid interrupted her friend. "She kicked us out. What can you expect? They lost their queen mother and their prince, and the ruling council and citizens suffered greatly in Durga's attempted coup."

"On the way to fix one mess we've let sit, we walk right into the muck we left in our wake," Grant said. "What else is new?"

"Guilt," Brigid spoke up quickly. Kane took a deep breath, showing her that she was right. "The baggage of everything we've done is starting to catch up to you?"

"Destroyed enclaves and wrecked societies have practically become a part of our job description," Kane admitted glumly. "But Kondo and his people were good folk. It was their commander, Orochi, who had gone too far with his experimentation, releasing some truly bad shit in the process."

"And except for Durga and his followers, the Nagah were proud of their human kin and those given the 'gift of Enki,'" Brigid added. "But we showed up at the right time for their world to fall apart, and Hannah told us to leave because she knew we'd be a reminder of their loss."

"I'm just wondering if we're returning too soon," Kane said.

Grant took out a bottle of water from the war bag in which he hauled extra ammunition, grenades and a couple of heavy weapons for use in conflict with the troubles that Kondo stated the Cerberus explorers could expect to encounter. Acting as rear security for the group, he was also the slowest with his burden, but it gave him room and solitude to keep his eyes open on the back trail. This area was known for bandits and though they were a small group, Kane's slashed path was one that could easily be followed.

Certainly it was paranoid, but the postapocalyptic world *was* filled with dangers, and cold-blooded killers stalked the land. It was something that none of the three people wanted to endure, and they wished that they could cleanse the cursed Earth of the predators stalking in the shadows, returning order and peace to lawless lands. The problem was that struggle was often derailed by the omnipresent menaces that sought the enslavement of all humankind or destruction of the whole world. Regional thugs had to be left to the side. Two examples of that problem were the aforementioned Enki's brother, Enlil, and more recently Ullikummis, his son. They were symptoms of a vastly different affliction, one dating back millions of years, even before the apes chipped volcanic glass into the first primitive knife. Humankind was born from the bosom of the Earth, but others had come to take advantage of the lonely pearl of life in the solar system, seeking its resources. The Annunaki and the Tuatha de Danaan were two of the most formidable extraterrestrial races that the Cerberus explorers had encountered in their journeys, and their influence had led to the near extinction of humankind, and continued to threaten subjugation to this day.

The two races created a race called the Archons, but only one Archon remained—Balam. Other servitor races, such as Enlil's Nephilim, and Enki's children, the Nagah, had been encountered, as well. Where the Nephilim were mindless drones, as befitting an interstellar tyrant such as Enlil, Enki's Nagah were intelligent and quite human in thought and form, save for the mixture of cobra DNA that made them into armored warriors, held in reserve to prevent Enlil's subsentient soldiers from attacking the world unopposed. With the discovery of the Watatsumi in the wiregrass swamp of the Florida Panhandle, Kane and Grant had come to the conclusion that the Japanese reptilian men were somehow related to the Indian serpent men they had met. It was highly unlikely that the "sons of the dragon" had evolved independent of the cobra men of India, and given the relative geographic proximity of Southeast Asia to the subcontinent, one could have been a lost tribe of the other.

"Hannah told us that we might never be allowed back in," Kane reminded his companions, even though Brigid never forgot a thing and Grant had just pointed out their current relationship with the Nagah. "Maybe she's right to see us as a poison to her society, but I can't help but think that we have a chance to heal some of those wounds."

"Kondo said his city was in conflict, so you think that by reuniting the two races we might give them both something to work toward?" Grant asked.

"If anything, an influx of immigrants has historically proved to further destabilize societies," Brigid brought up. "Just because they both appear reptilian, and thus could easily be seen as brothers, there are cultural and biological differences, according to your descriptions. One need only look at the Irish who came to America in the 1800s to see the kind of violent infighting that could arise."

"It couldn't hurt to know that there is backup out there that looks and feels like you do," Grant countered. "Back in Magistrate training, the number one rule for surviving any fight was not just to bring a gun, but to bring along all of your friends who have guns."

"The more the merrier," Kane added with a shrug. "We're also not going to have either side uproot and move in with each other."

"That still brings about one fatal flaw to this plan," Brigid told them. "The people we are allies with tend to catch a lot of hell. Need I mention the dilemmas that have befallen New Edo as exemplars?"

Kane grimaced. "That's because this whole world is broken to pieces. United, we could stand fast against bandits, against the Millennial Consortium, we could even take the battle to the overlords."

"He's right," Grant added. "The world's a large place, but we have the mat-trans units, Mantas, Deathbirds, the interphaser—"

"And the Nagah's substantial fleet of aircraft," Brigid spoke up. She narrowed her eyes. "When we first came, you seemed enthralled by the transport helicopters that they possessed. Even more, you were fascinated by the fact that they possessed the means of launching a one-way space trip to deal with *Tiamat* when she had lorded over the Earth in orbit."

"Between Aten, New Edo, New Olympia, Cerberus, the Manitius scientists, we have the makings of a technology renaissance," Kane explained. "Robots, nanobot medicine, aircraft, global communications. Humanity can get back together."

"You say back," Grant said. "But that never had been the case. Or don't you forget the cold war that made skydark possible?"

"We can start the conversation, start the bartering," Kane said. "There are enough mutual enemies that even if we're separated by cobra and lizard DNA mixed with regular old human, we would be pure idiots to ignore what we *do* have in common."

Brigid nodded solemnly. "Ullikummis showed us that we're not invulnerable, that we can be torn apart."

"We've been lucky for five years," Kane said. "What happens when we're stopped for good? What happens when the latest menace doesn't get our attention and brings us running?"

"So we go to Hannah, and ask for her help in locating Ryugo-jo," Grant said, referring to the subterranean home of the Watatsumi.

Brigid frowned. "And hope that we can convince her we're still their friends. Then we hope that we can solve the problems of the Watatsumi."

"And that enough of them survive to make this trip worth it," Grant concluded grimly. "We aren't always successful."

"How many times have we faced the impossible without giving up?" Kane asked. He turned to Brigid as she took a deep breath and pointed at her to cut her off. "That was a rhetorical question, Baptiste."

The flame-haired archivist's cheeks reddened for a moment, then she smiled wryly. "No fair. You get to show off your muscles and noble nature, but I can't give you an accurate account of our adventures and successes to date?"

Kane shook his head in disbelief. "I'm just saying that risk is what Cerberus is all about. Taking the chances and daring the wilderness in order to bring about the betterment of the world. We were outnumbered by the barons. We were overpowered by the overlords—"

Grant raised a hand, interrupting Kane. "Don't worry about me, Kane. I got along great with Kondo and his men. I care about them. And I care about the Nagah."

"Just talking to hear yourself bitch and moan?" Kane asked.

Grant managed a smirk. "Something like that. And reminding myself about what's at stake if we fumble. We have friends at stake on both fronts."

"So let's do our best to fix up old mistakes," Brigid commented. "Before we can actually build this utopian ideal Kane's set up in his imagination, there's still miles of jungle to traverse."

Kane nodded in agreement, accepting the bottle of water from Grant. He took a long, deep pull from it to replenish the fluids he'd lost through perspiration. "The sooner we get moving, the sooner we get to correcting our fumbles, as you put it, Grant."

Grant put the bottle away in his war bag, then held out his hand to Kane. "Speaking of fumbles, give me that machete."

"Still sore about getting smacked in the face?" Kane asked.

Grant plucked the chopping tool from Kane's grasp. *"Bakayaro?"*

As his partner began slashing through the rain forest, Kane smiled. The grin drew a quizzical glance from Brigid, even as he shouldered the heavy war bag in Grant's stead.

"What?" she asked him.

Kane leaned in close for a conspiratorial whisper. "He's asking me who the asshole is, right?"

Brigid nodded in response.

"Then tell me how come I got Grant to spell me for a couple of miles?"

Brigid looked at their large friend as he carved a path ahead of them with ease, as if he were walking through gossamer threads of spiderwebs. She put her hand over her mouth once more to suppress a bout of laughter.

EVEN BEFORE HIS EYES opened, Kondo felt the hurt in every bone in his body. At first, he had no clue where he was, but he was lying atop a broken body covered in silken, soft down. The smell of fresh grass and blood assaulted his nostrils.

Experimental movements of his arms and legs answered him with a sensation of being pulled like dough, muscles stretched to their limits. Flame burned slowly along his muscles with each gesture. The best he could do right now was to roll himself off the feathered body, or at least its torso. Wing bones cracked beneath him as he flopped on his back.

The sun was much lower in the sky than when he'd been up in the crow's nest. Time, hours in fact, had disappeared while he was out cold. The dull throb that pulsed through every muscle began to subside, so he was able to blink without feeling as if he'd been slapped in the face.

Once more, he tested his right hand, reaching for his radio, but his fingers were numb, lifeless sausages stuck to a molten lava ball that was his elbow joint. The self-diagnosis was easy—he'd broken the arm. He fumbled for the communicator with his left hand.

Once the general background pain subsided, he was able to locate where he'd truly suffered injuries. The right side of his chest burned with the unmistakable signal of broken ribs. His leg hurt, but it was not the sharp stab of a bone fracture.

"Broken arm, fractured ribs, sprained knee," he said, tallying his injuries. Taking deep breaths for meditation was contraindicated by his current condition. Instead, he distracted himself by biting his lower lip. Focused, he brought the radio to his mouth.

"Captain Kondo. Report," he rasped.

The ominous silence on the frequency was as informative as a complete situation report. In the time he was gone, his men either retreated from the ventilation and manufacturing fortress, or they had fallen in battle.

He clumsily turned the knob, dialing in to another channel. "Kondo to base…"

There were shouts on the other end. He could hear the call that there was a survivor from central command. "Captain Kondo? Where are you?"

"Flat on my back, no view of the surrounding area," he answered. "Where are my men?"

"Can you walk?" the comm officer asked, ignoring the query. From the cheers over his comm, and the lack of an answer, there had been plenty of death.

"If someone helped me to my feet, I could limp," Kondo returned. "I've got a broken arm and ribs, though. Rising under my own power is going to hurt too much."

He let the radio rest in his hand, listening for what was said on the other end.

"What happened?" the comm officer asked.

Kondo winced. If there hadn't been a report, then it was unlikely his men stuck around, or those who stayed behind as a delaying action were lost.

"I took on some kind of winged dinosaur. It's got a wingspan the height of two men, and plenty of muscle," Kondo said. "However, if you drop two hundred pounds on it from a hundred feet up, you can kill it. I've got the specimen right here to prove it."

"We're sending you a recovery team," the man on the other end said.

"How many were lost?" Kondo asked.

There was that long, uncomfortable pause. The silence stunk of dread.

"Four stayed behind for a delaying action. We lost contact with them while the others got the civilians to safety," was the answer.

Kondo lifted his head, glancing around. The fortress stood, smoke billowing through the latticework roof. The wall had been hammered down, a fifteen-foot hole bashed in it. The power of the acrocanthosaurus had proved itself once more. He could see the top of a prone body, the unmistakable hips of a fallen dinosaur. Holding his head up proved too painful, and he rested it again, breathing slowly so as not to exacerbate his rib injuries.

"They killed one of the acros," he croaked into the radio. "Did all of the workers get out?"

"No casualties among the civilians," the radio officer returned.

"I'll be waiting here," Kondo groaned.

A new weight made his spirit sag even further. He had been unconscious while his men fought and died, doing their duty by protecting innocents. Kondo grit his teeth, trying to fight off the wave of self-loathing that gripped him. This time, he was certain that he might surely drown beneath this dread.

Chapter 3

The humans had returned, and Naji Hannah was torn. Kane, Brigid and Grant were the only members of this meager expedition, meaning that they were here not so much for a friendly reunion as for business. They were at once friends, allies who had stood with them against the rebellious actions of Durga's "pure-blooded renaissance," but they had also exposed deep societal wounds among the Nagah. There had been other horrible injuries, as well, the loss of Matron Yun and the near crippling of her true love, Manticor, not to mention the deaths of citizens and politicians in a bloody, brief civil war.

The good and the bad hung about the trio like a stink. They had come for the purpose of an alliance, a friendship that would help with the growth of a brave new world out of the wreckage of the old. Now, what had been a relatively advanced and capable city-nation was buckling under the strain of a loss of transportation and the True Pools. The cell-altering baths were filled with their god Enki's wondrous technology, which transformed a human mammal into a Nagah.

"They offered no resistance when they encountered our people and made their weapons polite," Captain Rahdnathi, the commander of Hannah's Royal Guard, spoke.

Hannah had unified the royal protection details and the pseudomilitaristic police of the Nagah nation, but a small rift still remained. The survivors of Matron Yun's protection detail held too many reservations about the absorption of one group into the other, while Manticor's fellow surviving regent protectors had felt Durga's isolation of the groups had led to his ability to do so much harm with his attempted coup. As such, the captain before her seemed uncomfortable with his address to the young queen.

Again, the grim memories of a fractured golden age welled up within her. "They say they come in peace, but they said that last time."

"My queen?" Rahdnathi asked.

Hannah reproached herself. "Bitter memories, Captain. The Cerberus party is no enemy to the nation of Garuda. Let them come in."

The captain nodded. The visit of the humans had been far too recent for anyone to have doubts about the essential goodness, and the potential for danger, that the three people represented. Whatever the trio brought, Hannah knew that it would bear the weight of a world and its fate with them.

SURROUNDED BY A CADRE of guards, the warriors of Cerberus relaxed, not so much in that they felt protected, but they knew that with their history among the Nagah, there was the possibility that any tension displayed might be a precursor to edgy nerves among the cobra people. It wasn't the easiest task in the world for Kane, Brigid and Grant to shut down their natural wariness, but for the sake of peace and the Watatsumi, they had to do it.

"I hate feeling like a pariah," Brigid Baptiste whispered, audible only over her Commtact. "It's as if we failed in our trip here."

"Failed how?" Kane asked. "We protected them from exploitation by the millennialists, stopped Enlil's plans for conquest and put an end to Durga's plans for ethnic cleansing and racial purity."

"Sometimes the cost is too much," Brigid returned, looking around. Major sections of the wall, the ancient Sanskrit once detailing the history of this ancient society, spawned from the brilliance of Enki, had been scoured, damaged by battle or otherwise broken apart by the need for providing new housing. It had been nearly a year since their visit, and here were the signs that life was still rebuilding. The once-proud fleet of transport aircraft in the underground city's hangar was gone, having suffered major losses due to internal sabotage and outside assault. There were helicopters, and a badly damaged Annunaki skimmer, but in the end, that which had lit the fires of possibility in Kane's mind was dangerously depleted. The airborne transport craft, the means by which nations could skirt radioactive wastelands and ground-based marauders, were nearly gone.

The histories, the data passed down over thousands of years from Enki himself, which could also have created a whole new era of prosperity, seemed gone. She knew that the True Pools—Enki's pools of alien nanotechnology capable of healing horrific wounds or mutating mortals into nigh unstoppable gods—had been destroyed in an effort to slay Durga.

"This is a warmer welcome than we expected," Grant said. He sounded hesitant, something unusual for the big man. Brigid turned her attention to him. "What's on your mind?" she asked.

The brawny man shrugged. "Something has to be bothering me?"

"Now you're sounding like an old Jewish man, answering a question with a question," Brigid pressed. "You've got something eating at you."

"I thought it was just that we were cutting into his happy time with Shizuka," Kane spoke up.

Grant nodded, but Brigid wasn't convinced. "You're the one who pushed for a way for us to find Ryugo-jo, Grant. What's making you stop and fuss now?"

"If I tell you, it might be let out," Grant answered. "I don't want Kondo to get in trouble."

"For what?" Kane asked.

Grant tightened his lips.

"You mean you know how to find the city?" Kane growled, coming to a stop.

The guards paused, still maintaining their formation around the humans.

"Keep walking," Grant grumbled. "Otherwise, they're going to think we're up to—"

"Fuck that," Kane snapped. "We went on an unnecessary trip through a hostile jungle, and you're holding on to—"

Grant stepped forward. "Listen, the Watatsumi are not interested in having anyone from the outside world traipsing into their city, not when they're already at war with a cannibal offshoot of their race. I don't want Kondo to have to commit seppuku because I didn't do my best to help him out."

"Kane," Brigid said, putting her hand on his biceps. "Kane, take it easy."

"You couldn't just trust us," Kane said.

Brigid could hear the tension in her friend's voice, and she stepped before him, scowling. "Not here."

"Then when?" Kane asked.

Grant scowled. "When we have the time, which is something we haven't had in too long. I've been sitting on this until we got a chance, and now things are too damn desperate. At least that's the way you're acting."

"Grant, I understand a little bit," Brigid replied.

"I'm not looking for sympathy," Grant told her. "But I also wasn't looking for a fight."

"We will have this out," Kane grumbled, closing the topic of conversation.

"My apologies," Brigid told the commander of the unit taking them to Hannah.

The officer shrugged. "You came to us. Maybe you should have been a little more prepared."

Brigid considered rattling off the string of emergencies and wars that had erupted since their last visit to the Nagah, but it would have seemed like only empty excuses. She simply nodded, acceding to the inappropriate nature of the argument.

The throne room was open to them, and the royal court was assembled, complete with Manticor in a wheelchair with inward-tilted wheels. His arms were thicker than when they had last seen him, which Brigid surmised was due to his use of those brawny limbs to get around. She recognized the design of the chair as one used by handicapped and injured soldiers for use in playing wheelchair basketball. The inward-tilted wheels allowed for swifter, more agile turns. He was the queen's consort, and befitting his station, he had a scabbard and holster built into the chair for his duties in protecting her. Hannah's slender figure, once covered in glimmering, jewel-colored scales, had dulled somewhat, and her belly showed the slight swelling of early pregnancy.

The royal bloodline, the family that had been nearly destroyed by Durga, had one more chance with this generation.

"We bid you a happy return to our humble city," Hannah spoke, trying to sound lazy and disinterested, but Brigid could catch the acid tinge beneath her words. She had told the Cerberus visitors that it would be *her* decision to summon the humans back to the underground civilization. Their arrival represented a direct repudiation of her mandate.

Still, if she were harboring ill will, she could have simply refused Kane and the others admittance into the damaged city.

"Thank you," Brigid said, keeping the tone diplomatic, even though she could feel the hot flash of annoyance emanating from Kane. "We bring you good news this time."

Hannah tilted her head, the thick hood muscles on one side of her neck flexing as she did so. The cobra woman was obviously intrigued. "Go on."

"Do you have a legend of a lost or missing tribe?" Grant asked. "Brothers who left for the East?"

Hannah looked toward Manticor "Yes, yes, we have."

"You're not surprised that we're aware of all of this," Kane grumbled. Brigid could still feel the hurt feelings hanging around him like a dismal aura. "You've been hearing them communicate?"

"We first started hearing global transmissions—they're encrypted—but we've been hearing them," Manticor spoke up. "The one thing that was left untouched during your last visit was our set of ears."

"Again, our apologies," Kane spoke up. "Do you have any coordinates for us?"

"Only a general area. Whoever they are, they are pretty well organized. There'd been a lot of chatter going on a while back, transmissions bouncing from relay to relay from what used to be the coast of China to the Florida Panhandle and on toward the Bahamas," Manticor explained.

"That died out about a month and a half ago, right?" Kane asked.

Manticor nodded. "You were there, weren't you? During the period that Cerberus went dark?"

Kane shrugged. "You'll have to ask Grant about that."

Grant may have been flustered, but it didn't show on his face. "We were there. That's when we met up with the Watatsumi. They had traveled to the Panhandle to investigate biomechanical technology in a human base called AUTEC. They claimed that they were under siege and were hoping to utilize a mind-control program to deal with their opposition."

Hannah frowned. "Watatsumi…"

"The Japanese dragon deities of the ocean," Grant translated. "There were three of them, for the upper, middle and lower kingdoms. That sounds sort of familiar."

"Zeus, Poseidon and Hades in Greek mythology," Manticor interjected. "And we know who posed as those three. The Annunaki."

Brigid nodded. "We think that one of the three gods they named themselves after may have been Enki, rather than Marduk or Enlil."

"And if they honored Enki, then they may have been an offshoot of the Nagah," Hannah surmised. "That's an interesting idea."

"I know that you suffered great losses in the war that occurred during our visit," Brigid said. "But maybe this is a chance to offer amends, a reunion of sorts."

"I'm sure you've discussed this among yourselves," Hannah said, "but we're not in a good position to be entertaining refugees."

"But I'm sure you can use a new trade partner," Kane countered. "Any trade partner, actually."

"You have commerce to trade?" Hannah asked.

"Right now, no," Kane explained. "And maybe that's

the case for the Watatsumi, too. But wouldn't it be good to bring everyone together into a better community?"

"We've hidden ourselves from most of humankind for thousands of years," Manticor said. "This was for a very good reason. Humans tend not to react favorably toward reptilians like us."

"We have," Brigid countered. "And right now, with the world in the state it is, people will be a lot more open to new friends and allies."

"And you will have someone like you out there," Grant added.

"That helped so much in clashes between Pakistan and India. Their differences are probably even more slight than ours to the Watatsumi," Hannah grumbled. "I know how things are with humans, and we are very much human."

"And you are intelligent, reasonable beings," Brigid pressed. "Racism is endemic to every race, and those prejudices are simple survival instincts. However, other survival instincts can override the fear of the different. The world can be rebuilt. It was on track in the year 2000, it can be on track today. Otherwise, we've fought all for nothing."

"You can stay for the night, and we'll do what we can to help you in triangulation of the island," Hannah conceded. "You have had a long, harrowing trip to return to us. Rest now."

"Thank you, Hannah," Kane said.

With that, the humans were taken away to temporary quarters.

GRANT SLOUCHED, DRINKING from a goblet of weak wine, his frown conforming to the downward horns of his gunfighter's mustache. Kane was sitting across the room, looking everywhere except at his lifelong friend. It may have seemed petty, but Grant knew that Kane was hardly the

type of man to engage in needless conversation unless
something really struck him hard.

Keeping knowledge from Kane about anything was
something that had never even occurred to Grant; the two
men had shared nearly everything since they bonded as
partners enforcing baronial edicts in Cobaltville. It made
sense, if only that any hesitation of communication of important facts could mean the difference between life and
death.

Still, Grant knew that Kondo could likely be in the position where he'd be executed for sharing any amount of
knowledge about Ryugo-jo. Kane would only be inconve-
nienced by a side trip. Nevertheless, Kane had managed
to pry that information from Grant.

Grant took another sip of his wine, still frowning. "You
a little better now?"

Kane nodded.

"I'm sorry," Grant said. "You can understand—"

"Yeah," Kane cut him off, still sounding a little raw,
but he didn't have a sharp tone of voice anymore. "It's stupid of me to feel betrayed like that. You've never steered
me wrong, and you were just trying to keep someone else
out of trouble."

Grant nodded.

Kane stood up and walked over to him. "So, you going
to share some of that wine?"

"The alcoholic content doesn't make it much better than
grape juice from the cafeteria back at Cerberus," Grant
answered.

Kane shrugged. "We can get drunk back home. What?
I can't have a couple of sips with my best friend?"

Grant smirked and held out the bottle for him. "I don't
want to add insult to injury, but there *was* another person
I told about the frequency that Kondo gave me."

"And let me guess—it was Bry," Kane answered. "The one man who is the least likely to ever step outside the redoubt, let alone trudge all the way to the Southern Cific."

Grant nodded.

"Great," Kane said, pouring himself a glass and taking a gulp. "So we haven't heard anything from them?"

"You heard Manticor. The transmissions are encrypted normally, and though we've been sweeping around the globe with satellites, nothing has proved strong enough to pierce the atmosphere for them to pick up," Grant said. He shrugged, taking another sip. "Of course, it's no mystery why everything went quiet."

"They don't have to transmit around the world," Kane said. "Not since their Florida expedition returned home."

"Otherwise, the Nagah would have had an easier time of triangulating their position," Grant added.

"We *could* call them," Kane offered. "But that would end up negating whatever you did for Kondo in keeping things secret."

"Now you can see my dilemma in telling anyone," Grant muttered.

Kane shrugged. "So, let's get creative. They obviously have access to one of the mat-trans units. Otherwise, they wouldn't have been able to set up shop in the Florida Panhandle. We overlay the area where the Nagah picked up their transmissions with redoubts in the area."

"We'd been looking at the redoubts, but it had been a stab in the dark without having a transmission to trace," Grant said. "And we can put the Nagah's ears onto the frequency we do have."

Kane nodded. "That's one way to do it."

"It's the easiest way I've determined," Brigid said from the doorway.

"How long have you been listening?" Kane asked.

"Ever since we were given our quarters. I was half expecting you two to brawl it out," Brigid said. She smiled. "It's nice to know you can talk it out."

Kane shrugged. "Evolution is a wonderful thing."

"We won't need to call back to Cerberus now," Grant said. "I forgot that Brigid doesn't forget."

"So you already have a map of the redoubts with working mat-trans units, and a means to triangulate what the Nagah have a record of," Brigid added. "That is, if we've still got their approval."

"Knowing Hannah, she'll want to send someone with us," Kane said. "We were quite helpful to the Nagah in their last conflict, but we had to rely on some of their resources to even the odds. We might have an ally or two on this who don't happen to be Watatsumi."

"You make this sound like a good thing," Grant noted.

Kane nodded. "Well, we are heading into a war situation. Who's to say that the Watatsumi's enemies don't have people on the inside? I'll reserve my judgment."

"But after our adventures here, in New Olympia, in Aten, you're going to expect the worst," Brigid concluded.

"I'll practice my surprise face for when the bad guys do pop out of the woodwork, but I'm going to be ready," Kane said.

"Not that you're cynical or anything," Grant added with a chuckle.

"It's my turn now to be the 'I told you so' guy?" Kane asked.

"He's back in a good mood," Grant told Brigid. "Something shitty is about to happen."

"If only life were that predictable," Brigid answered.

Klaxons suddenly blared, their howl so harsh and sudden, Kane and Grant launched their Sin Eaters into their grasps.

"You were saying?" Kane asked.

CAPTAIN RAHDNATHI grimaced, noticing that the three visitors from Cerberus had left their quarters in the middle of a red alert. Ideally, Kane and the others should have been kept behind a lockdown, and Rahdnathi had been tasked with their protection. Of course, things never would go that easily.

"Please, turn around and stay away from the perimeter," Rahdnathi snapped as they approached. As much as he wanted to rush to the throne room and to his chosen task of defending the queen and her consort, he had received his orders directly from Hannah's lips. He would have sooner carved out his own liver than disobey a direct order, failing her wishes.

"There's trouble afoot," Brigid countered, "and we don't sit on the sidelines."

"What's the situation?" Kane asked.

Rahdnathi took a deep breath, the hood, which stretched from his shoulders to the crown of his skull, flexing open in the instinctive threat response. "The millennialists had invested too much time and effort into invading us on their last attack. As such, they've set up a small hidden camp within spitting distance of our city."

"But you can't find them," Kane returned.

Rahdnathi shook his head. "And since the destruction of the nano baths, we have had a growing pure human, as opposed to those who had taken the plunge."

"Which means you could have infiltrators among your human minority," Grant said.

"Not that it had been a minority in the first place. The Nagah have always been a plurality," Rahdnathi replied.

"Enki knew that if we'd completely isolated ourselves from regular humanity, we would be unable to complete our task as the protectors of humankind. Unfortunately, since the consortium found us, it means we now have to have our heads on a swivel."

"Sorry," Grant offered.

Rahdnathi looked at the big man, then waved off the words. "It was Durga's doing. If you hadn't set off the explosives, he might not have been weakened enough to be killed."

"So how does the consortium usually hit you?" Kane asked.

"They plant high explosives to sabotage rebuilding or new construction," Rahdnathi explained. "But right now, everything's been compartmentalized. We have hit a full lockdown, and as part of the Royal Guard, I'm in on the only operating communications network."

"Doesn't that interfere with emergency operations?" Brigid asked.

"The Royal Guard is much more than a bunch of gun-toting thugs," Kane told her. "They will be the heart of the communications network, and all of them will be background checked to verify that they aren't going to betray the Nagah."

"Just like the Magistrates?" Brigid asked. "Because I seem to remember a failure...."

"Damn it, Baptiste," Kane snarled. "You were complaining about me?"

Brigid glared at him but held her tongue. The communications were as secure as they possibly could be. And Kane hadn't betrayed his oath as a lawman so much as he rebelled against a partially human cadre of despots. "So we're stuck on the sidelines for good."

"Not necessarily," Rahdnathi returned. "Communications are filtered, and travel is restricted by blast doors, but there's no telling exactly where the attack has taken place. Hang on."

The chatter was coming in from all sectors, according to his headset, and that meant that he was as likely to have the Millennial Consortium saboteurs in his lap even as he spoke. He drew his pistol and shot a warning glance to Kane and Grant. The two men didn't need words of explanation, and as they readied themselves, so did Brigid.

"They're going all out," he told the Cerberus warriors.

That's when the explosion spit concussive force through the tunnel, lifting the people up and flinging them about like leaves.

Chapter 4

Kane had been caught near to enough explosions that he knew exactly how to minimize the brunt of a concussive wave force. He allowed himself to go limp, knowing that any effort to keep his body tense as the force of the blast hurled him along would make certain he broke bones when he came to the inevitable sudden stop against a wall, a floor, any projection.

He flopped flat against the corridor's wall, and having spread out his body mass across a broader surface, his weight didn't impact on any point of his body. The shock-absorbing properties of the advanced polymers in his shadow suit buttressed that level of protection, making his abrupt landing something he could easily weather.

Kane dragged himself from the floor, looking around. His ears rang, and his vision was blurred, but thankfully not from head trauma. Smoke was making his eyes water, and he blinked the fuzziness away, relying on his extremely well-honed subconscious to compensate for his less-than-optimal mental condition. Two quick glances informed him that Brigid and Grant were quickly recovering from their shock, gathering themselves back to their feet.

"Check on Rahd," Kane ordered Grant, knowing the big man was slightly more adept at first aid than the rest of them. The reptilian sentry, however, was crawling to his hands and knees.

"I'll be fine," Rahdnathi grunted, bringing himself back

to his feet. "When Enki remade the Nagah, we were given more than scales and fangs."

"I'd presume a pliant endoskeleton with far more flexible cartilage, just as in regular *ophidia*," Brigid spoke up as she did a quick check of her body and gear, making sure she was all together.

"Off day?" Grant quipped with a snort. "Sounds like the old man was *on* that day."

"*Ophidia.* Serpentlike," Brigid countered, looking in one direction down the hall as Grant checked the other end of the corridor.

He turned back to her and gave her a poke in the shoulder. "It was a pun, kiddo."

Brigid turned back for an instant, giving him a wink, letting Grant know that she was kidding with him.

Rahdnathi shook his head in dismay. "Taking time to joke, yet still paying attention to their surroundings. You always have to crack wise?"

Kane shrugged, his features serious, his gaze distracted by something in the distance, signs of hostile enemies, wounded allies or both. "There are wounded within what looks like the initial blast's shrapnel radius. Looks and sounds like four people."

Rahdnathi looked confused, but for all their banter, the Cerberus explorers were on the ball, moving quickly down the hall to provide aid to the injured. Grant and Brigid immediately set to work giving triage to the floored victims of the blast, leaving Kane and Rahdnathi to the important task of looking out for the perpetrators of this act of terror. The bloodied Nagah were sorted from superficial bleeding and one case of an arterial rip. Both Grant and Brigid swiftly applied their skills, tearing cloth in order to apply a pressure bandage to prevent the bright red, vital blood from pouring out.

As Rahdnathi scanned for secondary explosives meant to take out first responders to the attack, he spoke. "It's a self-diagnostic tool, the joking, right?"

Kane grunted in assent. "If you can joke, then your thought processes tend to be clear. It also keeps you from concentrating on fear and pain."

"Understood. I usually don't say mine out loud," Rahdnathi said. "Course, you need to communicate that information to the rest of your team."

"It's not for everyone, or every occasion, but as long as we're helping people and getting work done, we can dispel doubt and fear for ourselves and others," Kane said. "It also makes us look braver and more devil-may-care than we really are."

"True of any fighting man," Rahdnathi replied. He turned his attention to helping Brigid prepare a compress and pressure bandage for the arterial bleeder while Grant went to work on other victims. "You're said to have preternatural senses, Kane. You see anything about who set this fucking bomb to hurt my fellow citizens?"

Kane would have answered, but his focus was elsewhere, checking each shadow, each subtle sound that made it past the ringing in his ears, even scents and vibrations that he could feel through the soles of his boots. He listened closely to his subconscious, the ever faithful point man's sense, which picked up danger signs with far more acute skill than his conscious instincts. By shutting down his conscious thoughts, ignoring them, he freed himself to live in the moment, the state of mind that Shizuka, Grant's samurai lover, called *zanshin,* the state of relaxed alertness, or place where his most primal combat skills and his senses were at their sharpest. It was a mind-set that samurai struggled and meditated all their life to achieve, but Kane was born to it.

As such, when there was the merest scrape of a boot on the floor that was out of place from Rahdnathi, Grant and Baptiste, he whirled toward it, Sin Eater snapping into his grasp with lightning speed, its muzzle trained like a laser on the chest of an Indian man wielding a machete. The millennialist infiltrator stopped cold in his tracks, eyes wide as he was caught red-handed, arm cocked back, ready to deliver a limb-severing chop.

"Drop it or die," Kane growled. The would-be assassin was scarcely three strides away, and the Cerberus warrior knew that he was well within the lethal arc of the bared machete blade. Even a bullet right to the heart wouldn't be enough to stop the killer cold, but the snarled threat gave the man pause. With the speed of a mongoose, the ex-Magistrate kicked the faux Nagah-kin in the chest, the power of Kane's leg and all of his weight lifting up the killer and bowling him onto his back.

"Incoming!" Kane bellowed, catching the movement of others out of the corners of his eyes, his clarion call alerting his two partners.

Brigid continued to press down on a pressure dressing, but Grant's hands were free and he shot to his feet, rising to his full height. As he did so, his hand shot out and clamped around the throat of a millennialist saboteur, snatching the man off the ground and dangling him in empty air. The massive ex-Magistrate twisted, letting go of his opponent and bringing his fist hard under his opponent's sternum. The consortium's killer folded over the mighty punch, rolling away to the floor like a pile of discarded laundry.

"Get them!" another voice cried out as Grant had clutched the man's throat. Kane knew the owner of that voice brought a pistol up and around, aiming at the larger, easier target. The Sin Eater in Kane's hand barked once, the bullet following its shooter's gaze, a 240-grain slug pulverizing wrist and forearm bones to make the killer's handgun fall away, lifeless fingers opening up even as the paw dangled on cords of muscle and sinew.

Kane's shot had been merciful, but it wasn't out of kindness that he didn't blow a massive hole through the almost murderer's head. This group of killers were not on their own, and they had been engaged in a long-standing campaign to terrorize the Nagah in the time since their last visit. Kane wanted to know why the Millennia Consortium was so intensely interested in the cobra people of India, even in the wake of the destruction of much of their cherished and enviable technological treasures. So far they now had three prisoners, one of whom seemed to be in a position of authority.

Movement flickered out of the corner of an eye, and Kane's instincts instantly locked on. It was the last of the saboteurs, and the man was lunging at Rahdnathi, whose hands were full with his own first-aid efforts. Even though the cobra man was facing his attacker, he had no weapons, and his grasp was tight around a bloody wound. Kane willed himself to spin, but the last of the attackers was just too fast, and he was facing too far away from the knife-wielding saboteur.

The Nagah looked his opponent right in the face, and his lips barely parted, venom sacs unleashing twin streams of eye-burning fluid. Rahdnathi may have been a little too far back to have benefited from Kane's protection, but his cobra physiology was an effective form of self-defense. The millennialist infiltrator screamed as the venom spray caught him in the eyes, his diving effort to stab the first responder dissolving like mist in the blazing sun. The bomber collapsed, clutching his agonized features, tumbling to the side of Rahdnathi and the injured Nagah.

Kane returned his attention to the man he'd shot through the wrist, clamping his hand around the bloodied stump in an effort to control the bleeding. "You're not dying that easily, murderer."

The millennialist struggled, but Kane hammered him hard in the side of the head with his forearm, calming him with a skull-rattling impact. A quick twist, and he had the prisoner facedown on the ground and was constricting the shattered limb with a loop of plastic as a tourniquet. There wasn't going to be any rescuing of the almost severed hand, so the crushing of blood vessels and nerves was no concern. Kane pressed his knee against the Indian's lower back.

"Four prisoners," Kane said. "We will get some answers out of this lot."

"The obvious reason for this attack is our arrival," Brigid spoke up, finishing her desperate measures against arterial bleeding, trusting her partners enough to continue her work without lifting a finger to defend herself. "The Nagah are a nice sitting target, but adding us to the mix…"

"I figured as much," Kane grumbled. "You all right there, Rahd?"

The cobra man nodded. "I'm perfectly fine now that I have this bleeding stopped. That's more than I can say for these men if we don't get the right answers from them."

"Torture won't provide information. They'll say anything under duress," Kane argued.

Rahdnathi narrowed his eyes. "Who said anything about getting answers? If they're not going to talk, they're going to suffer for what they did to innocent women and children."

Kane mused for a moment. This wasn't an act for their prisoners, but right now, Rahdnathi was caught up in the moment. It was one thing to talk roughly when your adrenaline was heightened due to the proximity of injured neighbors and in the wake of an attack. He could see a momentary pang of regret cross the yellowed eyes of the Nagah even as he spoke.

Rahdnathi sneered at the blinded man on the floor. "Turning me into an animal?"

"Keep it under control, Rahd," Kane said, hand out to keep himself between the Nagah and the helpless man.

Rahdnathi glowered. "I am fine, Kane. It took me a minute to remember the kind of tactics these scum employ. They make it so that the defenders of the realm don't have qualms about torture or inflicting undue pain, and soon the government that serves the people begins to feel it can push those people around, making them servants. Then the Millennial Consortium can pass themselves off as better than the Royal Family."

"True," Kane acknowledged, but still blocked the Nagah and their prisoner.

Rahdnathi turned his focus to the radio. He gave it a couple of hard raps, frustration showing on his scaled features. "They must have a jammer."

Grant shot a glance to Kane. "The millennialists are getting smarter. They're blocking our frequency, too."

"Maybe someday the fused-out bastards will get smart enough to know not to fuck with us," Kane growled. "Please tell me that there's a way around the lockdown."

Rahdnathi nodded, but he wasn't going to talk in front of the prisoners. "Grant, could you babysit these murderous bastards?"

Grant sneered with dreadful mirth. "Yeah. Go do what you have to do. These pricks try something, they'll learn how pissed off I am."

"Good. Kane, Brigid?" Rahdnathi invited.

The Cerberus warriors followed the Nagah security officer as they ducked from the scene.

"One thing that the Royal Guard did as soon as we suspected infiltration was to give ourselves a means of access to all parts of the city," the cobra man said. "We'd kept the hidden tunnels to the throne room a secret in the wake of the first attack on Matron Yun."

"But you explored them," Brigid concluded.

"It's our personal rapid transit system even under the worst of lockdown conditions," Rahdnathi responded. "Where do you need to go?"

"Where the trouble will be the worst," Kane answered. "And we should have been there five minutes ago."

"The throne room," the Royal Guardsman growled.

The trio of guardians raced to where they needed to be.

AT THE FIRST DISTANT CRASH of an explosion, Manticor pivoted his wheelchair, spinning swiftly to put himself between the sound and his love, Queen Hannah. The royal consort was certain that Hannah hadn't lost a single scintilla of her fighting skill, nor her courage, but her belly was full and swollen with the next generation of the regal rule of the Nagah, and if the duty of protector to the royal family were not enough, he was the father of those unborn children.

He would die to protect them, and he was not intending to go to his eternal rest any time soon. Death would leave him unable to stand the line between his family and their assailants.

Though in a wheelchair, he was in the throne room, and the area was smooth and unbroken. Even without an unmarred floor, however, the wheels of the chair had heavily knobbed tires that allowed for greater traction and control, making the gripping of rubble and mud easier. His arms and shoulders had grown considerably in strength, and he was thankful for all the Nagah who had been through the vats or born with the mutations that made them more serpentine, either through boneless legs or fused lower bodies, which necessitated the continued development and innovation of technology for the handicapped.

While many had strived to increase their lower-body strength so that the fused trunk provided by their conjoined legs was all the support they needed, there was still the acknowledgment that a pair of wheels was far more advantageous than even the fastest of slithery opponents. This boosted the bonus to those who had been wounded and crippled, such as Manticor had been when enemy bullets had shattered his femurs and knees.

"Darling, I think you'd better get into the safe room," Manticor said as he plucked his pistol from its holster on his left shin. He glanced toward her, and noted the beginnings of an argument form in his wife's eyes. Luckily, logic won that argument even before she moved her lips. Her role as regent and the safety of her unborn children were too important to risk in an egotistical need to prove herself as no longer requiring a "babysitter." Manticor had been that sitter for a long time, before the events of Durga's attempted coup made any furthering of his feelings for her acceptable. Now, the princess's knight had been raised to the status of queen's lord. It was lip service to the fact that he was not of royal birth, but he still had earned respect, from his fellow Royal Guard, and in private, intimate moments, Hannah called him her king.

Hannah, regret stricken, moved to the curtains behind her throne where two members of the guard flanked the secret passage into and out of the royal court. One had it open while the other held his rifle at low ready, covering her approach. The doorman ushered her through the hole into the covert corridor as another guardsman took his place.

Manticor grimaced. He was accorded nearly the same prestige and protection as his pregnant bride, and that guard motioned for him to join Hannah in the safety of the secret passages. Reluctantly, he returned his pistol to its shin holster, freeing up both hands to operate his wheelchair. Fingers wrapped around the tacky, traction supplying knobs on the chair's tires. The design for these wheels came from sport bicycles, meant for off-road work, and made movement around the underground city easy, even with large patches of tunnels left unpaved or ungraded. With a powerful shrug, he pivoted the chair and was up the ramp with one explosion of effort, so efficient was the wheelchair design. The chair and his training made each pump of his corded arms swift and economic. As he neared the hatch, there was a thunderous bellow, buckling the court's ornate, but armored, main doors.

Temptation to stop, wheel around, and face this danger tugged at him, but every second he delayed was another moment that the Royal Guard's warriors had to divide their attention from protecting him and dealing with the callous threat that was setting off bombs around the city, forcing the Nagah's subterranean domain into a lockdown.

Another hard push, and an angry grunt from the effort, rocketed Manticor through the escape hatch and in a heartbeat, the security hatch locked behind him. Composite armor, formed from sandwiched polymers and rolled and extruded steel, now stood between the enemy and his family.

"Core!" Hannah called from a door down the corridor. She was busy latching an armored vest with extra protective panels around her swollen, pregnant belly as she stood at the entrance to the Royal Guard's emergency command center. She'd also stuck her personal sidearm and knife into sheaths on that armored vest, a shoulder-stocked submachine gun dangling from its sling around her neck.

"I'm fine," he replied. "Stop blocking the hallway, please."

Hannah's nose wrinkled as she jerked her head in a motion for him to hurry up and join her. The couple entered the small room that had been stocked with monitors and encrypted communications equipment. An arms locker was open in one corner, and a staff member quickly tossed him the queen's consort's royal battle armor. It was a vest adorned with hard composite plates down its chest, mimicking the pattern of his natural chest and belly scales. There was a sheathed combat knife and filled pouches with spare ammunition for his pistol and the rifle he carried.

The staff member waited until Manticor had pulled the vest over his head to throw him his battle helmet, complete with faceplate. The helmet was based on the design that—in what used to be America—had been used for the Magistrates, containing optics and communications, as well as providing head trauma protection. The helmets had to be redesigned slightly to accommodate the hooded heads of the Nagah, but they had proved effective in every test since.

Fully ready for combat, Manticor spun his chair to look at the cameras that had been situated in the throne room. In time with the second rumbling vibration that worked through the floor and up through the wheelchair, he could see the throne room doors topple, smoke billowing through the arch-shaped scar in the chamber. Shadowy figures advanced slowly, firing from the hip with deadly automatic weaponry in an attempt to wipe out any resistance.

"Your mistake," Manticor whispered, knowing that the millennialists wouldn't be able to hear him. The thugs hired by the would-be technocracy were well-equipped, and probably were even able to shoot fairly straight, but they hadn't anticipated the level of preparation that the Royal Guard had gone through, especially when in conflict with the Sons of Enlil. Two of the invaders suddenly twisted and writhed as their bodies were peppered with aimed, accurate streams of bullets, directed by a dug-in and prepared defensive force. The guard was made of smart, professional fighting men and their knowledge of the dangers of civil war and cultist insurgency had made them ready for such an attack on the regents in their own quarters. Only four of the Nagah warriors remained behind, but the cobra men had the home-field advantage. Not only did the enemy have to run a gauntlet, herded through a single entrance that walked them across the guardsmen's combined fields of fire, but the attackers had little to respond to. Each of the defending soldiers was nestled behind thick stone columns, which concealed much of their bodies from view and were able to stop all but direct hits from the rocket launcher that had taken out the huge armored doors.

The consortium's thugs were bogged down in their effort to charge the queen, which allowed Manticor to turn his attention toward movement in the secret hallway. Newcomers were on their way, but gunfire didn't erupt, a familiar voice calling out.

It was Rahdnathi and the Cerberus visitors, at least two of them. Manticor bristled at their arrival, but knew that Kane and his companions were already aware of the hidden tunnel system, having been present when Enlil sent two of his Nephilim assassins to murder the previous queen, Matron Yun.

"We're on top of the situation, Kane. If you run out there, you'll just stumble into the path of the good guys.

They're so busy dealing with the insurgents, you'll either catch lead or make them hold their fire and get killed by the attackers," Manticor warned.

"That's not a problem," Brigid responded. "However, we're not certain that the Royal Guard's new transit system is entirely secure."

Manticor looked to Rahdnathi for an explanation and got it without further prodding. The Nagah guardian spoke quickly. "Kane and Brigid reminded us that these were originally used by the Enlil cultists. And the Miliennial Consortium is not above allying themselves with psychopaths."

"The Sons of Enlil definitely would have a good reason to temporarily ally themselves with the consortium," Kane added. "Afterward, they could always call in their 'papa' to deal with the pesky mammals."

Manticor shared a long look with Hannah. His wife, usually an open book to him, had grimly darkened, her face an inscrutable mask. "My queen?"

"Since most of our backup plans and fallback positions depend on this maze, we have to sit it out here," Hannah said. "That means everyone is on full alert. We can't be any more prepared than full body armor, helmets and shoulder-fired guns. If the Sons of Enlil do make an effort to hit us here in the tunnels, at least my citizens will be out of the cross fire."

Manticor nodded toward the two humans.

"*If* Kane and Brigid are right, then they came to us to help, putting themselves in the line of fire. They may stay," Hannah added. "I still trust you, if not most humans. However, let us hope that you are wrong."

"You're not the only ones hoping so," Brigid added.

Kane suddenly jerked, his keen, predator-sharp eyes picking up movement. Even as he was in motion, his lips curled into a sneer. "Hope is taking another shit on us, Baptiste. *Get down!*"

Manticor lunged, pushing himself out of his chair with one arm and hooking his pregnant bride with the other. Even as he fell across her as a living shield, the control room shook violently, electronics sparking and sizzling as shock waves ripped through the wall.

Kane was gone, but Manticor knew that the Cerberus warrior wasn't abandoning the Nagah royal family.

He was hurling himself into the line of fire.

Chapter 5

Kane saw the consortium-backed insurgents on-screen, and they had an old Russian-made RPG rocket launcher being loaded and readied. He had only enough time before the first shot to warn the others and brace himself. Then the rocket slammed into the armored door and, thanks to their proximity to the entrance, he had to ride out a head-spinning blast that hurled people off their feet and caused television monitors to crack under the overpressure produced by the high-intensity explosives. A second shot, hitting the door, would knock the heavy hatch off of its hinges, and the subsequent blast wave would, at the very least, render everyone insensate with burst eardrums.

It was time to act, and he could beg forgiveness later.

Air was less resistant to compression than water, the only thing that had kept the initial explosion from rendering him senseless with the first hit. It still transmitted vibrations well, and the dense molecules of the stone walls ferried tremors through them to the point of making the electronics in the command center suffer from the thermobaric warhead. Kane threw himself at the hatch, snapping open the heavy bolt mechanism, which thankfully had not been bent by the first impact. Even as the door swung open, Kane pushing on it with all of his might, he could see the millennialist thug shoulder the reloaded rocket grenade, aiming to finish the job of exposing the queen and her defenders in the covert tunnels.

Thought became action, and the Sin Eater machine pistol he'd retracted into its holster to free both hands to open the hatch rocketed into his palm, the exposed trigger of the folding weapon striking his hooked index finger. The hydraulic motors shoved the gun hard enough that the Sin Eater's forward momentum pulled the trigger for Kane. That instantaneous action and reflex spiked a powerful 9 mm slug into the millennialist's chest, breastbone shattering.

The rocket launched, but instead of striking the hatch, it sailed into the vaulted ceiling of the throne room. Stone and dust vomited from the detonation, raining down in a thick, choking cloud that cut the chamber's visibility to mere inches, but the blast was far enough away, its energy directed elsewhere, sparing Brigid and the Nagah royal family the effects of a second shock wave.

The dead rocketeer's companions still had to be dealt with, and Kane was by himself in the smoke. Obviously the Royal Guard was out of commission; otherwise the guardsmen wouldn't have allowed the rocketeer to loiter in the doorway unmolested, especially with the lines of sight that he'd seen. On instinct Kane wove through the swirling dust toward one of the defensive positions that he'd seen on the monitors in the command center. Within a few heartbeats, he'd located one of the niches in the wall where the Royal Guardsmen had been holed up. He was down, and his armor was bloody from the feel of it, but the man's chest rose and fell with a regular rhythm. Kane didn't hear any gurgling of strained breathing, so the blood might have been from a superficial wound.

Taking time out for emergency first aid would allow the dust to settle and he and his opponents to be on an equal footing, the kind of thing that he avoided when outnumbered and outgunned. Kane knew that things such as tactics and strategy were only polite terms for getting an unfair advantage during the worst moments of a person's life. When he fought, he fought to win, and with decisive force.

He could hear the scuff of sandals close to him. Shoes were generally not needed by the scale-soled Nagah, so that meant his opponent was human. Even so, he didn't want to accidentally take on a trusted half-formed guardsman whose Nagah transformation had left him with humanoid feet. With a lunge, he reached out and snared the man in the mist, one arm snaked around his throat, his fingers plunging between very human-feeling lips to muffle any response. If it had been a Nagah, he would have felt the scales and held up on his assault, knowing that jamming his hand into a pair of venomous fangs would mean a painful end of his adventuring days.

This was a man, and as such, Kane used his jaw as a lever to control him, twisting the millennialist to the ground even though teeth struggled to grind on his knuckles. Kane's grasp was strong, and his fingernails dug into the man's tongue, cutting off any semblance of bite force. With a hard shove, he hammered the attacker's head into the floor with a thud. Skull fracture and head trauma turned the would-be killer into a puddle of limp limbs.

"Seti?" a voice called through the dust. That was the only warning that Kane had before he rose from his unconscious foe and stepped back. A burst of automatic fire cut through the churning smoke where he'd been a moment earlier, the millennialist's muzzle-flash giving away his position. The Cerberus warrior raced toward the gunfire, sliding his combat knife from its sheath at the small of his back. There was grumbling from two other voices, cursing in Hindi about their partner's panic fire, but he wasn't there to hear it.

Kane snagged the barrel of his rifle, using it as a handle to yank the gunman closer. Twelve inches of razor-sharp steel whipped through the dust cloud about them before disappearing with a wet slurp into soft viscera. The gunman's momentum at being yanked forward allowed Kane to maximize the force of his stab, compressing soft tissue and allowing him to open up a yawning, deadly wound that would have left him sliced in two had he taken another moment. As it was, the rifleman's diaphragm muscles had been severed, so he had nothing with which to croak out a cry for aid. At the same brutal slash, the millennialist's aorta was opened up, arterial spray jetting out crimson droplets to disappear into the gray haze about them.

"We've got five wounded in there, according to infrared camera," Brigid's voice said over his Commtact. "The Royal Guards and the one whose head you bounced on the floor."

"Thanks," Kane subvocalized, hoping to maintain his element of surprise a moment or two longer.

"Insurgent to your right, five paces," Brigid announced.

Kane swiveled his head in that direction, realizing that he hadn't noticed the foe because he'd gone instantly still.

The ex-Magistrate wasn't the only one using senses other than sight to locate an enemy in the dust cloud. The millennialist trooper had gone still, which was why Brigid had been able to notice him before he could. They knew something was up, from the odd cracking noise and then the sudden burst of gunfire. This consortium gunman was smart enough to pause and use his ears.

Kane could wait, but the dust cloud was starting to thin. He could see the millennialist's vague outline, a darker shade of gray than the surrounding obfuscation. But what Kane could see, he could shoot. The Sin Eater snapped into his grasp, and the blur jolted backward at the sound.

A brief rip of automatic fire filled the air as the frightened gunman cut loose, but he was shooting from the hip, and he was not like Kane, whose Magistrate training allowed him to focus his first shot without using the sights. The Sin Eater fast-draw shot that popped from the level of Kane's waistline struck the gunman's center of mass, and he sprawled backward, filling the air with a burst of gunfire that only sprayed the ceiling.

Kane's muzzle-flash gave away his position, and he heard his last opponent scurrying to one side, turning to open fire. Instinct and experience impelled Kane to move the moment he fired his shot in the murky mists of the throne room, and the segment of cloud he'd occupied a moment earlier was simply empty space as bullets sliced through it.

That last blaze of gunfire drew the Cerberus warrior's aim and he fired off a few more shots, the Sin Eater tearing through the head and upper chest of the hired gunman.

Within moments, the cloud had thinned enough so that it was a mere gray haze. He could see Brigid in the doorway of the secret tunnel, crouched with her weapon out, ready to lend assistance. As it was, her attentiveness on the infrared camera gave Kane all the advantage he'd needed.

"Thanks, Baptiste," he whispered, so that only she could hear it over their Commtact frequency.

All she had to do was smile. The two were close enough that oftentimes, words were not needed to communicate the messages that really mattered. They were bonded, not only in this life, but in the quantum-physics realm of reincarnation, two entities that had been entwined, as friends, lovers, family, across the history of humankind, perhaps even further back. They were old souls who had been reunited by happenstance as much as by Lakesh's interference in their careers as Magistrate and archivist for

Cobaltville. Grant was a part of that cosmic, transcendent mesh, as well, and in speaking with a young engineer named Waylon, Kane had been convinced that their measure of success against nearly impossible odds was due to the fact that they were part of a grand equation. Lakesh had pointed out that when they worked together, they experienced a "confluence of fortunes," which made them far more than the sum of their skills and abilities. Waylon's quantum physics interpretation went deeper.

"You are elements of a force of nature," the slightly built young black man had told them. "You are avatars of a universal constant, the means by which the balance of power is evened out. That's why you, at this time, in this place, have become so successful in toppling the barons and resisting the overlords."

"So, we have some kind of charm?" Kane returned. This had been after an encounter that left Kane's ribs sore and his back strained. "Because if you ask me, I don't have luck."

"No. You're human. Nothing more, nothing less. Well, except for Mr. Grant," Waylon answered. "But what your bodies aren't, your minds and spirits are. You're aspects of a greater whole, the representation of humankind, its champions."

"Great," Kane muttered. "We're not invulnerable, but we still have to be the line in the sand against dinosaurs, robots and aliens. Smart species that chose us."

"Species. Planet," Waylon answered. "Maybe even a universe, Mr. Kane."

As he looked around the shattered throne room, Kane knew that the young engineer who constantly called him a superhero wasn't entirely off base with the whole "right people at the right place at the right time" theory. Dressed in a skintight, high-tech polymer uniform, with a gun that could be drawn and fired with just a thought and a silent, hard-to-spy-upon means of communication with the rest of his team, he almost could forgive the nerdy, but brilliant, kid for his deference.

Then he remembered the injured, the people he wasn't able to help. He rushed to the aid of the bloodied Nagah man in the corner. The guardian had lost an eyeball from shrapnel, his scaled face scarred and torn by that single, deadly projectile's many companions. "Baptiste…"

The archivist had already gone to check on others, while more Royal Guards entered, bearing first-aid kits.

Thoughts of being a hero faded as the need for a real hero reminded him of what needed to be done. It didn't matter to Kane who called upon him, how he was called or why he was called. He had a job to do, and right now, that meant easing the suffering and blood loss of a fellow warrior.

KONDO'S BROKEN RIBS WEREN'T so completely damaged that he was required to stay motionless in bed, but he still had his torso wrapped and was confined to a wheelchair. Medical treatment came first for the Watatsumi warrior before he was swiftly debriefed by the intelligence officers. He was one of the few who had gotten a close view of the new creatures that the Dragon Riders had brought into this seemingly eternal battle.

The injured Kondo opened a small book relating the tale of Lone Wolf and Cub, trying to distract himself from his current state of uselessness and his failure to the men under his command when there was a knock at the door. It was a nurse, slender scales flowing and bouncing on her shoulders as if they were made of spun, flexible rose-colored glass. "Sir? Do you mind if I interrupt you?"

Kondo closed the miniature manga collection and

smiled at the woman. "Not at all. Is it time for my medicine? Bandage change?"

She shook her head, the hairlike scales rustling against their neighbors and producing a soft whisper that promised so much more when he ran his fingers through them. Kondo said a small prayer of thanks for such a pretty distraction. "You have visitors. No less than Tatehiko and Remus the Wanderer."

Remus the Wanderer. That was a heart-stopping revelation, that he would actually show up to speak with one of the troops. Remus was much like the rest of the Watatsumi who had lived in the Spine of the Dragon, except he held himself with an imperial bearing that belied his silent near inactivity in anything but battle against the Riders on their assaults. He had shown up around the time of the first Riders' appearance, the beginning of their attacks on "civilized" Ryugo-jo. There were always hints of the coincidence of his arrival, and why he kept to his own counsel, rarely speaking with the other troops.

Remus claimed he was ancient, though he looked as young as Kondo himself, physically in his midthirties, with long, straight limbs laden with tightly packed muscle. He was lean and sleek, and in combat, he was a living whirlwind, demonstrating the strength to seize one of the Utahraptors by the lower mandible and tear it off, despite jaw muscles capable of delivering eight-hundred-plus pound bites. That kind of strength and savagery in combat with the Riders had belayed most of the doubts about him, and he had proved to be a great asset to the Watatsumi *bushi* in their defense of the citizens of the underworld tunnels.

Remus regarded him with quiet, seemingly deferential respect. Kondo had seen few emotions on his stoic features, yet he was as like them as possible. His skin was much more finely scaled than a typical dragon man, and he was half a head taller than even the most statuesque among the Watatsumi, who topped out at five-eleven. His scales were reddish-gold, and he didn't possess the chest plates such as the rest of them. His eyes were a piercing blue, and he had visible ears that were pointed. He walked everywhere bare chested and barefoot, though he had on slacks that were rolled up so as not to constrict or interfere with the flexing fins around his ankles. The only sign of emotion in him generally showed itself through agitation of the slender, three-inch-long wing-fins.

"You did well," Remus said softly in a voice Kondo had rarely heard at such close range. His voice held a rumbling timbre, strong and soothing while carrying the weight of countless years.

"Thank you," Kondo answered, his brow bent in confusion.

"This is not congratulations, Kondo," Remus added. "You did not fail anyone with your efforts. You fought and bought time for those you have sworn to protect. You warned your men. Think not upon any doubts."

Tatehiko regarded the taller dragon man out of the corner of his eye, bristling with annoyance. "Kondo knows that his efforts are valued, Remus."

Remus's gaze never left Kondo. He was silent now, having spoken more than Kondo had heard in a year from the tall, powerful champion. His nickname "the Wanderer" came from his claims of having been everywhere on the surface of the planet. Some noted that the Western alphabet spelling of his name was backward for Sumer, a region where humankind first ascended to a city-building civilization, perhaps as a hint to his origins.

"Again, thank you," Kondo repeated. Those words, despite their shock, had the weight to sink into his psyche. He still felt the ugly, bitter pit of self-loathing simmering in his gut, but Remus's pep talk had made the sour taste in his mouth fade a little.

"We came as a show of appreciation to your efforts," Tatehiko said. "As such, we were thinking of giving you a boon, something from Remus's secret stores."

"A boon?" Kondo asked.

Remus held forth a small pill, his pointed fingernails surrounding it like a crown of horns. "Healing."

Kondo reached tentatively for the small tablet, then put it on his tongue. He wasn't certain what he'd been offered, but Remus held no menace, or malice behind his poker face. Even as he swallowed, he could tell that the pill was sweet, and dissolved just on contact with his tongue. Any questions within him began to fade as the throbbing ache in his ribs increased. Something was moving under his skin, like an army of fire ants, their feet long and clawed, tearing at the nerves. Kondo clenched his eyes shut, his body tensed.

"Relax," Tatehiko ordered. "Otherwise it may not—"

"Don't worry," Remus cut him off.

Kondo's molars ground against each other in the back of his mouth, his fingers clutching handfuls of his sheets. Every tendon and muscle tightened as the burning sensation in his rib cage grew and grew.

"You may cry out if you wish," Remus spoke, but Kondo didn't want to. A single tear wove between the scales on his cheek, trailing down to his chin. To give in to his agony would be a betrayal to his commander, Tatehiko, and the soft-spoken giant who had offered him this body-rending pain.

Kondo sucked in a deep breath, then realized something. Such an inhalation would have paralyzed him with the stress on his fractured ribs. Though they ached, the stabbing, agonizing knives of fire that usually accompa-

nied such a sigh were gone, submerged beneath the pinprick swarm buzzing in his chest.

"Feeling better?" Tatehiko asked.

Kondo could only nod as the fire-ant march turned to
a gentle caress of angel feathers.

"It will take some time, but by this evening, you should
be back on your feet and ready to continue your contribution to the defenses of Ryugo-jo," Tatehiko said.

"See me," Remus added. With that, he turned and left
the hospital room, his great presence no longer swelling
within the confines of four walls that could barely contain such an energy.

Tatehiko didn't bother watching his companion leave.
It was as if, having bathed in that sunlight, his skin had
toughened, darkened to accommodate such a blaze.

"Sir?" Kondo asked his supreme commander.

"I've been remembering what you said about the humans," Tatehiko finally spoke up. "Did you do anything
to betray our presence to the ape-kin?"

"No," Kondo replied immediately, cursing himself that
it sounded too fast, too sudden a response. It sounded like
the lie that it was.

Tatehiko didn't take notice if he did hear the jangled
nerves in his response. It could have been passed off as an
effect of the pill, whatever this wonderful thing was that
helped him breathe painlessly, could also restore feeling
to the foot beneath the broken femur. "Did they give you
anything to contact them?"

"A frequency," Kondo said. "He called it an 'emergency
phone number.'"

Tatehiko smirked. "They gave you a means of locating them?"

"No. They have a ring of satellites that can listen for
transmissions," Kondo returned. "And this is one of the

friendly lines that they regularly monitor. This way, we can call to them to set up a meeting on safe ground."

"Safe ground," Tatehiko mimicked. "So, Grant knew about our need for secrecy, our distrust of the world above."

Kondo nodded. "I love my people too much to betray our secrets, but I also care about them enough to request aid from afar."

Tatehiko frowned. "Yes. We could use help. Our manufacturing ability is too limited, despite the years we've spent rebuilding. There just aren't enough people, especially with the defection of the Riders."

Kondo frowned. "Could we send out a call?"

"Perhaps. We already have the disadvantage that we are in proximity to the mat-trans that sent the expedition to Florida," Tatehiko responded. "If they were able to monitor our communications…"

"They hadn't known about us, though they did mention a similar species," Kondo said. "They spoke of the Nagah."

"The rumored cobra men. Yes, you mentioned that when you returned from America," Tatehiko mused. Where Remus had been tall and light, Tatehiko was short and dark, his scaly hair nearly jet-black, and his eyes a deep, liquid brown. He was broad-shouldered and stocky, and his face was free of the humanlike foliage that even Kondo displayed. He always seemed deep in thought, his mind racing in the gleam behind his eyes. "Perhaps…"

"Our myths of a lost tribe mention our journey from another realm," Kondo said. "And maybe their closer proximity, on the Asian continent, could be helpful."

"We already have enough divisiveness that we continue to lose defectors to the Riders," Tatehiko responded. "Could you imagine a new species joining our fractured family?"

Kondo nodded. "It would be nice to have friends to rely upon. You know about the menaces out there."

"Yes. All too well," Tatehiko said. "Get some rest, and when you feel well enough, go before Remus. I'm certain he has things to question you about along the lines of this conversation. Let me know what his advice will be."

Kondo nodded again in confirmation of receiving that order. Tatehiko turned and left the *bushi* alone with his thoughts, considering the strangeness of the man's request.

Remus was a stranger, but he and Tatehiko always seemed to be working together, as if the tall wanderer was the Watatsumi commander's conscience. The Wanderer bore authority, and Tatehiko seemed to defer to his judgment, but other than that, little had ever been said about his background, as if he were a secret.

Taking inventory of his old aches and pains, he found that he was feeling much better. He could stand up if he wanted to. He tentatively rose to his feet, and while his femoral fracture tickled as he put weight on it, it was feeling much better, no muscle spasm forcing him back into the wheelchair.

It was a powerful gift bestowed upon Kondo, the ability to heal almost instantly from injuries that would have left him an invalid for months. But was it a form of bribery, or a reward for courage? Tatehiko seemed to hold suspicions about Remus, so it could have been the former.

Kondo sat back down, wondering if too many strangers were being added to the caldron of the besieged Ryugo-jo.

Chapter 6

Brigid, Kane and Grant finally returned to their quarters, limbs hanging numbly at the ends of their arms, exhaustion beckoning them toward the comfort of mattresses and pillows. Ever since the first explosion put the entirety of the subterranean city on lockdown, they had been on the move, providing first aid or battling with the Millennial Consortium and their allies. The city was quiet now, safe now that the bombers who had made their moves to engage in terrorist activity were put down or captured, and the wounded had been at least sent to medical care after being stabilized.

As it was, the tally of the day was a harsh one. The consortium's bombs and guns had taken more than twenty lives, of both full-skinned Nagah or their human kinfolk, and a hundred more had been wounded by shrapnel and bullets.

It was a brutal, grim reminder of the kind of cunning and callous disregard for human life their opponents in the Millennial Consortium had. The group was emboldened, strengthened by at least a temporary alliance with Erica van Sloan, but this had few of the machinations and subtlety of one of her plans. The Dragon Queen would have built a shadow government by now, or had enslaved dozens of the Nagah with her mind-control webbing. This infiltration from without was too clumsy, even if the millennialist assassins had been aided by the disenfranchised Sons of Enlil.

Kane pushed open the door to his and Grant's room and paused, shocked by the sight of the pregnant queen of the Nagah sitting on his bed. Brigid noticed Kane's sudden arrest of movement, then poked her head in over his shoulder.

"Pardon my intrusion," Hannah said, her long, lithe legs crossed despite the swell of her belly.

"I don't mind," Grant answered. "You're not sittin' on my bed."

With that, the Cerberus ex-Mag pushed past Kane and dropped himself facedown on his mattress, brawny arms encircling a pack of pillows as he groaned with relief. Kane had seen Grant applying his enormous strength to lifting fallen debris off trapped and injured people, his sinewy might all that had prevented several people from being crushed by fallen I-beams or heavy slabs of stone.

Kane leaned in the arch of the doorway, his head tilted to rest on the doorjamb with the tall, willowy Brigid resting her chin on his other shoulder. Kane didn't mind that sudden intimacy at all. It was akin to brother and sister, best friends offering physical support to each other. "To what do I owe this honor, Your Majesty?"

"I wanted to begin with a word of thanks, for having done so much for my people today," Hannah replied. "Not only am I grateful for the work you've done for my subjects, but for protecting my husband and myself."

"Saving people's asses has been my calling for a long time," Kane replied. "Except now, I don't have any baron telling me who the bad guys are. First aid and going toe-to-toe with murderers is business as usual for me."

Grant lifted his head. "Fuck his nobility. I accept the thanks, and add in a dose of appreciation for how comfy these beds are."

Hannah and Kane shared a momentary smile at that remark. Brigid didn't make a sound, but he could feel her reflexive shrug as she restrained a chuckle. She gave him a poke in the kidney to emphasize Grant's mock derision.

"What else did you want to say?" Brigid asked now that her poke had provided a pause in the conversation. "I'm sure you're exhausted from all this, especially carrying all that."

Hannah's scaled lips turned up in a subtle, demure smile as she patted her belly. "I came to tell you personally that I've retrieved the records of encrypted transmissions that our scientists have picked up in the time period you describe."

She handed over a small booklet. "Coordinates and frequencies."

"That was fast," Kane noted, taking the book. He looked over the pages and was disappointed that it was an endless string of coordinates and numbers, something he'd need a map to reference. Luckily, Brigid was right behind him. He held up the book and she plucked it from his fingers. He didn't doubt that her near computer-like mind was already transforming all of those numbers into a detailed map. She would have the home base of the Watatsumi within moments. "Or did you already have this ready?"

"There are elements of Nagah society that are growing more and more distrustful of the nonmutants among us, the untransformed humans," Hannah explained. "They feel that, thanks to the infiltration by the Millennial Consortium, that all humans are suspect."

"Elements?" Grant asked. "How many?"

"The exact numbers are unknown, despite having my government taking polls. My investigators hear things, but this is a representative republic, as well as a monarchy. I wouldn't want to impose martial law or engage in unwarranted searches of my people's homes," Hannah said. "The rule of law must be tempered by acknowledging the basic freedoms of all people, regardless of whether they wear scales or hair."

"That sounds like you're following in the footsteps of Matron Yun," Grant said, sitting up as he realized that he wasn't going to get any sleep thanks to the queen's intrusion into his quarters. "What about the prisoners we captured today?"

"They'll be spoken to by true interrogators, not torturers, if that is what you're asking," Hannah answered.

"It might have been a concern," Kane returned. "Mind you, I wouldn't be averse to putting a little extra oomph into questioning considering the damage and harm they've caused."

"Revenge comes later. Answers, however, are paramount," Hannah explained.

Grant smirked. "My kind of lady."

"Something tells me that those elements among you that don't like humans wouldn't mind torture to get answers out of the prisoners," Kane said. "And they would keep torturing until they received the answers that they wanted to get, not the truth."

"Absolutely," Hannah confirmed. "Depending on their agenda, they might not be satisfied until every human was expelled from our tunnels, or worse, exterminated."

"Which is why our efforts today were so welcome by you," Brigid said absently as her brilliant green eyes scanned the pages of the booklet Hannah had provided. "You want some help from Cerberus."

Hannah frowned, her eyes heavily lidded as she tried to fight off a wave of melancholy. "The state of things at the end of our last encounter made continued contact with outsiders from the other side of the world difficult, politically. I knew that you had done all that you could, but we were licking our wounds. Now, the consortium has been making use of the free society we live in, and the willingness to accept immigrants into our tunnels. I doubt that the millennialists want us to completely disappear from the surface world, but the council is growing more and more isolationist with each attack."

"Showing us as being helpful brought the image of humans being good and caring back to the forefront," Grant spoke up. "If humans from the other side of the globe were seen as tending to the injured or placing themselves in the line of fire to save lives, then the concept of humans being secondhand citizens suffers a powerful blow."

Hannah nodded. "I've already gotten several medals and commendations for our untransformed kin who engaged in rescue operations postattack. Even so, the hospitals have received six victims of venom sprays in the eyes over the past few hours."

"Antihuman sentiments turned to vengeance," Kane said. "Any fatalities?"

"Only one, and she was bitten," Hannah answered. "Of the others, three have been permanently blinded."

"Damn," Grant muttered. "Still, that's only six incidents."

"Ones that don't have eyewitness accounts, thanks to venom in the eyes," Kane returned. "So there are at minimum two violent, antihuman racists on the loose."

"Why two?" Hannah asked.

"One primarily blinded his victims, while another took the opportunity to commit murder," Kane said. "When was the murder in the order of the attacks?"

"The guardsmen are still working on it, but they ascertained that the murder was among the first of the attacks," Hannah said.

"The first," Kane repeated. "So we have five attacks based on bigoted sentiment, and one murder that doesn't fit."

"Criminals generally tend to escalate in violence. Once they've killed someone, they rarely dial back the intensity of their attacks," Grant replied.

"I forget that the two of you were first enforcers before you were explorers," Hannah said.

Grant looked to Kane. "Maybe the woman who'd been bit was on to something?"

"Do they have an exact time line from when she was attacked?" Kane asked.

"I'll get more details from my guardsmen," Hannah replied.

"We should have Sela and Domi come in for this," Grant said. "Sela has actual investigation experience, and Domi can smell a rat a mile away."

"Which could free us up to find Kondo and his people," Kane added.

Grant nodded. "Plus, more humans might actually prove beneficial. Especially if they trend more toward being women."

"So we're not going to have Edwards stick with CAT Beta?" Kane asked.

"He'll be along, but the face of the new human presence will be softer, friendlier," Grant said. "Not some ugly mug like you."

"Ugly, eh?" Kane probed.

"Positively revolting," Brigid spoke up, her eyes closed as she calculated spacial equations based on the frequencies, their strength and location. Kane wondered if she had overlaid a globe of the planet under that map, a three-dimensional relief chart kept updated by the satellite network that Lakesh had maintained before he arrived at Cerberus all those years earlier.

"Yeah. Edwards is positively cuddly compared to a scruffy bastard like you," Grant continued.

"We'll see what we can do," Kane said.

"In the morning, we'll fly you back to the parallax point so you can return home," Hannah offered. "And when your people next arrive, we'll be listening to pick you up."

"Sounds good," Kane added.

"Now, if you do not mind, my endurance has nearly reached its limit," Hannah apologized. "I am off to retire to my quarters."

With that, the regent left their quarters. Royal guardsmen passed by the doorway, leaving Rahdnathi to stand watch over the visitors.

"Scary how we didn't notice the extra security at our door," Grant muttered.

"They're bodyguards. They're supposed to be unnoticed. Even so, don't say *we* didn't notice them. *You* didn't," Kane answered.

Grant rolled his eyes. "Yes, O grand eyes of heaven."

Kane smirked. "I liked you better when you were cussing me out instead of that fancy Japanese-style cursing."

"You were getting used to my f-bombs," Grant replied with a shrug. "Besides, I did notice the guard force. The Royal Guard isn't just transformed Nagah. There are plenty of humans in their ranks. Trusted humans."

"I calculated, based on their representative numbers, around forty-two percent of the Royal Guard is comprised of the Nagah-kin," Brigid said.

Kane grunted in assent. "So you both saw that she had untransformed Nagah with her."

"Yeah. That means she knows all too well what's going on among the citizens who haven't been born of Nagah parents, or transformed within the baths," Grant mused. "Then again, her husband is the son of a transformed Nagah."

"You think that the murder was separate from the 'retribution' attacks?" Kane asked.

"I'm doubting it," Grant returned. "We've been among these people, and only the most ardent of believers would be behind any form of unrest. I think the other attacks might have been a cover-up, a distraction by the Sons of Enlil, to cover up the first murder. You think so, too?"

"That's why I mentioned the Royal Guard's human members," Kane said.

"The deceased woman could easily have been an undercover operative tasked with investigating the Millennial Consortium's infiltration," Brigid added.

"Hannah didn't come out and say it, but she did give us the information that the dead woman was one of the first. She played a little dumb about the difference between the killing and the venom attacks and the order of escalation in violence," Grant added. "She was sending us a message without having to say much."

"This way if there was a traitor within, she wasn't giving away her suspicions," Kane replied, "while still dropping enough hints to give us a lead."

"We'll transfer this on to CAT Beta, then," Grant said. "Then we move on ahead to Ryugo-jo."

"Once Brigid stops chiming in and gives us a location," Kane returned.

"I can multitask, Kane," Brigid said coldly, her eyes open now. "I've narrowed down the closest mat-trans to where Ryugo-jo's transmissions originate from. It's still a considerable distance, which means we're going to have to utilize alternate transportation."

"Mantas?" Kane asked.

Brigid nodded.

"Then let's get some rest and set out in the morning," Kane suggested. "I don't think we're going to have much more chance to snooze until we've finished solving the Watatsumi's problems."

Grant rolled onto his back. "Eat, drink and be merry, chums, for tomorrow we dine in dinosaur hell!"

With that cheery thought, the Cerberus warriors went to their beds and slept.

KONDO FOLLOWED THE TUNNEL where Remus the Wanderer made his home in the subterranean tunnels of Ryugo-jo. It was a long and winding path, taking him away from the main residences of the rest of the Japanese dragon men, to the point where there was nothing beyond bioluminescent fungi to provide any illumination. The last of the electric wiring and bulbs had long been left behind.

However, toward the end of the tunnel, he began to see a glow akin to the lava-lit outside tunnels. A stench of mold, humidity and sweaty life rolled to meet his nostrils, a sickly, thick scent that made his nose twitch uncomfortably. It was growing warmer, a hot, wet breeze meeting him the closer he got to the lava lights that churned through the roof of the cavern known as the Spine of the Dragon.

Judging by the incline of the tunnel he'd walked down, and the smell, this corridor had to have opened up out in the jungles, where heavy, thick, hyperoxygenated air made it possible for the beasts of primordial times to thrive and flourish in perpetuity. Kondo reached the light and saw Remus, standing on the edge of a cliff, looking down into the mighty forests of the subterranean continent. The air pressure, heat and humidity were far more oppressive than anything Kondo had ever felt before. Just moving made him feel like he'd been dipped in a bath of perspiration, each breath coming in with a cloying scent of wild saurian life and ancient flora that threatened to gag him.

He coughed, and Remus turned to greet him.

"Welcome, warrior," Remus said, extending a hand. His grip was anything but what Kondo had expected for a man so large, so powerful, so muscular. It was gentle, tentative, as if he viewed all other creatures in his presence as being fragile as eggshells, and he was a looming beast tiptoeing among them. This was not a man who felt the need to test his strength against others, and from the brawn apparent on his long, rippling limbs, few beings would be able to match him in might.

"Sir," Kondo returned, coughing again.

"I apologize for bringing you down here to my balcony," Remus replied, "but I wanted to speak to you freely, without fear of consequence for your words."

Kondo looked at him quizzically. "You think we would be spied upon, sir?"

Remus frowned. "You worked with Ochiro when you traveled afar, to the land of the Americans. He acted without honor, with little care for any but his own agenda. And he was not working alone."

"Who would he be working with?" Kondo asked.

"Who would benefit from the loss of an egalitarian society such as the one you and your ancestors have built?" Remus riddled in return. "Self-rule and personal accountability have been the way of the Watatsumi since the great dragon god formed us in his fearsome image."

"You are Watatsumi?" Kondo pressed.

"We share paternity, warrior," Remus said. He turned and looked out over the jungle canopy.

In the distance, hanging on updrafts with their wings spread wide, Kondo could see airborne pterodactyls and pteranodons. He felt a jolt of apprehension at the sight of them, broad membranes stretched out to capture warm, rising air to glide effortlessly in slow, gentle spirals. From a distance, without the malice of the earlier dinosaur attack, they seemed almost beautiful, even though every instinct within him commanded him to run for cover.

"They will not attack," the Wanderer assured him. "They are far from us, and easier prey awaits their hungry bellies."

"You knew about the presence of these creatures?" Kondo asked.

"I knew of them, yes. But they are generally fish-eaters, if over the water, or they seek small mammals and lizards crawling in the high branches of their arboreal range," Remus explained. "The ones who struck, the one that you killed, are a species I was not aware of."

"But you seem familiar with them," Kondo said. He tried to drain all the suspicion from his words, but once more, in the space of two days, he knew failure.

"I live here, on the edge of their forest, to not only spy upon the riders of the dragons, but to learn of the ecology of this continent," the Wanderer announced. "Do you see the end of this forest?"

"Barely," Kondo returned. "But it looks as if there is more sky, the lava tubes curving, disappearing past the horizon."

"The Spine of the Dragon extends far. Six million square kilometers, running north, to the fallen sky, and farther south, toward a land so savage even the Dragon Riders fear to tread there," Remus told him. "Thus, there is room for a myriad of species to have survived and adapted in the millions of years since the last of these creatures' terrible tread resounded on the surface of Earth."

Kondo looked up to the fin-eared giant. Thousands of

questions sprang to mind, each of them fighting for precedence, but he couldn't sort them all. He couldn't speak.

"It would take a person hundreds of years to explore this wondrous terrain," Remus continued. "From snow-capped heights to dark, dread lands where the lava trickles in streams amid blackened forests of gnarled treelike shells built by sulfur-breathing worms."

"Hundreds of years," Kondo repeated.

Remus looked down at him.

There was nothing that needed to be said. Kondo realized that the tall reptilian form beside him had lived those centuries, and had walked the depth and breadth of this uncharted continent, alone, seeking knowledge and gazing upon wonders that even the Watatsumi's darkest legends could only hint at.

Lightning flashed, only a mile distant, Kondo judged by the swiftness of its crackle reaching his ears. Thick gray clouds flared inside, and the rustle of falling torrents sounded in the distance, driving the winged saurians from their flights toward clearer air.

"This is huge," Kondo whispered. "It's amazing that no one has ever stumbled upon it."

"Some have," Remus answered. "But the tales were so astounding that those who lived in the world above relegated them to flights of fancy, instead of the true exploits of men such as George Edward Challenger or David Innes."

Kondo watched the nearby thunderstorm fall. "This feels almost too perfect. As if…"

"As if it had been hewn from the earth by the hands of ancient gods," Remus concluded the thought. "You are most perceptive, young warrior."

"This was man-made?" he asked the Wanderer.

The tall being shook his head. "Made by men? No.

Made by those who aspire to godhood? Yes. This was built before the first apes on the continent known as Africa utilized twigs to scoop termites from a mound. The beings who fashioned this continent were travelers across the void of deep space, visitors who come from a star that humankind called Nibiru."

Kondo nodded. "I've heard…similar things. Tales from humans who have traveled the world, like you have."

"Our paths have not crossed," Remus said. "But then, the recent past has found me here."

"Sir, would these gods have called themselves the Annunaki?" Kondo asked.

Remus's scaled lips stilled into a thin, bloodless line, his emerald eyes glimmering as his irises contracted.

"Sir?" Kondo pressed, even though his stomach tightened. The height, around seven feet, and the incredibly powerful build, these were things that Grant and Kane had mentioned as attributes of the alien overlords who were striving to conquer Earth, or rather to recover their control in the wake of losses and infighting. Was Remus known by another name? Was he one of the nine overlords?

No. Remus had been with the Watatsumi in the Spine of the Dragon since the original Ryugo-jo had been stricken by the war of the humans. The Annunaki had only recently awakened, according to the Cerberus travelers, and assumed the form of the overlords.

The nine overlords, however, were not the only Annunaki who had been present on Earth. There were others, such as Enki.

"I am sorry," Remus spoke up. "That is a name that I had not expected from the lips of a Watatsumi. Yes, this was originally built by an Annunaki. It was they who created the obsidian glass tunnels that make this cavern glow as bright as day. It was they who populated the forests with their experiments, with teeming herds of maiasaurs and forests of worms. The Annunaki are present?"

"Only a few, according to Kane," Kondo answered.

Remus frowned, looking down into the forest canopy below. "This changes things. And this explains much."

"Sir?"

"Tell no one of this conversation, please," Remus said. "Say I spoke to you of making you one of my personal cadre."

"To do what?" Kondo asked.

"To join me in exploration, to assist me in going into the heart of the Riders' territory," Remus answered. "I cannot think, right now. Just as your world was changed a few days ago, mine has been altered this hour."

"Are you—?" Kondo began.

"Please, ask me no questions," Remus returned. "I have no mind for further words."

Kondo turned away from the vista of the primeval forest, and saw that this cave had a niche, a Spartan bed resting upon a shelf of stone. There were books in a pile, others contained within sealed plastic cartons, and only one other thing, one personal possession hanging on a hook from the wall.

Kondo knew the proper name for the sword. It was the *nodachi,* the legendary field sword of the samurai. Its handle alone was a foot from pommel to cross guard, and the leather sheathed blade was four feet tall. Only the strongest of warriors could wield such a weapon, and the rare blade was nearly impossible to properly make, due to the extra weight of the steel.

Still, armed with such a sword, a lone man could slice a horse in two or carve a swathe through the ranks of even the most heavily armored soldiers.

This had been the only weapon that Remus had been

known to carry. In his mighty hands, from a distance, it appeared to be simply another *katana,* but now Kondo knew the truth, having met with the great Wanderer close up.

Were he an Annunaki, Kondo reasoned, he would have access to greater weaponry. Were he a conqueror, he might have more luxurious accommodations.

But this was just a cave overlooking a dense forest, with a canopy of trees so thick, the ground was merely a rumor. A being who claimed to live for centuries could have built a palace in that jungle. The Dragon Riders would not be the only humanoids to work, to slave, for an Annunaki overlord.

Was this strange, lone entity friend or a foe living under the guise of a humble man, biding the patience of an eternity for his chance to strike?

Kondo left, returning to Ryugo-jo, leaving Remus alone with his own thoughts.

Chapter 7

Sela Sinclair bristled at the presence of Mohandas Lakesh Singh on this mission to the Nagah city, though Domi swore that the old scientist would not interfere with their investigation.

"He can talk with the locals easy," the feral albino woman said. "He's our interpreter."

"Interpreter," both Sinclair and Lakesh spoke up at the same time.

Edwards shrugged off the simultaneous response. "I knew what she was saying. And we have translators in our Commtacts."

"We'll be underground, which may limit our access to the linguistic software back at Cerberus," Lakesh countered.

Again the large, shaved-headed former Magistrate shrugged. "All right, then. So he's useful. And Domi says she schooled him in using that pistol on his belt."

"Schooled and being a combatant are two different things, Edwards," Sinclair returned. "I know you've been here before, and I know you've in the middle of dangerous missions, too, but you were there working alongside Kane and the others. Those three are good enough that they could pick up even your slack."

"We do what we can, friend Sela," Lakesh said. "I'm here to provide my linguistic skills and my observational capabilities."

"Also worked with Hannah and 'Core before," Domi said. "They'll trust him more than you."

Sinclair sighed. "Okay. Kane already went through most of this with me, anyway. I'm just saying, no one better come running to me when some snake man pumps them full of venom."

Lakesh smirked. "Dearest Sela, that would be the furthest from my mind."

"You know what I mean. I'm responsible for my team, and adding you to that mix is not going to make things easy," Sinclair returned. "We're going to be looking for insurgents. Dangerous people who may or may not have fangs that can spit poison that can burn your eyeballs out. If you get the idea to wander somewhere alone, carve it into your brain that alone means Domi is sewn to you at the hip."

Domi grinned, probably at that mental image. The ruby-eyed young woman grew serious and elbowed her lover in the side. "She means it. I mean it. No running off alone."

"And if that doesn't work, then I'll sit you," Edwards spoke up. "Excuse me. I mean sit *on* you."

Lakesh swallowed. "No need for such draconian measures. I know my limitations, and I know the volatile environment we will encounter."

"Like I said. Been there before," Domi repeated.

Sinclair nodded as she tapped her foot on the floor of the ancient temple. As soon as they had landed, brought there by the interphaser, she had sent out the call to the Nagah for a helicopter ride. Pressing the recall button on the tiny pyramidal device, she ensured that Lakesh's invention would not fall into the wrong hands, especially if there were Nagah who could still be working under the aegis of Enlil. She didn't know if the overlord needed an interphaser to make travel easier, especially since Lakesh had told her of the Annunaki's threshold, a crystalline device that enabled its user to leap between parallax points around the planet, even to other worlds or an orbiting dreadnaught such as *Tiamat,* which had been destroyed, as far as they could determine.

Enlil and the other overlords had been sent scrambling, searching for new means of renewing their power on Earth, and in the recent battles between the Cerberus rebels and the Annunaki, who knew what Enlil or his kin had lost or rediscovered.

"Hear their bird," Domi spoke up, even though it would be a minute before the heavy yet familiar vibrations of a transport helicopter reached Sinclair's ears. If there was one thing that made the woman feel better about going on this mission, it was that she was allied with two of the deadliest people in the redoubt who weren't named Kane or Grant. Edwards was a huge, brawny beast of a man. Like Kane and Grant, he was a former Magistrate. His combat training, experience and phenomenal strength could be counted on in a pinch.

Domi, however, was the exact opposite of the muscular giant. She was short and slender, her limbs seemingly wisps of shadow as they were clad in the black polymers of the shadow suit. Sinclair knew, however, that Domi was a creature of the Outlands. As such, she had the instincts and reflexes of a lynx combined with the ferocity of a pit bull. Her skinny arms and legs were tightly corded muscle, and Sinclair had been present when the feral albino showed Edwards that size and brawn weren't always the best weapons in a fight.

Sinclair herself was a former Air Force lieutenant colonel. Having lived through the tumultuous eighties and nineties, she had received counterterrorism training.

"Hannah said i used to be a cop, but i was a beat walker

with a slice of SWAT team training, compared to you," Kane had told her. "You actually have investigative experience."

"Don't put yourself down, Kane," Sinclair had answered. "Beat cops have some of the sharpest eyes for clues that I've ever known. You've already gathered a lot of information that some CID officers would have let fly over their heads."

"We need the help of the Nagah," Kane emphasized. "If we can solve the mystery of who's doing all of this garbage to Hannah's people, we can add someone else to the list of allies."

"And if we get enough, then we can build the world back to a semblance of civilization," Sinclair answered. "I know. You think I don't miss not having to live underneath a mountain, worried that we have to fight off alien invaders or bandits?"

Kane frowned, forgetting that Sinclair was a woman well versed in what Earth had lost in art and civilization. The Cerberus redoubt was not lacking in creature comforts, but it was still a hideout, a hidden fortress tucked underneath a mountain, sharing the same Spartan, airless quality as a prison. Even then, twentieth-century prisons had windows where sky could be seen through the bars. "Sorry."

"I'm only saying that I know what's at stake," Sinclair said. She offered her hand. "Shake and make up?"

Kane nodded. Sinclair was a spirited woman, like so many of those he had met in his adventures since first encountering Brigid Baptiste.

Now, she looked for the distant helicopter, seeing it as a speck, a bug on the horizon, making a beeline for the temple.

"Cobra people in helicopters," she mused, a smirk crossing her lips.

"What's funny?" Domi asked.

"Just that one of my favorite helicopters is the Cobra gunship. They have anything like that?" Sinclair asked.

Domi shrugged. "Just Deathbirds is what I saw."

Sinclair sighed. "Oh, well. So much for irony. Let's get this show going, people!"

BRIGID BAPTISTE SAT IN THE back of the Manta, cramped into position as the high-tech aircraft were not meant specifically for passengers. Her long, willowy form and athletic build made it relatively easy for her to fold herself away in the tiny compartment behind Kane's pilot seat, but it was still a tight squeeze, and she was glad that the orbital craft were transonic, making what could have been a long journey seem that much shorter. She watched as the Manta inverted itself; what should have been the sky was now filled with the turbulent glowing blue-and-white ball of Earth seen from afar. Ahead, over Kane's shoulder, was the nearly infinite blackness of space. On Earth, next to a strong light source, the sky often seemed empty, and out in the wilderness, the night was dotted with a spray of diamond dust on a black velvet background as stars shone through the planetary atmosphere.

Here, infinity was not empty. Twisting, ruffling clouds and snow-flake unique galactic bodies represented a universe that stretched back billions of years, the light from distant corners of the universe only now finishing its journey to reach her eyes. Brigid's photographic memory had a huge collection of constellations that had been recorded by ancient astronomers, but what she gazed upon now was a whole new map. For once, she was looking at a sky full of surprises, an ever-expanding sprawl of nebulae and interstellar bodies that blurred past as the Manta tore through the upper edges of the ionosphere.

"Hope that the coordinates you gave us are good," Grant spoke up. Brigid's Commtact picked up his words, the static of charged ions thin enough that she could hear them, despite the hundreds of feet separating them from this Manta.

Brigid smirked. "They're approximations, which is why we are making our transit via aircraft."

"Any excuse to swing these babies into near space is good enough for me," Grant returned.

Kane looked over his shoulder at her. "Don't mind him. If he's not asking if the worst can happen, we'll probably end up stepping into the worst."

The archivist restrained a giggle. "Just keep your eyes on the road."

"What could we run into all the way up here?" Kane asked.

"Turbulence. Electrical discharges from all the ionic activity. Annunaki spacecraft."

"That's what radar is for," Kane answered, but he still returned his attention forward. "So you have nothing to share with us about myths of dragon men in Japan or the city of Ryugo-jo?"

"Not much that can supplant the knowledge Grant's accumulated," Brigid answered. "The traditions of New Edo are quite complete, detailing the history of the land they left, cherishing it and keeping it recorded for the sake of their future generations. Knowledge of their ancestry is vital to the samurai culture that they've nurtured."

"Really?" Grant asked. "I'm glad that we're so high that I can't crash into anything. You could have knocked me out with a feather."

"You were extremely thorough in your personal research, Grant," Brigid returned over her Commtact. "I am impressed."

"He had a good teacher," Kane said.

"That almost sounded like a compliment," Brigid said, patting him on his shoulder. "You feeling okay?"

Kane shrugged. "Perfectly fine. You know, all the time we've spent together, we're having things rub off on each other."

"So that's why I feel like having flings with Sky Dog's squaws," Grant interjected.

Brigid and Kane both snorted out a quick laugh. She watched as Kane sent an unmistakable bit of sign language out the cockpit window to Grant. "Just like you can shoot, punch and kick well enough to nearly keep up with us, Grant and I are both reading and doing some preemptive learning in case we run into certain opponents again."

Grant's chuckle filled their ears over the Commtact connection they had. "Don't get too impressed. The really big aid in my research was that my teacher is Shizuka."

Kane glanced back to share a knowing look with Brigid. "Nothing makes learning go down better than a pair of milky thighs and a soft, heaving bosom."

Brigid grinned, then affected a breathless tone. "I declare, Mistah Kane, you do make a woman's head turn when you get naughty like that."

"I'm a shallow, muscle-bound dude," Grant interrupted, now a sign of annoyance present in his usually grumbling voice. "But learning is learning."

"Amen and pass the ammo," Kane declared.

"Okay, boy and girl, put your trays in the upright position and fasten your safety belts. ETA on atmospheric reentry is ninety seconds on my mark. Mark," Grant said.

Kane scanned the controls of the Manta, watching the instruments and making minor adjustments in course.

Below them was the southern Pacific Ocean, and Brigid could see the shores of southeastern Asia. They were high enough that she could see the spread of the remnants of the Philippine Islands, their destination. Grant had managed to knock a few bits of information loose in casual conversation with Kondo. While the Japanese islands had been drastically damaged by earth-shaker nukes, atomic weaponry set to penetrate the planet's crust and cause enormous seismic activity, the Philippine archipelago had fared better, if only because the 7100 islands had already been subject to tectonic upheaval during the epoch of their formation.

The Pacific Ring of Fire had proved vulnerable to the nuclear missile salvo that hammered the United States and its Southeast Asian allies, and though the Soviet Union of their time line knew that the Filipinos were indebted to the U.S., they were scarcely a united military force that could lend aid to the Americans, especially with the KGB tugging at the puppet strings of Muslim radicals, Communist dupes and other assorted insurgents within the country. The forward bases that had been present, and but winding down at the end of the twentieth century, were for communications. Even the largest close to the most powerful volcano in the archipelago—Nichols Air Base—had been closed before a legendary mount exploded in 1991.

Mount Pinatubo was on the island of Luzon, and by the fact that it released enormous stresses, it had been stabilized so that even the disruption of the Pacific Ring of Fire didn't cause massive earthquake-related destruction on the Philippine isle ten years later. Other ICBMs and nuclear bombs had been diverted away from Luzon for years during the shutdown of the U.S. military's presence in the archipelago nation, sparing it most of the destruction that had scoured vast tracts of the world.

Unfortunately, the Philippines hadn't been left untouched by the effects of the nuclear strikes. Earth-shaker bombs had hurled massive tsunamis at Luzon, inundating and eradicating the coastal population. The vast clouds of fallout, ash and airborne dust that followed countless atomic detonations had introduced a chilling winter to the tropic islands, causing even more death as unprepared citizens, crops and domestic animals were caught, unable to adapt to the massive climate change. The smaller islands of the archipelago suffered far worse, tidal waves destroying fishing villages, shattering fleets of vessels that the nation depended upon now that their agriculture had been devastated by the proverbial skydark, the charred, sun-strangling cloud that wrapped Earth in darkness and chilling cold.

Brigid had surmised that Luzon and specifically Mount Pinatubo were the most likely means of passage from Ryugo-jo to the surface world. There they could locate the now-abandoned redoubt that Kondo had mentioned to replenish their armory and supplies of equipment, as well as utilize its mat-trans unit to travel between this side of the planet and the Florida peninsula.

The Mantas finally slowed, hitting their retro jets. The atmosphere was thick enough to push against, and the jolt was stomach churning in force. The pair of supersonic aircraft were built for this, but transitioning atmospheric layers was still something that required finesse and skill. Fortunately, both Kane and Grant possessed the necessary attributes. Even so, Brigid was locked in an area that wasn't designed to ferry passengers. Her only saving grace was the presence of her shadow suit. One feature of the high-tech uniforms was its capacity to take extreme changes in gravimetric forces, such as high-velocity turns, and keep the wearer from being mangled by his or her own internal fluid mass.

"You all right back there?" Kane asked. He had a deep tone of concern in his voice, as he knew that the shadow suit he wore was being supplemented by the Manta's pilot chair, itself filled with a gelatinous substance akin to the advanced polymers of the second skin, making piloting the craft far less jarring.

"Feeling shaken up, but I'll live," Brigid answered. "Thanks for asking."

"You'd gone quiet for a moment," Kane said. "I worried that you might have passed out or something."

"I don't have to spend all my hours running my mouth," Brigid returned. "Besides, you had work to do."

Kane nodded but didn't say anything. It was a cold, abrupt end to their conversation, and a sign that there were things on her friend's mind, but he was a stubborn man. While quick to voice an opinion if he felt something was wrong with anyone else, he also would hold his tongue and never speak, even under pain off torture, should he wish to keep his thoughts to himself.

Brigid pressed her lips tight, the overwhelming gravitational forces of their deceleration easing up. She no longer felt as if she were frozen inside a plastic shell. A glance over Kane's shoulder showed the Pacific Ocean, shining like a mirror as they dropped through a thin layer of cloud. Beside them, Grant brought his Manta closer until only a span of her spread arms separated the two supersonic craft.

"ETA at Luzon and Mount Pinatubo will be around five minutes, give or take a few ticks concerning headwinds and turbulence," Grant announced over his Commtact.

"Fine by me," Brigid said softly, knowing that even keeping her voice low, the vibrations through her mandible were picked up and amplified over the cybernetic communication system.

"We won't land right away. I want a good look at what's

on the ground down there," Kane said. "Depending on a few centuries of tidal damage and volcanic activity, we might be looking at a pirate cove or twenty."

"Pirates and dinosaur men," Grant spoke up. "Kondo didn't mention any hostile encounters. They have been working pretty hard at avoiding contact with humanity, until Ochiro decided to expand the scope of the octo-slug experiment."

"Also, we're looking at Manila as being our main interest," Brigid responded. "Pinatubo's only fifty-five miles from Manila, to the northwest."

"And you're sure that Pinatubo will be some form of highway?" Kane asked.

Brigid nodded. "Yes. There is a good chance that the earth-shakers might have either accentuated preexisting tunnels or created new passages to Ryugo-jo, allowing them to come up close to the Luzon redoubt."

"Got an eyeball of Manila," Grant spoke up. "Putting the image on your screen, guys."

Brigid leaned forward and saw that the city was scoured away. This was nothing new to her; she'd already pored over photographs of the city, then and now, memorizing them as she worked against the list of redoubts in her memory. "Luckily, the redoubt was much farther inland. It was settled beneath the old National Defense College of the Philippines, which was more than ten miles inland."

"So it would still be there?" Grant asked.

"The tidal action ripped fifteen miles inland," Kane said, "but when the flood abated, only seven miles of the landscape remained submerged."

"Part of the placement of the redoubts was not only to make them relatively safe from nuclear attack, by dint of significant natural barriers, but also to deal with natural disasters," Brigid added. "The redoubt location should be active on your monitors now."

Kane nodded as the programmed position showed up on his screen. "Got it. The coast is, literally, clear."

"This province of Manila was heavily industrialized, predark, mainly because it was a flat coastal plain," Brigid stated. "There wasn't much heavy forest to get in the way of urbanization."

"And most of it's gone now thanks to tidal waves," Kane said. "Though, from orbit, you'd think that this part would have been shielded from anything that had hit Japan."

"Japan was only one of the U.S. allies hit by earth-shakers," Brigid said. "Waves also were generated by attacks that caused seismic activity in the Indian Ocean and Oceania...New Zealand and Australia to be exact."

"So Manila is replaced by grasslands," Kane mused. "How many people lived here?"

"Ten million spread across the main city and surrounding communities," Brigid returned.

"Humankind was stupid enough to throw away that many lives, even when they weren't aiming at a shooting enemy?" Grant said with a thinly disguised sneer. "Makes me wonder why we're trying so hard to rebuild."

"Because it wasn't the fault of the ten million here, and the billions elsewhere who had been exterminated. It was leaders who had been influenced, mentally poisoned by Enlil's long-standing orders," Brigid explained, her voice brittle as she held back her outrage. "The nations of the world had been convinced by puppet masters that others were looking to steal from them, creating a balance of power that allowed them to exploit humanity with minimal effort. The mind-set of the cold war also made it easy for them to hit the reset switch as society was growing smarter and more capable, able to reflect on itself. If the war hadn't been triggered at that moment, humankind might have gotten enough of a clue to shake off the Archons and hunt down the sleeping overlords."

"It may have happened in a dozen, even thousands of other casements, but right now, all we have is our world, the one we're fighting for," Kane said. "No one is going to walk in from another time line to give us the fighting chance we need."

"Except for when your future self sent Sindri back to us," Grant corrected.

Kane frowned. "You and Kondo pull a rabbit like that out of your hat, I'll be a happier man."

"Speaking of rabbits, take a look at that. I think we've found the hole where the redoubt was," Brigid said.

There was an area of ground, only the bases of walls and foundations of buildings remaining after the tsunamis, that had been churned up. There were signs of excavation, the remnants of a camp, still lasting after a short period of months, at most three years.

"Grant, sweep a perimeter," Kane ordered. "Hang on, Baptiste. We're going in for a landing."

Brigid gripped the back of the seat tightly as Kane brought the Manta to a low hover.

"Where angels fear to tread," she barely said, lips mouthing the words so softly even the Commtact didn't pick them up and the vibrations of the hover jets drowning out any noise she'd made.

She looked around at the scoured cityscape. "Where angels fear to tread, we rush in."

Chapter 8

The trail was months old, a cold but still noticeable path that tracked off toward Mount Pinatubo, crawling in a straight line north above Manila Bay, where it would inevitably curve back south toward the volcanic caldera. Kane had followed the path for the better part of two hours before cementing the evidence he needed to confirm his instincts that Brigid had been correct.

The trot back to the redoubt was only a quarter of the time pursuing the track that the Watatsumi had taken, and once more the trio of Cerberus explorers was off, slower this time, utilizing the Mantas' hover capabilities and ground-effect radar to sweep the terrain for signs of the wagons that the Japanese dragon men had used. The trail, already intuited by Kane's sharp point man senses, was delineated by the ruts cut via wagon wheels laden with men and equipment, especially the gear necessary to open up an entrance into the redoubt.

The exploration of the dig site had been only cursory. Kane and the others had realized that knocking on the door of the underground base would be a waste of time if there were Watatsumi present or if they could find their way into the redoubt. Later, they could have the leisure of roaming through an empty redoubt or bargaining with a possible rear guard. Time was better spent in travel, reaching Ryugo-jo as soon as possible.

Skimming along at fifty miles per hour was as fast as

Kane would lead the flight of the Mantas at an altitude of only a few dozen feet. Any higher, and the ruts left by the expedition's wagon wheels would have faded in with ground clutter under the directed radar beams of the ship. Any faster risked losing a sudden turn in the same clutter or clipping a wing against the remnants of the tidal-wave-ruined city or its surrounding town structures.

The Watatsumi had to have known of the location of the redoubt, because there was scarcely any variation of their course as they curved around the north shore of Manila Bay. Other expeditions had to have come here over the years, and the only limitations of the entrance they had created and the effects of a tsunami crashing through the slender entrance of the bay around Corrigador had made it so that the larger hangar entrances were unable to be opened up.

Tons of rubble had been washed by a wall of water large enough to plunge more than fifteen miles inland, rubble that settled in tightly over the depression where the redoubt could have had the doors necessary to allow through vehicles such as Sandcats and helicopters such as the Deathbirds. As such, the Watatsumi had been limited to what they could build, or rebuild, in their subterranean realm. Kondo had mentioned that they were hardly primitive. After all, they had the communications necessary to transmit around the globe, even through the interference caused by radioactive areas and ionic storms in the upper atmosphere.

"One thing gets me," Grant said, cutting into Kane's musings. "They talked about the Dragon Riders."

"Yes?" Kane asked.

"So who pulled their little trolleys?"

Kane looked over his shoulder at Brigid.

Brigid's reply was only a few moments in the formation, her brilliant intellect plucking a possibility from the collection of facts. "We're presuming that the real threat of the Riders is that they've tamed carnivores for use as both riding animals and attack beasts. Where there are carnivores, there has to be prey. In the latter half of the twentieth century, paleontologists were postulating the possibility that these creatures had intellectual capabilities akin to animals we already can train—dogs, falcons…"

"Not a lot of herbivores are put to work for humans," Kane returned.

"On the contrary. Elephants were discovered to have their own form of language as complex as the songs of cetaceans. Horses had been observed capable of doing simple mathematics. Even the much maligned ungulates—cows and buffalo—have shown the capacity to learn daily regimens, such as placing themselves in position to be milked on motorized, rotating carousels."

"So you're saying they hitched a harness to a brontosaurus…" Kane began.

"Apatosaur," Grant corrected. "A brontosaur was actually a mismatched collection of sauropod bones."

Kane grimaced. "But I like the name brontosaur."

"Regardless, it is quite possible that they might have utilized a smaller-scale sauropod or a normal-size hadrosaur as a beast of burden, depending on their sturdiness," Brigid said. "That would also explain the consternation of the Dragon Riders' use of raptors and carnivorous theropods—a 'brontosaur' as you call them would be meat on the hoof for the barbarians' pets. Travel would necessitate an uncanny amount of alertness because dinosaur herbivores were not known for their speed, which would be further compromised by being 'in harness.'"

"I wouldn't say that they were slow," Grant interjected. "I've seen a trachodon, one of those duck-billed hadrosaurs, move about the same speed as a Sandcat could while being chased down by a ceratosaur pair."

"Sandcats can pull off over forty miles per hour," Kane mused. "And we've seen stagecoaches pulled by teams of four horses do fairly well in the speed department, but not that fast."

"As fast as the hadrosaurs sound, their predators were often by necessity quicker, or at least clever enough to herd a panicked animal into a waiting trap, made doubly dangerous by the combined hunting skills of humans, rather humanoids, and the packs of raptors they have tamed," Brigid added.

"Grant, do you remember when it was the two of us being lectured?" Kane asked.

"Yeah," Grant answered. "Why? What's changed?"

"Now it's the two of you giving the info dumps to me," Kane remarked. "I feel like the slow kid in class."

"Shizuka and I live right next door to the biggest dinosaur habitat we'd thought we'd known on Thunder Isle," Grant countered. "Knowing the capabilities of those critters is akin to me knowing how hard I can wring out this Manta if I have to. That's need-to-know everyday business for me, not you."

"Thanks," Kane muttered.

It was an hour and a half by the time the Mantas were in sight of the four-mile bowl that used to be a mile-tall volcano. Pinatubo's eruption at the end of the twentieth century blew four hundred yards of solid stone off of a mile-plus-tall mountain. The terrain had grown more forested in the centuries since the depopulation of Luzon, though this area had already been a Philippine national park.

The Watatsumi had cut themselves a trail, or expanded on the remnants of an older trail. The supply and equipment wagons had cut trails troughs in the dirt roads, but there was still no sign of any footprints of what had pulled them.

That was just a detail. The real reason they were following this road was because they led back to the tunnel where they had risen from the underground.

"Terrain is getting harder to read on the radar. The ground's too solid for tracks to have been made," Kane announced. "Baptiste, I'll land. You remember your training on this?"

"Just as long as you don't want me to fly this through a volcanic tube at supersonic speed, I can handle it," Brigid returned.

"Good," Kane said. "Now we're going to see what a world without sunlight gives us."

KONDO SPOKE, TALKING FREELY, spilling out the story of Remus taking him as a confidant, of asking him to become a part of a cadre in order to begin more direct punitive strikes against the Dragon Riders, and Tatehiko ate it up. The Watatsumi wasn't certain why he'd listened to the Wanderer, but there had been something in his voice, a loneliness that conveyed a desire to be trusted, to find someone to trust.

He was giving the Wanderer a chance, and at the same time, giving Tatehiko an excuse to take Kondo into his confidence. It was a dangerous tightrope, because what Kondo wanted to know might have been in the bailiwick of either of the two respected Watatsumi warriors. He needed to know why Ochiro, the disgraced leader of the expedition to Florida, had been so callous, so careless about the lives of innocents, and why he had set in motion the potential for a world-wide plague of demons controlled by the parasitic entity known as Kakusa.

Ochiro belonged to someone, and that someone retained influence and power enough to protect the *bushi* from the punishment he'd earned. Because of his actions in exceeding the scope of experimentation, Watatsumi warriors died and humans had been infected and killed under the control of the godlike hive mind known as Kakusa, or the Hidden.

Ochiro's goal had not been to release a powerful, ancient alien loose on Earth, but to experiment with the power of mind control on human beings, as well as on saurian beasts, engaging in instant conquest of enemy predators. The original plan was to use the octo-slugs as weapons that would latch onto a Dragon Rider raptor or acrocanthosaur and bend its primitive mind to the will of the defenders of Ryugo-jo.

Manipulating the minds of humans was something that showed an ominous plot at work. Whoever took responsibility for Ochiro would be likely to be involved, but there was also the dread knowledge that the Watatsumi, while strong and skilled, could ill afford to lose a commander of his experience while the Dragon Riders were still railing against their isolated, besieged plateau. Ochiro might have been on his own, or his mission could have been sponsored.

Kondo was alone. Isolated as Remus appeared to be. That made siding with and opening up to the Wanderer so dangerous. If he was guilty, if Remus was the man who wanted to usurp the rule of the pitiful remnants of the Watatsumi society, Kondo's confession of doubts might make him a victim of the tall, strange loner. Another possibility, one that chilled Kondo even more, was that Remus could twist his loneliness, use it to seduce him to the philosophy of the Dragon Riders, showing him that the ways of honor and discipline that he'd vowed to follow as a *bushi* of the Watatsumi were a lie and that in his heart he was a barbarian.

The attraction of living in the jungle, struggling and surviving in the verdant, lush primeval world, was there, in opposition to simply existing inside the tunnels of Ryugo-jo. But Kondo could not escape the disdain he held for the Dragon Riders, those brutes who didn't want simply to live the life of a wild man, but raid and attack those who did not agree with them. They were not barbarians, but despoilers.

Even the term *predator* was a denigration of honest, hard-striving creatures who hunted to survive, to feed their families. Despoilers took from others without care, without honor, without need of anything except the desire to destroy and ruin.

If Remus recruited Kondo to the Dragon Riders, then he would join, but only to the point of getting into position to destroy them. *If* Remus were to draw him into the Dragon Riders.

Supposition of guilt might be even more disastrous. Kondo was in a quandary, and thus, he kept everything bottled up tightly.

If Grant and Kane ever showed up, maybe he could confide in them. Until then, he had to watch his step and keep his emotions tightly under wraps.

Tatehiko wrapped an arm around Kondo's shoulders, his voice low, intimate.

"Go with him on his journeys. It will be fascinating to see where he travels and how he deals with the Dragon Riders without my eyes upon him," the *bushi* commander told him. "If there is any hint of impropriety, make certain that it reaches my ears, even if you must bloody your hands as he does."

Kondo nodded, impassive.

"You seem armored against something, Kondo," Tatehiko said.

Kondo nodded again. "You ask me to spend my time with someone who is observant, a proved and skilled loner. I dare not betray even the slightest bit, lest he murder me with nary a thought."

Tatehiko's eyes narrowed. He sized up the *bushi* lieutenant for several moments before curling the corner of his mouth up in a grin. "I like your style. Shrewd, kid. You'll last long in this business."

Kondo remained impassive. "Business?"

"Politics," Tatehiko said with a sneer. "I am a general of an army whose sole goal is the defense of our city-state. And instead of being given leeway, I'm tugged at by politics. Power brokers try to bend my ear so that I can give them the best chance at profit or political power, while they hold back resources or permissions to try new tactics or equipment."

"Why?" Kondo asked.

Tatehiko shrugged. "We're in a struggle for our existence, and yet all for a few votes, these so-called leaders hem and haw like nattering old women over the slightest of trivialities."

"All I know is that I've been on the front line, and I know that sometimes our needs go unmet, but we still give all for Ryugo-jo," Kondo returned. "Maybe they don't realize the seriousness of the threat posed by the Dragon Riders."

"They do," Tatehiko replied. "It's just that they feel a few losses can be acceptable."

"That is bullshit!" Kondo burst. "My men *died.* No losses are acceptable to a Watatsumi *bushi.* We fought to the death to save the civilians we were charged with protecting. If they can't see that…"

Kondo realized that keeping his emotions bottled was a lot more difficult than he figured. It was all he could do to unclench his jaw and his knotted fists, restoring the calm that was the natural condition of a wary, skilled warrior. "My apologies."

"I understand," Tatehiko said, resting a gentle hand on his shoulder.

Kondo managed a weak smile, knowing that his plans of uncovering deception were in grave danger if he couldn't keep his feelings close to the chest.

"Come, we'll visit Remus together," Tatehiko spoke up, distracting him from his doubts. "Chances are we'll be proved wrong, and he won't be against us."

Kondo shrugged. "Whether he is or he isn't, all that matters is that we detect the problem immediately."

"Then we tarry no longer!" Tatehiko exclaimed.

With that, the two dragon warriors made their way to the lair of the Wanderer.

Once back in the Manta, Kane followed Grant's lead as the two transatmospheric vehicles began their rapid trek through a volcanic tube that was a generous twenty-five yards in diameter, more than large enough to accommodate the aircraft. The walls seemed as smooth as glass, but there was a trail below them that was made of a rougher form of igneous rock, at least to Kane's touch. The "ground" was easily capable of providing traction to herbivorous beasts of burden, and provided more than enough room for even the largest of wagons to be tugged behind them.

"Though the sauropods are generally seen as quite huge, only the most extreme examples of the species topped out at slightly taller than this tunnel," Brigid said as the two craft jetted through the tunnels.

"Which was that?" Kane asked.

"Brachiosaurus, which ranged between twelve and sixteen yards tall, provided that their heads were not extended forward like their kin the diplodicus," Brigid answered. "There's some debate…"

"We'll discuss that when we're not flying at two hundred miles per hour and threading a needle," Kane said. "As far as I can tell, this is level ground, making any journey easy, even by wagon."

"Forward-looking radar is picking up the presence of small encampments every thirty or forty miles along this. You can figure each length was actually a day's journey, allowing their animals to rest for the night," Grant said. "That kind of puts the use of sauropods out of the picture. To carry enough feed, they'd have to use two wagons just for a long trip. Those things vacuum up enormous amounts of foliage."

"Yeah. The books I've read said they chew their cud all day," Kane responded.

Grant grunted. "Nope. Actually they have gizzards. Their flat molars grab leaves and strip them off branches. They roll it into a ball, and they roll it down into a sub-stomach filled with stones that they swallow, giving them a set of choppers designed to mush up plant material."

"That's only speculation, Grant," Brigid said.

Grant chuckled. "Observation on my part, Brigid. I've seen them selecting stones and swallowing them whole. The ones they belch up and discard are smoother than polycarbonate. They're practically gems, if you ignore that they've been vomited."

"Wait…was the stone you gave me one of those dinosaur pukes?" Kane asked.

Grant remained silent.

"Thanks a lot, Grant," Kane grumbled.

"Anything for my best friend." Grant grew serious immediately. "We've got an opening up ahead. We've been going a half an hour, we're 120 miles northeast from Pinatubo."

"By that reckoning, the Watatsumi had to have migrated—" Kane figured the math in his head, then spoke over his shoulder to Brigid for confirmation "—fifteen hundred miles?"

"We are talking over the course of centuries," Brigid responded. "Depending on the level of the catastrophe and available transportation, they could have covered quite a bit of distance. Don't forget that it merely took forty-eight years for the United States to expand from Appalachia to the Pacific Ocean. That was a distance of 2500 miles, and the settlers had neither twentieth-century technology nor the impetus of a lava flow guiding them."

The Mantas burst from the tunnel, and within moments they were soaring over a mountain range, lit from above by glowing yellow veins of liquid fire that stretched out ahead of them, creating a striated sky that was perpetually lit. The cavern they had entered was huge, and cloud formations were visible in the distance as the mountains below them faded away, submerging beneath the black, lava-light absorbing canopy of a great forest.

"No wonder they went underground," Brigid spoke up. "I don't think those channels of lava turn off for the night. In the tunnels, they can control the situation so that they have a diurnal existence."

"To the left appears to be the range that Kondo described," Grant added. "That is a huge plateau."

"Patches of forest appear there, but no industrialization evident at this range. It is remarkable. I'm reminded of the Andean Plateau," Brigid said.

The two Mantas soared, maintaining a distance of a

hundred yards from the ceiling of this strange subterranean world.

"Those lines, that's magma behind obsidian glass, right?" Kane asked. "You can't tell me that this was a natural formation."

"It's not. The striations are too evenly spaced and too completely covering this area," Brigid said. "This has to be artificially constructed."

"Man-made?" Kane interpreted. He shook his head. "The overlords?"

"Who else?" Brigid asked. "Or the Tuatha de Danaan."

"Likely the Annunaki," Kane murmured. "I'm reading the humidity and temperatures below, and it's hot and sticky there. Perfect weather if you happen to have scales."

"Oxygen levels are high, too," Grant spoke up. "Up here, at around four thousand yards, we should be at the limits of comfort, but it's regular atmospheric pressure. Down on the floor it's got to be short of walking through water."

"Which might explain the presence of dinosaurs and other prehistoric creatures," Brigid said. "The forest floor could easily be the home of legendarily huge insects."

"I thought giant bugs were unsustainable mutations," Kane returned.

"Not when they're existing in a hyperoxygenated atmosphere," Brigid answered. "We go down low enough, we can find the equivalent of seven-foot centipedes and dragonflies capable of picking up small children."

"So what is this, a game preserve? An underground zoo?" Kane asked.

"An ant farm for a god," Grant said softly, as if in answer. "Marduk's terrarium, except instead of praying mantises and turtles, he's got dinosaurs and God knows what other monsters."

"And we've never heard of this kind of a place?" Kane asked.

Brigid cleared her throat. "We have, sometimes in fiction, other times in mythology. This could easily be either Atlantis or Lemuria's inspiration. Countless fiction writers have called such a domain as this the Lost World or Pelucidar, or simply the Center of the Earth."

"Jules Verne wasn't pulling that story out of his ass?" Kane quizzed.

Brigid shrugged. "Apparently not."

"So, we've got a bird's-eye view. We've got the likely tableland they're hiding out in, but that's how large?" Grant asked.

"We fly," Kane said. "Hopefully, something will show up."

"Keep your sensors peeled," Brigid called to Grant. "We blink, we could be searching for weeks."

Chapter 9

Sinclair felt almost relieved the moment that the ominous shadow loomed over her lightly sleeping form. Her investigation had been going slowly over the course of the day, and patience was not one of her strong points. The shift of a body close to her bed had tripped her instincts, and she knew that any member of her team would not make the mistake of standing over her while she slept. She had been the chief of security at Redoubt Yankee, so her senses were naturally sharp, even while she dozed off.

It also helped that she was not only sleeping in a strange bed, but resting her head on a pillow that was shaped for the neck hoods of a cobra person. She could already feel the cramp in her neck. The wet sound of fangs extending, folding forward in a Nagah mouth, was everything that Sinclair needed to hear for her reflexes to snap into motion. With a surge, she rolled backward, her elbow striking the tough, hard belly plates of the Nagah even as her other hand whipped up, jamming under the chin of the leaning, mostly off-balance assassin.

"Dunno where you wanted to bite me, asshole, but your Dracula impersonation sucks!" she shouted, hoping that her bellow would reach the ears of the rest of her compatriots. Her elbow was sore from where it had struck one of the large, thick scales that adorned the cobra man's abdomen, but her rapid response had done its trick. The Nagah assassin's knees buckled as he staggered backward, one hand rubbing his stomach.

Sinclair knew that if her elbow hurt *that* much on her end, and she had initiated the strike, then her opponent had to be in a world of pain. Not bad for a reflexive, unaimed jerk.

"Soft-skin, you're going to pay for that," the silhouetted figure hissed, coughing and gagging, obviously feeling the effects of a *shuto* strike to his windpipe. Sinclair knew that she wasn't the same size and strength as a man, so she had to fight dirtier. As it was, she discarded the idea of a hand-to-hand battle with a full-grown Nagah man who was fanatically devoted to Enlil. Instead, she leaped from her mattress to the bed table, scooping her Beretta 92 into her grasp. As soon as her fingers closed on its handle, she pivoted and aimed at the Nagah assassin, only to find him rushing toward her. She pulled the trigger, knowing that her opponent was on the move and had momentum behind him.

Her single bullet created a brilliant muzzle-flash, illuminating the cobra man's face, not that she could tell any details of his scaled, semialien features to recognize him later. However, the momentary flare caused him to recoil, swerving away from the handgun aimed at him. Sinclair hoped no one she cared about stopped the bullet she'd missed with, but more urgent matters were on her mind. She whirled and lashed out with the barrel of the pistol, feeling it strike his hooded neck, missing the more vulnerable neck bones. Even so, she felt the snag of the front sight blade on scales, and the wet tear of skin as she pulled the Beretta free.

"Coming, Sela," Domi hissed over her Commtact connection.

"Careful," Sinclair warned as she stepped back from her

bloodied opponent. She tried to aim for the Nagah's center of mass, but one powerful, armor-scaled hand clamped over her gun hand's wrist, the other set of plated knuckles swinging for her head. Sinclair twisted her body the moment that her opponent grasped her, but even then, the grating, sharp edges of the scaled fist shredded a section of her forehead. Blood poured freely from minor scratches, and Sinclair counted herself fortunate that she had managed to move her skull enough so that she'd only suffered a glancing blow.

The freezie woman twisted with a grimace once more, throwing all of her weight into the Nagah's single hand grasping her wrist. He was strong, but hanging on to a full-grown woman with one hand while she used leverage, mass and physics against him was impossible. She popped free and rolled to the floor, somersaulting away from him. "Domi!"

In a flash, another shadow, gleaming ruby eyes flickering like the lights of hell, was in the room with Sinclair and the assassin. Something heavy and meaty resounded, and the hissing cobra man once more gargled out choking pain. The telltale whistle of an aluminum, telescoping baton slicing through the air told Sinclair all she needed to know about what the feral albino woman was doing. She was glad she'd introduced Domi to the weapon, as in her hands it was potentially less lethal in dealing with people they didn't want killed, but the ruby-eyed wild woman was still brutally powerful with it.

The baton fell again. Sinclair winced at the wet crackle of forearm bones shattering under the hundreds of foot-pounds of force that Domi's considerable, bestial might focused into the slender, nearly inflexible shaft of the weapon. Sinclair knew that she was able to burst a cinder block with her own baton training, and she wasn't someone who had used a machete to fight for her life against implacable hordes.

She felt almost sorry for the creature that had tried to kill her as she heard the whip-snap of a rib being fractured by Domi's attack.

"No more!" the Nagah rasped. "No more."

Sinclair activated the flashlight mounted beneath the barrel of her Beretta, and she saw that the snake man was slumped in the corner. His right hand dangled as if the forearm it was attached to were made of limp noodles, and blood trickled over his lower lip. He breathed rapidly, shallowly, eyes wide with horror as the Nagah struggled to get enough oxygen to feed his lungs despite broken ribs.

"Domi, frisk him," Sinclair ordered. "You move, I blow your damn head off."

"She won't get the chance to," Domi whispered, menace glinting in the reflected glow of Sinclair's gun light. "But you'll wish she had."

The Nagah snarled in pain, wincing at the feral woman's rough handling, slender white fingers clawing under his simple waist wrap and across his body. "He's clean."

"Tie him down," Sinclair said with a sneer. "You don't have to go easy on his broken wrist, either."

"You soft-skins are as soulless as our god says you are," the Nagah hissed with grim sibilance.

Domi rested the length of her baton across the would-be assassin's throat. "Your god? Enlil? Walking luggage. Hasn't got us yet. Think you can, broken snake face?"

There was a growl of agony as Domi punctuated her point by binding his wrists behind his back, the ugly grating sound of broken bones audible even over the pained exclamation of the Nagah.

"You will be extinct," the Son of Enlil threatened.

"You and what army?" Sinclair asked, hauling him to

his feet by the crook of his arm. The pressure was enough to draw more grunts of discomfort from the prisoner.

The captured killer had been standing for only a moment before his forehead exploded under a bullet impact. The corridor outside and all the lamps showing through other doorways plunged into immediate darkness. Domi released a growl that would have been at home issued from an angry panther, and she had to activate her own LED torch, the blackness so deep and complete that even her eyes were incapable of penetrating it.

Sinclair made certain of their prisoner's status, but the sudden jerk, the ugly rattle of a final breath, gave her all the answer she needed as she looked at the top of the Nagah's skull, flipped backward like a leathery trapdoor, the mush of the corpse's brain splattered all over the room.

"Domi?" Sinclair asked.

"He's gone," came her clipped response.

"Lakesh, Edwards. Report," the CAT commander said.

Lakesh sounded startled, drained. "I'm fine."

"Couldn't catch the shooter in the dark. Heard him, but he was too fast," Edwards reported. "We screwed this up."

"No. We have something for Rahdnathi to go over," Sinclair answered. "Even if it is just a corpse, and how that corpse died."

Sinclair turned her torch away from the bloody mess spread across her floor. It was going to be a long night.

KONDO HAD BEEN WATCHING the skies already, wary for the presence of the winged raptors that had been responsible for his inability to fight alongside his men. He grimaced at the thought of pushing off the blame for their deaths onto someone or something else, but both Remus and Tatehiko had convinced him that he was blameless, that his warning allowed most of his soldiers to survive.

Two streaks flashing across the glowing lines of magma drew his attention, and he whirled, bringing his rifle to his shoulder, shoulder and back muscles protesting at the rapid shift of nearly thirty pounds of the steel antidinosaur weapon. "Remus!"

The Wanderer turned his head, drawing back the string on his bow, an obsidian glass-tipped arrow already nocked on the line. The sound of the inflexible sinew cord bending the dense arms of the bow seemed like the guttural snarl of a small cat, reminding Kondo of the 350-pound draw of Remus's personal bow. The arms had been constructed from the horns of…some beast. Kondo didn't know what the creature was that the Wanderer had utilized to craft this simple but effective missile weapon, but if it were alive, he would have loved to have it at his side when going against an acrocanthosaur.

"They're not the pterodactyls," Remus said, relaxing his grip, the long lines of his arms no longer swelling with the seemingly effortless force that it took to bend the bow. "Aircraft?"

"Aircraft?" Kondo asked.

"Two small, unusual planes," Remus answered. "Flying ma—"

"I know what aircraft are," Kondo cut him off, a little more impatiently than he'd intended. "Apologies, sir."

Remus, if he'd been offended by the sharpness of Kondo's initial response, didn't seem affected, his golden eyes narrowing, as if he were extending his vision farther. "They are not of Annunaki design, as far as I can tell."

"How long has it been since last you saw one of their craft?" Kondo asked.

The directed question did get a reaction. "The overlords are quite conservative, maintaining designs over the course of millenia. Their skimmers are smooth skinned, like sizzling droplets of mercury slithering across a flat stone. These planes are similar in shape to earthly creatures, stingrays or manta rays."

"Mantas?" Kondo repeated. He'd heard that term somewhere before. "It's them."

"Who?" Remus asked.

"The humans who I met and fought alongside in America," Kondo answered. "Grant and Kane and Rosalia. One of them, Grant, stated that he'd do what he could to find us here. I hadn't given him much in way of finding us, only a few of the most subtle of hints."

"Such as?" Remus quizzed. Kondo noted the tension suddenly in the Wanderer's muscular form.

"I mentioned a redoubt we'd discovered in the Philippines," Kondo said. "And we're five hundred miles away."

Remus's taut shoulders eased, and he looked up. "They are clever."

"And maybe they had help," Kondo said. "They mentioned others, possessing technology different from theirs, and also a network of satellites."

Remus's scaled lips managed a tight smile. "Satellites, a list of redoubts and likely a knowledge of the kind of disruptions in the Ring of Fire, and the potential for volcanic tunnels, like the one that took our expedition to the surface."

"So, how would we contact them?" Kondo asked. "We could turn back toward one of the industrial centers."

"That would draw the Dragon Riders to interrupt us and our initial meeting with them," Remus answered. "Surely their eyes are on the same craft."

Kondo grimaced, then opened the breech, fitting a cartridge into the chamber. He then brought up his rifle. "I hope you can hear this."

Remus looked at the Watatsumi *bushi* aghast, but it

was too late. Kondo fired the powerful fifty, and a tracer round streaked skyward, his windage putting the line of the round ahead of the two Mantas. It was a dim hope, but the red, burning slug left a trail of sparks behind it, smearing the sky with a bright streak.

"See it, see it," Remus repeated, watching the aircraft as they arced toward the lone, soaring tracer.

THE MANTA'S SENSORS weren't picking up anything, even as Grant guided it through the sky at a leisurely 250 miles per hour. Any faster, and there was the possibility that radar and infrared wouldn't latch onto anything. He kept his eyes peeled, scanning out of the cockpit. The sensors were set to give an audible alert for anything for any potential threats incoming.

"Come on, Kondo," Grant muttered. "Give me a sign...."

The infrared picked up a significant source of heat, releasing a sharp bleat that drew his eyes to the screen. The source was small, but blazed at over 550 degrees Fahrenheit. Grant looked out the screen toward the heading of the contact and saw a dim red streak. The infrared, however, was able to pick it up much better.

"Grant, what's triggering the infrared scanner?" Kane asked.

"Someone fired a tracer round. We're not getting a comm contact from the ground, but Kondo might be under radio silence," Grant said.

"So he fires a gun?" Brigid asked.

"Radio silence, or no other means of reaching us," Grant guessed. "I do know that he recognized this ship."

"How?" Kane quizzed.

Grant sneered. "Because I drew its outline in the sand

and told him that if we couldn't reach him by mat-trans, we might have to use the Mantas."

"Makes sense," Kane said, sounding satisfied with that explanation. "Give them a radio ping, just to be sure."

Grant tuned the Manta's comm system to the frequency that Kondo said he'd be listening in on, then raised the microphone to his lips. Even as he did so, he slowed the Manta to hover. Kane took a little longer to stop, swinging around in a lazy orbit about his jet.

"Kondo?" Grant called.

There was silence, and Grant frowned. He didn't want to say any more, in case there was other traffic on this channel, even though things sounded quiet, almost abandoned. Kondo had been sharp enough to provide a frequency that wasn't in use, but if the Watatsumi had been away from any comms, then he simply sent out a message to empty space.

At least the miles of stone above them would keep any signal reaching the wrong ears on the surface. According to the Manta's sensors, they had descended six miles on a relatively steady incline. The volcanic vent they'd come through had been hewn from basalt, a dense, highly stable stone that was able to withstand seismic shocks, at least as Brigid described it. Because of the surrounding stone composition, she explained that they were in the Oceanic crust, which was a thinner, lower shell around the planet. The Continental crust was thicker, and made of "lighter" granite. If granite was light, Grant mused, then he didn't want to see what dense rock was.

This was a bubble that had been forged underground by the power of the Annunaki, and after having seen *Tiamat* up close, after his memories of his journey to the court of Humbaba, he knew the kind of wonders that the aliens from Nibiru were capable of. His jaw set.

"Kane, keep an orbit. I'm following that tracer's track back to its origin," Grant asked.

"And if it's an ambush?" Kane returned.

"If it was an attack, then they don't have a lot of firepower," Grant answered. "They fired one shot without knowing what kind of weapons these ships have."

"They don't have any," Kane said.

Grant shrugged. "They don't know that. Just keep the nose pointed at my position, like you've got a set of guns. And if they have millennialists with them, or Annunaki pawns, then I'm fuck out of luck, Cerberus is down one Manta and you two get out of here and seal off the goddamn tunnel."

"Still be careful," Kane growled.

Grant throttled up, guiding the Manta along the tracer's back trail, picking up two humanoids on the ground.

KONDO SHIELDED HIS FACE from the downwash of the Mantas, knowing that he and Remus were hedging their bets on whether the aircraft had been friendly. His stomach had sunk when the tracer round's so-called brilliant flare died out after what seemed like only a few hundred yards of flight under the yellow-orange glow of the magma lamps above them.

However, the halt of the two aircraft restored that moment of hope, and after his nervous wave of nausea passed, the two ships turned and approached their position. Remus still had his arrow nocked on its string, awaiting his mighty arms to apply the hundreds of pounds of force necessary to cock and then fire its lethal missile. With the kind of velocity that the bow's kinetic energy could release, Kondo had few doubts that it could puncture the hide of the mightiest of saurians, or even the skin of a light fighter jet.

Whether a single arrow and his .50-caliber rifle could

take down one of the ships should they turn hostile would be a moot point. One of the Mantas hung back, hovering, its nose pointed at them.

"I cannot tell what armament these planes have," Remus admitted. "Let us hope that whoever mans their guns comes in peace."

"If not, we won't suffer more than a moment of pain," Kondo replied.

The Manta's landing gear extended, and it settled on its wheeled legs, gracefully and gently. Kondo's mouth went dry. He couldn't imagine men like Grant or Kane having the tender touch to steer a fighter plane with such precision and skill.

Then the cockpit hissed open, and a familiar shape peered out.

"Son of a bitch, he didn't look that agile," Kondo muttered. "Grant!"

"Kondo!" the big human shouted, tugging himself out of his pilot's couch with one hand, then hurling himself over the side of the nose to the ground.

He made a display of putting his hand to the Commtact plate on his jaw and speaking. "Kane, come land. We're among friends."

Grant sized up the pair, and as soon as he studied Remus, his shoulders stiffened, wary caution racing across his features. "I hope we're among friends."

Kondo glanced to Remus, who returned his arrow to the quiver that hung between his shoulder blades. "He's with me. This is Remus the Wanderer."

As tall as Grant was, Remus was maybe half a foot taller. There was a look of faint recognition in the human's eyes, even as the other Manta swung in low, dropping to the ground with a decidedly less pinpoint and perfect landing, even if it was still a gentle return to the cradle of the plateau.

"A pleasure to meet you, Grant," Remus said, extending a long, corded arm toward him.

Grant looked hesitant, but he didn't push it to the point of rudeness. He shook hands with the Wanderer. "A friend of Kondo's is one of mine. Where is everyone?"

"Underground," Kondo answered. "You'd think there was enough 'undergrounds' with one set…"

"But a twenty-four-hour straight daylight isn't good for the human mind," Grant concluded. He continued to glance at Remus, except this time, it was more questioning than skeptical. "Excuse me, sir, but just what the hell are you?"

Kondo held his tongue, turning his attention toward Remus, even as Kane and a red-haired woman exited the other Manta. For a moment, Kondo wanted to quiz who this new stranger was, but as she didn't look like she could tear a man in two, he decided to await the Wanderer's response.

"Is that…" Kane began as the two closed with the group. He looked closer. "No. He doesn't look quite right."

"Quite right for an Annunaki, you mean," Remus said solemnly, his tone grim and sonorous. "I am not. I am merely a half-breed. There is nothing to be gained by disguising my parentage."

"That is why you seemed so shocked at the mention of them," Kondo said softly.

The woman with the flame hair and the athletic build of a young goddess stared at the Wanderer intently through emerald eyes that looked like focused lasers. She spoke briefly. "You are an Igigu, perhaps?"

"I remember them," Grant murmured. "They were in the court of Humbaba. One of them was his chief of fucking people up."

"That is a name I've not heard in millenia," Remus said. "Humbaba? Then you speak of Shamhat the Cruel, if you have named him."

"The Igigi were referenced in Sumerian myth as the younger gods of heaven, if not the servants of the Annunaki themselves," Brigid explained. "Shamhat is the one who was the bane of Grant's and Enkidu's existence."

The Wanderer narrowed his eyes, studying Grant. "Enkidu... By the gods, I thought you seemed familiar."

Grant looked warily at the tall man. "So you hung with Humbaba's court?"

Remus nodded, but showing shame on his features. "Like myself, and Shamhat, we were mixed-bloods, the results of interbreeding with lesser creatures. Humbaba was the son of an Anhur princess, the sister of Arensnuphis..."

"Menhit?" the woman prompted.

The Wanderer smiled, regarding her. "Your knowledge is great, young one."

"I thought that Menhit *was* Anhur's wife, since Arensnuphis is one of that particular god's many names," Brigid quizzed.

Remus grinned, extending a hand. "Arensnuphis was one of many Anhur who visited Earth at the peak of the Annunaki's command over this world. And as the chief representative of the race, he was oft referred to as the race itself. I am certain you would find many contradictions in the tales of the time of the overlords. But enough of me. What is your name, child?"

Kane remained tight-lipped. "Baptiste."

Everyone looked at the Cerberus warrior, shocked by his blunt response.

"Brigid Baptiste. You may call me Brigid," she said.

"Brigid it is," Remus said, immediately losing interest

in her and turning toward Kane. "You wonder if I am a pawn, a servant of your enemies? Enlil, Marduk, Lilitu…"

"She's dead," Kane said, barely controlling a sneer. "And hopefully, this time she'll stay a corpse."

Remus raised a scaled eyebrow. "How many of my ancestors have you faced, Kane?"

"Enough to know not to trust you," Kane answered, his gray-blue eyes lit from within by cold, icy hate. "Kondo…"

Remus held up his hand. "You need say no more. If you wish to speak, then go ahead and maintain your own private counsel. I shall stand away. Kondo here has his own secrets, feelings he's kept bottled up inside during his time with me."

Kondo felt his blood turn to frigid water in his veins.

"Just remember, I could have attacked you as you left your aircraft, and did not," Remus added. "My name is the antithesis of Sumer, the lands where I had been exiled from."

"Which would mean nothing," Kane responded. "Especially if you wanted to get back into Enlil's good graces."

Remus nodded. "Go. Speak."

Kondo took a deep breath, preparing to walk off with the humans from Cerberus when a nearby copse of trees exploded with the flap of wings and squeals of flying creatures.

The cause of the sudden burst of avian activity became apparent when he felt, through his sandal-clad feet, the heavy, ominous tread of something huge.

"Time for talk later," Kane snapped. "Big trouble's coming fast!"

Kondo readied his rifle, even as the tree line rustled with encroaching movement.

They were a quarter of a mile away, and even then, they could see the huge heads of a trio of great beasts. Huge sets of jaws adorned each monstrosity, while a tall, stiff fin of spines rose from necks trailing behind them. Each of the horrors stood, upper body and small arms dangling in counterbalance to a long, rigid tail.

"Acros," Kondo and Grant whispered in unison, moments before the superpredators lurched forward, their long powerful legs accelerating them to up to forty miles per hour.

Chapter 10

At first sight of the trio of megapredators charging across the plain, both Kane and Grant made a beeline to the Manta that Grant had flown in on. While Brigid Baptiste had been stowed in the back of Kane's jet, Grant's storage area had been used to ferry in the war bag that the two former Magistrates had packed for a journey into a primordial pocket. As much as she liked to rag on the two men's continual need to bring along heavy firepower, the flame-haired archivist had little recourse than to admit that in their travels around the world, it was a necessary evil.

"Can we ride out..." Kondo began as he steadied himself, the heavy Barrett rifle held at a low ready. "No, they're probably too small. Most of the space is probably taken up by engines."

"It was a tight fit for me, and I'm nowhere nearly as large as your friend," Brigid stated. She looked at the pistol in her hand, instantly drawn at the sight of the acros, who were closing in quickly. Breaking into an open run seemed futile and foolish. The beasts were faster than any normal person. It wouldn't be a matter of outrunning them, as by the time one of the humans ran thirty feet, one of those giants would cross the same distance in two strides.

She clenched her fist around the grip of the Iver Johnson autopistol she'd chosen to carry in recent times. Against a multiple-ton predator, it lacked the kind of authority she wished she could have had. A Copperhead would likely be no better.

"Baptiste! Catch!" Kane called, lobbing one of the Cerberus arsenai's SIG AMT rifles to her. "It kicks more than the Copperhead, but I set the selector to single shot. Hang on tight and counter the recoil with your weight."

Brigid grimaced. "You had me familiarize myself…"

"Hundred yards!" Remus shouted. As he did so, he drew back the string on his bow. Brigid watched as the seven-foot scaled humanoid held his aim for a moment, then loosed the arrow so fast, it was as if the feather-tailed shaft blinked out of existence. A knot of "silencing" tassels on the cord puffed out as they stilled the vibrations of the whipcord's motion.

One of the acrocanthosaurs gave a bellow, its course wavering momentarily.

Kondo cut loose with the Barrett, and Brigid winced at her close proximity to the big weapon's discharge. At the Manta, Grant's own heavy .50-caliber rifle boomed forcefully.

"Between the Mantas. We'll use their frames to shield ourselves!" Kane called out.

Brigid ran toward his side, even as the Cerberus explorer triggered his AMT, pulling the trigger on the rifle as fast as he could. He was able to get a higher rate of fire from the sleek Swiss weapon than Grant and Kondo, but the acros didn't seem as impressed by the 7.62 mm flyspecks spattering against their armored flanks as they were avoiding the hammer blows of the twin fifties and Remus's bow. One of the acros had a bloodied shaft jutting from its shoulder, and Brigid could tell that these creatures had a sense of tactics and self-preservation. Once they began receiving pain from their targets, they broke off from their straight charge and began circling the group of five and their aircraft, long legs powering them in a perimeter around them.

"These bastards are pretty damn fast," Grant said. "I'm trying to hit the rib cage, but they're just blurs. When they were head-on, even then…"

"Shut up and shoot," Kane grunted. Even so, he'd stopped peppering the air with his AMT's brass, realizing that he was having no effect, either from cold misses or just insufficient firepower to harm six tons of theropod.

The acros slowed, keeping themselves in the shadow of the Mantas, knowing that if they were still while in sight of their enemy, they would be injured. They also must have sensed that their human quarry were under the same worry. At this distance, with their great strides and the reach of those massive, curve-fanged jaws, exposure on their part would prove equally as perilous.

"One is hurt. That arrow sticking out of its collarbone is spilling blood," Kane noted, peeking around the Manta's landing gear. "There's some blood on the others, too, so you and Kondo must have scored a couple of hits."

"A couple of hits from a Barrett and they're still walking and stalking us," Grant answered. "You trying to tell me this is good news?"

"Wounded carnivores are angry and dangerous," Remus added. "Though, I'm likely stating the obvious here."

"That is from the file marked 'no shit!'" Grant countered. "I'm going to try an implode gren."

"Gren?" Remus asked.

"Grenade," Kondo translated.

"Baptiste?" Kane asked. "Think a gren's a good idea?"

Brigid glanced around a wheel on the Manta. The creature by their Manta limped, its thigh gouged by a bloody spot. "Shrapnel would do less than the rifles utilized by Grant and Kondo. An implode bomb…I'm not sure. It could cause severe internal trauma, or it could only raise their ire further."

"So much for knowing everything," Kane grumbled. "Okay, Grant. If this just pisses them off…"

"Hold on." Grant stopped him and shuffled through his war bag, seeking another bit of ordnance. "Brigid, think these acros would be turned away by capsicum?"

"Tear gas?" Kane asked.

Brigid nodded vehemently. "Yes. The family theropodia were well-known for their pronounced olfactory bulbs, indicating a sense of smell akin to a wolf."

"Tear gas," Kane repeated.

Brigid gave him a slap on the arm. "Their hides are thick enough that most of our bullets just bounce right off of them. However, we're dealing with scent-based hunters, who obviously caught our spoor from a quarter mile away. Capsicum extract, such as in tear gas, causes excruciating swelling among the mucus membranes, not just on humans."

"But since these things are probably taking huge breaths after a twenty-second quarter mile, they'll suck up CS-CN by the gallon," Kane returned.

"Tossing!" Grant called, popping the pin on one of the canisters, whipping the tear gas sidearm across the dozen yards where it struck one of the acros in the side of the face. Cottony clouds puffed and stretched from the canister's nozzle, and the predator, irate and curious about the object that had smacked it in the cheek, brought its nostrils down to it.

In a moment, twin streams of chemical ejecta were slurped into the nasal cavity of the massive allosaur, and it reared up, unleashing a shrill wail. Brigid felt as if her ears would burst from the sonic pressure wave put off by the pained acro. Its mighty head thrashed toward the Manta that she, Grant and Kane were taking cover beneath.

Neck muscles intended to snatch up a thousand-pound animal and shatter its spine with a brutal shrug proved more than sufficient to sweep the transatmospheric plane off its landing struts and flip it onto its back. The resounding thud and the near passage off the tormented superpredator's snapping jaws forced the trio of humans to scatter. Even Brigid opened fire as she scrambled backward, away from the blinded and bleating dinosaur.

With that sudden flash of activity, the other two acrocanthosaurus split up, flanking the other airplane, bearing down on the Cerberus travelers. Grant spun, his Barrett thundering rapid-fire, his biceps and forearms swollen with the effort of controlling the heavy blaster. The acro bearing down on him shuddered as the heavy hammer blows of the fifty creased its scalp over one brow, shattered its right cheek and found three more rounds deflecting off its collarbone, tearing furrows in its armored belly.

The salvo of gunfire slowed the surging monster just enough that Grant was able to dive out of the path of those six-foot-tall jaws, the acro's lower mandible tearing up a sheet of sod as tall as Brigid. With a violent jerk, the stymied predator hurled the grassy divot from its mouth and right at her.

The Cerberus archivist had no intention of seeing what the full force of such an earthen missile could do, even with the impact-mediating properties of her shadow suit, and she leaped away, only a moment slow enough for the corner to clip her across the shoulder blades and hurl her face-first into the ground. A simple glancing blow felt like being in a crashing aircraft, and she clawed to get dirt out of her eyes. She tasted blood on her lips, but she was in such a state that she didn't know where it was issuing forth from. All she could do was grope blindly for the rifle, even as the ground shook with the footfalls of giants.

Her prior encounter with the ceratosaur on Thunder Isle had been harrowing, but there she'd had the safety of a forest, and that solitary theropod was only one-third of the mass of an acro. As Brigid scurried, trying to blink her way back to sightedness, her ears and sense of touch were assailed by earth tremors and the roars of monsters and weaponry.

Then something else hit her, grabbing her and yanking her off her hands and knees.

For the first time in a long while, Brigid Baptiste screamed in fear.

KANE WONDERED ABOUT THE merit of rescuing Brigid as her peal of fright split through his skull. He was surprised that he could hear her, even over the deafening cacophony about them. Luckily, Brigid was quick witted, and realized that these were human arms, not the body-smashing mandibles of an acrocanthosaur, wrapped about her.

"Damn it, Kane!" she spit, bringing her palms to her eyes once more as he deposited her on her feet.

"You have nothing to be ashamed of," Kane returned, giving her a shove on the shoulder with one hand, clamping his AMT to his hip and triggering it with the other. For all the effect that the rifle had, he might as well have just thrown grains of rice at the monsters. Still, he was in a fight for his life and the lives of his friends. If the gun didn't have the power to injure the giant assailants, then at least it could distract and confuse the creatures.

Kane's recent burst of fire had been directed at a monster who was looking to tear Kondo in two, while the others were focused on other matters. Out of the corner of his eye, the beast that had inhaled several cubic meters' worth of tear gas was doing an insane dance, its face scraping into the ground, trying to use the grassland as a towel to wipe the agony from its eyes. The other was slow, measured, roaring a challenge at Grant, who had opened up its skin, bloodying it head and body, even though the man was without the powerful tool that had injured it.

The acro that had formerly been interested in Kondo whipped around, ferocious hazel eyes focusing in on Kane. Apparently the AMT was able to break skin, but the tiny trickles dribbling from its snout were scarcely more than an annoyance. He let the emptied AMT fall to the grass and extended the Sin Eater. The sidearm's heavy 9 mm rounds had proved more than capable of damaging the cockpit or the rotor shaft of a Deathbird. Maybe, if the creature charged, the machine pistol could punch through the roof of the giant's mouth and reach its brain.

It was a slim hope. Out of the corner of his eye, he saw Brigid, bringing her rifle to bear, unwilling to leave his side. He was simultaneously annoyed at her stubbornness to stay in the line of fire and heartened by her presence at his side. If they were going to die, Kane felt better that he wasn't alone, and he would go protecting his loved ones.

A sharp thwack split the air, and the acro facing down Kane suddenly recoiled in pain, whipping its face away. The movement was so violent and sudden, the former Magistrate triggered the Sin Eater, blazing a quarter of the weapon's magazine into the predator before it swung back around, forearm claw lashing at the shaft of an arrow jutting from its cheekbone.

To the other side, Kane noted that Remus was nocking a new arrow into his bow.

"Get to cover over here!" the Wanderer commanded.

Despite his prior misgivings, Remus had just penetrated the heavy skull of a six-ton monster with one of the most primitive missile weapons on Earth. That bought a lot of trust for the half-breed scion of the Annunaki, and he grabbed Brigid by the shoulder and got her started in a run to the Wanderer's side.

Even as this was going on, Kondo's rifle unleashed its clash of thunder at the terrible lizardlike titan that Grant had wounded. Round after round hammered into the limping creature, and one of its forearms dangled at the end of a bloody mass of smashed gristle and threaded sinew. The Watatsumi's persistent gunfire bought Grant enough time to find and reload his Barrett.

The mangled acro stood its ground. The leg it had presented to Kondo was bloodstained from a half-dozen impacts, which meant that it couldn't flee, and even if it did manage to kill the humans, it would be the predator's last meal.

"Grant, you gotta put that thing down," Kane ordered as he skidded under the wing of the other Manta.

Grant's answer over the Commtact was immediate. "If I can get a brain shot, I will stop its suffering. But its head is still moving around too much."

Kane extended his Sin Eater, leveling it, trying to get at the whipping head of the crippled opponent. By now, the other two creatures had given up their fight. Remus's "pincushion" was gone, trotting away on healthy legs, likely hoping to dislodge the arrows sticking in it, or at least salving those wounds with a wallow in mud. The tear-gassed predator staggered, almost drunkenly, grunting out sneezes as it made its escape.

The last of the predators looked around, realizing that it had been abandoned. Rather than cringe and back off, it believed that it had to finish this fight. If it ended the threat of the invaders, there was the likelihood that the others would return and help it nurse itself back to health.

Kane grimaced, remembering a discussion with Sky Dog over the naming of one of his tribe's youth as Winter Goose.

"Why a goose?" he had asked. "All I've ever heard is that geese are damn silly."

Sky Dog looked at him and in all seriousness answered "In our lore, the goose is a noble, reliable friend. Even in the coldest of winters, if one of the flock is too sick or injured to fly to warmer climes, another goose will stay with the ailing bird until it either recovers enough to travel or it has died. The other goose will bring it food, but most of all, stand by it, keeping it company and placing itself in danger to protect the infirm animal. To be named Goose means that the lad will be ever faithful, even through the darkest, most chilling of winter seasons."

Brigid also had explained that modern birds and dinosaurs were divergent paths of the same evolutionary chain. Paleontological records and live sightings on Thunder Isle had confirmed that these mighty, ancient rulers of the prehistoric past had the cleverness and emotional complexity of their avian descendants.

"Grant, if we don't kill it, those other two are going to come back the minute their heads clear," Kane said. "They were already angry and looking for a meal. Now they might just stomp us into jelly to protect him."

"Loyalty to the flock," Grant agreed. "I can't get a shot."

Kane tracked it, then triggered the Sin Eater, cutting loose with five quick shots. The wounded beast shuddered as a gory hole was punched through one of its orbits. Blood and pulped flesh burst out of the dying monster's head, and in an instant, it slammed into the ground, landing with a resounding crash.

Finally, there was silence in the clearing. In the distance, a baleful howl was released at the dreadful death impact.

Kane looked, seeing the arrow-stricken giant in the distance, at least three hundred yards away. It tilted its head up and sang a mournful note.

"We killed a dinosaur," he said numbly as Brigid rested a comforting hand on his shoulder.

"We survived, and it's not suffering anymore," she whispered in his ear.

Kane's lips curled in a disgust he aimed at himself. "No, but its family is. I thought we were going to just kill these lumbering things and be happy about it."

"You'd rather it slew us, Kane?" Remus asked. "This is not a reason to rejoice, but it is a reason for us to take a breath of respite."

Kane turned to the Wanderer. He tried to put aside the anti-Annunaki prejudice he bore toward him, remembering that one of the overlords, Enki, was not a tyrant but a Prometheus, bringing boons to humankind. If Remus was part Annunaki, that didn't make him automatically half devil.

It simply made him half alien, which was hard enough to trust.

"We must leave. They will be back, but without the urgency to rescue their brother," Remus said. "They will cry, and they will feast, and we will not have fear of hungry giants at our heels."

"Vengeful?" Kane asked as he gathered up his fallen gear.

Remus shook his head. "Revenge and spite are the traps of the so-called advanced mind. They will be wary of us, but sustained hatred is too complex for even their cunning brains."

Kane looked at the overturned Manta. "We'll need help flipping this back upright."

"We have beasts of burden back at Ryugo-jo," Kondo said. "And I would hope none of the Dragon Riders have the skills to pilot such a craft."

"Even if he did, there's no threat from this, short of crashing it into a village," Grant offered. "The only guns on board are ours."

Kane glared at his friend, but it was the truth. If there was going to be any sort of cooperation between humans and the Watatsumi, then there was going to have to be honesty.

"You merely acted as if you were protecting your friend," Remus said, shouldering a bag of supplies from the upright Manta.

Kane looked to the acro that waited on the horizon. The huffs and sneezes of the other gave proof to its presence, though it had disappeared behind a row of trees. "Grant's my family. And man, Igigu or theropod, family fights for its own."

The humans, Kondo and Remus started back toward the tunnels of Ryugo-jo.

Chapter 11

Rahdnathi folded his arms, regarding the lifeless form on the operating table. The head, what was left of it, had been removed, as per autopsy protocol. His face had been photographed and recorded. The dead assassin had no record of civil strife, and by all appearances was just another custodian.

"I don't suppose we can match his fangs to the wounds on your human operative," Sinclair said, knocking the Nagah from his reverie.

He shrugged. "I couldn't tell you. He doesn't even look like a Son of Enlil type."

"What, because he's half-mottled?" Sinclair asked.

Rahdnathi nodded. "The Sons of Enlil are purists. They don't even like the children of 'new skins.'"

"The ones who had been changed in the cobra baths," Sinclair said.

The Royal Guardsman leaned closer to the body, prodding a patch of exposed human skin. "That's correct."

Sinclair walked around the corpse on the table. "No known associates."

"A repair crew. We're interviewing them now, but in the wake of the attacks, people are making things tough. The custodial staff are needed, and citizens are reporting odd behaviors."

"A glut of sightings producing too much static to the signal to figure out a pattern," Sinclair mused.

Rahdnathi glanced up at her. "You acquitted yourself pretty well against him, so we do have a little bit of knowledge."

"That some of the members of this group are anything but highly trained insurgents."

Rahdnathi nodded. "Other than that, we've got dangling leads all around."

Sinclair poked again at the dead body's skin. "This look right to you? Even among a partially transformed Nagah?"

"What?" Rahdnathi asked as he watched her flick off a piece of dead scales. The Royal Guardsman leaned even closer, his mouth turning down in a deep frown. "The scales of a Nagah are not much different than normal human skin. The transformation is simply due to an increase in the density and thickness of the keratinocytes as they form. The scale...the underside doesn't look as if it were a dead cell disengaging from the stratum corneum."

Sinclair looked at the Nagah for a moment. "You know quite a bit about skin."

"It's one of the core pieces of transformation for us," Rahdnathi returned. "I went through the baths, and was given a course on the exact changes made to my body, such as the alteration of my salivary glands behind my incisors, and of course, the skin. This looks like stuck-on flesh."

"So we should ask to see if anyone recalls the dead man having a patch of untransformed flesh," Sinclair mused.

"His face was normal," Rahdnathi spoke up, looking at the bared skull and the flat, lifeless mask. "What could do that kind of thing?"

"The cobra baths?" Sinclair asked. "If they could alter the species on a scale like, well, from me to you, how about if they could alter someone's features, provided some form of programming?"

"But they were destroyed in Durga's rebellion," Rahdnathi explained.

"One that you knew about. What if the Sons of Enlil decided that they could make use of a body- or species-altering solution?" Sinclair suggested. "They draw off a little bit…"

"So they stole it a teaspoon at a time," Rahdnathi mused. "I'm going to look through my files."

"On the Sons who you captured or killed," Sinclair concluded.

Rahdnathi nodded. "We might be able to figure out who started funneling out to make their own special batch of the cobra baths, and then we can also see if they figured out a new interface."

"This could help immigrants become full Nagah if they want to. It'll help give your breeding population new genetic material."

Rahdnathi managed a smile. "A chance to grow and to heal back. People who've suffered crippling injuries have also been able to be restored by the use of the baths in the old days, though some who became serpentine in their lower-body transformations often took it as a sign from the gods, from our father Enki, that they were especially blessed."

"Allowing for things like Manticor's wheelchair," Sinclair mused.

"A happy coincidence," Rahdnathi returned. "At least for him, and others who have been injured in battles for our hidden world."

Sinclair pursed her lips. She wondered how Kane and the others were doing in their quest to penetrate a hidden world.

As the two left the morgue, Sinclair made a turn away from Rahdnathi and started back toward her quarters, where the others had set up a station to communicate with Cerberus and to collate information from their investigation. Her Commtact beeped a quick, short alarm and she adjusted her jaw, opening up the circuit.

"What's going on?"

"Edwards here," the big, almost brutish Magistrate's voice came over the communicator. "Domi and Lakesh just came back from looking at the dead guy's locker along with some of the guard."

"What did they find?" Sinclair asked, picking up her pace.

Edwards gave a noncommittal grunt. "It wasn't what they found, but an absence of evidence. The guy was clean. Like he never even thought about raising a ruckus."

"You can't prove a negative, Edwards," Sinclair replied.

She could hear the shrug in his voice. "Maybe, Sela. But the way these two described it to me, we might be wrong."

Sinclair sighed. "All right. Shoot."

"His locker was full. He was set on the night shift, brought in his lunch two days ago, there about," Edwards explained. "Two-day-old lunch does not smell good in an unrefrigerated locker."

"It's all Indian food to me," Sinclair replied. Her stomach was still feeling a little sour after the previous night's chicken vindaloo. Only three beers had been able to douse the burning in her gut.

"Lakesh said that no one in their right mind would let their food set that long," Edwards replied. "Also, his service keys were still in the locker."

"So he had a ring full of ways to unlock every door, but he leaves them behind," Sinclair answered. "He could have made copies in order to allay suspicion."

"Might be. But his logbook ended two days ago, about when he'd stashed his lunch. The logbook might be a little slapdash, but he was keeping his hours in it. The times of his repair jobs aren't up to date, but he did keep every note of when he clocked in or out," Edwards replied.

Sinclair frowned, slowing. "The Royal Guard looked at this, too, right?"

"They were looking more for ciphers, and the lunch bag was tossed in the trash," Edwards returned. "Domi and Lakesh wouldn't have noticed it except her nose is sharper than her knife."

Sinclair noiselessly convulsed in a chuckle. "Was it deliberate, or just hooked into the can to get rid of the stink?"

"They were watching. The guardsman who ditched it took a whiff after opening the bag, actually managed to turn greener then threw it out," Edwards told her.

"So why aren't Domi and Lakesh telling me this?" Sinclair asked.

"They went outside," Edwards responded, his voice dropping a few octaves.

Sinclair winced. "They didn't ask permission."

"Nope, and I don't think they were going out for some funny business. They told me to play dumb, and I figured I might as well give you the heads-up, just in case," Edwards responded. "What did you find out?"

"That the Sons of Enlil might have the technology that the Nagah thought they'd lost," Sinclair responded. "The ability to transform willing humans into cobra people, and to repair major damage."

Edwards snorted. "This is good news?"

Sinclair shrugged, then grimaced, realizing that her compatriot would not be able to see her response. "I'd say so. The Nagah decided to cut all ties with Cerberus because of the destruction and loss of this technology. Now, we get back into their good graces, and we also have a high-tech-capable healing facility…if one's needed. I like DeFore and the Moon-base doctors, but even they have their limits."

"Now all we need to do is find a replacement for the air fleet they lost," Edwards grumbled. "Then the Nagah will be good as new, and we might actually have a place to go to upgrade or repair Cerberus's own vehicles."

"If that works out, it'll be a good thing," Sinclair said.

"So what now?" Edwards asked.

Sinclair looked at her watch. "I should get some sleep."

"But it doesn't sound like you're going to follow your own advice."

"Nope," Sinclair answered. "I'm going to try to follow Domi and Lakesh. And hope they haven't wandered into a shit storm."

"So play dumb again," Edwards groaned. "Well, it's not like the Nagah have been disposed to seeing me as some kinda genius. Be careful, Sela."

"You, too. Watch your back and keep an eye peeled. They murdered one of their own assassins. They might want a second crack at us," Sinclair responded.

"Figured that much," Edwards said. "I only play dumb. I'm no caveman."

Sinclair smirked, then checked her notes on a way of escaping the underground city and rendezvous with the other members of the Cerberus expedition.

THE JOURNEY BACK TO THE entrance to Ryugo-jo was long enough that the three Cerberus explorers and their companions, Kondo and Remus, were forced to stop and make camp for what passed for evening. The glowing tubules of lava shed the equivalent of a cloudy day's sunlight. Even so, Kondo was quick to put up a tent to provide shade and shelter from the winds that occasionally whipped across the "tabletop" of the plateau. With camp made, and luckily

little need for a fire, Brigid Baptiste was able to sit back
and think over what was happening.

She returned her attention to the images of the acrocanthosauruses who'd assaulted them. There had been no sign
of the so-called Dragon Riders who apparently impelled
the creatures by unknown influences. The acros, as Grant
and Kondo had named them, had neither saddle marks nor
signs of prodding by sharpened hooks or slapping crops.
They all bore the signs of damage on their unusually tough
skin, remnants of battles with prey or other predators, for
the most part. She'd requested some information about the
usual movements of the supersized predators, and Kondo
had explained that until a few years earlier, even the Riders hadn't utilized them in attacks.

Brigid pictured the monsters in her mind's eye, stretching out their skins to make a map of injuries, seeking out
commonalities in their flesh.

Almost immediately, she found circular ligature marks
encircling their massive necks. By the state of the injuries,
all three acros had suffered lacerations or friction burns
along the skin. Obviously, these three creatures had been
lassoed, as if in effort to be captured akin to the horses that
Sky Dog and his tribe had. Brigid remembered that some
of those wild mustangs had similar burn or cut marks,
and that those wounds had been attributed to such spirited resistance to captivity that they broke the cords used
to snare them.

If the acros bore similar wounds, then it was likely that
the Dragon Riders had driven the small group of hunters
to the plateau with failed attempts at capture, or had lost
control of the animals since bringing them up here. Brigid
rolled out a map of the tableland and looked around the
sides, finding the potential for a half-dozen paths to climb

from the canopied rain forest below to the grasslands that served as the roof of the Watatsumi.

Either way, the acros, unable or uncertain about how to return to the lower jungle, where the thicker, warmer air would grant them more comfort and allow them to stay out of the light, had been forced to survive in the sparse forests up here. The sound of the Mantas landing and the smell of humanoids had to have been just enough temptation for them to risk their lives in a dangerous attack.

That they weren't under outside control, such as the mind-controlling parasites that Kane and Grant had encountered while on the run from Ullikummis, was apparent in that those who could had chosen the better part of valor, retreating from opponents who had harmed them and showed the potential to cause even greater injury upon them. A predator attacking prey that could return wound for wound either needed to escape, or end up crippled, unable to seek out another meal.

Brigid recalled the bitter, somber scene when the acro with the badly wounded leg had to be killed outright. The creature, unable to run away like its kin, had to stay and fight to the end. It was just too hungry, and Grant and Kondo had been too capable at crippling it, to escape. Its fate, ultimately, was a bullet in the brain.

Brigid frowned as she knew that, despite their former allegiance, the mourning pack mates would return and make the best of the situation. The dead acro was meat, and it was sustenance and survival for several more weeks.

The Dragon Riders hadn't directly caused the deaths of these animals, but their efforts at capture and captivity, driving them out of their natural territory, had doomed the acros. How many other creatures had stumbled into inadvertent doom because of this war?

"Kondo," Brigid spoke up, "the Dragon Riders utilize rope to control their mounts?"

"The dinosaurs?" the Watatsumi asked. "Yes. Ropes. Leather straps, perhaps cut from the hide of other dinos. Saddles."

"What kind of rope would they use?" Brigid asked. "And would they be able to produce cords capable of lacerating or burning the neck of an acrocanthosaur?"

"That would have to be wood fibers. They're nonstretching yet flexible. Wound tightly, they are, inch for inch, as strong as steel cable, and could cause injuries to dinosaurs," Kondo explained.

"Why is this important?" Remus asked.

"The acros might have been herded here, driven by Riders attempting to capture and tame them, or they could have escaped captivity during training," Brigid told him. "I'm trying to make sense of the time line for how the Riders are raising this army of monsters."

"They'd have to be pretty good to train winged hunters," Grant said.

Kane grumbled. "People have trained falcons, eagles and owls to hunt on command. They did it for centuries before firearms and gunpowder were introduced in Europe, as far as I can tell."

"They have hoods and leather gloves. I don't think even Remus could hold up a creature like Kondo described," Grant countered.

"Unlikely," Remus answered. "But that presumes capturing the flying hunters in the wild, as adults."

"Raised from chicks," Grant said in realization, wincing that he'd missed the obvious.

"The Riders were people who rejected the ways of the Watatsumi, correct?" Brigid asked.

Kondo nodded. "We had grown soft. Because we had

become so civilized, Ryu punished us with the destruction of our original home."

"Who?" Kane asked.

"The dragon god, upon whose spine rest the islands of Japan," Brigid answered. "Before skydark and the development of seismology, the ancient Japanese believed that earthquakes were caused by the sleeping giant Ryu, stirring in his slumber."

"A few dozen nukes, especially earth-shakers, would go far in waking up a bastard like that," Kane mused. "So they decided that if any tech was bad, they'd go back to enslaving animals."

"And trying to destroy us," Kondo added.

Kane looked across the plateau. "This is a lot of land. And there's jungle down there, where they'd found most of these species, that they were fine running around there, and capturing and taming superstrong, massive reptiles—"

"Dinosaurs are not reptiles," Grant interrupted.

"They're still taming raptors and acros and flying beasts," Kane returned sharply. "They can do that in a tropic, jungle paradise. Why fuck around with a plateau that's mostly grassland and trees? There's little enough wildlife up here, right?"

"When we first arrived, before the rift, we'd managed to procure breeding stock for the more…sedate creatures," Kondo said. "Trachodons, for the most part."

"For both manual labor and for food?" Brigid asked.

"Mostly labor. They took the place of oxen and horses," Remus spoke up. "Food, actually, was the cause of a rift between the Riders and the Watatsumi. You'll note that there are several rivers and lakes on this table."

Brigid nodded. "Fisheries?"

"Exactly," Remus answered. "When you have carp and salmon that weigh in at forty to fifty pounds apiece, growing in warm, oxygenated water, chasing down dinosaurs for beef really doesn't make sense."

"Yet you have a bow and arrow seemingly designed for such activity," Grant said.

Brigid turned to the large ex-Magistrate.

"I've been training in the use of the bow," Grant explained. "Your weapon is amazing. I don't think I could even begin to bend it to string it, let alone launch an arrow."

Remus sized up Grant with nonchalant interest. "Perhaps."

"Like the bow of Odysseus," Brigid remarked. "His wife made it a contest, that any suitor who could string Odysseus's bow and fire a shaft through a dozen ax handles would be worthy of her hand in marriage. Only Odysseus possessed the might and the skill to accomplish such a task."

Remus blinked, his gaze focused intently on her. "I would know nothing of that."

"This guy is a Greek myth?" Kane asked. "Like Ulysses…I saw that old vid. Cyclops, magic and that big bow."

Kane looked at Remus. "Sure doesn't bear a strong resemblance to Kirk Douglas."

Remus rubbed his fingers over his lips, but Brigid could catch the light of humor in the stranger's eyes. Greece was not far from Sumer, and if the Igigi had lived since those ancient days, then surely he would have been around at the time period alluded to in Homer's *Odyssey*.

"Why do you ask about rope technology?" Remus interrupted Brigid's musings.

"I am trying to determine whether the Dragon Riders are only making a show of their eschewing modern technologies while controlling the dinosaurs," Brigid responded.

Remus frowned. "So you want to know how the riders are giving their beasts orders."

Brigid nodded. "Any ideas?"

"We've been examining corpses of acros and raptors," Kondo spoke up. "So far, there's no signs of any devices. No radios. No computer implants. And we've sawn them apart top to bottom."

"We are thinking human technology," Kane said. "What about Annunaki toys? The threshold operates similar to our interphaser, except it doesn't possess electronics."

"And don't forget the control setup of the various ships they use," Brigid added. "Or the navigator's chair we discovered in Louisiana."

"Focusing gems and metaorganics," Remus murmured. "Those doing the autopsy work might overlook the presence of gems or even pocket them, not realizing what precious stones are doing inside an animal's anatomy. The same would go for the synthetic life-forms operating parasitically inside them."

"Would the Annunaki have had such a means of mass mind control?" Grant asked. "Outside of what they locked away beneath the ocean."

"We have tales of an ancient enemy imprisoned beneath the ocean," Remus said. "My memory could be better. I am long-lived but not infallible. Even with my healing elixirs, my brain is no longer as sharp as it used to be."

"Head trauma?" Brigid prodded.

Remus smirked. "When you live across three millennia, you try survival in a hostile world without a few knocks to your head."

Brigid frowned, touching the side of her head. Her skull still held the imperfections from the impact of an iron bar, wielded by an ancient, mad Nazi. Her journey to the Antarctic, seeking out a World War II-era redoubt hidden beneath the million-year-old permafrost of the barren continent, had nearly been her last. She'd survived, but days in a coma and odd, vivid dreams of another lifetime had haunted her ever since. "I feel you. And I'm only less than three *decades* old."

Kane's sharp gray-blue eyes fell upon her, and she could sense the worry in his otherwise impassive features. Though they rarely spoke of things out loud, she and Kane possessed a bond that was far stronger than any romance or blood relation could ever be. Their paths had intertwined across different lifespans, in multiple histories and universes, where they had met as lovers, as friends, as family. Each had died in the defense of the other, lives glimpsed through the fever dreams of passage through the mat-trans, and more recently during exposure to the universes between dimensions when they had sought out the location of Grant's tesseract, when his shadow-body had been hurled back to the dawn of humanity in Mesopotamia.

Even her normally photographic memory and prodigious intellect had been able to grasp only a few images or hints of the lives that were visible, the quantum strings of history that had been observed as they tumbled in the weird, barren spaces between the third and sixth dimensions. She retained some half realized, incredibly complex concepts, but trying to organize them into her current three-dimensional existence was like trying to explain a ball to a two-dimensional image. Her psyche had been strong enough to allow her those glimpses of that travel, but Kane, who had also taken that journey, was isolated from that experience, his mind shutting that door securely. His subconscious knew that usually three-dimensional minds were incapable of such comprehension. Only the level of mathematics she'd utilized had given her the mental stretch to at least visualize a framework of what the membranes between worlds resembled.

The thought of that temporal journey brought her back to Remus. She wondered if there had been any recollection on the Wanderer's face when he first met Grant. Unfortunately, she'd been in the air, waiting to come in for a landing as the big Cerberus warrior met with Kondo and the Igigu stranger.

If there were, however, that might not mean anything. In her experience, with the few jaunts through time, any effort to make changes simply resulted in a variation, the creation of a new universe.

Their trek back to the court of Humbaba had bothered her in that it was nearly unknown to have discovered artifacts from prior journeys, but it had been Grant's coat and sidearm that had given them a location in time and space to seek out his body.

Then again, the time trawl had done more than simply beam Grant's body to one location and insert his identity into the present day. The original Grant had been deposited somewhere outside the fifth dimension, which was the hypothetical plane where lines of time could diverge into multiple histories and universes. Because of that malfunction, they had been able to go to a point in their past and return, all without changing the history of their present reality, even to the point where Grant's lost gear had been left to journey forward in time.

The math required to understand that transaction would have been utterly impossible, save for the fact that they had recovered the spark that had been Grant himself, which had its own tether to the tesseract that had incarnated as a human body. Any future journeys, having no such silver thread between incarnations of a temporally displaced organism, would prove nigh impossible.

The trouble with whether Remus would be familiar to Grant was mediated by the fact that the man had predominantly been a simple shadow of himself while in that time, a shadow that had fleshed out, maintaining all but Grant's ego, a body that had incarnated itself in one of the Nephilim breeding vats. If Enkidu—the time-lost tesseract shadow—had encountered Remus, then there would be little chance for Grant to remember him, and importantly, remember which side the Wanderer had been on, either as a servant of Enlil or a follower of the more benevolent Enki.

Still, she could try. Later, in private, should they make it to Ryugo-jo, she would try her hand at hypnotic interrogation, hoping that Grant's subconscious somehow retained its experiences from the dawn of humankind.

For now, Remus seemed friendly.

Too many times, those amicable first encounters proved to be facades.

Brigid hoped that this wasn't the case, and she would keep her attention on the Igigu.

"Baptiste, I asked if you minded if we got some sleep," Kane interrupted. "We've been up for over seventeen hours."

She blinked. "No, not at all. I guess I'm spacing out myself."

Kondo would sit for the first watch.

Even so, Brigid's gaze didn't leave Remus until the heaviness of her lids brought her to the realm of dreams.

Chapter 12

Edwards was left behind to cover for Sinclair, Lakesh and Domi as they went aboveground to search for a potential Millennial Consortium base. That also left him holding the bag when dealing with anyone else. At least he could provide the excuse that the other three, having had their sleep interrupted, were attempting to catch up on their rest, and he'd only been fortunate enough to draw the short straw for staying awake. It wasn't as if he did more than spot the man who'd silenced the assassin.

Holding down the fort was task enough, but there were other things to be done. Rahdnathi sent a couple of Royal Guardsmen to keep him company, but Edwards and the Nagah were scarcely conversationalists, even with the translation capabilities of the former Magistrate's Commtact. Aside from discussing their gear and weapons for a few minutes, there was little more that could be spoken of without betraying the Nagah's state secrets or Cerberus's own operations, not that the two cobra men didn't drop a few hints to lead him into a verbal trap.

Edwards was glad that their general opinion of him was that of a thick, all but mentally useless lump of flesh who was best pointed at a target and told to go wild. He, like Kane and Grant, was a Magistrate, meaning that he had training on multiple high-tech military vehicles, such as the Deathbird attack helicopters and Sandcat armored personnel carriers. He'd also earned a lifetime's worth of street wisdom in his career, roaming the Outlands or fighting against criminals and insurgents in the wild Tartarus Pits.

Part of Edwards's armor against the Nagah's inquiries was his comfort in long, awkward silences. One-word answers, relentless, penetrating stares and keeping his craggy face impassive brought down a curtain that was as good as iron between the Cerberus expedition and their curiosity.

"Your friends are asleep," one of the guardsmen said, his voice cracking from lack of use and reluctance to try to glean anything from the human rock sitting before him.

"'Bout two hours," Edwards said, stalling. "If you want to go wake up Sinclair, you could go in there."

The two Nagah brightened at the idea that they could bring someone else in, but then realization dawned on their faces as they remembered the woman's response to a cobra man leaning over her in her sleep. Even if the assassin hadn't been shot through the head, he'd received a flurry of crippling blows from both Sinclair and Domi.

On edge from the prior attack, it was likely that if they did disturb her, they could end up with a bullet through the head if they were lucky, or a slow-healing, job-ending injury like a pulverized shoulder joint. They would have one saving grace—the swing of a collapsible aluminum baton would have a hard time causing vertebral trauma, thanks to the sheet muscles on the sides of their head, extending down to their shoulders.

"No, thanks," the other said sullenly.

"Since you two are here, I'll see if there's anything to eat," Edwards spoke up.

The Cerberus visitors had been quartered in the Royal Guard's central complex, but they had been limited only to living and common areas. That meant there was no access to communications, records or the armory. Edwards didn't need guns, wasn't interested in listening to hours of radio chatter and hadn't felt like reading, so that didn't affect his plans.

What he did do, however, was keep his eyes open.

Like most of the "centers" in the Nagah city, a series of buildings were built in blisters hewn in the caves. Each blister radiated transport tunnels, enabling movement throughout the city, though there were emergency doors all about, in order to deal with emergencies. Edwards likened it to the structure of the baronial villes, which were rigidly stratified. Here there were similar upper levels, and the buildings he saw were at most two stories in height. He saw a larger cavern, which was the hangar, but there was no sign of any other multistory blisters. The hangar, he understood, accommodated multiple types of aircraft, all of which had been damaged, as well as the need for extra "air" because of fuel fumes. Vent holes, both powered and unpowered, showed in the ceiling, giving a means of refreshing the breathable atmosphere in the city.

There was another giant cavern, Edwards reminded himself, but it had been off-limits. The Garuda Memorial Center was where Kane and Durga had finished their fight to the death. Annunaki technology had granted the monstrosity rapid healing powers, immense strength and the ability to absorb mass to form himself into a forty-foot, python-bodied killing machine. Gunfire and grenades had done little to seriously impair Durga, but an improvised explosive attached to the eternal flame of Garuda's statue had produced a fuel-air explosion that finally killed the mad royal.

Guardsmen stood at the entrances to the center, grim duty keeping them alert and ready to prevent people from idly trespassing into the ruins.

Edwards would have loved to know what was in there, but he was too big to slip past the cobra soldiers' notice.

There were not even workmen going through to the damaged section.

The place was Durga's tomb. He was a royal, so he had inherited that level of respect, being the son of two beloved leaders. He was also a monster who had brought a tragic civil war to his people, and his death was a dark stain on the history of the Nagah. Manticor had explained that much to the Cerberus visitors, catching them up on what Brigid Baptiste and the others hadn't briefed them upon. He didn't go into detail exactly why the center was cordoned off so completely, but Domi and Lakesh had a theory.

"Durga had been changed. He was a monster," Lakesh explained. "His hide was as tough as the stone he absorbed into his body, and even after grenades and gunfire had shattered that extra mass away, leaving him as a normal Nagah, the nanobots in his bloodstream were still able to protect him from a fighting knife imbedded between his eyes, directly into his brain."

Anyone who could survive twelve inches of steel in his skull was something that was just too dangerous to allow to live.

Edwards didn't need anyone else to do the math for him. The Nagah were frightened. Enlil and Enki, the gods of their mythology, were real, and they had both survived for thousands of years. Even in death, they had been able to reincarnate, growing anew as different races.

Edwards had personally seen Grant strangle a megatherium, a twenty-foot-tall mass of muscle, armored skin, with claws the size of swords. If the bronzed-skinned giant couldn't beat Marduk, Enlil's Annunaki brother, then the snake faces were truly terrifying. Edwards remembered being under the control of Ullikummis, a seed having been implanted in his head, sapping his will. Ullikummis had been genetically altered to assassinate Enlil's father and was another creature who had shown himself immune to gunfire and grenades.

Durga was supposed to be dead, and even Kane himself seemed to sound as if he wanted to add "I hope" to every mention of that enemy's demise. The dead royal traitor had also been the leader of the cultists staging the current insurgency in the Nagah city-state before his death.

Of course, no body had ever been discovered, apart from a few scales and fragments of bone. Semtex high explosives, combined with natural gas, produced a blast just short of atomic levels. No matter how fast the nanites had been able to reconstitute Durga's injuries, a fuel-air explosion was capable of destroying buildings or sections of forest in a nine-hundred-foot circle.

Durga's body wouldn't be recovered from that kind of explosion, but there was still the doubt that such a violent, vehement monstrosity was capable of being killed. The Royal Guardsmen didn't slack, and Edwards had to wonder if that was because of their professionalism—something that had impressed the big former Magistrate—or because they knew what kind of nightmares could be unleashed.

Further exploration led him to check out what kind of power grid their quarters had been based upon. Depending on who had access to turning on or off the lights the night before, during Sinclair's attack, it would thin out the list of potential suspects. As far as he could tell, the main command and control, not the one that was secreted behind the throne room, had its own power supply while there was an alternate grid devoted to living and support services areas.

There were guardsmen looking over different power boxes, looking for interference or tampering with the system, just like Edwards knew he or some of his allies would have been made to do should there have been violent, lethal hijinks in the Magistrate barracks. Since Edwards didn't stick around to observe too closely, they paid him little mind, even though he was sure that they'd compare notes back at their debriefing, again, just as he would have done.

They were making a thorough investigation, which was not any proof for or against an infiltrator within the ranks of the Royal Guard. A single investigator on the scene might have been more than enough to obscure and blur the trail forensically. Edwards wandered closer to another junction box and saw that it had scratches on its locks before he turned and headed into the canteen. That no one was actively looking at the box was a sign that others had to have been carved up similarly, to make it look as if there were break-ins at every junction box, further frustrating investigations. Edwards tightened his lips as he put on an act of deciding what beverage he was going to choose. Ice-cold water and beer were the only two things he preferred, and since he was on duty, he was going to avoid imbibing alcohol.

On his way back, he confirmed that multiple junction boxes had been tampered with, even as he sipped cold water. That gave him more than a couple of facts to weigh.

One was that whoever had killed the assassin was not alone, and he was working with a communicator. There was no way the lights could have been shut down and a bullet put into the head of the would-be murderer in that space of time. There were three killers in on the plan, perhaps even more. Only one was down.

The second point was that the killers were aware of the security protocols and the basics of investigations. At least one of them had hands-on experience, and could have transferred that knowledge to the rest of his team. While it was likely that one could have been a Royal Guardsman, there were also regular constables and private-sector business security that would have had the same skill set, especially since most private security staff were generally former law enforcement.

The third popped up as he thought over the communications network between the killer and his accomplice. The Nagah had shown a proclivity for spying on errant signals, having learned much of Cerberus's activities even before Kane and company's first visit. Whatever means by which they communicated had to have not only been secure, but on a frequency that had never been listened to by the highly sensitive ears of the Nagah's electronic intelligence networks.

Edwards frowned at that last bit of information, recalling Kane's account of Enlil's telepathic conclaves with Durga. The Nagah didn't drop any hints that psi-muties were common in their city, and the Annunaki were capable of mind-speech, though Kane had been contacted more than enough times that he could "hear" faint whispers of such conversations. Durga, having been exposed to that kind of psi contact, might have had pathways opened up in his brain, especially if the nanites made his body protean. If he could absorb tons of stone to change himself into an armored engine of destruction, then it was also reasonable to assume that the microscopic machines could have altered different nerve paths to make himself fully telepathic.

That was bad news, because then it would mean that Durga *could* have survived, slithering off into the shadows to reconstruct himself. Or worse, the blast had killed him, but his liquefied remains coalesced and were still rebuilt into…something.

"It's only one idea," he murmured as he twisted the cap off his bottle, taking another swig. "Maybe Durga wasn't the only one who was being contacted by Enlil."

He grimaced at himself. He'd been across the world

in his short time with the Cerberus action team, and he'd seen a lot of strange shit. He needed to be careful not to jump to the most extreme of suppositions just as much as he needed to guard himself from maintaining too narrow of a point of view.

Edwards took another sip. His life had gone from simple "serve and protect" to exploring abandoned cities and weird new parts of the world. The simple stuff was gone, but in its place came a regimen that worked into his mind, injecting life into his imagination, and though he rarely showed it, it returned a sense of awe, wonderment and joy of discovery. Sure, things seemed more clear-cut when it came to blasting away enemies in the Appalachian mountains, but he didn't feel like trading things in for a bland, pallid existence.

Edwards stopped himself, the hairs on the back of his neck rising. He'd been aware of the attention given to him by the Royal Guard as he wandered to and fro across the city. He wasn't cautious about their observations, and he actually welcomed them thanks to the fact that it made things easier for them to assume that his allies were in their beds, resting off a hectic, stress-filled night. When it came time for them to return, Edwards was to provide a further distraction.

That tingle of his senses was more than paranoia over the "good" Nagah's scrutiny. Something else was present, something laden with menace. Bringing the bottle back to his lips, he used the movement as an excuse to scan the area around him. He didn't have to look far to notice an Indo-asian man who was part of the large indigenous population of those who chose to remain mammalian, rather than visiting the cobra baths. Edwards tried to place what was different about him when he noticed a mottled shimmer of blue-green around one elbow, mostly covered by his work shirt but exposed when he scratched his head over his ear.

The man looked mostly normal, and it was possible that the Hindi was just someone who had attempted to alter himself but had failed, as per the nature of the cobra baths and immune system resistance or genetic anomalies.

Then Edwards remembered the briefing. All bits of transformation were welcomed, and proudly displayed, and it was warm enough inside the Nagah city that clothes were optional for the preservation of modesty, though the man was dressed in a work shirt, something to protect him from incidental problems—scratches, burns, caustic cleansers.

But the man had all the fidgety energy of someone who was worried over the chance of discovery—something that Edwards had seen almost every time he ventured into the Tartarus Pits or the less affluent sections of a ville. And just for that, he wanted to leap at the guy, put his massive hand around his throat and demand to be told what he was up to. He settled down, maintained his composure. Perhaps his escorts took notice, but Edwards wasn't certain. The flash of blue was only noticeable due to their proximity to each other, and Edwards's Magistrate instincts directed outward, looking for a sign of trouble.

That's when a second antsy shadow appeared in the corner of his eye.

"Business is going to pick up," he mused as he transferred his water bottle to his left hand.

This way, nothing would prevent him from grasping his Sin Eater the moment an emergency situation cropped up. As much as the Magistrates had trained to utilize and carry the reflex-activated submachine gun safely in everyday life, being nearly unerring marksmen with the sleek weapon, so too had they trained for the alertness necessary to distinguish between imminent danger and imagined threat.

For all the tyranny of the Annunaki overlords who had worn their neo-human guises as the barons of the nine villes, they had the prescience to realize that it took disciplined, capable warriors to protect their interests. Wild men who opened fire indiscriminately were hardly of any use when it came to defending the villes.

As such, Edwards was not on edge. Rather he was focused, wary of the behaviors typical of violent criminals or mayhem-breeding insurgents. The next man who had drawn the former Magistrate's attention was full Nagah, but like the Hindi, he appeared to be someone who was wearing the wrong skin, nervous and wired, touching his face and the large plate scales on his chest.

Sinclair's warning of the ability of the cobra baths to change humans and Nagah back and forth, perhaps allowing for one man to disguise as another, was a fresh alert in his mind.

Edwards decided to push the situation, turning toward the uncomfortable cobra man, locking him with a glare and standing his ground. This maneuver was an old tactic from patrolling the Tartarus Pits. It was the Magistrate behaving like a bull, an alpha male, hurling an unspoken challenge to draw an enemy into fight or flight. That kept him from unnecessary roughness and brutality, the throat-grabbing behavior he'd fought down before.

The Nagah's reptilian eyes drew wide at the brawny, tall figure before him. Edwards had to be careful. He was wearing his shadow suit, but there was little sign that even the antiballistic properties of the wonder material hugging his skin could do much against the savage bite attack of those inch-and-a-half folding fangs. He also knew that drawing and firing his Sin Eater before any sign of an attack would force the Royal Guardsmen who were following him to detain him, and Rahdnathi to send for the others.

Open conflict here and now would blow the ruse that Sinclair, Domi and Lakesh had counted on to keep their activities quiet. Edwards checked his Commtact, turning it on with a flex of his jaw, then speaking softly, subvocally, allowing the vibrations of his larynx to run through his mandible and be picked up and translated by the cybernetic communicator. "I've got two possible assassins on me. I'm in the open. Hurry home."

"Read you," Domi's curt response came. "We're almost back to quarters."

Edwards saw the uneasy Nagah, the possible Son of Enlil insurgent, shift his weight, sizing up the large human. "Move it. Business is about to pick up."

Suddenly, with a surge, the cobra man sprang at the former Magistrate. Edwards, free to go all out without risking the secrecy of his comrades, let the Sin Eater spring into his fist. He swung the compact machine pistol's barrel like a club to intercept the assassin's assault. A crunch resonated under the wet slap of metal on leathery hide, and the Son of Enlil spun in midair, his insensate form sprawling on the ground from the force of Edwards's pistol-whip.

Not trusting a single steel-framed impact to keep his foe down, Edwards sidestepped, then pressed the sole of his boot against the throat of his downed opponent, making certain to keep himself away from those venom-dripping fangs. He scanned for the other man, the Hindi, and was just in time to catch the blur of his small, brown form streaking forward, dagger bared.

Edwards swiveled, lowered the point of aim on his weapon and fired two fast shots that struck the blade-wielding attacker in the pelvis. Heavy slugs impacted on the cradle of bone that supported the torso's weight, connecting muscles to the legs, enabling a human body to stand erect. The two 240-grain bullets, designed to punch through even armor, splintered that part of his skeletal structure but avoided the femoral arteries.

Suddenly incapable of standing, let alone running and attacking, the Hindi killer tumbled to the ground, filled with agony, but still alive, still able to provide answers. Edwards had started picking up more than just bad habits from Kane and Grant; he'd been drawing on their knowledge of tactics, the minimum amount of force needed to bring a would-be murderer to the ground without silencing him forever. Racked with crippling pain, his knife handle rested in loose fingers, but the blade was soon kicked away by one of the Royal Guard shadows that Edwards had picked up.

The other guardsman pulled out a strip of nylon cable tie and flipped the Nagah whom Edwards had cracked in the face. Lying on his stomach, that cobra-headed assassin was in no position to lash out with his fangs, or rather his lone, remaining fang. Edwards's stroke with the frame of his Sin Eater had all but torn the other fang out by its root and muscles, yellow venom and blood seeping over the wounded prisoner's lower lip.

"Good eyes, there," one of the guardsmen said as he bound the wrists of the crippled Hindi. "How did you get them to blow their cover so easily?"

Edwards looked at the Nagah blankly, dropping into play-dumb mode. "I thought they just didn't like me."

The two guardsmen looked at each other, confused for a moment, then shared a subtle smile.

They were lawmen, too, Edwards knew. They didn't need a direct answer from the big man.

Chapter 13

Kane was on the morning watch, the last round of sleep for the long traveling explorers and their ally. The grasslands, surrounded by a crown of mountaintops as far as the eye could see, were beautiful. His one regret was that in a land of eternal sun, there was no way to see the beauty of the dawn.

It was no wonder that Kondo's people had once more driven themselves into subterranean tunnels. Without the diurnal-nocturnal cycle of life, the human mind and body, even those enhanced such as the Watatsumi and the Nagah, needed darkness. Underground, it was easier to bring in light than to cast the shadow of night under the relentless glow of the lava tubes.

He checked his map, having updated it with information from Kondo's and Remus's directions. They were several hours away from the entrance to Ryugo-jo. Most of the people lived in the honeycombed depths of the steppe near the edge, where a semblance of volcanic activity had created more tubes and tunnels, caverns through which the city of the dragon men could spread out.

He'd assumed it was artificial volcanic activity that had formed this tableland overlooking the rest of the thick rain forest sprawling outward like a flowing Victorian-era skirt. The ground that this pocket of prehistory had been carved in was the inside of a bubble of high-density basalt. Actual volcanic activity came from fissures and fractures in the lighter, thinner granite, where the glowing hot blood of Earth, magma, tried to expand toward cooler, less heavily packed exits.

For all the natural appearance of this lost world, still thousands of miles from Earth's core, it was not real. From the cockpit of his Manta, he could make out the token changes of environments, the shifts from rain forest to desert to inland seas. In the distance, hundreds of miles from the tiara of jagged peaks surrounding the plateau, he'd spotted an ugly, cloud-choked primordial hell, one that Remus had described as harkening back to an age before aerobic, oxygen-breathing life had taken to the surface of Earth.

"But there are living creatures in that toxic mist," Remus had promised. "The foulest of horrors, only barely imagined in the time of man."

The peculiar realm, carved by otherworldly technology and populated with samples of life from across the spectrum of the planet's existence, reminded Kane of the scope of the enemy that they had routed. Though *Tiamat* slept a dreamless sleep, stricken by deep, brutal injuries in the initial near destruction of the Annunaki bitch queen Lilitu, sometime, millions of years hence, the giant would awaken from its healing coma.

Lilitu herself had shown that the death of her Annunaki body was scarcely a hindrance to her continued plotting, especially since the overlords had been scattered by the same fiasco that had rendered the leviathan ship lame. Her essence had been divided, the shadows of her existence injected into three women.

"We can fight them tooth and nail, but still, we can't erase their manipulations from our world," he whispered.

A somber voice jolted Kane from his seat. "The stink of the Annunaki is a hard stain to rub out."

Kane regarded Remus with a hostile glare, informing the Wanderer of his lack of appreciation for such a surprise. At the same time, the Cerberus leader was fully aware that even his point man's instinct had done little to provide warning of the Igigu's presence just behind him.

"I'd have to wonder if you were interested in washing that away," Kane responded.

Remus managed a half smile. "Do you know your father?"

Kane frowned. "I *knew* him."

"He has left the mortal coil?"

Kane shifted under the Igigu's scrutiny. "He was killed. Stored in the Anthill by the overlord's hybrid incarnation for spare parts, organs, genetic material. He was used, just like the rest of humanity."

"But you spoke to him, once. In your distant youth."

"Yeah." Kane studied the stranger.

"My father was Annunaki. One of the thousands who had first come here, riding in the belly of *Tiamat*, brought across the empty void of deep space to populate a brand-new colony inhabited by—you," Remus explained.

"You almost called us apes," Kane noted.

Remus tilted his head. "Enlil thought of you as trained monkeys. Not my father. Not that it truly mattered."

"Because you were not as important as Enlil."

Remus nodded.

Kane narrowed his eyes. "So who was your dad?"

The Igigu's gaze wandered. This obviously felt like a sore spot for him. "Someone I didn't appreciate until it was too late. At least it felt that way."

"Sumer. Was it something from that?" Kane asked.

Remus scratched his brow. "I spent plenty of time there, when I was running away from what I should have been. I'd hung out with the wrong group. You said I nearly called you apes. And you're right. It was an old habit of mine. And I've gone back and forth since then on my opinions of humans. When you blew the surface to hell, that was the last I'd spent under the sun. I came here."

"Your father worked on this place," Kane surmised. "That is how come you wax poetic about the wonders of this little bubble in the basalt. And probably why you've taken to hanging out with the Watatsumi."

"They were fellow children of the dragon. A blind man could see our similarities, even though I'm taller, I'm stronger, I don't have the same features that they do," Remus returned. "And yet they have so much human about them. So much that my father admired about you scruffy little apes."

"It's hard to keep us down," Kane admitted.

Remus narrowed his eyes. "Kondo says that you've fought Enlil and his fellow exiles. That you've stymied them at almost every turn, across different incarnations."

Kane nodded. "Kondo makes it sound a lot easier than it really is."

"Doesn't matter," Remus replied. "You are here. After six years of conflict with him and the other outcasts, you are still here."

Kane frowned. "What happened when you turned your back on him?"

"I ran. This was one of the places I returned to. I've gone elsewhere. But I ran away."

The tent rustled above them, as if a strong wind had arisen. Both Kane and Remus looked up, but both of them knew that no wind would slice eight identical gashes in the shelter's roof. Each grabbed his weapon.

"Rise and shine!" Kane bellowed. In an instant, Kondo, Baptiste and Grant were scrambling to get up and moving.

A second impact, and the tent was torn up from its stakes, and both Kane and Remus aimed skyward, not toward the retreating canvas shelter, but toward the other pair of shadows that were now visible, power diving toward the explorers' encampment. Kane pulled his trigger in the same instant that the Wanderer loosed a shaft. Twin figures, winged terrors that were swooping down on them, jerked violently under simultaneous impacts. One figure twisted, impaled by three feet of obsidian-tipped wood. The other crumpled into a ball and crashed into the ground three yards behind Kane, its rib cage shattered by the burst he'd pumped into it.

The most immediate threat was out of the way, at least as far as the two of them could tell, but Grant gave a cry of warning as he spotted more menace.

"Riders!"

"No acros with them," Kondo noted. "Just Utahraptors and deinonychus."

"That good news?" Grant called to the Watatsumi.

"Smaller targets but harder to hit," Kondo returned. "Hate to say it, but the wild acros were easy."

Brigid sneered in disdain at that concept. "Then it's great news."

Nobody had to have her sarcasm explained. The Dragon Riders were horrors, and they were on the offensive. Kane grimaced. Though they had been at the edge of a tree line, the forest that their camp abutted allowed very little in way of cover. Shadowy figures flickered between trees, blocking off that avenue of escape.

"Gas 'em!" Kane called to Grant. "We need cover!"

As soon as the first word had left Kane's lips, Grant was digging in his war bag. By the time he got to cover, a tear-gas canister was in his hand, thumb through the ring on its cotter pin. With a smooth movement, he lobbed the shell toward the ring of hostile reptilian huntsmen circling them, a spiral of chemical smoke issuing from the end of it. The belch of capsicum mist from the grenade created a thick, burning cloud that the Riders, their steeds and their "hunting dogs" had little time to swerve to avoid. As soon as they plunged into one end of the billowing mass, there was the shriek of voices, rasping coughs, and the grunts and thuds of bodies slamming together.

Easily a dozen of the raiders were now caught in the eye-burning cloud, but there had been three dozen of them, and rather than make the mistake of charging to where their comrades had disappeared and been hurled into chaos, they stopped and held their ground.

A stone whistled past Kane's ear, and Grant let loose a grunt of surprise and amazement as another struck him.

"Slings," Kondo warned just before he let out a scream of pain, spinning to the ground. The Watatsumi wasn't moving, and Kane knew that trained hunters with slings were as deadly as anyone with a gun.

Another singing stone rebounded off Kane's shoulder, polymers of his shadow suit stiffening to alleviate the impact, but he could now understand the sudden shock of such a powerful strike. If one of the Riders managed to strike him or his allies in the head, he was fully aware that if they would ever awaken, they would be in a world of pain. The Sin Eater opened up on the reptilian huntsman who had struck him, ensuring that his marksmanship would never be a menace again.

The Dragon Rider fell backward, noiselessly, as if his vocal cords had been severed. The dragon man's scaled chest was a bloody mess from Kane's gunshots, and he was down for good.

That was about all of the reprieve that the four fighters would get as six of the deinonychus leaped into the fray, two of them bowling Kane onto his back, one of them showing enough wherewithal to latch its clawed hands onto

the Cerberus warrior's Sin Eater. That kind of swiftness
and skill stunned Kane, but not to the point of inactivity.
With a powerful surge, he punched the creature wrestling
for his gun across its long snout. The small, terrible-clawed
raptor whipped around, crashing to the grassy floor with
only a grunt as the air left its lungs.

The shadow suit's protective abilities finally failed
Kane, a hot line of burning pain suddenly appearing on
his left thigh. He gritted his teeth, rolling away from the
source of pain, just in time to see Remus's arrow piercing the head of the clawing beast. The Igigu's chest was
covered in welts that looked as long but not as deep as the
furrow that had been carved in his thigh, showing the true
endurance and durability of the Wanderer.

"Grant! Baptiste! Watch those claws!"

Around him, Grant's and Brigid's weapons chattered
violently, bullets ripping into the ground mostly as the
swift, agile predators darted between them. Grant had to
hold his fire, fully aware that the Sin Eaters had proved
able to slice through his polycarbonate Magistrate armor,
let alone the high-tech shadow suits. Brigid was equally
reluctant to cut loose, as well, the SIG rifle having similar
armor-defeating capabilities.

The flame-haired archivist spun, swinging the sturdy
stock of the AMT up and into the throat of another of
the deinonychus. The description of "small" was one that
Kane regretted using in his initial evaluation. Each of these
predators measured eleven feet from its nose to tip of its
rigid tail, and from experience, the one that had leaped
upon him to grapple for his gun was 170 pounds. They
were the size of an average full-grown man, though their
heads rose no farther than three feet from the ground as
they stood normally.

Kane whirled under another impact that spun him.

There was no fierce, cutting pain, meaning that the deinonychus's attack hadn't included those sickle-shaped hind
claws, deep tearing weapons that had been designed to cut
through the tough, scaly hides of their generally larger
prey. As much as he was glad that it was the "small" ones
that attacked first, he felt a cold pit of dread in his gut as
he realized that the Utahraptors, hampered as they were
with their human-sized riders, were even more dangerous.
Those things stood six feet tall at the shoulder, and from
Grant's explanations, weighed in at half a ton.

Kane looped his arm back, snagging the deinonychus
around its neck and throwing all of his weight into jamming it snout-first into the ground. The thing's vertebrae
disintegrated under his mass the moment its skull met the
ground. Broken-necked, the predator slumped into a clump
of twitching flesh. Another of the monstrosities launched
itself into the air, but the Sin Eater, an extension of Kane's
arm, erupted with hot lead.

It was as if the creature had slammed into an invisible
brick wall.

Amid the crackle of gunfire, the squawks of the drom-
eosaurs and the whistling arcs of sling stones, Kane surmised that these creatures and their masters were limited
in their avenues of attack by the trees. Certainly, breaking
into a run would prove disastrous. The deinonychus were
easily as fast as wolves or feral dogs, and amid the trees,
the humans would be dragged down and torn asunder.
Standing their ground was their best bet, using the thick
trunks as shields and cover against the smooth rocks that
sailed through the air, cracking bark as they struck.

Kane noticed that Grant had Kondo supported under
one armpit, his other fist filled with the fighting dagger
as he used himself as a barrier between the injured Watatsumi and a Utahraptor and Dragon Rider who had surged

into the melee. He started to aim at the rider with his Sin Eater when the snarl of an assault rifle erupted behind him. The gruesome sound of exploding flesh resounded, hot blood splashing against his cheek.

As concerned as he was for Grant's safety, Brigid had protected Kane from a pair of deinonychus that had slipped into the man's blind spot. Kane realized that he and Brigid would stand a much better chance in closer quarters. Even as he did so, he spotted a spear-wielding Rider come around the tree that Brigid had backed against. It would take a second for the deadly hunter to steer his steed and adjust the aim of his spear to pinion her against the trunk. Kane beat the killer to the punch, blasting two massive holes in the Dragon Rider's chest. His mount, the Utahraptor, whipped its large head around.

One-and-a-half-foot-long jaws, lined with curved, flesh-rending teeth, opened up as it lunged to avenge its rider. Kane shifted his aim and got off one shot before the thing jerked to avoid having its skull ruptured by his slugs. That did little to help the Cerberus explorer, however, as its thousand-pound bulk followed through, ramming Kane to the forest floor hard enough to jar his weapon loose. With an angry grunt, Kane snapped up his foot, driving it into the inner thigh of the beast standing above him. He didn't know if the thing had balls, but he did know it possessed a femoral artery.

The impact in the crease between groin and thigh caused a reflexive spasm that forced the Utahraptor to stumble. It sidestepped, and Kane watched as a foot laden with an eight-inch killing talon rose too close for comfort over his face. Brigid opened fire again, the AMT roaring as she pulled the trigger as fast as she could.

Half-ton predator or not, a dozen 7.62 mm rifle bullets in the ribs was tough to ignore. The Utahraptor whipped up its head, bloody froth foaming pink from its nostrils and from the corners of its mouth. Kane took the opportunity to snatch up his Sin Eater, cursing that the assault of the riders had exploded upon them so quickly that he hadn't had the opportunity to grab his own AMT.

As if to answer his question, the unmistakable thunder of Grant's Barrett .50 filled the air, and another of the Utahraptors crashed lifelessly to the ground. Kane craned his neck and noticed that the weapon was in Kondo's hands, but he'd only been able to get off one shot before having to resort to his handgun to shoot at a deinonychus.

Kane spotted the war bag, lying between the tree he'd found for cover and Grant's position. With a mighty leap, he hurled himself onto the satchel, hand diving into its pocket for another grenade. Guns and knives had been good for keeping the odds even so far, but they needed an ace in the hole, like the one that had handicapped one-third of the enemy force at the beginning of this fight.

Drawing out a frag gren, he popped the pin and yelled at one of the Utahraptors. The thing bellowed, a hideous intelligence and rage glowing in its eyes. These were not simple hunters like the acros of the previous day. Those megapredators sought only food and sustenance. The Dragon Riders and their allies were focused on one thing— cold-blooded murder.

Kane yelled again. The monster opened its jaws, and the moment he could see the thing's throat, he threw the gren hard and fast. The jaws snapped shut as it gagged on the hand-sized bomb, confusion making it shake its head. Seeming knowledge dawned as it opened its jaws once more, stomach convulsing as if to vomit up the high-explosive egg before it blew.

That kind of reaction left Kane with the sensation of cold water splashing in his chest.

The thousand-pound hunter exploded, its heavy hide dampening most of the blast, but thick petals of skin and muscle opened up, even as the creature's head disappeared in a cloud of gory mist. Kane, even behind the trunk of the tree, could feel the vibrations shake his teeth and rattle his senses.

It didn't matter. Explosives had proved just a little too much for the Riders. Their rapid assault had been broken, and in the thunder of clawed feet, they retreated.

Kane squinted, scanning after the dispersed raiders.

No one rode on the backs of the two remaining Utahraptors. Their saddles were empty, and unless Kondo and the Watatsumi were shown to be able to race with the speed of a horse, something was awry with this scene.

"Baptiste!" he shouted.

"I'm fine," she said. The shoulder of her shadow suit had been torn away, exposing skin from her neck down to her ribs, though she still had enough material to cover both of her breasts.

"Grant? Kondo?"

"Living," the two men answered.

Kane turned to see where Remus had gone to, but the tall Igigu had disappeared. A jolt of fear filled him and he moved toward where he'd last seen the Wanderer, and nearly stumbled over a body in the tall grass.

Remus was out cold, a bloody gash opened over his ribs. Kane didn't waste a moment of time, plunging into the war bag to retrieve a medical kit.

He tore open a bag of coagulant powder, gelling the blood deep into the wound to prevent further bleeding. A compress of gauze and tape followed to secure the injury with a pressure bandage. Finally he affixed an athletic wrap to prevent the further fracture of ribs. Kane's efficiency was rewarded by a low groan as Remus's eyes blinked.

"Still with us?" he asked.

Remus winced. "I will be. I will…."

The Igigu trailed off as he explored his own chest, sizing up Kane's medical work.

"You didn't look so good," Kane offered before Remus could even ask.

Remus's lips tightened. "Thank you. Please, help me stand."

"Normally, I wouldn't suggest it, but those bastards might be back," Kane answered.

Brigid was there by his side, concern darkening her features. Her prior bruises had a few more companions after this melee, as well. "Did you notice that none of the Riders survived?"

Kane nodded.

"And yet the predators turned and retreated, together," Brigid continued.

Grant was there, holding up Kondo. The Watatsumi's tunic had been torn open, and a patch of scaled skin had been bloodied by the impact of a slung stone. Beneath the broken skin, he was nursing either fractured ribs or a cracked clavicle. "Those species don't congregate on Thunder Isle. That's all wrong."

"You're bleeding," Kondo noted.

Kane grimaced as Brigid pushed him to a seated position. A packet of coagulant and a tight gauze wrap were what she applied to the situation.

"The cut didn't get down to the muscle, but it split the skin and fatty tissue," Brigid said.

Kane frowned. "I've got fatty tissue?"

"We all do, son," Grant grumbled. "Some just is more obvious, and gorgeous, than others."

Kane looked at his friend, then back to Brigid, who had tied off the ragged ends of her shadow suit's tear to keep her ample breasts private. As tall and athletic as Brigid was, she still possessed some fine curves, much to both his and her chagrin.

"Grant, remind me to tell Shizuka about that crack," she muttered.

The big man chuckled. He had scrape marks on his cheek, but they didn't look like the work of claws. Grant noticed Kane's attention. "A raptor's hip raked me."

"We're the walking wounded, and we still have a couple of hours to go to get to Ryugo-jo," Kane muttered. "With the raiders still about."

Something rumbled low and in the distance, cutting him off. With a grunt, he got back to his feet. He couldn't see anything moving among the waist-high grass, so he took a few stumpy handholds on the bark of a tree, raising himself up ten feet before he noticed a pair of beasts tugging carts behind them. They were escorted by Watatsumi with rifles, but they looked as haggard as he felt.

"We've got a ride coming," Kane said. "At least, I hope they're friendly. They look all beat."

Kondo nodded, returning to the remnants of the tent. He found his radio and keyed it.

Kane rested his forehead against the bark, letting the Watatsumi's rapid Japanese disappear into gibberish.

Things were pretty bad. They'd had an incapacitated Manta, and Remus was badly wounded. He and his allies were banged up.

He hoped that the medical facilities possessed by Ryugo-jo were as good, or better, than those of Cerberus. They were going to need that kind of help.

Because the Dragon Riders were not the true force

that was assaulting the Watatsumi. The renegade Japanese dragon men were puppets.

Something worse was out there in this forsaken pocket of prehistory.

Chapter 14

Rahdnathi didn't look happy in the least, but Sinclair was glad to notice that his ire wasn't directed toward her and the rest of the Cerberus contingent. If anything, Edwards's swift and decisive response to the two assassins had kept the Royal Guardsman from dealing with the headache of more bodies, even if they did happen to be killers.

When he looked over the freezie Air Force officer, his eyes narrowed. She hardly looked as if she'd taken a few hours to catch up on her sleep, though she was able to pass off her condition—sweaty and more than a shade sluggish—as the effects of having been awakened from a deep sleep and forced to rush to the scene of the murder attempt. Domi wrapped her arm around Lakesh's waist, tousling his hair in order to make it seem as if it was that way because of her affections, and not from a perimeter check around the surface of Nagah City.

If it was a convincing act or not, Rahdnathi held his tongue as he looked over the two men.

"These two men are matches for a pair of corpses that patrolmen located in a sewage runoff tunnel," he told the humans. "A third body was located along with them."

Sinclair looked over the third corpse, which had been rinsed off on the steel coroner's table. It was an identical match for the Nagah who'd attempted to murder her in her sleep, except for one thing. The patch of human skin that was on the dead murderer was absent on this man. She frowned.

"So he's innocent of the crime he was accused of post-humously," Sinclair murmured.

Rahdnathi nodded. "It'll be a small consolation to his family. His mother is still despondent."

Sinclair nodded. "Welcome to the real world, she said to me, condescendingly."

Rahdnathi raised an eyebrow. "Excuse me?"

"Old lyric," she answered. "People get murdered, and their deaths leave holes in lives."

Rahdnathi frowned. "That's why Hannah had your people sent away. It wasn't the loss of technology or the huge upset in our government. Good people died. We are a community, and we survive because we care about one another. We've fought so long and hard against bigotry between ourselves, between 'pure' and 'newcomers,' between 'scaled' and 'soft' because the world has enough against us."

Sinclair reached out and rested her hand on the cobra man's shoulder. "Humankind isn't as slow as you think. It's mostly governments and laws that make bigotry so easy to hang on. But people are essentially good, and this is a world that needs all good people, no matter if they're human, if they're black skinned, scale skinned, albino, Hindi, toe head like me…"

Rahdnathi's mood seemed to lighten as he threw her a smirk. "And now, these assholes are using the general distrust raised against the nontransformed to spread their terror, even though they're operating both as human and cobra."

"Anything from the prisoners?" Edwards asked.

Rahdnathi looked to the big Magistrate. "One has a hard time talking. You broke his upper plate. The other is still under heavy sedation from the damage you did to his pelvis."

Edwards sighed. "I'd have taken it a little easier, but I didn't want them killing bystanders if I didn't put them down right away."

Rahdnathi shook his head. "Don't apologize for that. Just be a little patient."

"Fair enough," Edwards responded.

Sinclair glanced over to Lakesh, who was looking at slides containing cells drawn from the skin of all three prisoners. As it was an electron microscope, he was able to zoom in to the point where salt crystals looked as if they were the size of cliffs. Right now, she saw the screen and noticed that there were bugs crawling around on a rocky shelf that looked as if someone had taken a night-vision photograph of the old Pueblo Indian ruins.

"So, they're full of nanites?" Sinclair asked, even though she could see the answer on screen.

"Leftovers," Lakesh stated. "This is one of the keratin cells that I'd drawn out from a scale. You can see from the blocky, hard-shelled structure."

"And that is not what this man was born with?" she asked, leaning closer over his shoulder.

"No," Lakesh replied. "Robotics and cellular biology are not my forte. Quantum physics are. But I can tell that these impostors came out half-baked."

"Hence the flaws in their skin," Sinclair said. "But why?"

"Excuse me?" Lakesh asked.

"They seemed to have changed species in a short time, seemingly only days," Sinclair continued. "So why have telltales such as scales on a Hindi man, or bare patches on a full Nagah?"

"A simple matter of inertia in programming. While the

bulk of the nanomachine suspension has the orders to alter appearance and species, there's still a current of them operating under the old rules," Lakesh answered. "As well, it's a known factor among the newly transformed that they are either not quite finished enough, or end up too finished."

"Fused legs," Domi added.

"Also, every Nagah who has been through the cobra baths has a small colony of mostly inactive nanites," Lakesh replied. "If they drop into a new transforming solution, they will multiply and breed."

"That true?" Edwards asked, wrinkling his nose at the thought.

"They're inactive but inert. It's something we live with as they're scarcely more noticeable than the huge ecosystems of flora and fauna living on regular human dermis," Rahdnathi said. "Between bacteria, truly microscopic mites and other entities, the human body is as densely populated as, say, Shanghai at the height of the twentieth century."

Edwards looked down at his bare forearm, frowning. "Great news there."

Sinclair gave him an elbow in the ribs. "You didn't feel or notice them before. You won't now."

Edwards shrugged. "True. I'll just know."

"Worlds within worlds, my dear friends," Lakesh said. He looked at the screen, lips pursed in thought.

"You've got an idea, sir?" Sinclair asked.

"I might, dearest Sela," Lakesh returned. "I'll get in touch with Bry and Philboyd back at Cerberus. We destroyed the previous interface with the nanomachines, but there is one available as far as we can tell. Otherwise they wouldn't have the ability to alter people. If we can reverse engineer the means by which they are controlling the machines, then we can locate their headquarters."

"What would you need?" Rahdnathi asked.

Lakesh looked at the sample full of nanomachines. "I just need to get these back to Cerberus, where we can have Bry and company look at them. I didn't realize that when we'd encountered you that there would still be microscopic samples of the original cobra baths that we could utilize."

"For what?" Rahdnathi asked.

"Duplication," Lakesh answered. "We could now return your people to the situation that they remembered, return your society where people lived as their species of choice, not stuck as an outcast because of the time they were born in."

Rahdnathi's lips tightened.

"Are you all right?" Domi asked.

"Then you do understand the damage left behind," Rahdnathi said.

Lakesh sighed. "Everywhere we looked, people were happy in the roles they had taken in this city. Only those who had been corrupted by the enticements of the Annunaki overlords and the cult Enlil had fostered so long ago had any call to demand change, to look at anyone who wasn't part of some imagined pure bloodline as something less simply because of a lifestyle choice."

"Who has to go back?" Rahdnathi asked.

Lakesh looked around the room. "Beloved Domi, would you mind terribly if I left you here and simply requested a Nagah escort?"

Domi made a point of seeming to think about it. "Return and wait for you and Bry to crunch numbers, or stay here and do something interesting."

Lakesh smirked. "Say no more, darling."

The albino woman winked to her true love. "Thanks."

Rahdnathi waved over one of Edwards's old shadows. "Rudyard, you go with Lakesh back to Cerberus."

He glanced to confirm that this would be fine with the head scientist. Lakesh nodded in agreement.

Rahdnathi looked at Sinclair. "So, did you three find the millennialist compound?"

"Friend Rahdnathi..." Lakesh began.

Sinclair lifted a hand to cut him off. "You'd have gone searching for the enemy yourself."

"That's why I'm not pissed at you and your team," the Royal Guard officer replied. "Maybe a fresh set of eyes would notice something we didn't."

"No luck," Domi answered. "If they're near, then they're invisible."

"By process of elimination, they must have some kind of operation inside the city," Sinclair added.

Rahdnathi frowned. "That's what we were starting to believe, but I was hoping that it was a case of disinformation."

"That way, if things turned out illogically, then you could lean on the one who was dropping a false trail," Edwards noted. "It'd make things a lot easier for you to work with."

"We already have someone to talk to," Rahdnathi returned. "Thanks to you."

Edwards smiled.

Lakesh shifted in his seat. "Edwards mentioned that there was an area blocked off to the public. It was Garuda's square, correct? Where Durga died?"

Rahdnathi nodded. "We are keeping a close eye on it. When it first had been wrecked, we had work crews on hand, but not on a constant basis. In between shifts, someone had gotten in and began setting up tributes to Durga."

"So you're not worried about Durga's cells regrowing from beyond the grave," Edwards asked.

Rahdnathi's eyes widened. Sinclair knew that the big

Magistrate had just hit on a thought that was too close to the surface to merely be the subject of an incidental inquiry.

"He was able to reconstitute his body from terrible injuries," Lakesh noted. "I saw him at his most horrific with my own eyes."

"Me, too," Domi added. "No body? No real death."

"Enough people believe that around here, too," the Royal Guardsman said. "That's why there's no lack of volunteers on hand, ready to open fire the moment there's a hint of him awakening from the dead."

"It ain't paranoia if you've seen the shit we've seen," Edwards added.

"How about maintenance tunnels running beneath the square?" Sinclair asked. "Any signs of activity in them?"

"We keep patrols going through, and we find signs of habitation. We leave booby traps behind to try to flush out any conspirators, but nothing drums up a response," Rahdnathi said.

Lakesh looked at the body of the conspirator, rubbing the gray-white bristles of his chin.

"An idea?" Rahdnathi asked.

"It's too preposterous," Lakesh said. "You've conducted an autopsy on the body already, haven't you?"

"Yes," Rahdnathi returned. "Why?"

"I was just wondering if the dead assassin wasn't just a spare body," Lakesh responded. "Part of a split consciousness."

"The remains of the Sons of Enlil are just Durga?" Rahdnathi asked.

Sinclair walked over to the corpse and gave it a jab. No response. "Like in John Carpenter's paranoid survival horror classic, *The Thing.* That creature was a shape-shifter and able to infect bodies."

"But we have three real corpses to accompany conspirators who have gone through reconstruction to take their place," Lakesh said. "Why not simply infect a body and leave it at that? No, he has to have accomplices."

"We'll work it all out," Sinclair said, prodding the body. She remembered the smell of its breath, the grunts, the strength in its hands before its head blew apart.

Could it have been someone pretending to be a living, normal person? Could Durga have been able to operate two of these monstrosities to attack Edwards at once?

The more questions that ended up answered, the more she could see dead ends that might not be dead ends.

There was the strongest evidence for cultists, but there were also red herrings that Durga himself could be alive. Was there also the possibility that Enlil wasn't through here, despite moving on once it had been shown that the combined forces of Cerberus, the consortium, the Sons of Enlil and Durga, and the Royal Guard had turned the city into a roiling mass of mayhem and destruction? And if not Enlil, the overlord had more than a few surviving brothers out there, aware of Enki's city, possibly even cognizant of his attempt at conquest.

Sinclair sighed. There was a reason why she liked older movies drawn from the writings of men like Chandler and Hammett. In those cases, if things reached an impasse, there was always someone with a gun bursting into a room to move the plot along.

Sometimes getting in the line of fire was the best possible way to find answers.

The only drawback was that survival was never assured when the enemy's guns blazed.

GRANT FOLDED HIS ARMS AS he looked over Kondo. The Watatsumi's bloody flesh had begun to scab over on the cart ride, and even as they took an X-ray of his broken clavicle, the medics noted that it looked as if this injury had been healing for weeks. Now Kondo slept soundly as Grant paid his friend a visit. The door to the hospital room opened, and in walked the half-breed Annunaki. Grant wanted to hate the being, it was a reflexive instinct brought on by memories of his tesseract's existence in the court of Humbaba, where an Igigu named Shamhat took great pleasure in testing the limits of that temporal shadow's physical limits.

But Remus had fought hard and bravely at their side, suffering wounds in the defense of Kondo and Grant, buying them time to reorganize and kill the dromeosaur opponents and their humanoid allies. He also entered, ignoring Grant's presence and casting his gaze upon the sleeping Watatsumi, concern evident on his face. If Remus were a menace akin to the Annunaki or the Igigi he'd previously encountered, it was unlikely. Those beings had nothing but disdain for creatures that they considered less evolved.

Grant studied Remus, whose wounds had sealed up so swiftly that his skin literally absorbed the gauze that Kane had used to bandage him.

This was close to the kind of medical technology that the Annunaki had demonstrated on multiple occasions. The only difference was that neither Kondo nor Remus had been placed inside an alien coffin lined with strange extraterrestrial gems and alloys.

Then again, there was no telling what manner of metabolism the Wanderer possessed, especially as he'd stated that he was part Annunaki, and had dropped hints of being many centuries old. Kondo's quick recovery was a little more unusual, but the Watatsumi said that he'd been originally restored by an elixir that had been mixed by Remus. Perhaps there were herbs here, or it could have been an extension of his Igigu biochemistry. Grant thought about nanomachines, but Remus didn't appear the type to have any close ties to technology, especially given his preference for primitive tools and a simple life.

The Wanderer, tall and magnificent, wore only a simple waist wrap and trod everywhere barefoot. Grant could understand. There were times, back before the discovery of the shadow suits on Thunder Isle, that he cursed the discomfort of his Magistrate armor, especially since replacement panels of the polycarbonate plates were taken off enemies, and thus built for smaller, more slender men.

The Wanderer's barefoot nature was doubly explicable thanks to the flexing, winglike fins attached to his ankles. Finding footwear that didn't interfere with that was likely a bitch and a half.

Remus looked down at his side, then grabbed a thread of gauze that had been swallowed by his healing flesh. He didn't even wince as he tugged, drawing it between the scales.

"So what is the elixir you gave to Kondo?" Grant asked bluntly.

"It is a complicated recipe that I'd be willing to share with you," Remus said. "Though one of the ingredients is quite rare."

"Your blood?" Grant pressed.

Remus smirked. "Astute. No wonder the young man cherishes your friendship."

Grant frowned. "What I don't get is what you're getting out of these people. They respect you and they show more than a little fear, but you're not taking advantage of it."

"Am I not?" Remus asked. "They are my allies in a war that I've been waging for over a hundred years."

"With who?" Grant fired back.

Remus sighed. "You might believe me. There are forces

at work behind the Dragon Riders. Tempters. In olden days, one may have called them sirens, succubi, all manner of dark manipulators."

Grant scowled. "What do you call them?"

"A dear friend called them the Mahar, but he was playing name games. Their true appellation was the Ramah," Remus said. "They are an ancient species, and quite elusive."

"Elusive? How so?"

"They control the will of others," Remus said. "As such, they stand far beyond the reach of reprisal. Their claws have not been sullied in single combat across three thousand years, according to the legends."

"They locals? Or are they part of the Annunaki reign?" Grant asked.

"Bastard children, far softer than an Igigu, merely the same as a human," Remus told him. "They're hardly anyone to boast of, but natural selection awakened a defensive mechanism in them."

"Mind control," Grant concluded.

Remus nodded. "They had been so much more powerful before, but there came travelers. They chipped away at the dominion of the Ramah."

"Enough that they were on the ropes until the Watatsumi showed up?" Grant asked.

"An influx of a new, sentient species gave the Ramah something to drag themselves back from extinction," Remus answered. "They were now able to fight back, by appealing to the disenfranchised."

"Fight back against what?" Grant quizzed.

Remus looked sadly at the floor. "The Watatsumi were not the only ones here. There were others before them, living in a relative state of peace with the Ramah. Like their ancestors, they sought out servitor races, though even with that, they were only barely able to make any conquests."

"But with intelligent warriors, instead of bestial humanoids, they proved to handle things better," Grant said.

"The Ramah control minds, but they also gain strength the more they 'network' those intellects. The more men they control, the more they can spread their powers," Remus said.

Grant frowned. "So with a small army of supposedly rebellious soldiers…"

"Not rebellious. Lacking in discipline, just enough so that they can be goaded emotionally into following the Ramah," Remus said. "They are sirens, as I said. They have been drawing those weak of spirit to their side, taunting them with how they are weak, or pointing out their minor offenses from others, fanning rage at the slightest, giving them the illusion of freedom as they release the beast."

"That's where the other animals are coming from? The extra brainpower of their new charges?" Grant asked.

Remus nodded.

Grant traced his gunslinger's mustache with his index finger and thumb, putting the math together. "And yet the dinosaurs retreated after we killed the riders."

Remus shrugged. "The network of humanoid brains that they have has grown. They appear not to want to lose any more fighting power than necessary. If they had to, I would bet that they'd utilize only one Watatsumi renegade as a lynchpin for their psychic control of the animals, but that wouldn't look right."

"So why haven't you explained this to the Watatsumi?" Grant asked.

Remus's dour mood deepened. "I've tried here and there."

"What happened to them?" Grant inquired.

Remus watched Kondo. "He has been the luckiest so far. The Ramah seem to be stronger than I suspected. Those who have hints of what truly goes on have been attacked viciously."

"You think that not all of the Ramah's thralls are out in the wilderness, riding on dinosaurs," Grant stated grimly.

Remus nodded. "I don't know who, but they are the relay here, within Ryugo-jo."

"Why?" Grant asked. "Why not just take the whole place over?"

Remus shrugged again. His melancholy grew, and it began to feel like a solid, oppressive presence in the small room. Considering that they had learned that the Annunaki could simulate psionic powers, it didn't surprise Grant that the Wanderer might be broadcasting his emotions unintentionally.

Kane rapped on the doorjamb. "Grant, Tatehiko wants to speak with us."

Grant nodded.

"How is Kondo?" Kane asked.

"Sleeping and healing fast. He'll probably be awake by the time we're done talking to Tatehiko," Grant answered.

Kane eyed Remus, seeing the tall being's brooding posture. "Is he all right?"

"I shall live, man of Cerberus," Remus said. "My wounds have already closed."

"Good," Kane said reservedly. He shot a glance to Grant, who nodded, indicating that Remus, as far as he could tell, was all right, not only physically, but likely someone who they could trust.

"Go. My colleague is less patient about tardiness than I," Remus said. "I shall watch over the young man."

Grant left the room and walked apace with his friend.

"I get a good vibe off him," Kane mentioned.

Grant nodded. "He's all right. You don't see Enlil checking in on the welfare of a lowly human."

Kane looked back. "For all the scales, they are just human. More so than the Nagah."

Grant shrugged. "Humanity is the one constant we've run into. We've met good. We've met bad. Even some hybrids have shown decency and courage."

Kane smiled. "So what did you two talk about?"

Grant thought about saying something, but so far, he had been isolated from anyone else who might have been a possible psychic puppet or spy for the Ramah. He had to shield his thoughts, and that meant keeping another secret from the man with whom he'd trusted his life on a daily basis.

"About the reasons he had for watching over Kondo, and for being with us," Grant said.

Kane's head tilted in curiosity. The man wasn't psychic, but there was no one else that Grant knew that could pick up on the subtlest of clues. Brigid had said that his almost supernatural sense for danger was based on his subconscious's ability to pick up on readily available hints in behavior, things that most conscious minds had long ago learned to tune out.

Grant cursed himself for letting any form of guilt show visibly over the omission of information.

"Tell me after we talk to Tatehiko," Kane said. He gave Grant's biceps a squeeze. "No worries about holding up any burdens of secrets."

Grant nodded. "Thanks."

That was the construct he would use. He wrapped Remus's talk up in a stone globe, thick and huge, and then rested that massive weight atop his shoulders, keeping it out of the reach of any spies.

Grant might not have had much to seal away thoughts from psychic probes, but if there was one thing even more legendary than his strength and grouchiness, it was the pure stubborn streak that would make even the most obstinate of asses throw up its hooves in dismay.

Let anyone try to break into his memories.

The Magistrate would stand strong.

Chapter 15

The meeting room was large, and Watatsumi guards, armed with short swords and machine pistols, stood at each entrance to the arenalike room. Tiered desks formed rings around the center, as evocative of a lectern as of a courtroom. Kane, Brigid and Grant were in the center, and the only representatives on the floor beside them were Tatehiko and a few others.

As opposed to their audience with Hannah and her court, the three Cerberus explorers were disarmed of anything larger than a hairpin. The frisking was thorough, and their war bag was kept separate. Kane could see the leadership of the Watatsumi, a civilian council, up several tiers, with plenty of wood and stone between the visitors and the politicians. Even if they managed to take down the armed guards on the floor, the bodyguard and the council would have cover and be able to react while the humans had to fight an uphill battle.

It was good, then, that the Cerberus group weren't there to start a war. On the contrary, they had arrived to provide aid against their enemies.

"Welcome to Ryugo-jo," Tatehiko said with official flourish, extending his hand.

Brigid, as always the pretty face put on any Cerberus interaction with other cultures, was the one who took the hand. Kane didn't mind, because not only was she qualified through her mastery of tact and diplomacy, but people were more likely to want to talk to her, in comparison to himself and Grant, who were obviously rough and ready warriors.

When there was a choice between dealing with someone who was soft, feminine and attractive, and a pair of brawny men, Kane always felt like erring on the side of chatting up the cute one. As a mouthpiece, Brigid had been worth her weight in gold, not counting her brilliant intellect, adept at dissecting duplicity, or her vast knowledge.

"We are pleased to finally discover the home of the honorable Watatsumi," Brigid responded.

Tatehiko was all smiles, but that didn't undercut the tension of the dozens of grim, armed *bushi.* Swords and guns were present, but Kane didn't doubt their ability to deal with opponents while unarmed. They were sharpeyed, and they stood firmly. Their uniforms were impeccable, which simply underlined their professionalism, as they were in battle dress, which was slick and practical, not flashy and needlessly complicated.

Kane understood the semimilitarization of this society. They were, after all, under siege. Even in Cobaltville, he had been responsible for not only the security of the baron, but also those whom the baron ruled and controlled. Without everyday people, their society would cease to exist. Warriors needed a cause to fight for, and that cause was first and foremost the existence of a normal world.

It was Kane's experience that, for the most part, those who enforced the law generally fell into the category of doing so for the sake of others, putting the needs of the many above their own. That had been proved out, despite grim, corrupt examples such as Salvo, who were simply examples of the predatory minority that not even an Annunaki megacull could drive into extinction. How many here were on the take, looking for the lure of easy power and prestige?

Kane couldn't read anything on their faces.

"So you say that the only hints given to you at the time of your first encounter with Ochiro and Kondo's expedition were of a redoubt accessed in the Philippines?" Tatehiko asked, stating the question loudly enough for their audience of councilors and bodyguards.

Kane looked at the *bushi* leader. He was a shade shorter than Kane, but still tall for a Japanese man. Again Kane was reminded as much of the similarities of the Watatsumi to the Nagah, and yet there were strong differences. If there had been a common ancestor, one branch of this family opted toward emulating the regal serpents of the subcontinent of India while the other took on the features of Oriental dragons, possessing mustaches, beards and manes of hair that were reptilian scale variants on feathers or mammalian fur.

"That's correct," Kane answered, speaking up now that Brigid had done the yeoman's work of building a bridge of dialogue. She shot him a glance out of the corner of her eye, once more admonishing that he had a history of burning such bridges with the wrong, rash statement in exactly the right place. "We had a whole hemisphere to search. We'd asked questions of a group of Japanese expatriates who settled in the islands of Southern California. They call their new home New Edo, and they keep the samurai tradition alive, as well."

Tatehiko tilted his head in curiosity. "How did you narrow things down?"

"New Edo didn't have anything to go on outside the legends of Ryugo-jo, and your race's nominal origin," Brigid said. "Watatsumi, the Japanese equivalent of Poseidon, in dragon form, of course."

Tatehiko smiled, impressed.

It was then that Kane felt the strange rustling in the back of his head, as if something were walking through his hair, feathery feet treading on his scalp. Telepathic contact had been made, something that his subconscious had been able to categorize and make a tactile sense thanks to several such communications with Balam. He didn't have the structures necessary in his central nervous system to initiate such communications, but he could "hear" it, especially if it were directed toward him, as was the case when he and Enlil engaged in a brutal psychic struggle back in India.

He fought the urge to tighten his muscles, and he turned his thoughts to Tatehiko's facial foliage, locking onto the intricacies he could see in the translucent streamers on his upper lip and chin. He let the thoughts spread and occupy the totality of his consciousness, losing himself in the tangle of the mustache. Kane's perception of intrusion seemed to go on for hours, but such was the nature of telepathic contact. Moments later, in real time, that soft, psychic caress was gone. No one else was in his head. Grant himself was still, as grim as a gargoyle and twice as imposing.

The room seemed to dip, as if he were a five-pound weight resting on a mattress, gravity buckling and swirling around him as he stood still.

"What we did have, though, were your communications with Ochiro," Kane spoke up. He realized that the whole incident had barely taken two seconds, a natural pause in the conversation. That made him wonder if Tatehiko and the others had been mentally swept, as well. "And we had one set of allies who have a remarkable set of ears to narrow things down."

Tatehiko tilted his head in curiosity. Kane tried to read that inquisitive look. Was it reaction to the probe that raised the hairs on Kane's neck, or was he perhaps an initiate of the psi-contact? Durga and the Nagah had little sign of any telepathic ability, and yet Durga had been on a mental hotline to Enlil.

You're looking for trouble based on past experience, he thought to himself. *Wait for a shred of proof before accusing people who might be allies.*

"The Nagah," Tatehiko prompted. "Kondo mentioned them on his return. It was their communications monitoring that allowed you to figure out where we'd set up a relay?" he asked.

Brigid nodded. "And given the vicinity of the redoubt on Luzon to a major volcano, we were able to correlate the relationship between the fabled undersea kingdom and your location."

"Resourceful," Tatehiko said. "That is part of why I opted to take you in. Your equipment will be on hand in your quarters."

"All of it?" Grant asked, finally speaking.

Tatehiko smiled, extending his hand to the big man. "You wouldn't be much use against an acrocanthosaur without that magnificent artillery you brought. We even replenished your supply of ammunition for your Barrett and SIG rifles."

Grant nodded, accepting the shake. "Thanks. Kondo had mentioned your state of siege, and in the space of a few hours, we encountered both an example of wild predators and the Dragon Riders."

"The Riders are insidious in how they have trained their mounts," Tatehiko noted. "I was surprised that five of you survived such an assault with only minor injuries."

Grant frowned. "Remus was badly clawed, and Kondo had a fractured collarbone when we first hailed the convoy. They took the brunt of their wounds defending us."

Tatehiko looked confused. and it wasn't like Grant to downplay Cerberus's contributions to anything, let alone a struggle for survival against a lethal enemy. Kane held his tongue, though. He knew there was a reason for Grant's behavior. It could be explained later.

Something crackled in the floor, and Kane whipped around, looking at it intently. Tatehiko and his personal cadre reacted to the sudden loud snap with equal alacrity.

"What the hell is that?" Grant asked. Both he and Kane had flexed their forearms in response to the threatening sound, a conditioned reflex to ready their Sin Eaters, even though they had been divested of the weapons. Something grated—a stone floor tile that heaved up an inch. "A bad case of moles?"

"We don't have vermin," Tatehiko responded. He snapped his fingers, and two of the Watatsumi soldiers unholstered their pistols and passed them over to Kane and Grant.

The tile suddenly heaved, four thick, armor-plated, undulating figures erupting through the two-foot-by-two-foot hole in the floor. Kane checked the load on his pistol by feel because his eyes couldn't leave the writhing, glistening black things that waved wire-cutter-shaped mouth parts blindly in the air.

"Good lord," Kane breathed. "Baptiste?"

"Some form of arthropleura," she answered quickly. "Six-foot-long centipedes."

One of them lurched free, another head popping up in its place. The suddenly escaped monstrosity, hard banded shells glinting in the light, rushed toward one of the *bushi,* who pulled the trigger of his machine pistol. Bullets scoured divots out of the concrete around the creature, and Kane could see the shudder of the enemy as one bounced off of its thick hide. The centipede monster looked as if it had been forged from the same polycarbonates that used to make up their almost-invulnerable Magistrate armor. It was bulletproof, and its dozens of legs propelled it along at high speed, snapping jaws clacking and gouging a bloody scar in the shin-armor of the Watatsumi it attacked.

"Son of a bitch!" the dragon man howled as it kicked loose, recoiling backward from his assailant. He took one step, and then his weight went onto the foot that had been bitten, and his knee buckled beneath him.

Grant discarded his pistol, realizing that gunfire was less than useless if a full-auto weapon hadn't been able to penetrate the hides of the squirming attackers. He instead scooped up a chair and upended it, bringing down the back of the chair atop the back of a second of the monster-pedes as it turned toward him. Those armor-slicing jaws snapped at the air, and it tried to stretch to get a taste of Grant.

Kane instinctively chose to stay with the gun, at least until he could think of a counterattack, and fired point-blank at the bulbous head of the arthropleura rocketing toward him. A bullet connected with the creature, rupturing its head segment, exploding it in a spray of viscous, foul-smelling fluid. The air in the hall turned thick with rancid, dizziness-inducing mist that poured through in the wake of the invaders. Brigid overturned a heavy table, its weight slamming into the ground just as a trio of them rammed into the top, sounding like the impact of sledgehammers.

"That stench!" Kane shouted.

"Hyperoxygenated air!" Brigid answered as she picked up a chair of her own to swat it across the thick, python-like predator. "It's what allows them to grow to a length of two yards!"

Kane turned his gun toward another, then recoiled as a pair of sharp mandibles sank into the pistol's slide, folding metal under crushing force. The Cerberus traveler grimaced and pistoned up his hand under what should be the thing's throat, suddenly feeling a half-dozen individual spines stab at his knuckles, even through the shadow suit. Kane didn't loosen his grip, instead wrenching with all of his might.

The six-foot horror's hind legs clawed at the stone beneath them, ten pairs of limbs scratching visible trails in the floor, but he was able to twist the thing from the ground. Utilizing all of his body weight, momentum and leverage, Kane jammed the black, ball-shaped skull into the floor below, that bullet-resistant hide cracking loudly. The combined weight of man and centipede left fractures in the tile, but those lines quickly filled with the ugly, fetid ooze of what used to be brains and blood.

His instincts suddenly impelled him to twist his head to the side, and a vicious snap resounded as the arthropleura's jaws closed on empty air rather than on a knot of neck muscle. Kane reached up and closed his fist around the thing's forelegs, instinctively attempting a shoulder throw. Had the enemy been a humanoid with two arms, two legs and "normal" proportions, his counterattack would have been ridiculously successful, shattering the assailant's spine over a table edge. Unfortunately, his opponent had a total of sixty legs and a sinuous torso. Claws jabbed his back and left leg, and even as Kane bent, the enemy's form followed his. He could feel countless needles of fire as the gigantic centipede's legs began to defeat the protective polymers of his suit. Given another couple of seconds, those legs, each of which was as long as a needlelike dagger, might cut through and pierce into muscle and blood vessels.

Kane switched gears and threw himself at the walled tier of the conference floor, throwing all of his weight toward the shoulder where he'd trapped the arthropod's head. This time, instead of actually doing more damage to his attacker, Kane found himself stunned as the compact, stout form of his opponent transferred his momentum right into his own shoulder.

With a grunt, he sagged to his knees. He could see two more of the hideous killer bugs scramble toward him. The things were nineteen inches wide, and with all their limbs touching the floor, they were a foot tall, able to raise up half of their bodies.

The two charging him were in full-on, pissed-off attack mode, which meant that Kane had to do something fast or their jaws would begin tearing through his arms and face.

With a swift surge, he stood upright, his free hand clamping over the head of the monstrosity clinging to his back. Those bolt-cutter-like jaws had closed on empty air again, and he took that exact moment to smother that mouth and use it as traction to twist the centipede's head. If he couldn't power through the thick chitin of his opponent, then he'd strain the connecting tissues between armor bands and body segments.

The thing's piercing legs squeezed painfully on muscle clusters along the back of his leg even as he applied torque. A brutal crack split the air, and the head twisted off after what felt like an eternity of fighting against the bug's musculature. Even headless, the arthropod wouldn't release, and Kane had a severed head in his fist to show for the effort.

He brought up one boot and kicked one of his two attackers in the face. At its full length and speed, the ninety-pound arthropod hit the sole of his foot and nearly dislocated his knee with the impact. Putting all of his strength behind his leg muscles, Kane shoved the six-foot bug backward, rolling it onto its back, dozens of legs kicking helplessly at the air.

The song of sword steel filled the air, and the second

of the arthropleura bearing down on Kane was suddenly a stump. Kane knew that Japanese *katanas* were at a level of sharpness that made razors seem dull, and given the strength and speed of its wielder, it could go even through the heavy polycarbonate of Magistrate armor.

Tatehiko drew his spare sword, offering it to Kane, handle first. "Blades, not bullets."

Kane accepted the *wakazashi,* eighteen inches of finely honed, slightly curved steel. The wave pattern of the steel along its edge was proof of the task of the thousands of hammer blows that forged the folded metal into a weapon that was designed to focus enormous force, even through bamboo and rattan armor. Strong hands gripped the squirming corpse of the arthropod still clinging, headless, to his back, and suddenly, he was free of the dozens of agonizing pinches that slowed him.

Grant hadn't acquired a sword, but he had a broken table leg, its jagged end soggy from where his powerful muscles had driven the wood through monster armor. "Next time I'm bringing some fucking DDT along!"

"That would kill us, as well," Brigid said, striking another of the huge centipedes across the upper foot of its body with her own table leg. The wood connected with chitin with a mighty crack, but all it did was send the multilegged horror toppling to the ground. Grant pivoted and brought down his own club, connecting with deadly, brutal force that crushed the front third of the enemy away from the back of its body.

"You familiar with these things?" Kane asked Tatehiko as the two men turned their swords against another of the attackers. The gleaming black bands of armor still deflected most of the force of their blows, but it also drove them toward seams in the enemy's armor, and the finely honed steel carved through, even though the effort made cutting leather with a machete seem easy.

"Never saw one of these monsters in my life," Tatehiko said, his voice filled with an uneasy tremor. "Ryu preserve us…"

"Clear the floor!" The order came from above, and Kane spun, throwing himself over the railing to a higher tier. Those who could, did likewise, though Kane could see three bodies sprawled on the floor, flesh and bone chewed to pulpy messes by the unyielding jaws of the attackers.

The thunderous bellow of heavy rifles filled the air, and the black cable bodies of the killer arthropods twisted under impacts that even their armor couldn't deflect. Gunfire rained from above, heavy bolts of .50-caliber and 7.62 mm lead crashing into the deadly nest of creatures as they struggled through the opening they'd created. They didn't seem to want to retreat, but *bushi,* carrying canisters of gasoline, appeared on the same tier where Kane and the others had taken cover.

The smell of gas filled the air as fuel splashed on the sinuous bodies below. Matches flared and flames burst on the floor amid the bugs. It was hell, and the death squeals of the monsters grated on every single one of Kane's nerves.

"One hell of an insect attack," Grant murmured, looking down at the inferno that finally drove the attackers into retreat. He was panting, his long, muscular torso heaving as he sucked in air to replenish his spent strength. Tears had been rent in the big man's shadow suit, and superficial cuts were slashed along the skin beneath.

"Arthropods. Centipedes don't qualify as insects," Brigid returned.

"How the hell did those things get in here to attack us?" Tatehiko snapped. "Anyone?"

"Most likely they burrowed through the earth and came up here," Brigid said. "But who directed them...I wouldn't have a clue."

"It's not like you can train bugs," Grant said breathlessly. "Bugs is right, no?"

Brigid nodded, leaning on a rail. She lowered her forehead to rest on her arms, exhaustion threatening to take her. "Yeah. Bugs is right."

"Does it matter?" Kane asked Tatehiko.

"How they got in? Yes! The whole city could come under attack," the *bushi* leader said.

Kane pointed to Brigid. "I mean the why and how."

Tatehiko looked around. "Four men are dead because of this attack. I don't want it repeated, and if this is another assault by the bloody Dragon Riders, then why haven't they used this before...and how did they direct them?"

Grant shrugged. "Maybe we should go ask them."

Kane swallowed. "You up for that now?"

Grant looked at his arms as they hung limply at his sides. Even the massive club he'd used to bludgeon the monstrous arthropods into messy pulps only seemed to stick to his hands by stubborn inertia, as his grasp on it was half-open. "Fuck no. We need rest. Medical attention. We've been attacked three times in two days."

"We're not the only ones," Brigid muttered. "But I wouldn't say no to a little pampering for a change."

Kane nodded. The scorched bones of the Watatsumi who had fallen to the centipede horrors mixed with the curled, charred exoskeletons of the attackers. The stench of hyperoxygenated, thickly humid air and postcombustion gasoline and corpses threatened to make him vomit.

Grant looked even more haunted than he was before. Something was eating at him.

Something even more insidious than six-foot-long centipedes.

Chapter 16

Deep within the bowels of Nagah City's maintenance tunnels, Domi was in a familiar, comfortable element. As much as she enjoyed belonging to the Cerberus team, traveling with Kane, Brigid and Grant or with Sinclair and Edwards, or alone with Lakesh, she still had feral, solitary instincts that often sent her into the nooks and crannies of the Bitterroot Mountains surrounding the Cerberus redoubt. There she engaged with nature, capturing her own game, and after a while, taking up more esoteric pursuits, such as her cave of collections.

It was there that she engaged her nascent reading abilities, having been schooled at Lakesh's knee or in a classroom during sparse snatches of Brigid Baptiste's free time. Though she had grown up without such an education, rendering her functionally illiterate, when those two brilliant minds had combined, her reading aptitude had grown.

Perhaps it had been because of their love of knowledge and learning, or the simple joy of passing on the lessons of their lifetimes. Either way, while Domi was never going to be able to configure a pan-dimensional matter-transfer beam or have an encyclopedic knowledge of the history and sciences of humankind, the albino woman accepted the gifts given her with aplomb.

While she was rising from the level of wild woman, she still exercised her feral instincts and skills. They were what had kept her alive, helped her to combat the forces of earthly and interplanetary tyranny that Cerberus battled.

The stench of the sewer threatened to make her gag, even despite her time surviving in the Tartarus Pits, which itself had raw runoff and human waste running through open gutters. Still, the smell was more than just the effects of a vindaloo on a Nagah's digestion. Something else was down here, something that had not been alive for days.

She closed in on it by smell, then touch, the slosh of sewage lapping at the unmistakable bulk of a grown man's corpse. Domi was glad that the man she'd discovered had reptilian skin. Even in water, the scales had a leathery quality that held the insides together. Even so, muscle and fatty tissue beneath the surface sloughed, a mush that told the tale of a longer stay in the tunnel than a mere day.

The corpse was in a sewer tunnel adjacent to where other bodies had been discovered, and yet it was definitely older than the others in the morgue. She risked a moment with her LED flashlight to look at the body's face. While it was illuminated, she took another device from a secured pocket on the belt swashed around her waist, dangling across her hips at a rakish angle. The device was a compact digital camera with a transmitter. Lakesh had been stating that there was a need for real-time visual intelligence so that Cerberus could collate data much more quickly. There were times when verbal descriptions weren't enough.

Luckily an engineer named Waylon, a freezie from the Moon base, had found a way to piggyback images on the Commtact's signal. Utilizing remote camera microtechnology that had been on the bleeding edge back in the 1990s, he'd developed a palm-sized device to send and receive images over a long distance.

She felt for any sign of current, but it was slow, stagnant water. The only way she could determine where the body had drifted from was the splay of the body's limbs as it was jammed against a corner. Swinging the light, she looked back the way the corpse had drifted from, her mouth drawn tight into a frown. The end cap button clicked, and she was back in darkness, relying on her ears and nose to guide her through the inky black. She'd noticed something in the tunnels, something outside her own motions in the sewage.

Her free hand went to the combat knife in her belt sheath, but she didn't draw it, simply keeping her fingers tight around the rubberized grip of the keen, deadly bowie. Here, in the midnight black of the sloshing, knee-deep water, she eased forward, heel to toe, her movements barely making a ripple. Something was out there.

The sound carried well in the sewer tunnel, and now a tangible sound reached her sharp ears. There were the grunts of two figures, hauling a weight between them, their boots scuffing on stone. Domi eased through and caught the faint glow of an incandescent light bulb around a corner.

"He's not making it easier for us to keep a low profile," one voice said in heavily accented English.

"Oh, you'd rather have a corpse stink up our headquarters?" another returned.

The response to that was a grunt, but it was filled with such emotion that Domi could imagine the shrug produced by the issuer. He didn't seem at all concerned with the sanitary conditions of his hideout, so much as he didn't enjoy the idea of slogging a corpse through the stinking sewer. Domi reached the intersection and could see two figures silhouetted in the dingy, amber glow of the bulb. She brought out her camera and took a quick snapshot of the scene, keeping her lips pursed tightly as she melded with the corner.

Slimy mold along the walls stunk less than the fetid

murk of the normal sewage, and even as her bare cheek touched it, she could feel the tingling presence of tiny tendrils reaching out to adhere to her flesh. She backed away, giving the skin a rub to scrape off the mess.

Two figures were being manhandled by the burly shadow men, both young women. Domi tried to place them, once more envious of Brigid Baptiste and her eidetic memory. She took another picture of the grisly scene, then ducked back, increasing the resolution on the camera's liquid crystal display. The first thing she noticed that the women were full Nagah, and they had been gagged. One had her eyes open, wide with fear.

"Fuck," Domi growled. These animals were taking them into the tunnels first before killing them. Drowning in sewage was about as horrifying an experience that she could imagine, but the two brutes hauling them around probably had more than just murder planned. Neither of the slight, helpless girls was clad, even in the wispy thin wraps that female Nagah donned for propriety's sake.

She put the camera away, sealing it back in the waterproof pouch.

"We got to do it where we dump them?" one of them asked. "It's dry here."

"That's an idea," the other mused.

That was all the feral survivor needed to hear. The blade was out, and as the two-man disposal team looked up from their victims to the sudden splash of movement at the intersection of sewage tunnels, only her ghostly face and battle knife were visible in the halo cast off by the dying bulb. Going from total blackness to even the glow of a forty-watt bulb would have been hard if she hadn't inured herself to the light by looking at it. The two men, on the other hand, had come from a place of illumination, and their senses hadn't sharpened to deal with the dim conditions. Even so, they jolted in reaction to her sudden appearance.

Even as she'd been taking their pictures, Domi had measured the two brutes. They, too, were Nagah, each sporting the cobra hood of muscle that flexed between the tops of their heads down to their shoulders. They also undoubtedly had fangs with full sacs of venom. Each was about the same size, as well, closing in on two hundred pounds and topping six feet in height. The brawny scaled men would prove to be tough if it came to unarmed combat.

But this was Domi of Cerberus, and as long as she had her blade, nine inches of razor-edged steel, she was a match for any mountain of muscle on the planet. She got within jumping distance and her spring-steel tight leg muscles launched her into the air toward the thug with the conscious girl. The cobra man let go of his prisoner, bringing up his forearm swiftly and decisively, brass ringlets adorning his wrist clanging as her knife was deflected. Luckily Domi was on the attack, her body a living missile that followed through, plowing into her opponent's chest. Though less than a hundred pounds soaking wet, Domi had fired herself forward with all of her strength. Mass plus velocity combined to overwhelm the Nagah traitor's balance, toppling him backward under her weight.

Even as the thick, muscular trunk of her foe struck the concrete platform, Domi tucked and rolled off him, gaining some distance before the other one clawed at her with outstretched fingers. The albino woman, clad in her skintight shadow suit, had little to latch onto, even if she had stood in place, but she had been in too many fights when a larger foe had gotten a good hold of her and ended all chance of resistance.

She rose to a crouch, knife held across her forearm as a

shield in an ice-pick grip. Crimson eyes glinted like blood jewels in the night. "C'mon, pussies."

The Nagah who had missed grabbing her saw the razor edge, then clawed at his belt for a weapon. Domi didn't take a moment to discern what he was going for, pouncing again, but this time going low, at her enemy's knees. The bowie knife shot forward as she punched at his leg, and she felt the parting of armored scales and muscle, only the heavy thickness of his femur stopping the brutal slice. Blood gushed from the wound, spattering her cheek in her passage between the Nagah's legs, and she was past him as the strength of his lower limbs failed, dropping him to his knees.

The other scrambled to get up, and Domi felt his nails rake across her calf as she shot free of his grasp. Both were on all fours now, but the feral young woman was as comfortable crouched and low as she was standing at her full height. The first Nagah sneered, then pushed off with both hands, leaping at her, hoping to get her off balance.

Domi countered with a pivot, whirling her body so that her right heel connected with the thick sheet of muscle that made up the Nagah's hood. The spin-kick grazed off the top of his head, and he smacked face-first into the concrete floor with an ugly crack. She immediately coiled back into a perched position, looking between her two foes.

The man with the slashed thigh let out an angry grunt as he finally drew his pistol from its holster on his belt. Domi had given up the conceit that she was going to allow her opponents to leave this sewer alive. Certainly, when answers were necessary, a minimum of force had been required to keep prisoners to question. But now, these two so-called men were openly intent on murdering two helpless victims, and Domi had long ago vowed to let no one fall prey to the physically strong but morally weak.

As the gun rose, Domi lashed out with her knife, spearing the Nagah through the back of his hand, the point striking the grips of the pistol hard enough to jar them from his fingers. There was a sudden jolt of pain that caused him to scream out as the lump of alloy was driven into the air. Domi twisted her bowie and wrenched it loose from the would-be killer's gun hand, bones and muscles separating. Fingers dumped onto the ground next to the fallen weapon, severed in anything but a clean manner. The twice-cut killer recoiled, eyes widened in horror at the savagery of her attack.

The first of the pair rose from the ground, blood streaming from his nose and mouth.

"You little bitch, I'm going to split your legs and get my blood back," the killer growled in threat.

Domi snapped a kick toward his face, but he moved with the speed inherent to his cobra heritage, dodging a second skull-rattling blow. She drew her foot back swiftly as fangs lashed in the air, his mouth coming far too close to her calf. The bowie flipped in her grip and she swept the blade in an arc to push him back. The cobra man recoiled, realizing that the sharp knife would have severed his jaw. He also remembered that he didn't need to close with the ruby-eyed woman.

With a flex of the muscles in his fangs' venom sacs, he unleashed a stream of toxic, acidic poison. Domi jerked reflexively, but she hadn't had enough of a warning to dodge completely. Even though she clenched her eyes shut, Domi couldn't contain the pain of burning agony that seared across her eyes, even through closed lids. The skin around them puffed and swelled painfully, and it was as if someone had lashed her across the face with a bullwhip.

She jolted backward, once more unable to see, clawing at the ground as her grasp failed on the rubber handle of her knife. Disarmed and denied one of her senses, she writhed on the floor, pushing herself into the sewage with a ugly splash. The world shut off and the thick, stagnant wastewater flooded everywhere, even into her mouth. If she survived the next few minutes, she was going to need to get inoculations against all manner of plague organisms.

That was if she survived, and through the water flooding her ears, she heard another splash. Fingers reached down to clutch her, seeking to snag her hair, but it was too closely shorn, not long enough to grab, let alone use as a handle to hold her under. The searing agony in the middle of her face was flushed from her tear ducts.

Domi thrashed her head, opening her eyes against her every instinct, and the nerve-burning toxins abated somewhat so that she could at least concentrate on something else. She reached out, fingers snapping around an ankle just as fingers began to squeeze at the base of her skull.

The murmur of gloating barely broke through the surface, and even if it did, the rush of water around her ears made any discernment of her enemy's words impossible. The feral woman didn't care; she just knew that she only had moments to act, as the grip on her neck and head were as solid as a vise. She had her own grasp on the goon's ankle. Without a knife, her options were limited, so rather than push upward, where she could breathe, she surged down, her teeth meeting the scaled flesh blunting her initial bite. The Nagah tried to regain his grip on her, but she had gone low, and he was off balance by the effort of trying to snag her.

Domi clenched her jaws tighter, scales tearing loose from the snake man's skin, peeled away by her teeth. Reflexively, the Nagah tried to pull his leg away from the source of the pain. Now, even further unbalanced, the enemy loosened his clutch at her, toppling into the sewage.

With a surge, she burst from the stagnant water and spit out fluid, scales and muscle tissue. The disgusting crap in her mouth spewed clear, she sucked in a fresh breath, looking back toward the stunned form behind her. Domi spit again, resisting the urge to vomit, and though she could make out the outline of the enemy Nagah in the water, it was through a dim, ugly fuzz thanks to the aftereffects of the venom. Pain still throbbed in the center of her face, tears working overtime to flush away the irritant.

The murderer struggled back to his knees, spitting out sewage, as well, shaking his head to fight off the nasty taste. Without a knife, Domi didn't have many combat options, but she did have the Detonics .45 in its holster. She plucked it free, reversed it so that she held the barrel like a handle, and swung toward the back of the Nagah's head with all of her might. Two pounds of steel, wood and ammunition impacted on the armored hide of the enemy's skull. She couldn't trust the pistol to function after its immersion in the choking water. Right now she only had a compact, tiny club, not much more than a fist-load, and even with all of her strength behind the swing, all she had done was elicit a stunned grunt from the snake man.

The scales and thick sheet of cobra-hood muscle blunted the strike. Another attack from this angle wouldn't do much to cause any head trauma to her opponent. With a reflexive surge, her opponent whirled, a back fist catching Domi across her hip and driving her back. The punch didn't have much more force or effect than the one she'd thrown, but it was enough to stagger her.

She collapsed backward against the stone platform where the two women had been deposited and where her fallen knife lay. Her vision was a blur, and all she could make out were dark figures, her blade nowhere to be seen. Her ears picked up on the slush of water as the Nagah rose.

"Having troubles, woman?" the Nagah asked, wiping his mouth. "No knife, a gun that's just a paperweight and you're so damn tiny."

Domi turned back to face the six-foot brute stalking through the sewage toward her. Half blind, half drowned and battered badly, she had nothing to make up for a hundred pounds of muscle and thick, reptilian hide.

The sound of a female grunt behind her rose to her ears, and the clatter of something metal skittering toward her followed a moment later. Domi turned toward the object, instinctively clutching for it. Her fingertips brushed the checkered handle of the fighting knife, and she clamped against it.

One of the girls had to have awakened, or had been watching all along. She'd managed to kick the blade over to Domi.

It was all she needed as the threatening cobra man lunged, fangs bared and ready to sink into her soft, human flesh. Knife in hand, she whipped it up, spearing into the reptilian face coming at her. There was the sickening crunch of bone collapsing in on itself as the steel point drove into the roof of her enemy's mouth.

Lurching backward, the killer clutched at his face, hissing and choking as blood flowed. The knife had to have missed his brain, but the pain he suffered was all consuming, at least for the moment.

The Nagah reached for the blade's handle, trying to pry the obstruction from his mouth. Once free, he'd return to the gruesome task of trying to murder her.

Domi exploded in a burst of strength and speed, focusing on the end of the knife. The heel of her palm struck the pommel of the weapon and drove it farther, deeper into his face. Bone cracked, flesh ripped. The Nagah killer stiffened, then toppled backward into the sewage.

Domi coughed, slumping back. She craned her head around to look for the second of the murderers, and heard a muffled scream. Her vision cleared enough to focus on the muzzle of a pistol aimed right at her eyes.

"Fucking little bitch," the gun-toting cobra man snarled, hand trembling. He'd permanently lost the use of one leg, muscles severed, and one hand was carved by her knife. "My gun works, yours—"

A thunderous boom echoed through the cavern, Domi's ears punished by the nearly simultaneous thunder of a steel door kicked open and the brutal shotgun blast that resounded right on its heels. Edwards stood in the doorway, watching the nearly headless corpse of the insurgent snake man collapse. He, too, had been searching the sewers and had come to her rescue when he'd overheard their struggle.

"You okay?" he grunted.

"Check the girls," Domi panted. She rested her forehead on the cool concrete of the platform, her lower body still in the wastewater.

Sinclair was on the platform, as well, and a couple of Royal Guardsmen. Medical kits had been drawn out, and they were put to work on the two Nagah women that Domi had rescued. Strong hands lifted her out of the water, and the albino woman blinked, puffy, venom-burned eyes barely making out Edwards's features close to hers.

"I said check the girls," Domi snarled.

"Guardsmen medics are on it," Edwards answered. "You look like hell."

Domi nodded, motioning for Edwards to put her back on her feet.

"We've got some stuff for you to look at," Sinclair said. Domi blinked.

She sighed, trying to, but failing, to dispel the ache and exhaustion in her small frame. "Back to work."

Chapter 17

Kane winced as he touched the bruised flesh revealed by doffing his shadow suit. He now wore a gray, loose-fitting T-shirt that was already clinging to his chest with perspiration. The temperature in the underground realm was slightly higher than that of the Kashmir forest he'd visited before the trip to the Nagah realm. In the shadow suit, he'd have been cooled off and been protected from the heat and humidity just as well as he would have been able to withstand even the biting, below-zero chill of the Arctic tundra in the depths of winter.

"Those centipedes did a number on your back," Grant said.

Kane groaned, acknowledging his friend's input but not saying much more. He mopped his brow with a cloth. "Crazy, fused-out man-eating bugs."

Brigid took a sip of water. "Actually, arthropleura was a plant eater. Those bone-crunching mandibles were meant to slice through tough vegetation stalks, as well as serve as defense against rival arthropleura."

Kane looked at her. "They tore people to the bone."

"Not out of hunger," Brigid responded.

Grant frowned. "Telepathy."

Kane nodded. "Remus told you about the Ramah. They can make raptors and acros travel in herds, and they can get giant bugs to murder people. I felt one of them in my head, too."

"We all did," Brigid said, pointing to Grant. "He told me while you were changing."

"Great. I'm not the only one going nuts," Kane murmured.

"Wonder if anyone else had that brush with the weird," Grant said. "I'd ask around, but Remus isn't sure if there are traitors within the ranks of Ryugo-jo."

"Isn't sure?" Kane asked. "You trust him?"

"You feel certain believing him," Grant said. "You took the story about the Ramah at face value."

"Only because I felt them, and we observed the Riders and their animals acting too coordinated to simply be human trained," Kane countered. "He could be lying, but telling ninety percent of the truth to support that story."

Grant shrugged. "Kondo trusts him, and you trust Kondo."

Kane nodded. "We dealt with him before, but anyone can be seduced or tricked."

"It doesn't seem to me that there's any relationship of that manner between them," Brigid interjected. "The two work together out of a bond of camaraderie and shared experience."

"I wasn't saying that the two were front to back, so to speak," Kane answered. "And I don't care if there is a man crush or something more there. It's just that when you're alone and you're surrounded by people who kept Ochiro in power, you look for some refuge."

"We don't have any proof of collusion between Remus and Ochiro, but Kondo has mentioned that Ochiro was under close scrutiny by Tatehiko," Brigid said. "Given Tatehiko's position of power—"

"He'd be obvious, but maybe too obvious," Kane cut her off. "He's a likely choice, but the Watatsumi militia is just too damn large. We know only a few names from the whole crowd. It could be anyone, especially if they're supposedly some form of relay for telepathic contact."

"That's even if they know they're being used as a psi-mutie puppet," Grant added. "Mind powers don't have to be showy and flashy as when Enlil used that telepathic comm to go after you in your own head."

"No," Kane agreed. He looked to Brigid. "So, we have a plan to deal with the Ramah?"

Brigid scrunched her nose. "Yes. Find them and shoot them in the head. Can't take over brains if they have none of their own."

Kane turned to Grant. "You got to know things are desperate when Brigid borrows our Plan B for her Plan A."

"Trouble is, if we do go after the Ramah, we're going to have to do it on foot, unless we cannot only fix our battered Manta, but call up a bunch more, and maybe equip them with air-to-ground missiles," Grant said.

Brigid nodded. "I didn't say that the plan was fully thought-out."

"They're telepaths, so they'd know we'd left or were on our way," Grant added. "Everyone else who Remus has told about the Ramah has ended up in a fatal accident or been killed on patrol."

"We're already targets by butting into this fight," Kane said. "Whether we like it or not, we're going head to head with them. He said that the Ramah were Igigi, similar to himself."

"Distant relatives," Grant returned. "Brigid?"

She shrugged. "The Manitius base had psi-scrambler technology, things that could shield our minds from external influence, but those headbands are back at Cerberus."

Kane grimaced, then threw his sweat rag at Grant. "You can pack everything else, but you leave that stuff behind."

Grant shrugged. "I didn't know we'd be fucking with muties. I came loaded for dinosaurs, not this stuff."

"Well, I gotta blow off steam somehow," Kane answered. "Better whipping a hankie at you than bottling up useless frustration."

"We should go see Remus," Brigid said. "He might have more answers."

"So we'll throw in with him," Kane returned.

Grant sighed. "We know he's got rotten family, Kane. We don't judge people by the sins of their fathers."

"No," Kane answered. He took a deep breath. "No."

"Come on," Brigid said, poking the two men to get moving.

The war beneath the earth would not wait for the heroes' prejudices. There was no room for bigotry when innocents' lives were at stake.

REMUS WAS ALONE ON HIS BALCONY, blowing a gentle tune into a pan flute. The melody was soft, lilting, deeply haunting as Kane drew closer. Even without lyrics, he could tell that there was a story of wanderlust undercutting the song he blew. It reached Kane, finding a sympathetic vibration in his heart of hearts.

"Welcome," Remus said, putting away the flute.

Kane had been sent alone, while Brigid and Grant went to check on Kondo, whose recovery was considered nothing less than remarkable by the Watatsumi medics. Even so, his injuries had taken much longer than Remus's to heal. The half Annunaki was at home, comfortable, sprawled on the ledge of his Spartan home.

"You didn't have to stop," Kane said haltingly. He wasn't certain how much of the tune had been for show's sake, but with such a stirring loneliness to it, Kane couldn't imagine anything less than honesty in the feeling. The man before him was an outcast, a kindred spirit.

"I don't have to play a melody that we both know so well," Remus answered.

Kane tilted his head, quizzical.

"The last time I remember meeting the spark that dwells within you, I was a gnarled, hunched figure, wrapped in the skin of an African. You bore my staff on a journey across wilderness and jungle, through city and environ, its stout might proving sufficient to bolster your step. Your journey continues today," Remus said.

Kane, as he was told this, saw the image, a memory flash of a time he had spent between universes, seeing the time worm of his existence stretched out behind him like a silvery highway into history and stretching on, far into the future. The staff was familiar; he could sense its weathered hardwood, a comfortable weight in his grasp, and he remembered the Puritan fanaticism that impelled him, one foot after the other, to push him across the globe in an age of provincial ignorance.

"I'm pretty sure I haven't seen your stick in a long time, Remus," Kane answered. "The others sent me to talk to you about the Ramah."

Remus nodded. "They may subconsciously remember the ties we bear. Or it may just be they feel your skepticism and count on it as an armor between any duplicity I may harbor."

"Do you?" Kane asked.

Remus looked at him. "Do I what?"

"Harbor any duplicity," Kane responded.

Remus smirked. "The skins you wear, traveler, have been different, but as always, your bluntness is refreshing. I have things necessary to keep to my own counsel.

adventures I am not proud of, mistakes that made me leave the world where the sun rose and fell."

"So you haven't always been so friendly to humankind?" Kane quizzed.

"I have. And I have paid for it. I have been scourged by eagles who feasted on my liver, which grew back every night to maintain my torment. I have crossed burning sands and weathered deluges. My eyes had been stricken from their orbits and my tongue severed."

Kane looked the Igigu over. "And still, everything came back."

"But the scars are never far from my mind or heart," Remus concluded.

"I need to know who you think is the Ramah's puppet. You've been watching this situation for years," Kane said. "Is he an active plotter or a sometime tool?"

"He is a conscious ally," Remus answered. "It's the only way I can see the Ramah working so effectively. The Dragon Riders are not completely innocent. The puppet masters have picked those who had the temperament, the lust for battle, to make them capable, willing pawns, improving the aggression in all concerned."

"Do you know who?" Kane asked. "And do you know why the Ramah would risk the awakening of the entity Kakusa?"

"I knew no creature by that name, but considering that Kakusa is the Japanese translation of 'the hidden' I can speculate on the original monster," Remus said. "Kondo and Ochiro said you destroyed him."

"We killed every cell we could find," Kane answered. "If he survived, he was reduced dramatically to lone organisms that didn't seem to have the power to reproduce."

"I hope so. If it is any of the Annunaki enemies that I suspect, then he could be trapped, unable to survive outside of a few specific bodies," Remus said. "If we finish with the war for Ryugo-jo, I will come to the surface, to help."

"About that," Kane brought up. "We need a council of war, how to deal with the Ramah, even if the others don't believe."

"I wish I had the confidence that letting the truth come out would inoculate the Watatsumi from reprisals," Remus bemoaned.

"Sunlight, often, is the best of disinfectants," Kane returned. "It did wonders for the soul of one man I met a few months ago."

"I've been around too long to believe in any salvation for my soul," Remus bemoaned. "There was even an era where I, in variance with the beliefs that drove me to exile, had me fighting for a nation devoted to slavery."

"Do you keep slaves now?" Kane asked.

Remus's face twisted in disgust.

"Then you've learned. Not everything is lost."

"Easy for you to say. You've only lived one lifetime," Remus said. He paused, then slapped himself in the forehead. "No. You have touched your past, your other existences. I've forgotten myself. I've allowed history to slip from me in vain efforts, and at such times, I've had the world change, disappear from under me. Lessons that should have been basic have slipped through my fingers with greater facility than my guilt. I've discarded good in exchange for a moment of peace from my memories."

"So, why run from your duties?" Kane asked.

Remus regarded the human. "Like you ran from your duty?"

"As a Magistrate? As a pawn of a liar?" Kane asked. "Not just the pawn of Baron Cobalt, but of a history, a world of tyranny. I didn't run from my duty. I found my duty, to war against those who usurped the ideal of goodness and justice that raised me."

"Run toward your duty," Remus answered.

"That means we've got to bring down the Ramah," Kane said. "They're the ones who started this war, and if you care about the Watatsumi, you have to bring this struggle to an end."

"I have no doubt what needs to be done, but if we say anything, we could have the Ramah launch a terrible attack," Remus answered.

"So what is the best way to strike at the psi-muties?" Kane asked. "This nickle and diming only hurts your society. It's created a sense of war, isolation, it breeds a paranoia, akin to what had been in the villes. We had been taught that those who lived outside the walls were lawless, loathsome parasites. And by buying into that, it made murder so much easier. I killed in the name of monsters. You sit here, fingering your ego, thinking you've done such horrible things. So have I. And I fix it by going where my skills are needed. China. Mars. The bottom of a continental plate."

Remus held out a hand to the human. "It matters not how oft you fall."

Kane helped the Igigu to his feet. "Just how often you stand back up."

Remus smiled. "I may just have a plan that keeps the Watatsumi safe, at least until we strike a telling, warchanging blow."

The two champions shook hands.

MOHANDAS LAKESH SINGH stalked through the door into the hideout of the two dead Nagah who had almost murdered their helpless captives. Domi looked bruised, but the same feral rage seethed in her ruby eyes. The doorway had been small, making it a wonder that Edwards had squeezed his bulk into the room.

As Lakesh returned to his full height, he spotted a small pile of what appeared to be black, obsidian glass eggs. He immediately recognized them as the control nodules that the Annunaki utilized to not only dominate their Nephilim slaves, but garb them in smart metal armor to increase their survivability and arm them with the sinuous, snake-headed ASP blasters.

Domi glared at the devices. "Here from last time."

"You certain?" Lakesh asked.

She narrowed her ruby glare. "Logic."

Sinclair folded her arms. "Enlil could have been generous with his supply of armor nodules. And in the wake of the last battle, these could have easily been assembled by the more conniving of the cultists."

Domi pointed. "Old bloodstains."

Lakesh looked at the spot where she had gestured. Sure enough, splotches of darkness had assembled down the wall and on the floor beneath the basket where they had been stored. While the glassy shells themselves showed little sign of soiling, they had easily sloughed off the old bodily fluids that had belonged to their deceased masters.

"Fascinating," Lakesh said, trying to subdue the disturbance that made his voice tremble beneath. He held up one of the egglike objects, examining it.

"The dead snakes didn't have one," Edwards added. "But they look like men who were reported missing. Something's really weird here. They held on to these, but didn't wear 'em."

"Well, they would be recognizable," Sinclair replied. "And the Nagah would keep an eye peeled for someone wearing Nephilim armor."

Domi frowned. "Don't like this."

"I know, dearest," Lakesh replied. "But we're picking up clues."

"So who had them? Who has been turned into other men, for no damn reason?" Rahdnathi asked. "Cultists?"

Lakesh frowned. "We could have gotten answers from these two."

"No," Domi said, cutting him off. Lakesh looked at her, and then saw two huddled Nagah girls through the doorway into the sewer. Their eyes were wide, full of shock, terror and relief. He could only surmise the reason why neither of the dead men was alive.

"I understand," he whispered in her ear. She stunk of sewage, but he didn't flinch as she wrapped her arms tightly around him.

"I wouldn't have shown mercy, either," Rahdnathi said, adding his touch to her shoulder. "We can take care of their carcasses at the morgue, dig deep into them and see what secrets their guts can provide."

"Do that," Lakesh said, distracted as he stepped away from Domi. She seemed less angry, now, but there was a nervous twitch in her, her eyes scanning for the slightest of clues, hunting for a reason why two innocents were nearly murdered. "Dearest?"

Domi stood up, pushing Lakesh aside. "Follow me."

With that, the feral woman bolted through the entrance and headed for the royal court. Lakesh, Sinclair, Edwards and Rahdnathi were confused, but since there were others on hand to watch the former kidnap victims, they took off after her as fast as they could get through the door. To Edwards's credit, his struggle through the tiny doorway had been only a minor impediment, his long legs pumping along to push him to the lead of the group.

Lakesh's mind raced even as his feet pounded the floor of the corridors leading toward Hannah and her husband.

The two women had to have struck a nerve in Domi's memory, and she was following that hint as swiftly as she could. There was little doubt that her sudden rush was indicative to the kind of danger that she anticipated.

Obviously she knew these girls, or at least what their stations had to have been from now, or a prior time. And if she was heading to the royal court, that meant that they had positions there as chambermaids or something equally invisible. That meant they could be with Hannah and Manticor at this moment, wielding knives a heartbeat away from the kill.

Rahdnathi brought his radio to his lips, rattling off orders to central command. Not only did he have to ensure Domi's safety, but also alert them to murderers in their midst. The feral woman drew her knife as she ran, her slender legs pumping with animalistic intensity as she swiftly disappeared into the corridors ahead.

Lakesh hoped that Domi wasn't biting off more than she could chew.

Domi's explosion of speed meant that her allies were falling behind her, but she heard Rahdnathi call ahead to alert the other Royal Guardsmen of danger in their midst. She had one idea, one clue as to who the two girls were supposed to emulate for the purposes of disguise. That was Manticor and Hannah themselves.

So far, there had been little information indeed, very little conversation between the prisoners and their captors, and it was as if they were in a state of shock. That could mean only one thing. The dead Nagah weren't being used for the basis of a disguise. They were the base for duplicates, blank slates who were crafted by external means, and under the most basic of control thanks to the technology that the enemy had access to. That was why there was little fear of a conspiracy being blown as assassins made their strikes against the regent or the Cerberus visitors.

Dead bodies or live prisoners, the captives had little more than basic language and free will.

It was a familiar, if chilling, concept.

The Sons of Enlil had the means to grow custom-adapted Nephilim bodies. The nanotechnology used to shape the nearly mindless drones had much of the same limitations as the cobra baths, resultant in patches of human skin on Nagah duplicates, or segments of scales on even human duplicates.

Domi saw the guardsmen at the entrance to the royal court, but the two men waved her on. Normally she would have thought it was a mistake to let a charging, knife-wielding maniac rush toward you, but the albino woman knew that they were prepared for her arrival, and that they had backup troops inside the hall. Domi still felt that they were tangle brained, simply because the enemy had shown the ability to disguise their agents.

She was in the chamber, and Hannah and Manticor were in their seats, handmaidens attending to them with trays. The sharp glance from the queen's consort showed that Manticor was in touch with his fellow guardsmen. He knew there were snakes in the grass, so to speak, and the blade-wielding Outland woman sized up the two Nagah women who reacted to her swift, explosive entrance. Manticor tensed, awaiting for Domi's evaluation.

Domi's ruby gaze swept across the woman, but seeing their faces quickly disqualified them as threats. "Okay."

Manticor reached out and took the elbow of the girl nearest to him, guiding her toward the relative safety of the hidden tunnel behind them. Hannah nodded, motioning for the other girl to get out of the way.

"Domi?" Manticor asked, rolling to her as the feral woman sheathed her blade, looking around the hall.

"Two maids copied. Originals not dead," she said, plucking the digital camera, turning it over so that she could show the man the small plasma display on the back. "Recognize?"

Manticor's brow furrowed. "They're with the queen's prenatal nursing staff."

Domi frowned. "Where now?"

Manticor pointed to the doorway that she wanted, and in the space of a heartbeat, she was gone again. She was on a mission, now, knowing that she may have been in time, but hoped that Lakesh or the others would get to explain further.

Someone wanted to plant a genetic link into the belly of Hannah, ensuring that Durga would return to the royal family.

Durga may not have been killed completely, but the rogue prince of the Nagah needed a new body, a brand-new birthright, and the maternity nurses were his ticket in.

Chapter 18

Out on the steppe, between the two Mantas that brought them to this peculiar realm, Kane heard Remus's familiar voice release a long, warbling call that rode the wind.

"So the five of us are going to launch an assault on the Ramah, no matter how many Dragon Riders and mind-controlled dinosaurs are between us and them," Grant stated glumly.

"Well, when you put it like that, it sounds like a suicide mission," Kane returned.

Brigid shook her head at Grant's complaint. "Remus undoubtedly has a support force in mind."

Kane turned, walking toward where they had killed the wild acrocanthosaur the other day. Its corpse lay, large chunks of flesh torn from its torso. The massive beast's companions had wailed their lonesome, mourning cries, but the dinosaurs had proved practical enough to return and slake their hunger on the largest known source of food available. It would have been a grisly act of cannibalism, but these were multiple-ton carnivores possessed of near-mammalian metabolisms, according to Brigid and Grant. They required protein to survive.

"Did Remus tell you what he had in mind?" Kane asked Kondo.

"Not a clue," Kondo said. "He mumbled something about Edgar and took off."

"Baptiste?" Kane was looking for some form of information. Remus had promised a thrust of nearly unstoppable power against the Ramah, something that could give them the decisive edge that they needed.

"Edgar," Brigid mused. She ran her thought processes through every bit of information she recalled about strange, underground realms such as Ryugo-jo, and any explorers or theorists who might share that name. Normally the flame-haired archivist could utilize her eidetic memory to draw up random bits of information at the drop of a hat, but now her smooth, high forehead wrinkled under the effects of concentration. "No."

She tilted her head up, listening to the cry of the tall Igigu, putting her fingers to her lips in dawning realization.

"What?" Kane asked.

"Of course," she said. Her eyes darted around as she was visually cuing similarities, meaning that she was on to the answer he sought. "No wonder he returned here. It was the last great jungle to be lord of."

"Going to tell me what Remus is pulling?" Kane asked.

Brigid nodded. "The Edgar that Remus is referring to is a late-nineteenth, early-twentieth-century author named Edgar Rice Burroughs. And Remus's call is in a tongue long lost to the surface world. The language of the Mangani, once a pseudo-humanoid, apelike race found in equatorial Africa."

Kane and Grant looked at each other quizzically.

"Remus must have been the inspiration for not only the tales of Pelucidar, but the stories of Barsoom and the supposedly fictional Tarzan of the Apes," Brigid concluded. "Judging by the vibrations coming through the ground, we're in for a magnificent surprise."

Kane looked into the distance. Kane was surprised to see Remus straddling the neck of an acrocanthosaur, one which bore the scars of recent battle with a bowman.

"I'll be damned," Kane muttered. "It's the dinos that attacked us and our ships, and he's made nice with them."

"I calculated as much, once his identity was made a little more clear," Brigid said. "Perhaps he is partly Tuatha de Danaan, which would explain some of the tales of Barsoom."

"Which is Mars," Grant said. "That's where Macaan ran off to, or hoped to, anyway. He wanted to go to his own dimension, which he had to access through the pyramid on Mars, and the interphaser he stole after he tore up Cerberus."

"John Carter, Warlord of Mars," Kane said. "I read the first one and thought the writer was off of his rocker."

"The opening words of Carter must have been Burroughs's statement of Remus's Igigu longevity, stating that he had always seemed to have been a man of his early thirties," Brigid mused. "You stated that he claimed to have deleted lifetimes of memories?"

Kane nodded. "That must explain his guilt. He, and Carter, had fought for the confederacy, to maintain slavery, among so-called other state's rights."

He returned his gaze to Remus and saw that the Wanderer was accompanied by more than the two beasts that they had battled. There were other monstrosities in this herd. There were long-necked beasts with bodies and legs reminiscent of elephants, and smaller, spike-adorned creatures. "Grant?"

"He's got some kind of theropod. Could be any kind of brachiosaur or apatosaur. He's got a small herd of stegosauri with him, as well."

"I've always wanted to know what those plates on their backs were for," Brigid said. "There are multiple theories regarding sexual display or heat dissipation—"

"Time for scientific study later, Baptiste," Kane admonished.

It took only a few minutes for Remus and his army of saurian beasts to come to the two Mantas. With a few barks and hand motions, one of the formidable theropods, easily standing twenty feet at the shoulder, strode to the overturned aircraft, scooping its tail beneath the sleek aircraft's frame. After a few minutes of jostling and struggle, wherein another of the long-necked, long-tailed dinosaurs added his strength, the Manta was neatly and easily flipped back onto its landing gear, wing structures and hull scuffed and scratched, but showing little significant grounding damage.

"These are the same tricks that you utilized to domesticate the Watatsumi's hadrosaurs, right?" Brigid asked.

"Correct, Brigid," the Wanderer said.

"One thing I want to ask. Have you always been scaled?" Kane asked the man mounted on the neck of a six-ton superpredator.

"It was a minor adaptation that many of us, like Fand, possessed. We can display the skin of either side of our parentage," Remus answered. "For example, most of my time spent among the growing society of humankind was spent looking far more human."

"You know about Fand," Kane said bluntly.

"I told you, I have known of you for a long time, old friend," Remus responded. "And I knew you when you were with my sister."

"You're her brother?" Brigid asked.

"A figure of speech," Remus responded. "The Igigi were always second-class citizens to the Annunaki, and we found little more comfort with the Tuatha de Danaan," Remus said.

"This family reunion is nice and all," Grant interrupted. He pointed to the relatively restless, healthy acro that bobbed and wove its head, looking over the humans who had inflicted such pain on him, and caused the injury or death of his companions. "That one looks on edge, and I don't know if I want to trust him."

"You can trust him. He shall bend to my will," Remus answered.

Grant looked at the Wanderer, suspicion in his gaze. "Then why didn't you stop them before?"

"They were hungry, desperate," Remus answered. "Even now they are anxious, wanting to return to the more comfortable lower forest. But in their need to feed, they would have been blind and ignorant of my pleas."

"And the Ramah just can't let you into the minds of the others, right?" Grant asked. Kane wondered if it was too neat and pat an answer to dilemmas that had plagued them. Remus could still be pulling a con on the Cerberus explorers, but obviously he intended to keep the trio around. Kane couldn't see the four of them surviving an attack directed by the Igigu, not with hundreds of tons of muscle, bladed tails and knife-long teeth at his beck and call.

"It seems as if I am making excuses for my failures, but you attribute too much malice to the acro you face," Remus said. He barked out an order, and the acro lowered his head so that Grant could climb onto its muscular, powerful neck. Grant gripped the ridged arch-shaped structure on the back of the creature's head, the very neck structure that its species had been named for, and used it to haul himself aboard, as if he were mounting a horse.

The acro rose gently, breathing deep before releasing a snort. Grant gently patted the thing's neck. "No malice?"

"If it is any consolation, all humans look alike to the relatively simpleminded acros," Remus said. "These have no more intellect and memory than a trained parrot, a necessity to outsmart their prey."

"There is a similar brain-weight-to-body-mass ratio with avians among the predatory dinosaurs," Brigid commented.

Kane and Kondo handed up gear bags to Grant, who slid them over his shoulder or rested them across his lap, as in the case of the Barrett .50-caliber rifle.

"Kondo, join Grant," Remus suggested. "Kane and Brigid, would you mind riding on the apatosaur?"

Neither complained. Remus had already wrapped vines about the necks or shoulders of the other mounts in order to make it easier for the Cerberus riders and Kondo to hold on or strap in their weapons and gear. Kane tested one of this thick tendrils, and it was taut. No amount of strength could move it, while it provided slack for the shoulders of the apatosaur to move freely as he loped along.

"The acros are full from their meal," Brigid whispered over his shoulder. "Thus, they will prove nonthreatening to the creatures we are with."

"Weren't these things supposed to be docile plant eaters?" Kane asked. "What happens if they spook or if a Ramah acro attacks them?"

"See that huge beam of a tail back there?" Brigid pointed out. "That thing is a gigantic whip, capable of lashing out with the strength to shatter tree trunks or to flay the hide of another dinosaur. You saw the strength they possessed while turning our other Manta upright."

"And attacks from the front?" Kane asked.

"Its forefeet are huge. They can focus thirty tons of force with one stomp," Brigid said. "Apatosaurs and other sauropods use their mass and strength as their means of defense. Few predators would attack an adult. As such, they will be hard to panic. We also can take up the slack with our assault rifles."

"That sounds like a plan," Kane returned.

"You still don't trust Remus?" Brigid asked.

Kane shrugged. "It's hard to tell. We went through two battles with these creatures, and he never mentioned an affinity for them. Now he's walking in off of the plains with his very own army, something he could have used against these so-called enemies for the centuries since the Watatsumi came here in exile."

"He did teach them to use the animals as labor. I'm also certain that while the utilization of their own dinosaur army would have been tempting, the Watatsumi knew that they were going to have to fight an uphill battle, so to speak," Brigid said.

Kane frowned. "What do you mean?"

"It's one thing to steer a hadrosaur with reins and a prod," Brigid said. "It's another to ride in combat. We know that the Dragon Riders are able to. Presumably the Ramah synchronize rogue rider and dinosaur to move and operate in harmony. As well, you've seen our preparations. We might need something to filter out dangerous levels of oxygen."

"The Dragon Riders don't seem to be held up by that," Kane mentioned.

"Perhaps they operate solely on the steppe here, or in the higher levels of the jungle, where the oxygen ratio is still nearly the same as Earth's surface," Brigid responded. "I looked at atmospheric sensors and was convinced that traveling more than a thousand feet down from this plateau would be dangerous."

"Too *much* oxygen?" Kane asked.

"The breathable atmosphere is a specific mixture of gasses, only a small percentage of which is the oxygen we require to breathe and process energy in our cells," Brigid responded. "Too high a dose can be as detrimental as too little. The initial effects start with a giddy, drunken feeling."

"All right," Kane cut her off. "Maybe it's a risk we have to take. Can the Ramah and Remus handle that kind of atmosphere at the bottom of this bubble, or what?"

"Annunaki metabolism might actually be more adaptable to different atmospheres. They already have the facility to travel between bodies as nothing more than a genetic code," Brigid said. "Given their increased strength and longevity, it's highly likely that we could be looking at simply a different environment for them, like us coming out of the rain under a roof."

"Beautiful," Kane groaned. "Hard enough killing the snake faces—now they can handle states a lot more dangerous than we can."

"I believe that the midrealm, just below the edge of the table, is a relatively safe four hundred feet lower," Brigid said. "Not only will the oxygen be present at a ratio our bodies can handle, but the air pressure will make things much less strenuous."

"Air pressure," Kane repeated. "Moving through that might just as well be trying to swim under water."

"Not to that extreme, but where the arthopleura came from, we would be beset by incredible heat, humidity and pressure. I was surprised that they lasted so long in the thin air of the plateau," Brigid noted.

"They had a tunnel leading back to their home, burrowed for miles and miles through rock," Kane said. "Maybe that gave them all the air they were used to and needed."

"A possibility," Brigid returned. "Remus has risked a lot for us. I'm willing to trust him for now."

"So can I," Kane answered. "But I will keep an eye on him, just in case he does turn dangerous. And don't forget—"

"I never forget. and I presume you're talking about his rapid recovery from the injuries he sustained." Brigid said. "Like Durga or Enlil himself, there might be a threshold where his healing powers are overwhelmed."

"Is everything all right?" Remus called out to Kane.

The ex-Magistrate lifted his hand, waving that he was set.

"Head 'em up, and move 'em out!" Remus cried to his compatriots.

Brigid squeezed Kane tightly around his narrow waist as the long, powerful legs of their steed pushed them forward, the swell of tens of tons of muscle beneath them jarring them for a moment.

Ahead lay a knockout blow in a war that had been raging for a century, and feeling the might of the apatosaur they rode, the two people had a glimmer of hope that they could accomplish this task.

KNIFE IN HAND, DOMI WAS on her way to Hannah's nursery. As she closed with the chamber, she saw the two "Naghani women" allowing another burly man, like one of the disposal crew, at the door with them. She paused, crouching to observe their interaction with the man, her Commtact's translator picking up their words and filtering them for her understanding. As much as every muscle in her yearned to leap into action, there was no telling if the guardsman was on their side. If this had been six years ago, Domi would have attacked without reservation, if only because the creatures before her were scaled, inhuman beings.

The Domi of this day and age was far different. She'd come to know the Nagah as generally benign beings, no better or worse than any other humanoid species as a whole. She knew the difference between callous monster and uninvolved bystander.

"Things are getting tight down here," the guardsman told the two nurses. "Hurry up and finish."

They looked at him and barely acknowledged his command, a sure sign that they were Nephilim blanks, creatures born from some hidden backup that had allowed Durga to create his own personal Nephilim shock troops to smuggle within the walls of the Nagah city.

With a sneer, the feral woman regarded the guard at the door, realizing that he was part of the conspiracy. This Nagah was under six feet, and he carried the usual submachine gun that the rest of the Royal Guard had. It was a good bet that this man had been part of Durga's personal cadre, and being in on the Royal Guard's comm network, he was aware of the potential threat looming in the regents' quarters. Through the door, Domi could see that one of the nurses held up a bag, a simple clear IV solution that would be the suspension for whatever vitamins or medicines that a pregnant, vulnerable woman would require.

The other took a needle and added a clear mixture to the solution. Whatever it was, Domi didn't think it would be for any Nagah's good interest. Disguised inside a sterile saline USP, the syringe's contents would prove to be either a poison or something far worse.

Domi just couldn't break the concept that the slender needle was injecting something of Durga into the saline. Hannah was back in the royal court, out of the line of fire. With a surge, Domi drew her Detonics .45 autopistol and exploded from the shadows.

"Damn it!" the rogue guardsman snarled as he tried to level his automatic weapon at the charging silhouette of the slender albino woman.

Domi triggered her .45, thunderous rounds ripping from the short barrel, smashing into the face and upper chest of the gunner, pulverizing muscle and bone in their wake, blowing wet, stringy pulps of flesh and tissue through exit wounds the size of her fist.

The guard tumbled backward, his dying reflex releasing a stream of gunfire into the ceiling above Domi and his own toppled corpse.

The nurse who held the IV bag turned her attention to returning it to the proper spot while the other mountebank turned her attention toward the commotion at the door, holding the syringe like an ice pick. Yellow eyes met Domi's fury-red gaze as the feral woman entered the doorway.

Even before the small Outland woman could pull the trigger again on her pistol, the false nurse hurled her syringe like a dart, the sharp, thick needle punching into Domi's shoulder. As the object had little mass or force, it wasn't enough to have an effect on the woman's momentum, but the sudden flare of pain sent her first shots wide of the drone.

In a heartbeat, the nurse scooped up an object and leaped closer to Domi, swinging it hard. She was able to recognize the bulk as a kidney-shaped medical bowl a moment before she blocked its passage toward her face. The tray, far heavier than the needle, impacted with Domi's forearm with incredible force, jarring the knife from her grasp even as she blocked. Had the kidney tray struck her in the head, Domi knew that her skull would have been fractured and dented. Even so, she was glad that at least one of the sleeves of her stretched out, damaged shadow suit was able to absorb the kinetic force, lessening it to a simply stunning impact rather than shattering the bones of her wrist and forearm.

Domi winced and pivoted, bringing her bare elbow around and under the ribs of the drone-turned-nurse, discovering that she was hitting something far more dense than normal human flesh. The last time she remembered striking something in the chest with that kind of resistance was in combat with the Nephilim, confirming her suspicions that these were blank-minded humanoid automatons with little more than self-preservation and the will to follow orders working between their ears.

That self-preservation, however, was a strong reflex, and the altered Nephilim lashed out again with its improvised weapon. Domi tucked herself in close to her opponent, catching only the force of the nurse's forearm across her shoulders, rather than being the recipient of a kidney-shaped bowl cracking into her unprotected shoulder. Domi struck again, this time jamming the muzzle of her pistol hard into the creature's kidney, pulling the trigger in the same moment.

A powerful boom filled the room, and the Nephilim assassin jerked violently, a fat slug ripping through the drone's lower abdomen unhindered by even the densest of flesh and bone. The creature shuddered, dropping its tray, and staggered away, clutching a gory exit wound in her belly.

Domi lifted the .45 to fire once more, but she saw that her gun was jammed out of battery, the impact of the barrel against the hard skin of her foe turning the multiple-shot pistol into a single-shot weapon. Now all she had was a small, all-metal club. With a grimace, she turned and saw that the other nurse had completed her task, and rushed toward the dead renegade on the maternity unit's floor.

A jammed pistol against a half-loaded submachine gun was a losing proposition, no matter how Domi looked at it, and she spun toward the Nephilim. With a surge of strength, she whipped the inoperative pistol like a boo-merang, the L-shaped hunk of steel and wood tumbling through the air, but maintaining a true, straight flight until it smacked the killer nurse in the head a moment before her fingers found the grip of the dead Nagah's assault weapon. The sound of metal crunching against armored dermis and skull was loud and ugly, the gun's front sight ripping open the scaled hide as it careened away from the enemy's head. Stunned and knocked off balance, the drone was incapable of holding on to the machine pistol, which clattered onto the corpse's belly.

Domi shifted tactics and dived for her knife, plucking it off of the floor from where it had been thrown. Her friends would be coming into the line of fire any moment, and there was no way that she would risk their lives, especially not Lakesh's, by getting them involved with this brawl. She pounced across the room, landing on the bloody-headed nurse with all of her mass, spearing the point of her knife into the drone's clavicle. Leathery flesh ripped and parted, nine inches of steel plunging deep into viscera, carving through blood vessels and air passages.

The murderous drone reached up, trying to pin her adversary, to provide one last final blow against the feral woman, but Domi twisted free, kicking with all of her strength against the stomach of her foe. With that leverage and the power of her body, Domi slashed the knife up, splitting the lower jaw of her enemy so that the mandible flapped apart as if they were parts of some hideous insect's mouth.

As she bounded free from the conflict, she realized just how lucky and prescient she had been. The enemy who had been gut shot somehow retained more than enough strength to lift a cart of medical supplies up and swing it down, crushing her drone sister with all the bulk of the steel cart and her natural Nephilim might.

The two survivors of this fight were off balance, but Domi gathered her legs beneath her as she regarded her opponent in the cold ruby rage of her albino's gaze. Blood dribbled over the bottom lip of the gravely wounded drone, but it stood straight up, regarding the smaller woman with abject hatred.

"You must die," the thing said in a monotone, a strangely male voice.

"Everybody dies," Domi answered. She charged the gut-shot Nephilim, knife slicing the air before her. The wounded drone tried to bring up her arms to block and counterattack. Domi's knife bit deep into the creature's forearm, and with a twist, the Nephilim assassin broke her own arm and wrenched the blade out of the feral woman's grasp.

A slashing fist barely missed Domi's head, brushing the slicked hair on her head. Disarmed, there was only one thing for her to do. She drove her other fist deep and hard into the belly injury of the drone. Blood and pulped flesh erupted from the wound as she struck it, and Domi's weight and strength was focused all in one spot, punching deep into the enemy's bowels.

The impact released a torrent of vomiting crimson from the mouth of her enemy and soaked Domi's hair and bared shoulder even further. She followed up with another punch, hammering the creature's kidney with everything she could. With a twist, she swept the enemy off her feet, wrenching her hand free from the grisly crater that had been excavated from the nurse's belly.

Domi staggered back, hoping that her foe was dead. Every part of her body hurt, muscles screaming for respite. If anything else attacked her...

"Domi!" Edwards bellowed.

She turned, reacting to her CAT partner. The big man looked over the room, keeping his weapon held low.

"Check bags," she muttered, pointing to the saline. "Injected stuff."

"Right," Edwards answered. "You okay?"

"Check bags!" she snarled, staggering back to lean against a gurney. "Be fine."

"You're the boss," Edwards answered, still keeping an eye on the belly-burst thing that Domi had risen from.

But for now, the Nagah city was quiet. The battles were over for this deadly night.

Chapter 19

The humans riding atop the mighty sauropod readied their rifles, making certain that the bandoliers of spare magazines they'd require would be readily at hand. The way the vine harnesses had been rigged up, Kane and Brigid also had the opportunity to set up small shields that would allow them to take cover behind heavy planks of wood, but neither felt that they wanted to limit their mobility. Their other options were either Magistrate torso armor or trauma-plate-laden Kevlar vests.

The expedition led by Remus might not have been going against opponents who possessed high-caliber firearms, but they had learned from recent conflicts that they were going to need every edge they could get against the terrible claws of the deinonychus and Utahraptors, as well as the aerial assaults conducted by the Ramah's new "air force." Kane, Brigid and Grant hadn't encountered the dangerous winged predators, but they had been briefed on the new flying assailants by Kondo, by Tatehiko and by Remus.

Grant had been left in the dust by Brigid Baptiste's evaluation of the airborne monsters as the Liaoningopterus, a toothy pterosaur with a five-yard wingspan. Deadly snatching claws and considerable strength had combined to make the winged hunter a considerable piscivore.

"A fish eater?" Kondo asked incredulously. "Those things were strong enough to snatch a forty-pound rifle."

"Which required considerably less effort than grabbing

a similarly sized gar or other bony fish from a lake or an ocean," Brigid countered. "That explains why it was able to bear your mass for as far as it could fly while injured. You seem to forget that fish are far stronger in water than we assume. A bass weighing a mere thirty pounds has considerably more strength than a similar sized human while swimming even at a fifth to a sixth the weight of said man."

"Liaoningopterus?" Kane quizzed.

"Named for the province of China where their fossils were first discovered," Brigid said. "It's fascinating. There are species from various parts of the globe and several prehistoric eras."

"Can't we just call the damned things pterosaurs?" Kane asked.

Brigid nodded. "For the sake of brevity in combat, yes. I would just prefer to know the precise species. I'm trying to figure why there is such a range of species from different realms and eras."

"Doesn't take much to figure that these are just specimens for some Annunaki's idea of a gigantic zoo," Grant replied. "The dinosaurs could have been present for only a few hundred years. Especially since they cleave so closely to specific animals from different eras. If it's one thing that the dinos knew how to do, it's adapt. They've been able to cope in behavior, but pretty soon, different physical features will pop up, even in the space of a few thousand years."

"Kept in storage until the Ramah retreated down here?" Kondo asked. "Makes sense. And then when we arrived, the Watatsumi as a race of refugees, they decided to dip into the stores and bring out the dragons."

Brigid nodded, mulling it over. "That's a plausible explanation. Remus?"

The Wanderer nodded. "My fellow Igigi would have preferred not to deal with opponents head-on. They could easily have tapped into the gene banks. The Annunaki take a shining to different species, and they like to keep copies on hand, similar to the old Doomsday seed vault project that humanity proposed in the late twentieth century."

Kane narrowed his eyes. "I thought you had disappeared down the rabbit hole long before that?"

Remus answered without a pause. "Archival knowledge that the Watatsumi had brought with them, scavenged and rescued from the destruction of their original home. It was in the design stages, but given the Continuity of Government facilities like the redoubts, the Doomsday vault might have been anticipated."

"Kane, if you're wondering about what kind of knowledge he shouldn't have, the Watatsumi came bearing a lot of information, as well as our trips searching for more redoubts," Kondo spoke up.

Kane nodded. "You've been noticing my paranoia, too."

"Right now, we know we can only trust Remus as far as we can get away from his herd of saurian muscle," Kondo said.

"We are fighting a mutual enemy, one utilizing methods I despise," Remus added. "I have had countless chances to harm you, and instead I have suffered injury in your defense."

"So, on the other hand, we have Tatehiko who wants to know what you're really up to, and why so many personal assistants have ended up dead," Grant countered.

"It's politics. Tatehiko is not sloppy. If anything, he is too cautious. He retained Ochiro, despite the claims that Ochiro might be working for another party within the Watatsumi," Remus told him. "Believe me, it would be incredibly easy to lay blame at my comrade's feet, but he works hard to minimize the losses. It was that kind of training that allowed Kondo and his squad to protect the factory workers, despite the Riders' surprise weapon. I can suspect an influence in his command structure, maybe even a subconscious influence upon himself, but there's someone else, something much worse, at nearly the same level of influence and military access."

"And as you said, fully aware of his interaction with the Ramah," Kane said. "But all this time, you said it had to be a conscious ally to them."

"Something wrong?" Kondo asked.

"Well, you said you had doubts about both leaders the moment you were brought into close contact with them," Kane said. He aimed a finger at Remus. "And you keep losing people you show trust to."

"Someone inside is playing us?" Remus asked. He frowned. "But I'd have noticed any psychic interference. I'm too strong willed…"

"Maybe," Kane said. "I only have the basic idea of what telepathy can do. I can feel it used on myself, or in close quarters to a parallax point, which increases mental sensitivity. It's like hearing a whisper or feeling a spiderweb you walk through. Can't hear things or make out details, but it's there. But those are minds that are trying to be heard."

"Something more subtle than mind control," Remus murmured.

"Infrasound?" Brigid asked. "There are frequencies of sound that are too low for the human ear to hear normally that incite paranoia and dread in people."

"Got ears sharp enough for that?" Kane asked.

"Not necessarily even sound," Grant butted in. "Maybe it's just a mental link that's not on a normal frequency that an Igigu mind recognizes. At least not one that hasn't been in isolation for a few millenia."

"Teleempathic broadcast," Remus mused. "Someone in Ryugo-jo is able to broadcast a mental note that resonates in paranoia and distrust."

"Not a puppet, but an actual Ramah, or some other refugee who came here," Kane said. "They have that in place, and we're looking at the real reason why you've not been concentrating on anything more than the enjoyment of your isolation. The more you're with people—"

"The more paranoid I get. But given my background, rather than lashing out, I retreat to my Spartan little cave, or take to the trees in the high forest," Remus answered. "But we don't have a suspect, do we?"

"We can save that for later, once we have our showdown with the Ramah," Kane told him. "Who knows what kind of resistance we're running into."

"At least some aerial," Grant said. "Look!"

The humans, Kondo and Remus all threw their eyes skyward, seeing a dozen V-shaped shadows cross a lava tube directly above them. Their appearance was singularly impressive, long membranous wings spread out sixteen feet from tip claw to tip claw. The stretched glider limbs weren't the most frightening aspect of them. Their feet had strong, clawed talons designed for penetrating tough scales, and their heads were two feet long, from back of skull to tip of tooth-laden jaws.

Brigid didn't need to shout a warning that the snapping jaws of their enemy were filled with powerful, naillike fangs that were easily two inches long, and also meant to tear into the armored skins of gatorlike fish or lizards, and hold them despite being composed of thirty pounds of thrashing muscle. Even through their shadow suits, those jagged hooks would leave terrible lacerations, and hurl them from the backs of their mounts in helpless dives a dozen feet to the ground.

These weren't some high-speed monster that could swoop down and slice them in two like living guillotines, but that didn't lessen their threat. Kane wasn't interested in testing the power of his Mag armor against the natural weaponry of the fastest diving of the pterosaurs.

The winged horror had tucked in its wings, turning it into a flying M that allowed gravity and its own momentum to turn it into a living missile, jaws spread wide. Kane extended his fist, Sin Eater snapping into place like a reflex. As soon as the gun extended, a burst of high-powered slugs ripped from its barrel.

Committed to its power dive, the Liaoningopterus couldn't flap and maneuver. The very movement that would have allowed it to tear deep into Kane's armor left it a sitting duck, the trio of machine-pistol rounds punching through its skull and powerfully muscled breast. Bone structures meant to take a ton of wing-flap force did a lot to deflect the 240-grain slugs, but the ricocheting rounds simply tumbled and ripped apart muscle and vital organs on their way through.

The initial crackle of gunfire was enough of a signal to make the pterosaurs scatter, wings flapping or pivoting, shooting each of the fanged hunters off in eleven different directions. The good news was that their attack formation had been broken. The bad news was that the number of angles that the Cerberus warriors could expect an attack from had grown significantly.

"Dismount!" Remus bellowed, loosing an arrow into the sky. The shaft zipped through the sky so quickly, the air released a zipping whistle in its wake. The impact was audible as the broad head punched into the round, muscular trunk of a pterosaur. Two of the enemy attackers had been eliminated, but that meant there were ten more flying killers to deal with.

Grabbing the vines that made up their harness, Kane and Brigid quickly got off the shoulders of their apatosaur steed, using the thick cables to rappel to the ground. Even as they cleared the trunk of their massive beast, swift zooming shapes wove away from its back. The pterosaurs had tried to recover their initiative, but they had to scatter for fear of crashing into its powerful bulk.

Once in the grass and amid the thick, tree-trunk legs of the giant sauropod, Kane and Brigid had a decent cover over their head and only needed to watch in two general directions for incoming threats. Off to the side, they heard Grant's Sin Eater snarl out its deadly message of high-powered slugs, and Kane caught the sight of one of the winged antagonists cartwheeling through the grass. It hurtled toward Kane, and it would have crashed into him had it not been for the snapping jaws of an acro deleting it from the battlefield. With a ferocious shake that dislocated joints, the predatory giant swallowed the crushed corpse in one mighty gulp.

Kane and Brigid turned their attention to the other side of the apatosaur, his Sin Eater and her autopistol booming out their powerful messages of destruction toward the flying horrors skimming toward them. Even as they shot down a couple of the enemy beasts, tails flailed across the paths of others. Be it the swordlike tail blades of a stegosaurus or the tree-trunk-thick whips of the apatosaurs, the Liaoningopterus were either driven off course or brutally shattered by the natural weapons of the herbivores that the Cerberus heroes rode with. Pulped corpses slammed into the ground, and as soon as the aerial assault broke, five surviving creatures climbed desperately into the sky.

Remus grimaced. He hadn't moved from the back of his acro, staying on its neck in order to give the wounded megapredator all the protection he could provide it. He could see movement, and the Wanderer's face was filled with hatred. "Riders!"

"Get on board?" Kane asked.

He didn't wait for an answer as he seized the vine of his apatosaur's harness, pulling himself up. The creature had slowed, bracing itself so that Kane and Brigid could climb its powerfully muscled forelimbs and haul themselves hand over fist on the ropey vines. It wasn't the most agile and graceful bit of acrobatics either had ever engaged in, but as they clawed back into their spots on the sauropod's back, they noted the sudden flash of small, dog-size bodies weaving through the grass where they'd been moments ago.

"Deinonychus!" Grant warned as he fired at one of the swift, agile creatures. His aim was true, but even as his target fell, three more emerged from the long grass, bounding at the acro he and Kondo rode. Kondo's submachine gun chattered, swatting a second of the assailants from the air.

Remus let out his battle cry. After only a second of the song, the two acros echoed his roar. A moment later, the entire attack formation of Remus's dinosaur army was bellowing, the air shuddering under a sonic assault from sets of lungs that were each as large as Kane himself.

Kane could easily see how the mass of the beasts they rode had more than a few advantages. The combined volume that the animals put out would have had a jarring effect, nothing short of a stun grenade going off in close proximity. The twenty combined beasts had the effect of dazzling the smaller animals who, among their arsenal of hunting abilities, relied on razor-sharp vision.

Dazzled and thrown off their attack, the herd of dinosaurs surged forward, massive apatosaur hooves catching the most stunned of their opponents underfoot, reducing them to squashed masses of flesh. Kane looked back to Brigid Baptiste, making certain she was okay as he felt the thunder lizard beneath him accelerate to a gallop. The last time Kane had felt such power and force beneath him was when he rode the shoulders of a New Olympus gear skeleton as it launched itself through the sky. His fingers were wrapped tightly around the straps of his improvised saddle, and he glanced to make certain that the gear he and Brigid might need was secure.

Relieved that nothing was lost, he checked behind the charging herd. The stegosauri and the two acros were struggling to maintain the pace of the long-legged sauropods, but they were only behind the group by about five to eight yards. The animals had hardly been obscured by the dirt and debris kicked up by massive feet.

"How long can they do this?" Kane called over his Commtact.

"Don't ask me! I never saw information about the ground speed of a brontosaur!" Brigid spoke up.

"Thought you said—"

"Just hang on!" Brigid snapped.

The living tank cavalry of Remus galloped on for what felt like hours, but after five minutes, they had lost their Ramah impelled pursuit. It wouldn't last for long. As quick as the apatosaurs had been, their enormous strides enabling them to cover more ground in a single step than a horse could in five, the predators would be back on them. There was also no doubt that the airborne part of the Ramah's terrible army was regrouping, recovering from their losses.

This was going to be a long, deadly march.

HANNAH AND MANTICOR had joined Lakesh as he and the royal physicians looked at the bags of saline solution that had been tampered with by the false Nagah nurses. Even under a microscope, there wasn't much to tell within the saline suspension. The only real advantage that they had was the syringe that one of the disguised Nephilim drones threw at Domi had been easily recovered and its contents put on a slide.

Domi was asleep in her quarters, being looked after by two of Rahdnathi's most trusted comrades, recovering from the battering that caught up with her. Lakesh frowned as he thought of how close she had come to serious eye damage from Nagah venom, in addition to multiple contusions that included bruising from her attempted drowning in sewage. As an albino, normally the feral woman would have had a fragile immune system, but Domi was a slight mutation from that norm. While she lacked pigmentation, which allowed for her eyes to seem so bright red from the blood flowing through the natural veins in her sclera, she was hardly a delicate flower. Life in the postapocalyptic Earth had forged her into a compact, taut package of muscle and sinew. As such, she could handle exposure to the elements and her life in the Tartarus Pits had already exposed her to more than her fair share of sewage-borne contagion.

That didn't ease Lakesh's concerns for his love, almost making him wish he were two people at this moment. He tightened the magnification on the microscope, noting that there were strange clusters within the syringes. He zoomed in on one of the clusters and noted that they appeared to be capsules, massed together. He could see that they were tiny globes, the surface adorned with a shell. He took a digital camera recording of the image and transmitted it back to Cerberus. It took only a few moments for DeFore to reply that he was looking at a retrovirus, information shot to him over his Commtact, leaving him in privacy.

Two places at once, Lakesh mentally repeated to himself.

"Well, this is obviously a case of genetic tampering."

It had been said by one of the Nagah doctors, a svelte, attractive cobra woman named Vimala. Lakesh immediately translated the name from Hindi: "pure, clean." It seemed a fitting name for a woman who sought to improve the health of the royal family, but she seemed on edge as she looked over her results. "Lakesh, do you have any idea what RNA is at work inside?"

Lakesh shook his head. "It could be anything from HIV to some manner of cancer."

Vimala nodded in agreement. "Do you think that this might be the Sons of Enlil trying to preserve the bloodline of Durga?"

Hannah grimaced at the mention of her former fiancé's name. At his best, Durga had been a rough lover, and at his worst, he had been a sexual predator who gloried in the power he wielded in the form of controlling her via threat and coercion. "One last chance to father a new master race with a pure bloodline."

Lakesh nodded. "The retrovirus could rewrite whatever nascent development has occurred in your ovum, pardon my bluntness."

Hannah nodded. "You are pardoned."

"One thing I don't get," Manticor said. "We know that he has access to the means of restructuring Nephilim drones. Why not simply make a new Durga out of one of those?"

"Perhaps it is a case of revenge," Lakesh mused. "Durga's followers hate the fact that you have fathered children with Hannah. This is their way of removing you from her bloodline."

Vimala sneered. "Sick."

"You were Durga's physician," Hannah said. "You know that while he was perfect in body, his mind was twisted."

Vimala gazed at her out of the corner of her eye.

Lakesh felt the uncomfortable silence in the room. Hannah had just struck a low blow against a man who, up until now, seemed to have little means of standing up for his reputation.

"Pure," Lakesh repeated, realization dawning upon him. "You were Durga's doctor."

The Nagah doctor smirked as Manticor swiveled to face her.

"What can I say?" Vimala answered with a shrug. "You now have one final victory of my beloved prince."

Manticor and Hannah both turned their attention to the pregnant queen's bulging belly.

"They are the sons of the true royal blood," Vimala answered. "I'd been biding my time."

Manticor pulled his pistol. Other guardsmen moved in to take her captive, but Vimala was not a warrior. She had accomplished her mission.

"Oh 'Core…" Hannah whispered, touching the scales over her abdomen. A tear welled up in one eye.

Manticor reached out, taking her hand. "It's… You'll be… We can try again."

"Who else was in this with you?" Lakesh asked, stepping closer to Vimala, anger crossing his features.

"Those who attend to the fallen prince, honoring his name, his bloodline, his power," Vimala returned. "I have no names, and those who have fallen are either mindless pawns or members of his old cadre. We struck, bringing the knowledge that they have not been abandoned, that there is still strength within the arms of Durga, no matter how he has returned."

"Durga," Hannah growled. "Is he alive?"

Vimala smirked. "Of course. But you will never find him. He has been borne to safety, far beyond these caverns."

"Damn it," Manticor cursed. He reached for Hannah's hand.

"How long?" Hannah asked. "How long have I been carrying…"

"Ever since your first diagnosis of a successful pregnancy," Vimala returned. "Any spark of the half-breed cripple has been long extinct inside of you."

Hannah's fists clenched.

"It was so good of the fools from Cerberus to return. To be here for your greatest loss," Vimala said. "The eggs within you, they will render your womb infertile. Never again will you bear another's child, unless you can find the very technology that Durga needs to rebuild his shattered body."

Hannah's lips parted, eyes wide.

"And the closer you get to that goal, the closer a true king comes to returning to life," Vimala continued. "You will be the mother of his offspring."

Manticor saw Hannah looking at a table full of medical implements. He rolled between her and whatever tools she could grab to cut the offending tissues from her womb.

"No," Manticor barked. "No. You cannot do that."

"But they're *his*," Hannah returned, her voice cracking.

"There are too few of us to allow rotten parentage to ruin the lives of the unborn," Manticor said. "It's going to be a hard choice, but these are still blank slates, and these still have the familial traits of not only Durga, but Matron Yun and Garuda."

Hannah looked down, touching her belly. "I don't want them to grow up to be monsters."

Manticor squeezed her hand. "We won't raise them that way."

Lakesh glared at Vimala. "Either way, you think you've won."

The doctor smiled callously. "The Nagah know their

prince lives. And either Hannah destroys innocent lives, or she nurtures the seed of a man she hates more than anyone."

Lakesh looked back to the queen and her consort. "There was a time when I would have felt that chromosomes were everything that mattered in the development of a person, but there are forces in this universe even Durga can't anticipate."

Manticor and Hannah embraced tightly, her sobs softly filtering through the laboratory.

Lakesh felt his anger fade as he continued. "And the strongest is the love of a parent, a love that doesn't see genes—it sees another chance to get the future right."

Chapter 20

According to the readout before Grant's eyes, the atmosphere was growing thicker. The shadow suit's built-in environmental controls were reporting that they were entering an atmosphere where oxygen toxicity was growing. For all of his life, the big man had only known oxygen as the means of keeping himself alive, the very breaths he took allowing him to display his great strength and vitality. Brigid had mentioned the dangers inherent in the lower, high-pressure, high-oxygen environment.

They had been at this altitude for six minutes, and according to her, this would be the onset of vertigo, extreme nausea and uncontrolled twitches and muscle spasms.

"You all right back there?" Grant asked Kondo.

There was a clap on his shoulder. "I'm fine, I'm just worried about our noble steed."

Grant patted the muscular neck of the acrocanthosaur. If it felt the contact, it paid him no mind. For what Grant had seen of how it had shrugged off armor-piercing slugs, he doubted that it considered Grant more than a fly landing on its shoulder. "According to Remus and Brigid, they feel that these animals are more used to a higher oxygen level in their atmosphere, somewhere between modern times and the era of the giant millipedes that attacked us. They can adapt and withstand it until we get the job done. And if it begins to show symptoms, we turn around and hie these boys out of here."

"You care about these things?" Kondo asked, seeming a little suspicious.

Grant nodded. "I've spent time on Thunder Isle, and its forests are a dumping ground for time-travel experiments, including a number of dinosaurs. After seeing them in the wild, and even seeing them here, I could see that these are just trying to live like we are. You might not feel the same, since the acros and the raptors are used as weapons against you."

Kondo nodded. "That doesn't mean we'll try to tame these behemoths. I couldn't even begin to think of how we can feed them."

Grant patted the acro again, an absentminded move. "I'm not saying to hold hands around a campfire. But I've learned that live and let live is the best possible strategy to use with wild animals of any sort."

"Even shooting at ones under Ramah control?" Kondo asked.

Grant grimaced. "In that case, it's live or die. I can't do anything for my friends or the Watatsumi if I'm dead."

Kondo and Grant scanned the sky, but the forest canopy had enveloped them overhead, limiting access to them by the Liaoningopterus. The trees were far enough apart at this height for the sauropods and smaller dinosaurs to walk between their trunks easily, but the branches above them provided little maneuverability for winged creatures.

Death wouldn't come from above, but that didn't mean enemies would not fly through the forest at apatosaur shoulder height. Their advanced optics allowed them to sweep for heat signatures, and tell the difference between flitting shadows and malevolent or benign creatures stalking the primeval jungle floor.

Their acro kept sniffing, snorting to clear its nostrils to inhale a new set of scents. It was aware that they were

enemy territory, and it swiveled its eyes. The acrocanthosaur was an active hunter, with excellent vision as in-
dicated by its two forward-looking eyes, a common trait
among predators like humans or big cats, allowing it to
gauge distance thanks to depth perception. That sharp vision and canny sense of smell were only two of its means
of looking for prey or danger.

"Remus?" Grant called.

"My acro is acting up, as well," the Wanderer said. "I
don't see or feel anything, except an empty dread."

"I'm feeling it, too," Kane cut in. "Unfocused fear, and
it's casting about for targets."

Remus glanced from his mount to Kane on the apatosaur. "So your paranoia is already focused."

Kane nodded. Grant hadn't felt that unease yet, but
Remus had a partially Annunaki mind, and Kane's exposure to Balam's telepathic contact had made him exponen-
tially more sensitive to psychic contact. The wild-animal
senses of the great predator that he and Kondo rode were
probably cued in to those same levels of dread.

Kane tugged on his apatosaur's reins, kicking his heels
hard into the mighty sauropod's shoulder to direct it forward.

"Where are you going?" Grant asked.

"To the very place that my instincts are telling me to
run from," Kane said. "The Ramah must be using the same
kind of mental influence that has the Watatsumi command
at odds with itself."

"Can we keep the animals under control?" Grant asked
Remus.

The tall, half-Annunaki wanderer shrugged. "I don't
know about the rest, but if we keep a steady hand on our
mounts, we might be able to guide them along."

Even as the two acros stepped forward to follow Kane's

lead, they noticed that the others, the stegosauri and un-
burdened apatosaurs, stood at an invisible line of demarca-
tion. Skittish eyes followed the expedition, and more than
once a long-necked beast dug the ground with a foreleg,
as if trying to dig up the strength to advance.

From now on, Grant knew that the humans' backup had
diminished radically. Rather than an unstoppable mass of
thundering muscle, they only had one thirty-ton, living
tank, and two six-ton super-predators along with them.
Even now, Grant could feel his jaw tightening, anxiety
rising within his chest.

He took a deep breath, squeezing the vine tightly. He
would not allow an alien mind to set him to flight.

THE WAVE OF INSECURITY and nausea swept over Kane like
a tide. Noting that the Ramah's initial assault had stopped
only the herbivores, except the one that the ex-Magistrate
prodded forward with kicks and yanks on reins, his stomach wanted to flip over. The vines strained in his grasp as
the apatosaur stretched its enormous neck forward.

It was struggling, as much as he was. In its primitive
mind, it was surrounded by hostile predators, and the sight
and smell of two actual hunters, the massive allosaur-like
acros, weren't helping things. He glanced side to side, noting that the twin carnivores were also anxious, their heads
shifting, as if they could shake off their own nightmare influences like they could break the natural ropes that held
their riders on board.

"Kane, if this thing panics, we can be thrown," Brigid
said. "And given the size of the feet, and the weight of
this thing…"

"I know, Baptiste. You don't have to state the—" Kane
bit off the rest of that sentence. "Everyone, we're starting
to get a lot more testy!"

"No shit," Grant answered over his Commtact. "Sorry."

"This isn't us. We're better than this," Remus responded. "I'm better than this."

Kane could feel the tension in the Igigu's voice and saw how he clutched the mighty bow he carried. His eyes seemed to actually glow in the shadows of the canopy. He was absorbing the brunt of the psychic assault, as if the other spawn of the Annunaki, the lost, refugee children of the old, mad gods, knew that their main opposition was the intellect of their distaff brother. He saw both of the tall wanderer's hands flash to his face, nails clawing at his armored forehead, scales bursting free from skin as he dragged them down.

"Remus!" Kane bellowed.

The Igigu was speaking in a language that even the computerized translator of the Commtact was unfamiliar with. His chanting was swift, crazed, unfocused. Kane felt the almost imperceptible whispers in the back of his mind. It was spillover from the proximity to Remus, and his own senses were acting like radios in proximity to flashes in the sky. He looked back to Brigid.

"Baptiste, hold on to Bronty," Kane ordered.

"But it's not a brontosaur..." the flame-haired archivist began.

It was too late, as Kane rose upon their steed's shoulders, took a few running steps, then leaped from the back of the apatosaur. It was a stupid, desperate move, and he was leaping from a height of sixteen feet, across a gap of ten, to the shoulders of a slightly shorter acrocanthosaurus. If he missed, he would end up with broken bones, or at least a sprained knee, and be on the ground, vulnerable to the Dragon Riders' raptors, if they were within range.

Kane sailed through the air, arms windmilling, torso twisting as he guided himself toward the neck of the con-

fused, wounded acro. The beast, its fears heightened by
the Ramah attack, was skittering, so at the last moment,
midair adjustments were necessary. Rather than trying for
the nearly impossible target that was the vines coming off
of the predator's harness, Kane aimed for Remus, a larger,
more secure figure to grab.

Kane's arms snapped shut around the Igigu's torso, and
his flight ended as suddenly as it had begun. The mad dive
had jarred Remus, his attention turning toward the human
that landed, literally, on his back. Golden eyes flared with
anger, but his unknown language disappeared, instead a
jumble of human words, all curses, flowed from the lips
of the powerful being.

"Right," Kane muttered as his Commtact tried to keep
up with the stream of multilingual vulgarity spewing forth.
He wrapped his arms under Remus's armpits, drawing
them together behind his back. Against another man, the
full-Nelson hold would have been an inescapable trap. Instead, there was a surge of strength as Remus burst loose.
Kane's fingers hadn't been interlaced yet; otherwise they
would have been shattered by the powerful shrug of his
ally, but he felt his muscles stretch almost to the snapping
point. "Remus! Focus on your mind! I'll keep you from
hurting anyone!"

There was a wild thrash of the Annunaki's arms and
back, pushing Kane off him. An elbow lashed around.
The Cerberus champion deflected it with a slap, and with
a quick glance, he noticed that the Igigu was no longer
talking, his eyes rolled back and glassy. He had been in a
struggle to control his mind while still preventing himself
from being utilized as a puppet, an out-of-control weapon
usurped by the Ramah.

The acro beneath them reared, its normally horizontal
form standing erect, akin to a man standing in a rubber

suit, tail dragging in the dirt. The sudden surge of muscle hurled both Kane and Remus to the forest floor, but the human managed to twist, using Remus's far denser, far more durable body as a cushion. As it was, both men were stilled for a moment.

Kane rolled away, gathering his strength and wits. The acro had taken four huge strides, and was away from them, its fierce golden eyes flaring angrily as it snapped at imaginary enemies left and right. Remus sat up as if nothing had happened, and started to quickly get back to his feet. There was a very strong possibility that Kane would have to resort to lethal force to keep the Igigu from tearing him limb from limb, but after the Wanderer had taken two steps, he froze.

"Remus, did you—?"

A hand was held out. "Come on. I don't know how soon they'll regroup."

Kane took the offered hand and was pulled to his feet as if he were as light as a child's toy. "Any idea where they are?"

Remus's steed stopped its attack on unseen foes and strode back to the two adventurers. The Igigu lifted a hand, brushing its jaw gently. "We can smell them. They're so close, they put everything they had into this fight."

"Kane!" Grant shouted. "We've got company on the way!"

Even as his partner spoke, Kane could hear the bleat and trumpet of assorted ferocious beasts mixed in with the angry shouts of men. The cacophony bounced off tree trunks, echoing, seeming to swell in intensity.

"How can they be breathing down here?" Brigid murmured even as she, Kondo and Grant opened fire into the depths of the forest.

"Pop some grens to slow them!" Kane bellowed as

Remus hefted him onto the back of the acro. "We've got a small window before—"

A sharp, piercing tone broke through his concentration. *Kill him! Kill him!*

Kane didn't need any further information to realize that he was being ordered to attack Remus. There was no internal, mental conflict. This was simply pure shouting, a bellow across telepathic links.

You know he is the enemy of your species! Why spare any of them?

Kane gritted his teeth. "Shut up. Shut the hell up."

Remus looked back. "They are desperate."

"So are we!" Brigid said over the Commtact. In the distance, grenades boomed like thunder. The other three, acting as the rear-guard, opened fire with everything they had. Where there were clusters of bodies, grenades landed, blasts splitting the ground and severing limbs with fantastic force. Where the others saw the massive bulks of Utahraptors or acrocanthosaurs, Grant triggered his Barrett, spearing armor-piercing slugs into their forms.

"Hold the line!" Kane growled. "You know where they are?"

Remus had only to point. They could see the mound, like a termite's nest, except even more massive. Its walls had been built up by slave labor, the Ramah utilizing the awesome strength of their theropod servants. With a glance, Kane looked back, focusing on the line of Dragon Riders hurling themselves to the defense of their masters. He could see that the Watatsumi had been so powerfully controlled that despite their convulsions and vomiting, they continued on. Despite oxygen poisoning, the humanoids still struggled, putting one foot in front of the other.

The dinosaurs had little response to the increased oxygen saturation and pressure of this realm. Kane felt the power of the creature beneath him, the acro surging forward toward the Ramah, hatred burning in its heart. Long, powerful legs ate up the ground, hundreds of yards disappearing in a titanic charge as tons of living predator became a missile of muscle and sinew.

It knew by instinct that the creatures within its walls had been the reason its pack had been driven from fertile hunting grounds, had been so terribly defeated as they sought prey for their starving bellies. Remus had prodded them along, their strength, their determination the core of the charge that had gotten them past the initial scout force.

With the waves of gunfire and explosions chattering behind, the roars of swarming minions surging toward the Cerberus expedition, the acro was giving Kane and Remus a chance to get at the Ramah. The charge, fully fifty miles per hour, came to a sudden stop as the acrocanthosaur hurled its powerful bulk at the wall of the Ramah's nest. Stone separated, hard-baked mortar shattering. The termites' nest had to have been eighty feet tall, and yet it still was beneath the soaring canopy of the forest above. The theropod's strength had dislodged tons of wall material, and now Kane and Remus were hurled inside.

The last Kane saw of the acro was the creature's bloodied snout withdrawing through the hole it had torn. Its attack on the Ramah had been costly, but its roar signaled that it was returning to join its brother on the line between the Dragon Riders and Kane. He turned to scan deeper inside the mound nest and saw slender, long-clawed creatures with slouching shoulders and eyes that glowed similar to Domi's own ruby albino gaze. Millennia without sun, in the shadows of a primeval forest, had turned the half-blooded spawn of the Annunaki into pale, weakened things that looked more like zombies than anything else.

The only sign of intelligence was the size of their heads,

large prominent brows that showed the mass of the brains tucked within their skulls. They wore no clothes, and except for slender shafts of filtered light spilling in from the ceiling, they seemed to have no need to see. Through telepathy, they had obviated the need for material items or physical labor. Servant creatures scurried around their knees, and the loathsome assemblage had gathered as one. They held themselves with confidence, reptilian lips curling into cruel smiles, revealing wicked, razor-sharp teeth.

Their unified telepathic voice was an enormous pressure behind Kane's eyes once more. *You had your chance, human. But remember, you are only human.*

The odds looked to be dozens to one, something Kane had faced before, but these were psi-powered opponents. They had engaged in a battle of wills with Remus, and had only been defeated because Kane had allowed the Wanderer to focus his full mental might on the battle.

Had they recovered? Or had the wasted limbs of the Ramah merely lessened the strength of their Annunaki heritage to average human might? If they actually retained any amount of muscle, the long, curved talons at the end of their gnarled fingers would be more than sufficient to slice through armored scales and polymer shadow suit alike.

"Fuck off, muties. If you're going to fight…fight!"

Kane wasn't going to give the enemy a chance. He swept up the SIG AMT rifle, stroking the trigger as fast as he could. In the close, dark quarters of the Ramah's lair, the muzzle-blasts of the powerful gun were flashing, burning balls of fire that illuminated the crowd even as he pumped bullets into them.

Pale, leathery flesh puckered, blood spraying on impact as the pale nocturnal telepaths lunged as one. This was not self-sacrifice; this was a group knowing that its only chance of success against gunfire was to swarm its enemy.

Beside him, Kane was certain he'd seen Remus load and fire his mighty bow five times before the first clot of the pale spawn swarmed him, long limbs wrapping around him and hauling him to the ground. Kane's own weapon had emptied of its 20-round magazine, and the enemy was within yards of him.

With no time to reload, Kane launched his Sin Eater into place, ripping out the machine pistol's heavy slugs into the closest bodies. His other hand twisted, reversing the rifle into a club to deal with the encroaching mass. As the Sin Eater ran dry, he got in one final swing, the frame of the SIG rifle bouncing off skulls with cracks that rattled in tune with distant gunfire from his friends.

Surrounded, Kane felt something hot burn across his side, clubbing paws blunted by the rest of his shadow suit. With a powerful surge, he backhanded the rifle's stock across a half dozen more faces, leathery hide tearing, fangs jettisoning from bloodied mouths. The maneuver had bought him a moment of space, and Kane released the Sin Eater, fingers clawing for a grenade on his belt. The machine pistol folded back into its forearm holster, leaving his hand free for gripping the handheld bomb.

His left arm protested, nerve endings wailing as he swung his club once more, bringing it down like a hatchet onto the head of another Ramah.

"Kane!" Brigid's voice cut through his Commtact. The pawns of the telepaths had gotten into close combat with his allies. He had only moments left to make some kind of dent.

The gren, an implode charge, arced into the air over a knot of the Ramah even as more bodies crashed atop him. Needle-sharp claws sank into his skin through his protective suit. His torso clattered as the Ramah's nails stabbed and clawed at the polycarbonate shells that he'd supplemented the shadow suit with, but his arms, legs and head were alive with prickly pain before the gren went off. The high-tech polymers could only do so much if one of those curled talons carved through and severed an artery.

The grenade blast was enormous, a wave of pressure crashing outward with more than sufficient force to push Kane and his closest opponents backward before the void left by the thermobaric explosion sucked in air, creating a secondary thunderclap as Ramah corpses were crushed into a small space.

For a moment, Kane's senses swam. He felt as if he were weightless, but even as he did so, he clawed for another of the miniature bombs on his harness.

To one side, Remus surged, bellowing with the rage of a berserker. Ramah bones shattered under his fists as he lashed out brutally, raging with all that he had. Kane rolled the next implode grenade beneath the feet of another staggered knot of the telepathic reptilians, then burst from the tangle of stunned forms around him. The second blast collapsed a far wall of the nest, chunks of the roof hurtling down in slabs the size of Kane's torso.

Only the ex-Magistrate's swift reflexes had saved him from a chunk of masonry that turned a pale, diminished Igigu into a sack of leather-clad pulp.

"Grant! Baptiste!" Kane bellowed. "If you have anything left—"

With that request, the roof shuddered again. More of the castle of the Annunaki spawn disintegrated, wails crumbling under the force of one weapon that Brigid Baptiste had access to—the massive whip-tail of the apatosaur. The long, powerful beam of muscle, sinew and thick hide sliced through stone and masonry like a knife, shearing through support structures in the nest. The roof rumbled as it broke apart, turning into a lethal storm of rock and dust.

Kane stumbled as a heavy stone smashed into his shoulder. The Magistrate torso armor he'd added was good for even rifle-strength calibers, but the size of this missile had been more than even he could take. He was forced down to a knee, his brain rattled again. On the heels of the implode grenade detonations and the tackle by a dozen of forms, his reserves of strength were failing.

He struggled to push off, to continue his run for safety as the nest folded in on itself. He slipped, the floor turned slippery, itself collapsing beneath him.

Before he could consign himself to being crushed and buried along with the Ramah, a powerful arm hooked him under one shoulder, lifting him back to his feet. It was Remus, and the pair of them were on the move in an instant.

The apatosaur's tail lashed down again, a guillotine of living weapon that chopped down behind them, crushing more bodies of the Ramah that struggled to escape their doom. The passage of the tail had cleared a path, though. Legs pumping, Kane and Remus hurled themselves out into the open just as the floor behind them caved. Thick, cloying dust vomited skyward as the Ramah's home turned into a crater, shattered by grenades and the rage of dinosaurs.

Sagging to his knees, Kane looked up to see Grant and Kondo, patrolling, looking at strewed corpses. The Dragon Riders had grown close, but once the Ramah no longer could impel their slaves, their courage had broken. The renegade Watatsumi had tried to run, but now they were sprawled, succumbed to epileptic seizures due to oxygen oversaturation in their bloodstream. The bulk of the carnage had been among the smaller raptors, here and there the massive bulk of a thousand-pound Utahraptor twisted on the ground.

"No acros?" Kane asked.

"Grenades and this bastard," Grant answered. "How're you?"

"Alive," Kane returned.

Just to make certain that the menace of the Ramah would be over, he plucked his remaining implode grenades off his belt, lobbing them into the cratered remains of their nest. The ground shook, but no more screams or hisses sounded in the tomb of the monsters.

Remus sighed. "They're extinct, Kane."

Kane smirked. "They said the same things about the dinosaurs, Remus."

No mirth rose from the scene as they looked around at the carnage.

Chapter 21

The acrocanthosaur pair remained behind in the primeval forest, healing and licking their wounds. According to Remus, and the sensors built into their hoods, the jungle had plenty of prey for the two recovering predators. The expedition had come across three more corpses of the giant predators, but there were tracks of others.

"There should be a viable breeding population for them," Brigid noted as they rode the back of the apatosaur. Two people or five, it was no bother to the sauropod who outweighed the mass of them by a factor of thirty. "They'll make it fine…I hope."

"They saved our asses," Grant said. "Brigid let out a cry that we were being overrun for a moment, then your boy charged in, stomping raptors into the dirt."

Kane nodded. "Glad for him."

"You sound like shit," Remus muttered.

"We all do," Kondo said. "We look like it, too."

"We'll get some rest when we return to Ryugo-jo," Brigid spoke up. "Once there, we can find the last of the Ramah's allies, then go home to Cerberus."

"Home," Remus muttered. "It will feel like home for a change."

"Not an exile?" Kane asked.

The Wanderer nodded. "I might even have to give up my sobriquet."

"if you have a place to stay, yeah," Grant responded. "Makes it hard to call yourself a wanderer."

"The Watatsumi, the Nagah, New Edo, we could really have a unified group to patrol and keep the Orient safe," Kane suggested. "Just an idea. If you want to help with that."

"I would be honored to help with that," Remus said.

Kondo nodded. "And I will pledge my sword."

Kane smiled. All they needed to do was engage in one more bit of mop-up to take down the spy that had assisted the Ramah in the direction of the Dragon Riders. Then the subterranean realm known as the Spine of the Dragon would be a relatively safe haven.

One last bit of work, something that wouldn't seem so dangerous, Kane mused.

He grimaced. Those kinds of relaxed thoughts always rode in just ahead of tragedy....

THE EXPLOSION WAS all-consuming. It wasn't just one blast; it was a half dozen. The sky split, the atmosphere seeming to crack under the multiple impacts.

The next thing Kane realized, he was sprawled on the ground, head swimming. The apatosaur that they had been riding was nowhere to be seen, but as he looked around, his face was coated in blood.

They had ascended the slope, crawling through the path that led to the plateau where Ryugo-jo nestled. The air was sweet, fresh, but still thick and wet. Kane struggled to his feet, looking around.

Brigid crawled to her hands and knees. She was coughing, dazed by whatever had hit them.

It took a moment for Kane to realize where the apatosaur had gone. The proud, mighty beast who had been instrumental in destroying the greatest threat to the Watatsumi lay on its side, bloodied ribs exposed to the air as the stench of roasting beef and leathery hide stung Kane's nostrils.

"Stop! It's us!" Kondo shouted, waving his arms. Kane whipped his head around to see who the Watatsumi addressed when the familiar punts of grenade launchers filled the air again.

An explosion of movement whisked Kondo off his feet, but it wasn't the blast of a grenade that carried him to the ground; it was the speeding shape of Grant, tackling the young warrior out of the path of a line of shells that hammered around them.

The groaning bulk of the apatosaur rose to a crescendo over the sounds of the blasts, but the loyal beast's mass once more had come to the rescue of the Cerberus explorers and their allies. Shock waves shook the air, but no shrapnel sliced through the sauropod's body.

Kane's throat tightened. This attack wasn't going to be unavenged. He scurried, climbing the hip of the dying animal, and looked to see a company-sized force of Watatsumi *bushi* assembled, their weapons bristling.

"Even *we* know the legend of the Trojan horse, humans!" Tatehiko bellowed from his vantage point atop the shoulders of a trachodon. With that exclamation, the reptilian commander of the subterranean warriors leveled his rifle and triggered a long burst.

Kane dived for cover, mere small-arms fire too weak and insubstantial to cut through the dying dinosaur's body. The apatosaur grunted, wheezing as its multiple wounds were already too much for it to hold on much longer.

"We're going to clean *him* up," Kane snarled, the Sin Eater launching into his grasp. "Remus! Where are you?"

There was no answer, and he swept the scene. He finally found the half-breed, in waist-high grass that was darkened from its dry tawny into a darker red. Kane whispered a desperate prayer that his friend was only drenched in the blood of the warrior beast who had fallen to a telepath's treachery. He rushed into grass, running broken-field style. Rifle fire snapped through the air over his head and he skidded, feetfirst, to the ground, landing beside Remus.

What he found was not a pretty sight. The tall Wanderer's left arm was gone, and several ribs were visible as skin and muscle had been peeled away by a nearby blast. With a sense of dread, Kane knew that Remus had taken the brunt of the explosion, saving the lives of the rest of the humanoids who rode the mortally wounded apatosaur. In a heartbeat, he was at the badly injured Annunaki.

"Remus, wake up, man," Kane said, giving the mauled Wanderer slaps on the cheek. "Don't go into shock."

"Not," Remus rasped. "Lowering my metabolism… Can't heal this."

"Damn it," Kane growled.

Remus reached up with his remaining arm. "Can't heal here…but have…a place."

Kane paused. "It'll rebuild your arm?"

"And chest…but can't last." Remus coughed. "But don't kill them."

Kane nodded. "We know that. We won't."

Remus smiled. "Maybe mop this up."

His gaze blanked, and except for a deep breath that he held, he was completely still now.

"Kane?" Grant called over the Commtact. "How's Remus?"

"In suspended animation," Kane answered. "We need to get him to help. There's a place he can recover."

"A healing chamber," Brigid said somberly. "The only thing between us and them is an angry, paranoid army."

Kane grimaced. "I didn't say this shit was easy, Baptiste."

He could see Kondo punch the ground, frustration evident on the young warrior's face. Kane scrambled back to where the others were.

"Kondo, can you try to reach them?" Kane asked.

The Watatsumi glared at him. "They're not accepting my radio signals. It'd be nice if we had a megaphone like Tatehiko."

"Even if we did get through to them, what?" Grant asked. "Because I can be pretty damn loud."

"Tell them that we're unarmed?" Brigid asked. "We can throw our weapons down and wave a white flag."

Kane and Grant frowned. "They sure as hell don't sound like they want to take prisoners."

Kondo shook his head. "We're supposed to be better than this."

"Hang on," Kane said. He scanned around, then saw what he needed. "Grant, you have to tell them Remus is dead. That might scramble the orders from the psychic."

"No…" Grant muttered. "You're not going…"

Kane's lips curled in distaste. "He's going to grow a new one."

Kondo's eyes widened in shock. He took a deep breath. "We have to use what we have. It might confuse them, or at least Tatehiko, if he's the only one receiving orders."

"The Ramah had to focus their combined mental abilities to control the large numbers of minions," Brigid said. "And Remus and Kane speculated there was one telepath in the Watatsumi ranks back at Ryugo-jo. It could be a one-on-one thing for the spy."

Grant grunted as another grenade salvo rocked the apatosaur corpse. Fortunately, the poor beast had passed by now. Still, beyond its death, it served to protect the humans it had come with. "Get the arm, Kane. This isn't fun, but we have to show them. It'll at least give the *bushi* reason not to continue their attack and question their orders."

Kane rushed for the severed limb even as Grant called out. "Remus is dead!"

The stentorian bellow made Kane wince, even as he raced away to gather up the mangled body part. As he picked up Remus's arm, he saw that the Igigu had to have suffered even worse of a hit than he'd originally thought. The scapula and a section of flesh hung off the upper arm like a grisly flag. That Remus had still been able to speak was astounding to him.

The Watatsumi gunfire immediately abated, and Tatehiko's voice came over the megaphone again. "He's dead?"

"We're not a threat to you!" Grant thundered. "Don't shoot! We don't want to hurt any of you!"

There was a distant cry. "Proof!"

"Sorry, old man," Kane whispered as he ran back, raising the bloody remnants of the Annunaki's back muscle and shoulder blade as a surrender flag. To add to his distaste, he had to climb atop the lost, trustworthy apatosaur to do it. As he did so, he felt a small wave of relief as he realized the Watatsumi were not firing on him. There would be no battle now. Kane wouldn't have the blood of would-be allies on his conscience, even though droplets of a friend's spattered on his head and shoulders as he waved the flag.

"Proof," Kondo repeated as he peered around the dead animal's bulk, scanning the company of *bushi*. He stretched, searching for the man who had made that demand.

"Only the Ramah conspirator would want that," Brigid said softly, looking over his shoulder.

Kondo scanned the faces of the large Watatsumi militia facing them. He didn't know each and every fellow member, but right now he was looking for one of them out of the ordinary. While men over six feet in height were rare among the dragon men, there were still plenty of them who filled the ranks of the defending army. Even among Tatehiko's number, there were a dozen, including Tatehiko himself.

The look on the militia commander's face was one of confusion and more than a little regret. Whatever doubts had been in his mind suddenly abated with the sight of Remus's carcass, or at least such a large piece of him that there was no way the Wanderer could survive. Kondo hated the fact that Kane had to wave it like a flag, a bloody flap of tissue at the end of what used to be a warrior's arm. Remus had risked much. Though he had remarkable healing abilities, and right now appeared to be in a self-imposed coma, he was not indestructible. Kondo couldn't imagine the pain that had accompanied such a wound, though the recent breaking of his shoulder and collarbone had given him a basis for such an impulse.

"There," Brigid said, tapping him on the shoulder, breaking him from his reverie.

There would be time to worry for the fate of the tall benefactor of the Watatsumi later. While everyone else in the company had lowered their weapons, looking on in awestruck silence, only one of the *bushi,* this one slightly shorter, but far stockier than Tatehiko, kept his rifle shouldered, staring down the sights. Even so, he hesitated.

There was no need to open fire on the "Greeks bearing gifts," and to do so would garner suspicion, the one reason that the mountebank among the Watatsumi intended to hide by killing those returning from battle with the Ramah. All of this could be passed off as a tragic mistake, and maybe Tatehiko could be demoted.

From the looks of the rifleman's uniform, he had the rank to move up the ladder of authority. Without a war to ensure his control over the society, higher rank would compensate for increased pay and perks. Kondo sneered at the type. "He has to die."

"Kondo, no!" Brigid admonished, squeezing his shoulder tight, squelching the impulse to rise and leap into bloody battle. "If we engage in violence now—"

Kondo pressed his lips tightly together.

"We have to make sure we don't threaten any more lives. The wrong move, and innocent soldiers die," Brigid continued. "We've already suffered enough losses, both of our groups. Further wanton death…"

Kondo nodded, keeping his gaze focused on the traitor. He finally put together a name to the features. It was Major Hanjian. His skill in leading successful interceptions of Dragon Rider attacks had pushed him through the ranks. With very few losses, he was able to get closer to the top. There were rumors that he would take Tatehiko's place if anything should happen to him, a rumor supported by the general himself. Hanjian turned his gaze toward Kondo, but he lowered his rifle.

The only sign of recognition was a wave of a hand across his face. To the Japanese, this was a sign of abject dismissal, the wiping of the offending person from their own eyes. With Remus down, Kondo was nothing more than a pebble in his shoe.

"Nothing wanton about this, Brigid," Kondo answered. "This is personal."

GRANT REMAINED SILENT as Remus's "remains" were tenderly and solemnly drawn through the gates of Ryugo-jo. He kept his gaze away from Major Hanjian, knowing that eye contact was likely one way that a telepath could easily communicate. Instead, he concentrated on the image of Atlas, holding his globe of secrets away. There was little doubt that Hanjian knew that Kondo was aware, and likely had warned the Cerberus delegation, but Grant didn't need to have Hanjian back in his head.

Grant remembered the wave of unease that rolled through him, the telepath rooting around through his surface thoughts as if he were in an office, looking for a pen. That was the image that bubbled forth in his mind, but Grant had managed to hold his thoughts. Even as Hanjian was inside his mind, there were the grim, deadly machinations going on deep inside, the thoughts of revenge, the plans of destroying an opponent who quite possibly was another Igigu, possessed of all the same strengths as Remus in addition to mind reading.

"Tatehiko," Kondo spoke up, jarring Grant from his reverie. "Sir, Remus told me of where he would prefer his body to be interred."

The general nodded solemnly, and Kondo began the procession toward the lonely Wanderer's quarters.

Tatehiko regarded Grant for a moment. "I didn't mean for this to happen. We thought that you may have fallen in with the Dragon Riders and—"

Grant shook his head. "This wasn't your fault. Not at all."

The *bushi* leader tilted his head, a moment of confusion showing itself in his features before something seemed to click behind his amber-golden eyes. Tatehiko glanced left, then right, before nodding in acknowledgment of the message sent to him.

Tatehiko lowered his head and his voice, so that only Grant could hear him. "I…I kept looking for evidence that Remus was secretly sabotaging us. There was someone giving away information about our defenses."

"I know," Grant answered.

"It wasn't him," Tatehiko whispered, more to himself. "But I was so sure. It seemed everyone around me had suspicions."

"Everyone but who?" Grant asked.

Tatehiko grimaced. "The major."

Grant remained silent as the Watatsumi commander's face lost its emotional cast. He was now stoic, frozen. "I won't say his name. I won't even think it. He wasn't saying a word. He didn't have to."

"No, he didn't," Grant responded.

"I didn't realize—"

"Remus did," Grant said, cutting him off. "He knew of them."

"Them?" Tatehiko's brow furrowed. "The riders?"

He shook his head. "No. He wasn't working with the renegades. There were others, the riders were intermediaries. They were a barrier between us and what we would instinctively want to kill."

Grant nodded.

"That's where you'd gone," Tatehiko murmured. "You ended that?"

"All except for the traitor, the telepath working for them," Grant answered.

He clenched his fists. "How could we be so blind?"

"Because he's been hiding for more years than your people have been on the Dragon's Spine," Grant said. "He is like Remus, a son of the so-called gods of old."

Tatehiko's eyes narrowed. "And why are we not shouting this out to the world? For all to hear?"

"He turned Ochiro into a one-man conspiracy, urging him to open up an ancient Annunaki weapon to release against the world. A weapon that only he could talk to.

Who knows what he could do if we expose him?" Grant
asked.

"And who will deal with him?" Tatehiko asked.

Grant remained silent.

Tatehiko didn't need to be clued in. Though Kondo had
been the last to ally himself closely with the Wanderer, he
had been required to operate the device to rejuvenate the
fallen warrior. Grant, on the other hand, had made a vow to
the younger *bushi*. He had crossed oceans, traveled to another world beneath Earth's surface. He had fought against
hordes of violent minions, buying Remus and Kane time
to weaken the Ramah.

"Godspeed," Tatehiko returned. He kept his thoughts
disciplined, his face stoic, samurai discipline slammed
down solid to shield his thoughts.

Grant could feel Hanjian rummaging in his brain. The
enemy was aware of the doom coming for him. That would
make his destruction all the more satisfying.

Now Kane and Brigid just had to make sure to even the
odds against the Igigu mind master.

REMUS'S INERT FORM WAS SET into the deep box. It looked as
if it were made of polished gold, an incongruous extrava-
gance in such a Spartan cave as the one he'd owned. It had
been hidden inside a niche, covered by a dirty, ancient rag
that split even as it was touched and brushed aside. Kane
stood back, Brigid Baptiste beside him. She looked at the
ratty, threadbare tarp that hung across the doorway as the
Watatsumi gently lowered Remus's body into the casket.

Kane didn't doubt that she had already memorized what
remaining patterns showed on the old cloth, and at the moment was filling in as much as she could utilizing symbols
from concurrent eras. Her attention to the door hanging
had to have been important, because her eyes stayed on

it. Perhaps she was tapping into whatever ancient knowledge was within the symbolism that even his sharp gaze could barely make out. The inks had faded over centuries, maybe even longer.

Kondo oversaw the process of interment. Somewhere in the time the two men had known each other, the young *bushi* had been told what to do if Remus had been injured beyond the scope of his normal abilities. The coffin looked the same as others Kane and the Cerberus explorers had seen, hidden chambers that possessed the awesome rejuvenative abilities that had saved the lives of allies, or extended the miserable existences of foul villains.

If they could hold on to a secure, easily accessible rejuvenation chamber, it could be a boon to the world, Kane imagined. The world had a need for healers, and the nearly magical powers of such a regeneration chamber would go a long way to making life easier for doctors. Medical technology was rare, but if it could be made more available, no longer at the end of a treacherous journey past forsaken deserts or beneath mountains and within mazes, then lives otherwise lost would be rescued.

Remus was one such life. The knowledge he bore, the lifetimes he'd led, the power in his heart and body, could spread. He would become one of Earth's mightiest protectors, or a teacher of unparalleled talents. There was no way a resource like him could be lost because of the treachery of a telepathic rogue.

Kondo nodded, and the other Watatsumi had leave to exit. As it was, the men looked down upon the fallen Remus, sadness in their eyes. Kane inwardly grimaced. Hanjian had heightened the sense of dread, the unease among the warriors, and doing so, he had overwhelmed them to the point that they pulled the trigger as soon as they saw a giant, living tank rise from the path to the lower forest. Any doubts disappeared as the soldiers saw who they had killed.

"He is not gone yet," Brigid said aloud. The Watatsumi pallbearers were jarred from their mourning, looking at the flame-haired archivist. "He can be back on his feet. This may look like a golden tomb, but it is a place of powerful healing."

The soldiers looked down at the long stranger who had fought so powerfully beside them.

Kane watched them file out of the healing tomb. They were somber, but no longer weighed down by guilt or sadness. Things would be explained. The world could turn out for the better.

Life had a chance to go on.

The chamber began to glow as a translucent screen closed over the inert Igigu. It was ready to instill new life, grow fresh flesh, to repair the wounded life within.

Cracks began to appear at the corners of the chamber, and Kane's instincts kicked in. He lunged across the casket, hauling Kondo toward him.

"Baptiste! Run!" Kane snapped.

She paused, looking in horror at the trapped Remus, but broke through the curtain. Kane, dragging Kondo, was hot on her heels.

Lightning erupted into the Spartan cave, sailing toward the open sky, out over the forest, the stone archway channeling the energy away from Kane, Brigid and Kondo. As it was, the sudden flash of heat was breathtaking, and even with their eyes shut, the world blazed brilliant yellow through jammed closed lids.

The stench of ionized atmosphere assailed their senses, and they were able to open their eyes. Broken, golden chunks littered the floor of Remus's quarters, strewed through the archway. The curtain had been incinerated by the lightning. Steaming mist made the interior of the other room impossible to see. Anything within had to have been obliterated, ionized.

"No!" Kondo roared. He struggled to break free of Kane's grasp.

Kane gripped the *bushi* tightly. "You can't go in there. Who knows if there's anything alive in—"

A single cry split the air. It was deep, inhuman and in agony.

"Keerg!"

Kane, Kondo and Brigid got one look at the figure, the huge silhouette standing in the middle of buzzing, glowing ionized plasma. From the unholy cry, and the swollen, savage pose of what stood within, Remus's body may have been alive, but its spirit had been replaced by something far more deadly.

The three people retreated from the chamber.

Chapter 22

Grant's trek through Ryugo-jo to meet with the man who was the insider who gave the Dragon Riders all the secrets of the Watatsumi. Hanjian was a telepath, and likely also a member of the same subspecies, the sons of the Annunaki known as the Igigi. He remembered, as though through a mirror darkly, the encounters his tesseract, the shadow who had been named Enkidu, and the Igigu called Shamhat. It was a hazy dream recollection, but the attempts to break his cross-time avatar had been enough to earn the enmity of Grant.

Certainly Remus was also an Igigu, the half-breed spawn of entities such as Enlil, but Remus had not been the one who nearly killed Kane and Brigid by launching a salvo of grenades. Grant wasn't a fan of being shot at, but those two were his family. No one tried to harm his family, not if they wanted to live much longer. Hanjian's assassination attempt had crippled Remus, but it had also succeeded in bringing down Grant's wrath.

"Time to reap the benefits of that success, motherfucker," Grant snarled. He let the shield of his thoughts drop. The telepath didn't deserve any chance of fairness, but Grant knew the advantage of making an opponent worry and fret.

Kane's voice bellowed over his Commtact. "Grant! Remus has been sabotaged! The casket exploded!"

Grant froze in his march. "But Remus?"

"Something is in there," Kane said. "But I don't know who or what it is."

"And you're not sticking around," Grant returned, glad his grimace was hidden over the radio contact. He'd been present for enough transformations, enough releases of almost limitless power, to realize that it may have seemed cowardly, but staying at ground zero of a maniacal god's birth was just another way to be pounded brutally to within an inch of one's life, and survival was only an option if you were incredibly lucky. "All right, I'm on my way. One crisis at a time."

A bolt of searing agony struck Grant between his shoulder blades. He staggered forward, grunting as pain rolled through his mind and body at the same time. He clawed at the wall, fingers clawing to grab hold of something, anything to keep him standing.

Gravity took hold of him, and almost without resistance, hauled the big ex-Magistrate crashing to the floor. Grant felt something wet on his face, and he knew it was his blood, but he didn't know where it issued from. All he could do was roll over onto his back, teeth peeled back in a rictus of agony. His bleary eyes locked on to a blurred, fuzzy figure striding over him.

"One crisis at a time," Hanjian said, leveling his pistol at Grant's face. "Too bad you forgot that you let me know you were coming."

Grant's vision focused on his features even as he saw the tendons in the killer's hand flexing, drawing the strength to pull the trigger.

KANE'S ATTENTION WAS SPLIT by the sudden, strangled cry of pain from his friend Grant, even as the corridor shook with a ponderous impact.

"Kane, Hanjian must have ambushed Grant," Brigid

said. She looked back toward the shadow that drew across the distant entrance of the hallway. "He could be in grave danger."

Kondo grimaced. "I can get to Grant. I have no experience fighting monsters."

"Except for dinosaurs," Kane returned.

"Yeah. But you beat Kakusa," Kondo returned.

Kane sneered, then waved Kondo off. "Hanjian's not going to be easy, either. Hurry!"

With that, Kondo took off, running like hell. He turned to Brigid, who was looking at the creature that had emerged from the wreckage of the rejuvenation cask.

"Give me some news," Kane muttered, the Sin Eater slipping into his grasp. The weapon was low on ammunition as he had not been able to replenish its magazines since the return to Ryugo-jo. The revival of Remus had been the priority there, but now all of that was out the window.

Even so, he kept the weapon pointed at the floor, awaiting some sign of what actually was going on.

Brigid nodded. "I'm recalling Remus's old facial features, and even with the enlargement of his body, the entity at the end of the hall shares at least eighteen of twenty points of visual reference with our ally."

"What happened?" Kane asked. He couldn't say he was glad to return the machine pistol back to its holster. Depending on what happened to the Igigu titan, he was still radically altered by the destruction of the device that had been meant to resurrect him.

"It was an alteration of the technology within the casket," Brigid surmised. "When we turned it on and began to stimulate Remus's tissues, instead of the usual gradual influx of energies to cause cellular reconstruction…"

"It overloaded," Kane finished. "And instead of a normal healing, we got a supersized version of Remus."

Brigid nodded. "We could try to reason with him, whatever is inside."

With that there was a pained bellow and a sudden surge, as if the plateau they were on experienced an earthquake. Kane grabbed Brigid before she could stumble and strike her head against the stone wall of the tunnel. As the two people looked down, they noticed a latticework of cracks stretch toward them.

"Oh, this is never a good sign," Brigid muttered as Kane pushed her along, racing back toward Ryugo-jo, fleeing the creature that had just struck the ground with the force of a bomb blast.

GRANT DIDN'T HAVE MANY options, not when he was in such pain that he couldn't do more than roll or extend an arm. Trying to sit up would only have brought him closer to the barrel that Hanjian aimed at him. The telepathic Annunaki-spawn wasn't carrying anything resembling the SIG-Sauer P-225 that had been the standard issue of the Watatsumi militia. Instead, he was looking down the deep, impressive bore of some odd, outsize pistol.

Hanjian scowled. "This is called an Automag. It's a treasure from the twentieth century, a gun that has been long out of production, even by the time humanity burned itself out. It has the power to punch through the heart of an automobile engine. I'm surprised that you're actually conscious."

"New technology, asshole," Grant spit. He lifted his hand, but his strength ran out, forearm folding across his chest. His face screwed up in pain. "Non-Newtonian polymers."

Hanjian smirked. "I'd heard of that. Fluid mass that solidifies under the introduction of sharp impact force."

Grant tried to lift his hand again. The Igigu kicked him in the elbow, flipping the limp limb back onto the floor. The Automag, whatever that monstrous piece of shining, silvery steel fired, had been more than capable of causing tremendous trauma, even through the combination of Magistrate torso-plating and impact-absorbing polymers.

Even as he lay on his back, he could hear and feel the crumble of shattered polycarbonate spilled beneath him. Luckily Grant and Kane had gone for the belt-and-suspenders approach, overlaying the Mag armor to provide additional protection against the deadly claws and fangs of the smaller, faster predators.

Hanjian looked at Grant's chest, then tapped the black, shiny armor with his toe. "I seem to remember these. How are you feeling, Grant?"

"Fuckin' peachy," Grant murmured. "Real fuckin' peachy."

If only he could lift his arm enough to aim his own Sin Eater, but the gun, normally an extension of his limb, was now a dragging weight. Powerful muscles were useless when broken bones and a jarred spinal column were at stake. The dual trauma made picking up a finger even harder.

Then the floor shook, heaving beneath him. The rumble drew Hanjian's attention from his slow, grim torture and the source of the distant thunder.

"Well, apparently Remus wasn't turned into a living tumor," the Igigu said. "I set his casket to overload."

"Overload…" Grant repeated. The longer he could keep the infiltrator talking, the more strength he could recover. It took every ounce of will for him to clench his fist. It was an improvement, a small glimmer of hope.

"I had two outcomes," Hanjian said. He set his foot on Grant's chest, right where the monster pistol had shattered the polycarbonate shell. Hanjian's weight normally wouldn't have registered, but even the shadow suit hadn't been able to spare Grant's ribs the battering induced by a high-velocity, high-energy projectile. "One was that Remus turns into an enormous, out-of-control tumor. Transformed into an agonized, completely alien entity, his own people kill him."

"Second?" Grant rasped.

"That's what's coming now. Remus is now easily as strong as a full-blooded Annunaki, maybe even stronger," Hanjian said. "But he's in blinding pain. And he's lashing out. That was him punching the plateau."

Grant blinked. "Punching the plateau."

"Are you some kind of parrot, Grant?" Hanjian asked him, looking down. "Oh, sure. Delay me. I'm enjoying the fuck out of this. I mean, who is going to sneak up on me? Who is going to stop me? Recover all the strength you want."

Hanjian leaned forward and tapped Grant between his eyes. "You're an open book to me now. No more of that stupid 'Atlas holding the world' static you threw down before. Here's a bit of advice for the next time you run into a telepath… Oh, wait. There will be no next time."

Grant gritted his teeth. "Gonna enjoy—"

The blast of the Automag made Grant flinch, but this time the roar and blaze of the weapon's muzzle didn't accompany a new spike of flaming agony in his body. He tried to turn his head, and caught sight of a Watatsumi soldier, sprawled down the hall.

"Sorry, someone wanted to interrupt me," Hanjian said. "One of the faceless little drones that Tatehiko and Remus cared about. By the time more come here, I'll have finished you off. If there are even any soldiers left after they throw themselves at Remus."

Grant shrugged with all of his might, his left hand wrapping around the turncoat's ankle. He squeezed, knuckles grown white as the leather of Hanjian's boot crackled under the force of his grasp.

Hanjian kicked loose and stepped back. "Getting more spirited, Grant?"

The ex-Magistrate rolled, propping himself up on one elbow. His forehead hung, brushing the floor. Ever since entering the Dragon's Spine, he hadn't had an ounce of coolness. Even the stone beneath his head had been warmed to body-heat temperature. Rather than providing a moment of refreshment, he felt the skin over his brow moisten with perspiration.

Hanjian kicked Grant's boot. "Come on. I want to be impressed. Stand up a little more."

"Hold your fuckin' horses," Grant returned.

The chuckle behind him told Grant that this man was cocky, self-assured. Another distant rumble transmitted through the floor, a vibration tingling against Grant's forehead.

"That didn't seem as strong as before," Hanjian pointed out.

Now Grant had a second elbow beneath him. This was living torture. Even if his arms and legs hadn't felt like leaden weights, threatening to tear loose from his torso, he was getting tired of the Igigu behind him. A sheet of white-hot anger crossed his vision, blinding and actually slicing through his sensation of pain.

The next flicker of sight that returned to him let him know that he was back on his feet, standing, swaying. Hanjian was nowhere to be seen, though. That didn't mean things were good. His fist hurt, and Grant wondered if maybe, in a fit of blind pain, he'd lashed out.

That wouldn't make sense; the Igigu infiltrator was armed with something that had the ability to defeat his armor. Only utter cockiness had kept Grant's head attached to his shoulders.

That's when he heard the sound of crashing in the distance. Grant took a step. It was uneasy, and it felt as if he were carrying a Sandcat on his shoulders. He grimaced and pushed through the pain, dragging his other foot out of the limb-sucking sludge that gravity had become. He could almost hear Brigid Baptiste whispering in his ear about the symptoms of spinal trauma and how this wasn't like that.

"Don't care why," Grant muttered to himself. "Got to stop Hanjian."

The floor shook violently again. Someone was bombing the hell out of Ryugo-jo.

But Grant did not fall.

He would not stop until Hanjian was ended.

KANE AND BRIGID REACHED the end of the corridor. At the other end, the pallbearers and the usual guard watch were at full alert, eyes wide with dismay.

"What's going on?" one of them asked. "Kondo tore past us like a bat out of hell."

"He's going to back up our friend Grant," Brigid informed them. "He wasn't running from trouble—"

"Remus is awake," Kane cut her off. "He's been poisoned with rejuvenative energy and is angry, in pain and extremely strong."

Another of the Watatsumi looked down the tunnel. "We could kind of guess the angry bit. But—"

"Right now we have to make sure that Remus doesn't

kill anyone. Get on whatever phone you guys use and order an evacuation," Kane said.

"What about Remus? Can't we just shoot him?" a sentry inquired. The other *bushi* glared at him.

"He is one of us, and he was betrayed," the first guard said. "Besides, it took a grenade to tear off his arm before, and he still lived. Bullets would only make him upset, wouldn't they?"

Kane looked back as the tremors of a ponderous tread shook the floor. "I don't want to find out. That's why I want civilians and *bushi* out of his way. I don't want him murdering anyone, and we have to find a way to stop him without killing him."

The dragon men nodded in agreement. Kane stood at the entrance to the tunnel, arms spread so he could hold the edges of the doorway. He peered into the distance.

"Kane, you didn't trust him," Brigid said. "And he is a threat…."

"As much as I'd love for this to be a case of black and white, it's not going to work like that," Kane answered. He let go of the archway. "Think about anything we have here. Is it possible that Remus wasn't the only one who brought in Annunaki technology?"

"You're thinking of a cure for him," Brigid murmured. "Some way to bleed off the excess energy driving him mad?"

"Yeah," Kane said. "What could we do?"

Brigid frowned, going through her catalog of experiences since they had arrived in Ryugo-jo. As it was, while the Watatsumi had considerable agricultural and industrial processing ability, there had been little sign of anything that could be construed as technology of the ancients, simply weapons acquired from redoubts on the surface.

"There's nothing," Brigid said. "I'm trying to think of analog to this situation."

"He's getting closer. About five hundred feet away," Kane cautioned.

"Durga," Brigid responded.

Kane looked at her. "Durga is the answer?"

"How we defeated him," Brigid explained. "We simply overloaded his body's healing factor. In that instance, it was a huge amount of nanomachines."

Kane grimaced in disgust. "So, telling the Watatsumi to fall back was a bad idea. We should pump bullets into him."

"No. Like they said, it took far more to injure Remus when he wasn't supercharged," Brigid answered. "We'd need grenades and high explosives."

Kane's brow furrowed. "Or something as powerful as he is."

"You saw how the ground shook. You'd need an apatosaur to face him down," Brigid said. "And mind you, it took every bit of kicking and prodding that I could to get our beast to go at the nest. It helped that a wave of hostile, attacking theropods were driving us back, but—"

"We have no access to that, and I'm barely a horseman, let alone a brontosaur rider," Kane returned. "Even if we could squeeze one into the inner depths of the city."

Brigid's eyebrows knitted together, wrinkles forming on her high forehead.

Kane quickly pushed her out of the way as a sudden jet of dust and stone vomited through the tunnel. The cloud dissipated, but Kane could feel where his arm and leg had been peppered by debris that had rocketed along at high speed.

"We have to get him back outside," Brigid said. "I know a path to the nearest exit."

"Draw his attention and get him to follow us?" Kane asked.

Brigid shrugged. "That will protect the city, for the most part."

Kane nodded. "All right. Can you contact Tatehiko and tell him about our plan?"

Brigid smiled as she pulled out a multiband communicator from the Kevlar load-bearing vest she'd worn to supplement her own shadow suit. "You went belt and suspenders. So did I. And I just looked at the frequency the guards turned to."

"Call him," Kane said. "And clear a path."

With that, the ex-Magistrate turned to go face-to-face with the rampaging beast that had once called him friend.

TATEHIKO'S COMMUNICATOR went off immediately on the heels of the first earth-shaking impact, and the streams of information were consistent, updating him every second. The underground city had been built on a plateau in the heavy basalt bubble, and by all rights, very few things should have been able to rock the superdense material that formed Earth's crust. Right now, however, tremors rocked the entire city, causing fear and minor damage and non-threatening injuries.

That's when Brigid Baptiste cut in over the radio. He could hear her Commtact translating over the line, but it was the Japanese that he focused on.

"General Tatehiko, this is Brigid Baptiste of the Cerberus expedition. There was an incident regarding Remus," she said.

Tatehiko took a deep breath. "Something to do with his casket. It was ancient technology, the casket of one of the old dragon kings?"

"Correct," Brigid answered. "You know the situation with Hanjian?"

"He must have sabotaged it," Tatehiko returned.

"Again, correct. You've received information from your men about evacuating people from the path of Remus," Brigid said. "Kane and I want to lead him through the tunnels to the nearest possible exit to the surface. This would be the surface access to generator seven."

"That sounds like a workable plan," Tatehiko responded. "I'll start working on it right away. Do you and Kane require anything else?"

"Kane is light on equipment. He could use something to keep Remus's attention focused," Brigid requested. "He wants to be the only one to engage Remus, though. This will keep your soldiers from coming to harm, and limit any real damage done to our ally."

"I'll dispatch a team," Tatehiko returned. "I haven't heard anything from Grant since he went after Hanjian."

"We have," Brigid replied. "But your men are better used to keeping people from coming to harm."

Tatehiko wrinkled his nose in distaste. "The Watat-sumi *bushi* are forever dedicated to protecting the people of Ryugo-jo. Anything less, and we would be unworthy of the name Sons of the Dragon King. My wishes extend to Grant's safety."

"Kondo is en route there," Brigid said. "Thank you."

Tatehiko grunted in assent.

There was crashing in the distance, and the general turned to see what it was. It sounded like a brawl going on. "Brigid, I think we've found Hanjian."

Suddenly a burst of booming gunfire sliced through the air. Tatehiko could feel the shock wave of air bursting against his cheek as a monster bullet zipped dangerously close to his ear. One of Tatehiko's lieutenants fell, his arm all but amputated by a single hit.

Kondo tumbled into the open, blood smearing down his face like a crimson mask.

Tatehiko drew his own weapon and started toward the hall where the young *bushi* had erupted. True to his suspicions, Hanjian was there, grim and imposing as he reloaded the largest handgun that the general had ever seen.

"Ah, hello," the Igigu infiltrator said in a singsong voice. "Let's see what kind of mayhem I can cause by decapitating this fool militia."

Tatehiko opened fire with his pistol, gun blazing out all nine of its shots. As the slide locked back, the weapon empty, he saw Hanjian standing there, not even a bruise on his chest.

He did, however, sport a malicious smile as he raised his reloaded hand cannon to aim at the general. "My turn."

THE THING ONCE KNOWN as Remus had been reduced to little more than a reactionary mind. Every cell in its body was not only swollen to the point of bursting, but was also aflame with internal fire. This had been the powerful surge of a CEM—or Charged Energy Module—which should have been filtered through the rejuvenation casket's checks and limiters. Instead, the fiddling of Hanjian, possibly the only other being in Ryugo-jo who had any experience with such Annunaki technology, had caused the CEM to pump all of that power directly into the explosion-ravaged body of the Wanderer.

Now Remus could see only hazy shadows backlit by a gleaming, blinding glow. He was able to hear only the sounds of his own blood rushing through his ears and the thunderous explosions as his feet struck the floor, every slight sound amplified as all of his body had been supercharged by the casket. And his skin itself—even the slightest caress of air felt like a slap, even though his re-formed hide was now easily strong enough to turn aside the impact of infantry shoulder-fired rockets.

He had broken every single bone in his fist as he punched the ground in an effort to stop the imperfections in its otherwise smooth surface from assailing the soles of his feet with what felt like a terrain filled with upturned daggers. Remus had been injected with the force to make him a god, seemingly all seeing, all hearing, all feeling.

The mere body of an Igigu was capable of holding all of that force and sensation, but the mind beneath was drowned, inundated by a violent lightning storm of data channeling through his nervous system. Consciousness was a long lost dream, at least the consciousness of a higher thinking animal. All that remained right now was the lower brain, the reptilian core that the Annunaki, the Tuatha and humanity had in common, the lump of nerve tissue that monitored pain, hunger and other matters of survival.

The beast cut loose with another roar of anger, outraged that the world burned his every sense. Had he more cognitive ability, he would have realized such a release would only exacerbate his own aural discomfort. Instead, the cycle of pain folded back and he punched the wall with all of his might. The rejuvenative energies coursing through his body had only barely reassembled the fractured stew of shattered carpals and metacarpals from the prior earthquake-inducing blow, and once more his heavy, powerful hide proved more than sufficient to keep the crushed bone matter inside one flattened sack of pulped flesh.

The only thing he was able to release was the screech of *"Keerg!"*

Who was he calling? What was he calling? Those were

what few semiconscious thoughts that bounced, dreamlike as the rest of his mind was buffeted by agonizing input.

"Remus?" a voice called.

He turned toward the sound. All he could see was a sliver, all but obscured by the reflections of infrared, ultraviolet and visible light that was everywhere so that even the darkened tunnel appeared to be ground zero for dozens of spotlights that seared his irises.

A rumble rose in his chest.

"It's me—Kane," the shadow spoke, low and soft. Even so, the tones of his voice hammered Remus's supersensitive eardrums. Had his body not been inundated with power that spurred the regrowth and repair of cells, his finely acute hearing would eventually have worn down. As it was, he would not be blessed with the partial deafness that most sentient beings knew in their normal life.

Remus bellowed again, lunging toward the figure.

It had caused him pain directly.

It had to be stopped.

Kane had to be destroyed.

Chapter 23

Grant staggered into the open and saw Hanjian raising his gun. Every part of his body felt as if it had been squeezed through an opening the size of a quarter, and yet the moment he saw Tatehiko's life in jeopardy, his instincts took over.

A flex of his forearm, and the Sin Eater snapped out into his hand. The swift hydraulics operated with such blinding speed that they allowed a Magistrate to simply think of shooting an opponent, and the bullet would be in the target before the enemy registered that sound. That was with normal humans, and that was for Grant at his top speed. Even though he'd been slowed somewhat, he was surprised at the sight of Hanjian suddenly whirl and step aside. The Sin Eater's slugs sparked and exploded against the wall where the Igigu had been standing.

Hanjian grimaced. "I thought you were still on the ground, Grant."

"Gotta kill one menace at a time, ass wipe," Grant challenged. Even as he did so, he triggered another burst, but he was still behind the curve. Hanjian was no longer there the moment Grant's finger flexed on the trigger.

Hanjian lunged forward and kicked the Sin Eater out of Grant's grasp, breaking it free from the hydraulic holster against his forearm. "That will be enough of that."

The telepathic Igigu backhanded Grant hard across his jaw, the blow snapping his head around and dropping him to the floor. First there had been the heavy Magnum slugs that pulverized his Magistrate armor. Then there had been the earthquake. Now all of this abuse dropped Grant to his knees, his brain swimming under the hammering he'd received.

Hanjian snorted in derision and turned his back on the kneeling, disarmed Magistrate.

Grant wasn't completely helpless. He still had his combat knife in its sheath, and he had the strength to stand up again. He just needed to refocus. He needed a means of getting his body and mind to operate at a level that the false *bushi* couldn't anticipate telepathically.

Zanshin. He had been training hard with Shizuka, adding to his already-formidable combat skills with the addition of the arts known to the Tigers of Heaven. The state of mind known as *zanshin,* literally translated as "remaining mind" was a Zen consciousness where the body focused on nothing and everything at once. Rather than engage in tunnel vision, looking for one particular threat, the samurai's mind was looser, relaxed, reacting without thought, but with perfect awareness of surroundings and situations. It had been an especially telling lesson in Shizuka's *kyudo* archery training. A samurai archer would loose his arrow perfectly on target, but immediately upon release, he would not be in a state of vulnerability after taking his shot.

It hadn't been that hard to bring himself to that level of thought and awareness. Much of his Magistrate Sin Eater training had been based on the principle of relaxed alertness, *kyudo* simply taking that mind-set even further.

Grant blanked his surface thoughts, dispelling everything that crowded for his attention. Pain, anger, frustration, all of it faded away, as did any plotting ahead, any plans he had to make. It was time to engage Hanjian the way only a true warrior could, and that was the final thought that Grant allowed to let slip.

The Igigu turned, glaring at Grant as his slumped form rested on its knees. "You still want to take first place?"

Kondo snarled in the distance. "We won't stop until you're finished, monster!"

Grant's eyes opened, and he saw everything at once, his subconscious mind taking in the whole scene. Kondo lay on the floor, his chest covered in blood where the Automag's rounds had broken the heavy trauma plates that supplemented his Kevlar and borrowed shadow suit. Tatehiko was in reloading, face grim and determined to continue his battle with the Igigu who had evaded his first few shots. And then there was Hanjian, looking back over his shoulder at Grant.

Grant didn't speak. He didn't form thoughts. He observed and waited, brown eyes taking in the world before him, ears picking up whispers, rumbles, tinny voices clamoring over radios.

Hanjian smirked. "Where did you go, Grant?"

The Igigu took a step closer, gun now leveled at Grant's head. "I'll tell you where your mind will be in a few seconds…."

Grant exploded to his feet, his rise as swift as a launching rocket. Hanjian's reflexes were just an instant too slow, and this time his shot wasn't exactly where it was supposed to aim. The blow struck Grant in the belly, and would have folded him over had it not been for the violence and speed of his motion. Momentum took him into the air, actually, his hand drawing the knife from its scabbard even as he leaped three feet up, crossing the yards between Hanjian and himself swiftly.

There was no pain, no slowing and sluggishness of his limbs as he hurled toward his opponent. Grant was in the moment, the blend of focus and diffusion of his senses making his actions a closed book to the Igigu. The massive Cerberus warrior lashed out with a palm strike that impacted Hanjian's inner wrist, swinging the Automag muzzle-first into the wall, where a second shot exploded, striking nothing.

The combat knife swept up, thrusting toward the Igigu's face and throat. Even without telepathy to anticipate the attack, Hanjian was quick and prescient enough to twist himself, his shoulder peeling open as the battle blade carved through muscle and sinew. The stab caused Hanjian to backpedal in pain, his arm hanging limply as the muscles that allowed the limb to move were severed in one swift, brutal slash.

Hanjian reacted with a psychic backlash, broadcasting his pain to all around him.

Grant noticed Tatehiko, Kondo and the other Watatsumi soldiers present all wince, curling up in agony, the psychosomatic impression seared into their brains so great that their arms fell limply to their sides. Grant felt the pain, too, but his *zanshin* cradled him, formed a breakwater against the powerfully focused sensations of Hanjian.

His momentum carried him forward, closer to the retreating infiltrator, knife whipping around in a backstroke that opened up Hanjian's forehead, his leathery Igigu hide parting easily under the razor edge of the blade. Staggered, Hanjian tried to continue his retreat, but he backed into the wall behind him. Grant's vector of movement continued, and he slammed into the Igigu with a powerful body block that sent both men bouncing off the immovable stone of the corridor and back to the floor.

That impact was more than enough to jar Grant from his Zen state, but even as they sprawled on the ground, he could tell that Hanjian was too rattled to do more than writhe and moan where he lay. Grant wasn't doing much better, the ugly knot of agony where the first Automag slug connected with him radiating fiery impulses that threatened to paralyze him. He tried to take a breath, but the searing flame in his fractured ribs cut that inhalation short.

Hanjian rolled over, hands clawing clumsily on the floor. Grant turned and saw that he was going for the hand cannon, or Tatehiko's fallen pistol, or any one of a group of discarded weapons. It wouldn't matter. Grant was a helpless target, ripe for a bullet through the forehead.

Gritting his teeth, he swung his knife out again, spearing his opponent through the grasping hand's forearm. The blade cut clean through and broke its tip off as it struck the stone floor. Hanjian grimaced and tried to recoil, only further mutilating his arm as he dragged it against the knife.

Hanjian clenched his eyes shut and focused, projecting and sharing that wound with Grant. The pain was so shocking, Grant released his knife, but it didn't help Hanjian much. The rubber handle of the blade stuck out from his torn limb, numbed fingers now drenched in blood.

"I'm going to rip your intestines out with your own weapon, ape!" the Igigu threatened.

Grant saw Hanjian exert his remaining stores of strength, wrenching steel from mangled flesh and bone. The sawtoothed back of the blade was clogged with stringy, torn sinew from the interior of the Igigu's arm. Around them, Grant made out the others in the intersection that Tatehiko used as a command center. It was as if a bomb had gone off, though no one bore the physical signs of injury, all except for himself, Hanjian and Kondo.

The *bushi* was on his knees, shakily holding a blurred object. His face had been split open in several places, the result of Hanjian pistol-whipping him, the heavy steel of the handgun tearing skin and leaving brutal lacerations.

One eye was gone, its sclera a milky pink trail that flowed down his cheek.

But the blurred gun stilled itself, coming into focus as Hanjian struggled to his feet, knife held to gut Grant. The ex-Magistrate saw the stainless steel of the Igigu's Automag for only a moment before a fireball spit from its muzzle.

Hanjian froze in midstride, then looked down at the ugly exit wound pouring gore down his stomach and thighs. His fingers loosened on the knife's handle, and he took a staggering step sideways. Kondo pulled the trigger again, and this time Hanjian wheeled around, as if his feet were a pivot. The Igigu crashed to the floor, spitting up a fountain of blood through his lips. Kondo collapsed into a seated position, the powerful handgun discarded.

Grant winced. He'd bought the young *bushi* enough time to recover from the earlier broadcast psychic assault, the crippling pain now forgotten.

The city shuddered. That meant Remus was still on the rampage, according to the now-dead Hanjian. And the only thing standing between the agonized godling and the deaths of thousands was his best friend, Kane. Before succumbing to unconsciousness, he sent his brother in arms a silent prayer of hope.

KANE KNEW HE WAS IN OVER his head when Remus's fist connected with empty wall yards away, and the sudden overpressure produced by that impact actually hurled him from his feet. Even so, there were too many people counting on him to let his fall slow him. He scrambled into a low crouch, realizing that something about him had induced an increased rage within his opponent. "Come on, old friend. Are you in there?"

Kane's skepticism about the swollen-limbed warrior before him had long since faded. The reality of the situation was that he was aware of his prior existences, even having received snippets of those lives thanks to the vagaries of matter transmission across the scope of dimensions.

All of that was irrelevant now. The creature before him held nothing of intellect as it swatted at empty air and reacted to the sound of his feet scuffing on the stone floor with glaring rage.

Kane stopped moving, going so far as to hold his breath.

For a moment, Remus seemed unfocused. It was as if the Cerberus explorer had disappeared, completely lost from the enemy's senses. Then a droplet of blood fell from Kane's upper lip and splashed against the stone floor. That minute sound made the gigantic humanoid wince at its intensity, and Kane had only a moment to leap for his life before a fist the size of a cannonball slammed into the ground at his feet.

Once again, Kane's ears were abused, his brain rattled by the proximity to the impact. He hadn't felt this rattled by anything less than an implode grenade going off in close proximity, such as back in the nest of the Ramah. If Remus were pained by noises as soft as a drop of blood striking the ground, Kane didn't want to imagine the kind of agony that the shock waves produced by his fists were creating.

As it was, Kane scrambled backward, his movements drawing the hulking beast along with him.

Even as he retreated, he activated his Commtact, speaking clearly. No point trying to hide his plans, as the thing before him operated on pure reaction to the impulses spiking through his mind.

"Baptiste! New plan!"

Brigid sounded flabbergasted on the other end of the communication link. "What?"

"Nobody comes close. That even means those guys you sent to resupply me," Kane snapped.

"What about Remus?" Brigid asked.

Kane looked back at the enraged being. "I can keep his attention on me. His senses seem superacute right now."

"Of course, everything about him has been enhanced, from his healing to his nervous system. He grew another arm in the space of seconds," Brigid said. "One can assume any attempt to lessen his sensory input would fail."

"Why?" Kane asked, breaking into a run. He knew each footstep was a drumbeat, a snare snap that spiked through the ears of Remus. He didn't have to look back, hearing each of his opponent's footsteps as he strode in pursuit. The Wanderer's leg muscles had swollen far too much for him to actually run swiftly, and any effort to leap would go nowhere, as the roof above was carved from the same heavy basalt that the rest of the mountain was. He could possibly leap, but he'd be stopped cold.

"He heals too swiftly," Brigid returned. "Human hearing degrades over time, and receives incredible trauma from intense sound pressure, further damaging our sensitivity. Remus has none of that. The same would apply for vision impairment. Neither chemicals nor intense light would last for long as his healing factor cycled in new cells to replace anything damaged."

"Are you saying I can do anything to him?" Kane asked, breathless as he continued leading Remus onward toward the surface.

"He'll feel it," Brigid told him. "But his wounds would heal, even if you did break his skin. He's a continuous explosion of pure rage due to the fact that everything hurts him. It's as if he were swimming in a river of lava."

Kane skidded to a halt at an intersection. He glanced back, watching as the huge clublike arms of the mutated

Remus slammed into a wall, caving it inward as if it were made of bricks rather than solid stone.

"We need to overwhelm his healing, don't we?" Kane asked. "But if we do that—"

"We need to get him away from others. Including you," Brigid responded. "Your speech sounds slurred. You must have suffered some trauma, as well."

Kane stumbled a few steps, then broke into a run again. Though he was in great physical condition normally, he'd been through the wringer over the past few days, having engaged in combat with all manner of monsters, from winged predators to six-ton titans with teeth like knives. His reserves of strength were depleted, but he still managed to put one foot in front of the other.

Something about the acrocanthosaurs crossed his mind.

"If we get him into the open, maybe he'll find a place of happy medium," Kane said. "Remember how the acros bore little animosity toward us or the sauropods?"

"They had fed, and they weren't under attack," Brigid agreed. "You think Remus could wander off?"

"I can hope," Kane said. "Right now, he's in a berserker rage, but the effects of the Charged Energy Module can't last forever. He's using tons of power lashing out."

"Keerg!" came the cry of rage behind him. It was the only semblance of communication that Remus even attempted.

"We can't even begin to imagine the rate of consumption he's utilizing, but we also have no idea how much energy he absorbed," Brigid responded.

Kane winced. The angry Remus had just slammed both fists into the ground, frustrated over the distance his quarry had gained. The overwhelmed mind of the creature seemed to pick something up, and Kane fired his Sin Eater, hoping to attract Remus's attention away from whatever hapless Watatsumi had drawn his focus.

The bullet struck Remus, seemingly with no effect. Kane also noted that he barely heard the shot of his own weapon. There was a ringing in his ears that he'd been ignoring thanks to adrenaline and other pressing matters. He absently touched one earlobe, and his fingertips came away coated with blood.

"Great. Burst eardrums?" Kane muttered to himself.

"What did the gunshot do to Remus?" Brigid asked.

"Confused him," Kane answered. "He's just looking at me now."

"Maybe that's good news," Brigid mused, but she didn't sound sure.

Remus's gaze leveled on Kane.

"This is not going to be fun," the Cerberus explorer said. He spun and raced, seeing the tube leading to the surface, at Generator Complex 7, according to Brigid's translation of the map.

Even as he ran, long legs eating up distance, he knew something bad was coming. A sudden gust of wind struck Kane in the back, lifting him off his feet but not hurling him to the ground. The concussion wave of some powerful impact had caught up with him. Only the shadow suit's non-Newtonian polymers and the environmental seal on the uniform kept him from being crushed by overpressure.

"Kane?" Brigid called, even as he sailed halfway up the tube to the surface. "That sounded like an implode grenade went off!"

"I don't want to know what Remus did to send me flying. All I know is that I must have crossed sixty yards before I landed," Kane returned.

"Kane, you have to run now!" Brigid ordered.

Kane didn't need to be told twice. The shadow suit and

his armor had prevented his crash to the ground from dislocating a knee or elbow, so he was able to get up and continue running. Even as he did so, he fired down the tunnel behind him, gunshots cracking violently through the air.

Remus's bellow came on the heels of those rounds. Even if they hadn't struck the enraged behemoth, they still hurt his ears. And that sent the rampaging hulk chasing after him all over again.

"Come on, Remus," Kane muttered. "Keep on me."

He reached the surface and exited into the lava-lit pocket atop the plateau. Brick walls surrounded him, as well as two massive turbines that spun, producing electricity for at least one section of Ryugo-jo below. Even as he took in the scene, he saw the bricks pulsate with vibration, the complex moving and adjusting to the ground shaking beneath. Kane grimaced, realizing that Remus was hot on his heels. He raced for the exit door, throwing open the bar that prevented the Dragon Riders and their monsters from penetrating into the complex, and consequently down into the tunnels of the city.

There was little need to bolster the defenses against an enemy that had been decapitated, and Kane realized that even if he dragged a dead apatosaur across the doorway, Remus would still plow his way through. Bricks tumbled from the wall as he made it outside onto the steppe.

"*Keerg!*" came the maddened cry from within the generator complex. Suddenly brick and mortar disappeared in a roiling pink cloud, Remus sailing through and landing amid the grasses. As his feet struck the ground, dirt swelled into a tide, soil like water rising and sweeping Kane off his own legs and hurling him to the ground.

Dazed, Kane looked at the mad being covering his face against the "daylight" of the pocket within Earth's crust.

Massive shoulders heaved as Remus buried his head in his palms.

"Remus," Kane subvocalized.

His head jerked erect, but snow-blinded eyes were glossy, insensate.

"Remus," he repeated. He hoped that those intensely sharpened ears hadn't been inundated with other sounds. Even so, he could feel his own heartbeat pounding in his ears. Kane realized his own heart had a strange echo to it. Focusing, he noticed that that pulse was coming from Remus himself.

He looked down at the shadow suit he wore.

"The environmental filters," he remembered Brigid saying.

All it would take was getting it onto the supercharged Igigu.

The leather-skinned giant was dealing with a flood of light and natural sound. Kane had one possible chance to ease the suffering of the being who once called him friend.

He cast aside his armor, then tore off his shadow suit and carried it draped around his neck. With a burst of speed, he rushed through the knee-high grasses. Remus howled as his ears were assailed with the rustle of blades striking Kane's legs. That momentary distraction wasn't going to last long, but it was enough for Kane to get behind the giant's back.

He leaped with all of his strength, landing on those broad, leathery shoulders. The scales on Remus's back were large enough that Kane could use them as handholds, and he gripped with all the strength he could muster. It was good that his grasp was solid as suddenly, both man and monstrosity were airborne, sailing high into the sky.

"This wasn't fun in Greece, and it's not fun now!" Kane snarled as he dragged himself higher. Remus's head was less than proportional with the rest of his body, but that was due to the fact that it was soft tissue that had been swollen with energy. As such, Kane was certain that he could stretch the shadow suit over the agonized being's head.

He surged, throwing himself at the back of Remus's head, yanking the material across the being's forehead. The giant's shoulders were so oversized with expanded muscle tissue that there was no way he could reach back and grab at Kane. The Cerberus warrior knew that any contact with those fingers would grind him into a bloody pulp. As it was, he was sure that once they landed, he'd be dashed to smithereens.

Another twist, another desperate tug, and the shadow suit material expanded, conforming to the new, alien head, polymers adapting to the wearer. A hard tug and Kane managed to bring it back over the Igigu's ears, folding them beneath the suit. Polymers stretched to accommodate the cartilage.

There was a sudden loosening, pain-taut muscles relaxing. Kane felt himself drifting away as the two reached the apogee of Remus's leap. He stretched, trying to grab on to those scales, and he prayed that the suit material had enough adaptive programming to conform to the senses of its wearer. It had been a long shot, but at least sounds and light would be filtered to normal human limits.

That might not be enough, Kane realized. Remus's figure tumbled end over end, and Kane kicked, trying to swim through the air to catch up with him. Maybe if he could hold on to the bigger entity, its body would absorb the fall.

"Remus, it's all you now," Kane muttered. "Don't go back to the city."

There was a grunt audible through the material, and a huge hand reached up, fingers as thick as Kane's wrists folding around his torso. Kane grimaced, realizing that he

wouldn't need to wait to strike the earth at terminal velocity. Remus would simply crush him like a grape up here.

He was surprised, then, when those fingers actually
didn't close with the force of a hydraulic metal press on
him. Instead, Remus pulled Kane against his chest. The
world spun as the Igigu adjusted his orientation in midair,
the finlike structures on his ankles actually acting like ai-
lerons. Suddenly capable of steering, Remus aimed himself and rocketed earthward.

Kane braced himself, gripping platelike scales on the
Igigu's chest like handholds. This time the giant didn't
seem to react to his touch.

From where he could see out of the cradle of Remus's
gigantic hands, he could tell that he was looking up at the
striated obsidian "lights" powered by glowing-hot magma.
Remus had angled himself so that he could land feetfirst
on the ground.

"Hope you know what you're doing," Kane whispered.

"Hope…too," a brutish voice returned, as if it were
pushing through an avalanche of snow that had buried it.

Moments later, Kane could see a splash of dirt and sod
all around Remus and him. There was the sense of deceleration, but superhuman muscles absorbed whatever impact that the shadow suit couldn't. Kane still felt the breath
explode from his lungs, and his bones wrenched as if he'd
slammed into a brick wall.

It was a far better fate than being turned into an ink
spot by impact with the ground.

Remus let go, and Kane covered his head as soil rained
all around him and the Igigu.

The precipitation of dirt and vegetation took a minute to
end, and straightening, Kane could see that a circle about
fifty feet in diameter had been excavated by the impact
of the pair against the ground. Kane took a deep breath

of relief as he realized that Remus had borne the brunt of the fall. He glanced back to see Remus's broken legs reknitting themselves.

Pained grunts issued from the Igigu, but finally both mangled limbs were long and straight once more.

"Are you in there?" Kane asked.

"Thanks," Remus answered, pointing at his head, and the material that deadened the sights and sounds of the world that had tortured him so. The huge entity struggled to its feet, and took a few tentative steps.

"Remus?" Kane pressed.

Remus shook his head.

"Friend," came the simplistic answer. There was no way to read his features through the all-black, all-encompassing polymer fibers. "Not good...be near."

"Remus, we can find a cure," Kane pleaded.

Though he couldn't see Remus's eyes, Kane could tell that the Igigu looked straight at him.

"Bad," Remus whispered. "Go away."

"But..." Kane began.

Suddenly, Remus launched, disappearing into the sky like a tiny dot. The leap carried the figure far away, sailing into the distance.

Kane doubted that even a Manta could keep pace with such a powerful jump.

"No, you're not good to be near, old friend," Kane whispered. "But it's not your fault."

Remus was gone, even his newly supersensitive ears no longer able to pick up his words.

"I hope that you find some peace," Kane added.

In the distance, a baleful note echoed, one akin to the jungle cry that had assembled an army of dinosaurs only the day before.

Kane grimaced, looking back.

It would be a long walk back to Ryugo-jo, but luckily there would still be a city left. Remus's pain and fury were under control, and were far away by now.

A war had been ended on this journey. Brigid Baptiste called in, informing Kane that Lakesh and the others were on their way back to Cerberus with news that somewhere, there was a new form of cobra bath that could revitalize the Nagah. Once Kane and the others recovered from their injuries, that would be on the too-long list of missions to complete in the postapocalyptic world.

There was hope for a new solution, though lives had been lost in the endeavor. So many things needed attention that it would take a while before answers could be found, both for the Watatsumi and the Nagah. Ryugo-jo still stood, but reconstruction would be necessary to return the subterranean metropolis to peak capacity. The Nagah were once more on speaking terms with Cerberus, but now they longed for the return of the semimystical waters that could reshape their bodies.

And though Hanjian and the Ramah had been destroyed, Durga's servants told of the Nagah prince's survival, stalking the shadows of the subcontinent.

There was a lot to do, and Kane felt tired, too tired to do anything but lie down and go to sleep.

He fought off the urge to lie down. Taking one step, Kane settled into the long walk home.

* * * * *